Praise For Bette Lee Crosby's Novels

A Million Little Lies

"Steeped in secrets and Southern charm, heartwarming and heartbreaking. A tale of forgiveness, family, and what it means to finally find your true home."
— Barbara Davis, bestselling author of *The Moon Girls*

"Crosby at her best! Masterful storytelling. A young mother builds her new life on a ladder of lies. Read it in one sitting."
— Marilyn Simon Rothstein, author of *Lift and Separate*

"Heart-wrenching and heartwarming. A novel to satisfy your soul and leave your heart feeling happier."
— *Linda's Book Obsession*

Emily, Gone

"Heart-wrenching and heartwarming. A page turner until the end."
— Ashley Farley, bestselling author of *Only One Life*

"An extraordinary book that raises questions about love, family, faith, and forgiveness. This one will stay with me for quite some time."
— Camille DiMaio, bestselling author of *The Way of Beauty*

"A beautiful story that will being you to tears! The writing is flawless! Definitely one of the most beautiful books I've read this year!"
— *Book Nerd*

A Year of Extraordinary Moments

"One of those rare books that makes you believe in the power of love. Filled with memorable characters and important life lessons, a Southern treat to the last page."
— Anita Hughes, author of *California Summer*

"Throughout this book, the author beautifully explores the theme of letting go of the past while preserving its best parts . . ."
— *Kirkus Reviews*

The Summer of New Beginnings

"This women's fiction novel is full of romance, the power of friendship and the bond of sisters."

— *The Charlotte Observer*

"A heartwarming story about family, forgiveness, and the magic of new beginnings."

— Christine Nolfi, bestselling author of *Sweet Lake*

"A heartwarming, captivating, and intriguing story about the importance of family . . . The colorful cast of characters are flawed, quirky, mostly loyal, determined and mostly likable."

— *Linda's Book Obsession*

"Crosby's Southern voice comes through in all of her books and lends a believable element to everything she writes. *The Summer of New Beginnings* is no exception."

— *Book Chat*

Spare Change

"Skillfully written, *Spare Change* clearly demonstrates Crosby's ability to engage her readers' rapt attention from beginning to end. A thoroughly entertaining work of immense literary merit."

— *Midwest Book Review*

"Love, loss and unexpected gifts . . . Told from multiple points of view, this tale seeped from the pages and wrapped itself around my heart."

— *Caffeinated Reviewer*

"More than anything, *Spare Change* is a heartwarming book, which is simultaneously intriguing and just plain fun."

— *Seattle Post-Intelligencer*

Passing Through Perfect

"This is Southern fiction at its best: spiritually infused, warm, and family-oriented."

— *Midwest Book Reviews*

"Crosby's characters take on heartbreak and oppression with dignity, courage, and a shaken but still strong faith in a better tomorrow."

— *IndieReader*

The Twelfth Child

"Crosby's unique style of writing is timeless and her character building is inspirational."

— *Layered Pages*

"Crosby draws her characters with an emotional depth that compels the reader to care about their challenges, to root for their success, and to appreciate their bravery."

— Gayle Swift, author of *ABC, Adoption & Me*

"Crosby's talent lies in not only telling a good compelling story, but telling it from a unique perspective . . . Characters stay with you because they are simply too endearing to go away."

— *Reader Views*

Baby Girl

"Crosby weaves this story together in a manner that feels like a huge patchwork quilt. All the pieces and tears come together to make something beautiful."

— Michele Randall, *Readers' Favorite*

"Crosby is a true storyteller, delving into the emotions, relationships, and human dynamics—the cracks which break us, and ultimately make us stronger."

— J. D. Collins, Top 1000 reviewer

Silver Threads

"*Silver Threads* is an amazing story of love, loss, family, and second chances that will simply stir your soul."

— *Jersey Girl Book Reviews*

"Crosby's books are filled with love of family and carry the theme of a sweetness for life . . . You are pulled in by the story line and the characters."

— *Silver's Reviews*

"In *Silver Threads*, Crosby flawlessly merges the element of fantasy without interrupting the beauty of a solid love story . . . Sure to stay with you beyond the last page."

— Lisa McCombs, *Readers' Favorite*

Cracks in the Sidewalk

"Crosby has penned a multidimensional scenario that should be read not only for entertainment but also to see how much, love, gentleness, and humanity matter."

— Gisela Hausmann, *Readers' Favorite*

WHEN I LAST SAW YOU

Also by Bette Lee Crosby

The Magnolia Grove Series
The Summer of New Beginnings
A Year of Extraordinary Moments

The Wyattsville Series
Spare Change
Jubilee's Journey
Passing Through Perfect
The Regrets of Cyrus Dodd
Beyond the Carousel

The Memory House Series
Memory House
The Loft
What the Heart Remembers
Baby Girl
Silver Threads

Serendipity Series
The Twelfth Child
Previously Loved Treasures

Stand-Alone Titles
A Million Little Lies
Emily Gone
Cracks in the Sidewalk
What Matters Most
Wishing for Wonderful
Blueberry Hill
Life in the Land of IS: The Amazing True Story of Lani Deauville

WHEN
I LAST
SAW YOU

A Novel

BETTE LEE CROSBY

BENT PINE PUBLISHING

ISBN-978-0-9981067-7-9

BENT PINE PUBLISHING
Port Saint Lucie, FL

Published in the United States of America

Dedicated to the memory of Lavinia Webb
and her eleven children

1968
Heatherwood, Georgia

Margaret Rose McCutcheon

I lost Albert a week ago Friday. It happened in the blink of an eye. One minute he was on the telephone arguing with a client; the next he was face down on the desk, dead.

He died the way he lived: trying to force someone else into his way of thinking. He didn't consider it arguing. He felt he was simply revealing the errors in the other person's viewpoint.

Albert was strong-minded and opinionated, but he also had a sense of fairness. That's what made him a good lawyer. He didn't just argue a case; he brought the judge and jury around to believing in both him and his cause.

I suppose he did the same with me, and in the end I came to accept that his dreams were my dreams. Little by little, I let tiny pieces of myself slip away until I came to where I am now—a woman alone. A woman with an abundance of wealth to live on and nothing to live for.

I loved Albert just as any woman who's been married to a man for 50 years loves her husband. He was a good provider, hard-working, and generous to a fault. Not once in all those years did he raise a hand on me, stray, or give me reason to doubt his love. But now I'm asking myself if those things were enough to make up for what I've pushed to the back of my mind.

I was one of nine siblings with a mama who loved us dearly. We were poor as church mice, hungry most of the time, and sleeping three or four to a bed, but we had each other. Some nights, when I was crowded in between Nellie and Louella, I'd lie awake asking God to give me a bed of my own. Now I look back and laugh at such a wish. Here I am in a house with seven beautiful bedrooms, and I'm still reminiscing about that lumpy old bed I shared with my sisters.

If you live long enough, you look back on life and think about what you would've done differently. By then it's too late to change anything. Today if you were to ask me which is worse—being poor or being alone—I assure you my answer would be a lot different than it was back then.

Loose Ends

At 8:30 in the morning, the doorbell chimed. Condolence callers seldom arrived at such an ungodly hour, so Margaret assumed the housekeeper had forgotten her key. She started down the stairs, and before she reached the landing the bong sounded a second time.

"Hold your horses," she called out, a whisper of annoyance in her voice.

When she opened the door she found herself face to face with Jeffrey Schoenfeld, now the law firm's senior partner. Not one of her favorite people. Before he'd been offered a partnership, she told Albert she thought him overly aggressive and too blustery for her liking. Albert agreed with a laugh and said those things were what made him a good lawyer, but that hadn't changed Margaret's opinion.

"Sorry," she said. "I thought you were Josie, our housekeeper."

"No apology needed. It's early; I should have called."

Yes, you should have.

"Nonsense," she said with a stiff smile, pushing back the door and inviting him in. "You and Albert never stood on ceremony before, so there's no need to start now."

He followed her down the hall and into the living room. Jeffrey took the large overstuffed club chair, and she settled on the sofa opposite.

"I know you haven't had a lot of time to think this through," he began, "but we should talk before the partners' meeting this afternoon. There will be questions about how we handle Albert's interest in the firm, and I need to know whether or not you're interested in a buyout."

"Why do I have to decide this right now?" Margaret said. "It's only been ten days since Albert—"

"I don't need an answer this morning, but I'd like to know before the quarterly distribution. If you decide to sell, I'm ready to make you a fair and equitable offer."

He's ready? What about the firm?

She let out a long exhale and leaned back into the pillow.

"Albert spent his life building that law firm, and I doubt he'd want me to rush into making a decision about keeping his shares or selling them. I'm going to need time to consider the various options."

"What options? Has anyone else approached you about this?"

She toyed with the ring on her finger. "No, but it's only been ten days. Albert always handled our financial affairs. With him gone, I might need to consider using a financial planner."

Jeffrey hesitated several seconds before speaking again. "Do whatever you think best, but I hope when it comes to your interest in McCutcheon and Schoenfeld you'll trust my judgment. I'd like to maintain control of the firm, because doing so is in the best interest of both the firm and our clients. While I can't force you to sell your shares, I will ask that you don't sell them to an outsider."

"What happens if I keep Albert's shares?"

"You continue to receive a percent of the firm's net revenues commensurate with the number of shares you hold. Of course, revenue share amounts can go up or down depending on the business, but with a buyout you're guaranteed a lump sum to invest in whatever you like. The stock market, real estate, bonds…"

Beneath the guise of friendship, Margaret heard the silvery sound of lawyer talk. It always came like a mudslide of words to cover a person's ulterior motive. Albert trusted Jeffrey, but she didn't.

"I'm not ready to make this decision. I need time to think it over."

"Okay, but bear in mind your decision should take into account whatever plans you have for the subsequent dissolution of the estate."

"Dissolution of the estate?"

Eyeing her over the top of his glasses, he gave a nod, reached into his briefcase, and pulled out a folder. "Here's a copy of Albert's will, which is what we need to talk about."

In more than one way, Jeffrey reminded her of the Albert she'd seen at work in the courtroom: sharp-edged and determined, his jaw set firm, his face expressionless until he needed to draw on the emotions of the jury.

Jeffrey's furrowed brow and look of concern was the same as she'd seen Albert wear during the Robinson trial. Eddie Robinson was a construction worker who'd limped into the courtroom claiming a scaffolding accident had left him unable to work. Thanks to Albert, he'd gotten a hefty settlement and walked away whistling. Afterward when Margaret asked if Eddie's injury was legitimate, Albert said he believed it was. Still, she had her suspicions.

A few weeks later, she spotted Eddie high footing it along Cameo Street, no trace of a limp. Later that evening, she told Albert what she'd seen and asked what he was going to do.

"Nothing," he said. "My job was to present the client's claim, not decide if he's telling the truth."

Albert's answer had irked Margaret and she'd told him so, but he stayed firm on his position.

"Life is not always fair," he said. "You don't get to judge another person unless you've spent time walking around in his shoes."

Jeffrey leaned forward, elbows on knees. "I hate to bring this up when you've already got so much on your plate, but unfortunately it's necessary."

Margaret left the folder lying on the coffee table. "I've already seen Albert's will, and I know he left everything to me. I can't see why there'd be any questions."

"The issue is not about the estate passing to you. It's about subsequent distribution. Albert's will did not have a per stirpes clause and without—"

"I don't understand. Distribution of what?"

"Everything. The entire estate, including his shares in McCutcheon and Schoenfeld."

With what she could almost believe to be a genuine look of concern, he reached across and touched her hand.

"Albert's will was drawn up in 1941, and, yes, he left everything to you, but he never updated that will so there is no directive regarding further distribution. Without having a per stirpes clause that directs distribution upon your demise, the entire estate could default to the state of Georgia."

Margaret's throat tightened. She'd barely come to grips with Albert's death, and now she was being forced to think about her own.

"That's crazy."

"Don't worry," he said in a less lawyerly tone. "There's an easy fix to prevent this from happening. Our office can file the paperwork transferring all of Albert's assets so they're registered under your name. Then we can liquidate anything you want to turn into cash and draw up a will designating the beneficiary to inherit your estate."

Margaret turned away, looking first at the ceiling then toward the window that faced out onto Pine Street. In all the years she and Albert had been together, they'd never spoken of things like death and distribution. They'd talked of planning for the future, but it was always about the things they'd do, the places they'd go, the wonderful adventures they'd have once he retired. Now with him gone and her heart already shattered into pieces, she was being asked to dispose of the estate he'd spent a lifetime building.

Just then she heard the front door click open and close.

Josie.

Jeffrey sat waiting for her answer, and in the quiet of that moment she could hear the heartbeat of the house. It was as sorrowful as she was.

"There's no one to leave it to," she said tearfully. "No family; no beneficiary."

"Surely there's somebody. A distant relative? Someone on Albert's side of the family?"

She shook her head. "Albert was an only child as was his father. Both of his parents are long gone; so are mine."

"What about you? Any siblings? Sisters, brothers, cousins maybe?"

Again, Margaret shook her head.

"At one time there were nine of us," she said, her voice quavering, "but after all these years… I know for certain Mama and Louella are dead. I don't know where the others are; I lost track of them a long time ago."

"Lost track?" Jeffrey's face was pulled into the same expression Albert wore when something puzzled him.

As Jeffrey rattled on about the need for a beneficiary, Margaret spied Josie, a dark-skinned figure wearing a simple cotton housedress, passing through the foyer. Catching her eye, Margaret nodded.

A nod or a wink was all they needed. The two women had been together for over 30 years, and they understood each other in a way that only the closest of friends could. In the weeks following Margaret's miscarriages, Albert had gone off to work and Josie had been the one to sit beside her as she gave way to tears. When she'd spoken about the excruciating pain of losing a child and the heartbreak of a lost family, Josie listened without judgment. In those dark days Margaret told her things she'd never even told Albert, and for all those years Josie had held tight to her secrets. There was a time when having an outsider know what had happened to her family would have left Margaret feeling ashamed, but with Josie it somehow seemed okay.

Breaking through her thoughts Jeffrey asked, "This estrangement, was it your choice or did they—"

"It wasn't a choice. It just happened. Not because we didn't love one another, but... After Daddy disappeared, we had to leave Barrettsville and each go our own way. Things were different back then, jobs scarcer, money harder to come by..."

Her thoughts drifted back to the two years in Barrettsville: the big house sitting all alone at the far end of Second Street; the room she shared with Louella and Nellie, all three of them in one bed; their window overlooking a weeded lot where in the early months of summer dancing fireflies made it seem like a fairyland. How many times had she and Louella fallen asleep at the window trying to count those fireflies with both of them wishing the magic of the moment would go on forever?

She hadn't wanted to leave Barrettsville. None of them did, but Mama said they had no choice. As the train chugged westward, heading home to West Virginia, she'd clung to Dewey and pleaded with him to make the train go back.

"I wish we could go back too," he said. "But we can't."

Hearing that, she'd sobbed all the harder. He wrapped his arm around her, pulled her close, and said, "Don't waste tears on something you can't have, Maggie. Once something is left behind, it's gone for good. Even if you go back, it's never gonna be the same."

"Regardless of what the situation was back then," Jeffrey said, "don't you want to at least try to locate your siblings or their descendants? It's a sizable estate, and if you don't do something…"

She thought of Dewey and the last time she'd seen her big brother. He'd kissed her cheek, promised to write, and disappeared into the train station. She'd never seen or heard from him again. Almost two years later she married Albert.

With sadness tugging at her heart, she shook her head. "It's a lovely idea, but I doubt it's possible. Sometimes we have to accept that the past belongs to the past and leave it that way."

"Do as you will," he said and stood. "But at least consider my buyout offer. Cash on hand is always a good option. Once you decide that, then we can figure out how to handle the remainder of the estate. If there's no family, you might want to designate a worthwhile charity as your beneficiary. Perhaps an organization Albert had an interest in; his alma mater maybe? William and Mary, wasn't it?"

Margaret nodded. "Yes, it was. I'll keep it in mind."

She followed Jeffrey to the door, thanked him for coming, then promised to get back to him as soon as she'd had time to process her thoughts.

"The sooner the better," he said. "And when you have a moment, if you could look through Albert's things and make sure he didn't leave any files here at home I'd appreciate it. They're the ones in the green folders."

Margaret noticed how he'd mentioned the buyout a second and then third time. He seemed more worried about the firm than her. Why was he so eager to move things along? Why couldn't he just let her grieve in peace?

If You Never Try...

Margaret stood at the window watching Jeffrey back out of the driveway. After he was gone from sight, she turned and headed back to the kitchen. Josie was just pulling a tray of cinnamon biscuits from the oven.

"Mm, that smells good," she said.

"You looked like you were having a stressful time in there," Josie said, "so I figured you could use something sweet to take the edge off."

"You figured right," Margaret said. "Jeffrey Schoenfeld has never been one of my favorite people. And now with Albert gone, I feel as though he's pushing me to do something I'm uncertain about."

Josie took two mugs from the cupboard and set them on the table. "Have you had breakfast?"

"Not yet. I'd barely finished dressing when he rang the bell. If I had known he was coming I might have been ready to…." Margaret dropped down into the chair, whooshed out a long and weary-sounding exhale, then continued, "talk about what happens to Albert's estate when I die."

Josie turned, her eyes wide. "When you die? Is there something—"

"No, no. It's nothing like that. He's talking about some time in the future, whenever it may be."

"Way in the future, I hope." Josie poured the coffee and sat opposite Margaret.

"I hope so too." Margaret tried to make it sound lighthearted, but the thought of how suddenly Albert had gone was in her head. "I guess we never know. The day before Albert died, he was talking about us taking a trip to Europe next summer."

"That doesn't mean you'll—"

"Of course not, but it does make me think about how suddenly something like that can happen, and, as Jeffrey said, I need to be prepared for the eventuality of it."

"In time maybe, but right now what you need to do is have some breakfast and stop fretting about stuff you can't fix. How about I scramble up some eggs?"

"No, thanks, the biscuit's enough. What I find awful about all of this is that Jeffrey seems so anxious to get on with business. He's even asked me to clean out Albert's office. I guess he's forgotten Albert hired *him*, because now he acts like he's the boss."

Josie patted her hand, and Margaret covered it with her own. "Truly, Josie, I don't know what I would do here without you."

"You wouldn't have breakfast, that's what. You need to eat something more than one little bitty biscuit. How about oatmeal? I could fix it with raisins and cinnam—"

"No oatmeal."

The longer Margaret thought about it, the more Jeffrey's request to go through Albert's office needled at her. Albert had spent a lifetime building the law firm and had made Jeffrey partner. Was Jeffrey worried she'd find a way to challenge his stake in the company now that Albert was gone?

Impossible, she thought, remembering how much Albert trusted him. *He just wants to get through all the formalities. Maybe…I wonder if Albert had paperwork on a beneficiary and just forgot to file it.*

"The sooner I clean out Albert's office, the faster Jeffrey will leave me alone," she said, thinking out loud.

"If there's any way I can help—"

Margaret shook her head. "Thanks, Josie, but it's something I have to do myself. Crazy as it might sound, it's like saying one last goodbye. When I'm in there, it's as if I can feel Albert's presence."

"Well, then, if you've no need of me, I'm going to sweep the walkway and clean up those potted plants on the front porch."

Margaret pushed open the door to Albert's office and stood there breathing in the scent of him. In time it would fade, but for now it was still here in the leather-bound books that ran end to end across the bookshelf and the stacks of papers and magazines lying about. For a moment she closed her eyes and saw him sitting behind the desk, his eyeglasses low on his nose and a ribbon of cigar smoke circling his head. She spoke to him just as she had the past few nights. With her face tilted toward the sky, she whispered, "Please Albert, help me to get through all of this."

She crossed the room and lowered herself into his desk chair. Countless times she'd visited Albert in here, but she'd always been in front of the desk. Sitting there in his seat, the desk seemed somehow bigger than she remembered, more intimidating, the drawers deeper, the handles heavier, scaled to fit a larger hand. Albert's, not hers. For several minutes, she remained frozen in place. Then she leaned forward, dropped her head onto the desk, and began to cry.

There was no way of knowing how long she remained there, but when she finally opened her eyes she saw a shiny brass object through a blur of tears. Raising her head, she lifted the paperweight. It had been a gift from his father, and Albert had kept it on his desk for as long as she could remember. The engraving on the top was worn and scratched, but still readable: "IF YOU NEVER TRY, YOU WILL NEVER SUCCEED."

Margaret brushed back the tears and sat up. Was that message only for Albert, or was it meant for her also? He'd tackled his challenges head on and succeeded. Was he trying to tell her she could do the same?

Placing the brass paperweight in the center of the desk, Margaret took a deep breath and pulled open the bottom right-hand drawer.

The drawer was stuffed with file folders, and even though they appeared to be client files none of the folders were green. Checking the dates on the top pages of each folder, she saw they were old, outdated. After she had emptied out that drawer, she moved on to the top drawer.

Folded scraps of paper and telephone message notes lay scattered about the top, and underneath Margaret found a box of cigars, two broken lighters, and matchbooks from a dozen different restaurants. Most were places where they'd dined together, but in the past she'd seen Albert jot a name and telephone number on the inside cover. She read each matchbook, remembering times when they'd shared a bottle of wine at one place or dined in a cozy booth at another. With stopping to revisit the special significance of one thing and another, then twice giving way to a flood of tears, it was late in the afternoon before she finished clearing the first two drawers.

She had just wiped the tears from her eyes when Josie looked in the office.

"I'll be leaving soon," she said. "I made a beef stew and left it on the stove. Make sure you eat. It's not healthy to be skipping meals. You'll end up sick for sure."

Margaret forced a smile. "I'm fine. Honestly."

Josie eyed her suspiciously. "I don't know. Your throat sounds scratchy, and you don't look so good. Maybe I'd better stay to make sure—"

"Go home. You've got a family to take care of. I'll be fine."

"Well, if you're sure…"

Josie started out, then hollered back, "Don't forget to eat, and call me if you need anything."

"I'll be fine."

Once Josie was gone, Margaret sat there studying the paperweight. She'd seen Albert do the same thing any number of times, holding it in his hands, tracing a finger across the engraving, almost as though he expected the words to magically change into whatever answer he was looking for. She closed her eyes and pictured him sitting at the desk. The look on his face wasn't confusion, it was determination. He wasn't looking for an answer; he was renewing his commitment to this one.

IF YOU NEVER TRY, YOU WILL NEVER SUCCEED.

It was a mantra Albert had lived by. When the firm was still young and on shaky ground, he'd stayed with it, working 14 hours a day until he'd built it into a thriving law firm. All those years he'd remained purposeful and dedicated, always moving forward, never losing sight of his goal. But it hadn't been that way for her. She'd followed along in his wake, accepting that his goals were hers.

She thought back on her earlier conversation with Jeffrey.

"Lost track of your family?" he'd said, making it sound like such a thing were ludicrous. Perhaps it was.

That thought was like the dinging of an alarm clock in her head, and she asked herself the question she should have asked decades earlier. Why hadn't she tried to find her sisters and brothers? Why hadn't they tried to find her? Was it because of what happened in Barrettsville? She was only nine years old when they left there; too young to remember the details of what happened but old enough to remember how they'd been a family.

They'd struggled through the hard times and made do with next to nothing, but they'd always had each other. After Barrettsville, everything changed. Their mama had decided to split up the family.

Why? What secret had to be kept? For how long? Did anyone still remember? Did anyone care?

Albert's Secret

Once the ghosts of the past began to pick at Margaret, it left her feeling more guilty than ever. She could remember the sound of Nellie's laugh, the warmth of Dewey's hand in hers, the way Oliver had carried her on his shoulders.

Where were they now?

She could only hope they were better off than they'd been back in Coal Creek, West Virginia. With Mama and Louella dead and buried, there was no one to ask. No one to say that Dewey had become a doctor just as he'd hoped or that Nellie had married well, that Oliver had raised a fine family and John Paul was a successful businessman. On days when those questions haunted her, she wondered whether she had abandoned them or had they abandoned her.

The last time she'd seen Dewey was at the train station. She should have searched for him, written letters to the army, asked around. She could have done a lot of things, but the bottom line was she didn't.

IF YOU NEVER TRY, YOU WILL NEVER SUCCEED.

With a heavy heart she placed the paperweight in the drawer and walked out, closing the door behind her.

A week passed before Margaret gathered enough courage to go through the remaining drawers of Albert's desk. It was a painful process. Everything she touched was a bittersweet reminder of what they'd once had and what she'd lost. Were it not for her fear that everything could end up in the hands of the state, she might have left the office door closed forever and simply pretended he was off on a business trip.

There were times when she could do that: ignore reality and fool herself into believing that tomorrow or the next day Albert would be returning home. But those moments disappeared in a heartbeat. Then she'd remember he was gone and she had to decide how to handle the estate he'd spent a lifetime building. When that happened, a strange new heaviness took hold of her and there was nothing she could do but give way to the sorrow. She'd lower herself onto the sofa or a nearby chair and cry it out, asking the Almighty to help her sort through everything.

In the earlier search she'd found nothing of value and no papers with instructions on how to handle the estate, but the bottom drawer on the left-hand side of Albert's desk was full of files. None carried the familiar McCutcheon & Schoenfeld label and none of them were green, a good sign. Taking her time, she went through the folders one by one but found nothing other than notes on old cases.

Near the back of the drawer, hidden behind a divider, Margaret found a thin folder with Bateman Investigative Services stamped on it. Inside were three sheets of paper, all of them invoices dating back to 1944. The year before they bought this house.

It was odd that Albert would have this type of invoice in with old files. He had dealt with private investigators from time to time, but it was always on behalf of a client. Those invoices were marked with the client name, case number, and specific details for the firm write-off.

Puzzling over why he would hire a company such as this, she studied the first bill. It was a standard invoice form with a few sparse details written in blue ink. It indicated 16 hours of investigative services totaling $440. Expenses came to $53.40 for a total of $493.40. The others were similar with only the number of hours and amounts changing. Not one of them gave a description of what was being investigated. That alone was odd…almost as if whatever Albert and the investigator were working on had to be kept secret.

The longer Margaret looked at those invoices, the more concerned she became. It had to be something significant for Albert to spend this kind of money. And the way he'd hidden the folder behind the divider also meant something. Was there a problem with the house? A fraudulent claim to the title? Albert's daddy died in 1943; could the investigation have something to do with the old man's partnership in the firm? It wasn't like Albert to hold onto meaningless bits of paper. If he kept these invoices and hid them as he did, they had to be important. But why?

Lost in thought, she was startled when the telephone rang. Jeffrey gave her a hurried hello then got to what he'd called about.

"Have you given my proposal any thought?"

"What proposal?" she asked, still preoccupied with the mysterious invoices.

"Regarding your shares of the firm. I hope you're not talking to anyone else. I've already offered you a buyout, and I'm willing to match any other price. You do realize that, don't you?"

"Yes, I know," Margaret said absently. "I just haven't made any decisions yet. I'll get back to you as soon as I do."

She was about to hang up when the thought that Jeffrey might know something about the invoices crossed her mind.

"Wait a minute, as long as I have you on the line, can you tell me why Albert would have been working with a company called Bateman Investigative Services?"

"Was this recently?"

"No, back in forty-four."

"The name doesn't ring a bell. But I was fairly new with the firm back then. It's possible he was working on something I wasn't in on."

"Would you have Eloise check his files? Maybe ask around the office to see if they've done work for anyone else at the firm?"

"Anything that far back would be housed in storage. Getting the files brought up would take a week, maybe longer. If you want to tell me what this is in reference to, I might be able to help. I could ask around, see if there's something more recent."

Margaret could have been mistaken, but she thought she'd detected a bit of reluctance in his voice. Perhaps he wasn't the one to ask. This might be something she should look into herself.

"I doubt it's worth the bother," she said. "Just chalk it up to a wife's curiosity."

He laughed. "Well, if you want me to take a look…"

"No need," she said, "but thanks for the offer."

After she hung up, she sat there for several minutes studying the mysterious pieces of paper and wondering what secret Albert was keeping. Unable to come up with even the most remote possibility, she picked up the telephone and dialed the number at the top of the invoice. On the second ring, a recording clicked on saying the number had been disconnected.

Thinking she might have misdialed she tried again, this time speaking the number aloud as she dialed. The recording clicked on a second time and repeated the same message.

Hitting a brick wall as she had only increased Margaret's curiosity. She pulled the county telephone directory from the bookshelf and searched Bateman Investigative Services. Nothing. She tried searching Bateman Detective Agency, Bateman Surveillance, Bateman Security, and the yellow pages. Still nothing. Returning to the residential listings, she ran her finger down the long list of Batemans. It began with Alfred Bateman and continued on until it reached Yolanda Bateman. Two columns in all.

It would take a day, possibly two, for her to call every one of these listings, and even then she could come away with nothing. Not discounting the idea altogether but wondering if what she found would be worth the effort, she replaced the directory on the bookshelf.

First, she had to finish cleaning out Albert's desk. There was only the top drawer and a few more file folders to go. Once those were done, she'd go back to searching for Bateman. Pulling the last of the folders from the drawer, she began leafing through them.

While she'd gone through the earlier folders page by page, careful not to miss a thing, these got little more than a cursory glance. A few prospectuses from companies he'd considered a solid investment, his daddy's death certificate, a copy of last year's income tax return. None of these things interested Margaret. She was still wondering about those invoices and what it was Albert needed to keep secret. She tossed the outdated prospectuses in the waste basket, closed the drawer, and returned to the telephone book.

"That top drawer can wait," she mumbled as she dialed Alfred Bateman's number. The phone rang nine times. Seconds before she was going to hang up, the receiver was lifted from its cradle. She could hear someone rustling around, but no one spoke.

"Hello? Are you there?" she asked.

After what seemed a long time, someone on the other end yelled, "Hello?"

The voice was so loud she felt vibrations in her ear.

"No need to shout," she said. "I can hear you just fine. I'm looking for Alfred Bateman."

"Which one?" he yelled.

Stumped, Margaret paused a moment. "The one who would be involved in the Bateman Investigative Services company."

"Can you give me that again?"

Holding the receiver a good distance from her ear, she repeated the request and added, "Can you please lower your voice?"

They went back and forth several times before she learned that the old man and his son were both named Alfred Bateman and had no connection to the investigation company.

"We're butchers," he said. "Always have been, always will be."

Margaret thanked him for his time and hung up.

A single phone call had used up almost 15 minutes. At this rate it would take a week to call all of the Batemans, and even then there was no guarantee of success. With a groan of resignation she moved on, dialing the next number.

After five no answers, one "temporarily disconnected" recording, and 19 people who had no idea what she was talking about, she dialed the number for Geneva Bateman. By then, it was after 7 pm.

Forcing herself to sound cheerful, she said, "Good afternoon. I wonder if you can help me. I'm trying to locate someone familiar with a company called Bateman Investigative Services. Does that name sound—"

"It's seven-fifteen," the woman snapped. "We're in the middle of dinner. You should have enough courtesy to call at a more suitable time, not when a family is eating their meal."

She slammed the telephone down—hard.

Margaret crossed Geneva off of her list, then set the telephone book aside. Tomorrow she could start over again. Right now, she was hungry, tired, and discouraged.

The thought of sitting alone at the kitchen table settled in Margaret's chest, and she could feel herself crumbling. Leaning forward, she lowered her face into her hands and gave way to tears again.

"Why, Albert, why?" she said through her sobs. "Why would you find it necessary to keep this secret?"

She thought back to that year: 1944. The year they bought this house. They'd gone through a rough patch the year before, and she'd been on the verge of leaving. Not because she didn't love him, but because they argued night and day.

Buying the house was Albert's way of trying to make things better. He'd started to do that sort of thing; buy her some ridiculously expensive gift, thinking it would smooth things over. Of course, it didn't.

The house was never the problem. She could have been happy forever living in the colonial they had. What she wanted was a family, but he refused to listen. For years they'd tried to have a baby, but it never happened. After two miscarriages, they gave up trying.

She begged him to consider adoption, but he wouldn't hear of it. He had a dozen different excuses. He was too old to contend with an infant. With just the two of them they were living the good life, and a baby would change everything. Somebody else's baby could never be the same as having their own child. The list went on and on.

She thought she'd learned to live with it, but the truth was she hadn't. She hadn't tried to find her siblings and had gone through life thinking one day she'd have her own family. When Albert wouldn't consider adoption, the empty spot in her heart grew larger. She'd explained that to him, but as an only child himself he either couldn't understand or chose not to. They'd stayed together, but it was years before she completely forgave him.

Margaret wondered if during those difficult years Albert had found other ways to satisfy himself. Was it possible he had a lover? Another family? He traveled and it was not unusual for him to be gone for two or three days at a time, but she'd never considered that it might not be all business. She'd lain next to him in the bed, their bodies so close that only a thought could pass between them, and she'd never suspected…

"Damn you, Albert!" she shouted. "Damn you for leaving me!"

She balled her hands into fists and hung her head.

Looking for Answers

Once the memory of that terrible year settled in Margaret's heart, it grew larger and more vivid. She thought back on how night after night she and Albert had climbed into bed with their bodies turned away from one another and a wall of silence between them. She'd cried until there were no more tears left but couldn't remember him shedding a single tear. At the time, she'd thought it was because he'd believed it unmanly to cry. Now she had to wonder.

When things were at their worst, she'd reached out to him, tried to make him understand why having a child was so important. She told him things she'd never spoken of before, explained how being separated from her brothers and sisters had caused an emptiness inside her soul, an emptiness that could only be filled with a family of her own. He'd taken her in his arms, held her face to his, and said he was her family. Then he swore come what may, he'd always be there for her.

Later on he'd asked why the family broke apart as they did, but she could never fully answer the question. She said only that times were hard, and after her daddy disappeared her mama did what she thought was right. He'd eyed her with curiosity, then turned away saying he found it hard to believe anyone could think sending children off on their own was right.

While she was struggling to move from day to day, he'd stood his ground and hidden away whatever it was he needed to keep secret. On their wedding day, they'd sworn to love one another for better or worse. She'd kept that promise and stayed faithful through the worst. Had he done the same?

Earlier Margaret felt hungry; now the thought of food nauseated her. She left the can of soup sitting on the counter and pulled a brandy snifter from the cupboard. Pouring a full inch of cognac into the glass, she swirled it as she'd seen Albert do then tipped the glass to her mouth and drank. It was the first brandy she'd had in years, decades maybe. Albert had enjoyed a nightly cognac, but she'd never found pleasure in it until now.

The heady brown liquid was sweet and satisfying. It eased the fluttering in her chest. She took another sip and then another. When the glass was empty, she refilled it and carried it into Albert's office. This was where he'd hidden those invoices. If there was anything more to find, this was where it would be.

She slid a note paper in the telephone directory to mark her place, closed the book, and placed it on the credenza. It was too late to call anyone now. She'd have to continue tomorrow. Bateman seemed to be a family name, so it stood to reason that the person who owned the detective agency was a Bateman. Sooner or later she'd find them.

Although she'd started her search hoping to discover some charity, organization, or person Albert might have wanted to be the next beneficiary of his estate, now she would be content to learn the truth about Albert himself. If through all of this she found nothing, she'd name a beneficiary of her own choosing; a children's hospital perhaps or, better yet, an adoption agency. A charity to help women with broken hearts find a family.

Taking another sip of brandy, Margaret returned to the task at hand. Tonight she would go through the one remaining drawer and tomorrow search the credenza and bookshelf.

She pulled open the small drawer and started sorting through a jumble of rubber bands and paper clips. Behind the box of pencils, she found a stack of note pads with "A.J. McCutcheon, Attorney at Law" printed at the top. A thousand times he'd used those same pads to leave her reminders: pick up the dry cleaning; pay the paper boy; have the car washed. At times the notes had been a source of aggravation, and she'd grumbled about him treating her like a servant. Now she'd give anything for just one more note signed with his scrawling "A."

The thought of never again seeing one of those notes, of never having *anyone* remind her of *anything*, was almost overwhelming. Fighting to hold back the tears, she downed a swig of brandy and dropped the note pads into the waste basket. She'd be better off without all those blank pages reminding her of how empty her life had become.

With the note pads gone from the drawer, Margaret spied something she hadn't noticed before: a packet of business cards banded together. The top card was from the trucking company they'd used when they moved into the house. She lifted the packet and as she did so the dry rubberband snapped, sending a spray of cards across the desk.

She spotted it right away: a business card from Bateman Investigative Services. It read, "Thomas H. Bateman, Serving you with discretion. Licensed, Bonded, & Insured." She thought the street address and telephone number on the card appeared to be the same as on the invoices. Taking no chances, Margaret checked and they were the same. She now had his full name but little else.

Setting Bateman's card on the side of the desk, she began to shuffle through the others. An electrician, a barber, cleaning services, two plumbers. Tradesmen Albert had dealt with years ago; nothing of any use. Seeing no value in these, she swept her hand across the desk and brushed the pile of cards into the waste basket. Her elbow hit Bateman's card and knocked it to the floor. When she bent to retrieve it, she saw a handwritten phone number on the back side. Realizing this number was not the same as the one she'd called earlier ignited a spark of hope.

She glanced at the clock: 10:30. Too late to call...or was it? If it were an office no one would answer anyway, and if it was Bateman's home she'd hang up and say nothing. In either case, she'd know if this was a working number. Pushing past the trepidation that had settled in her chest, she dialed the number and waited. On the ninth ring, a man answered.

Her plan to hang up was quickly forgotten.

"Thomas Bateman?" she asked.

"Yeah, who's this?"

"The Thomas Bateman who owns the Bateman Investigative Services company?"

"Used to. I retired five years ago. What's this about?"

"My name's Margaret Rose McCutcheon. You did some work for my husband back in forty-four, and I was—"

"If you're looking to hire a detective, get somebody else. I'm retired."

"I'm not really looking to hire a detective. I just want to find out—"

"It's damn near eleven o'clock, lady! I'm not interested in what you want; I told you, I'm retired."

"But if you'll just listen to—"

There was a click, and he was gone.

Even though Thomas Bateman hadn't been willing to hear her out, Margaret felt strangely optimistic about the next day. She now knew who the mysterious Mr. Bateman was and where to find him. She lifted the snifter, drained the glass, and started toward the bedroom.

⌒◦◦◦⌒

The two snifters of brandy enabled Margaret to drift off, but her sleep was fitful and the dreams disturbing. She saw herself standing at the edge of a room filled with people. At first they seemed strangers, but as she ventured into the crowd familiar faces began to take shape: her mama, Dewey, Louella, and, over on the far side of the room, Albert, eyeing her with a smug smile. She waved to him, grabbed Dewey's hand, and started across the room. As she was making her way through the crowd, she could see a great sadness on Albert's face so she called out to him and waved again. He looked at her, gave one last smile, and evaporated into nothingness.

"Albert!" she screamed and woke with a start.

The sky was still dark when she opened her eyes and sat up. A quick glance at the clock told her it would be another hour before it would be light and several more before she could call Thomas Bateman. Knowing sleep was now impossible, she climbed from the bed, pulled on a robe, and started downstairs.

She never liked being up at such an ungodly hour. It reminded her of the years in West Virginia when they'd left the house before daybreak and walked out of the hollow. Dewey had held her hand as they made their way along the long dirt road, but still she'd been frightened. He'd asked why, and she told him in the dark she couldn't see trouble coming. That morning he'd held her hand a bit tighter and said not to worry, that he'd always be there to protect her.

After Barrettsville and the family breaking up, he'd been the one she missed most.

Margaret brewed a pot of coffee, poured herself a cup, and sat at the kitchen table. She thought through what she'd say to Tom Bateman and tried to anticipate any arguments he might have. She wasn't going to give up, not even if he hung up on her again. It seemed unlikely that would happen, but if it did she'd drive over to his house, bring home-made cookies as a peace offering, and refuse to leave until he agreed to talk to her.

When the pale glimmer of a new day rose above the treetops, she showered and dressed. It was still too early to call so she sat at the table, downed a second cup of coffee, and after that a third. She'd originally thought 10 am would be an appropriate time, but by 9:30 she could wait no longer.

He answered on the second ring, and she recognized his voice.

"Mr. Bateman, I apologize for calling so late last night. I needed to speak with you about an urgent matter and didn't realize the hour. My husband died three weeks ago, and you did some work for him back in forty-four—"

"I'm sorry about your husband, but as I told you I'm retired. I closed the business five years ago. You're gonna have to find yourself another detective."

"No one else will be able to help me. I'm looking for information about a case you worked on."

"Twenty-four years ago?" He gave a cynical laugh. "I'm sorry, but you're wasting your time. There are days when I can't remember what I had for breakfast. I'm sure as hell not going to remember something that far back."

"But you have files. Perhaps if you checked—"

"Look, I was never really good about record keeping, and whatever files I do have are packed away in the basement."

"I'll pay for however long it takes you to go through the boxes. I'd like to know what it was you were investigating for my husband."

"If he wanted you to know, don't you think he would've told you?"

"You'd think so," Margaret replied sadly, "but he didn't. Now I'm trying to straighten out the estate he left behind, and I'd like to know if there's someone else who should be taken into consideration."

A lengthy silence followed. "By someone, you mean a kid he might have fathered?"

"That's something I won't know unless you're willing to look through those files."

"Even if I go through those boxes, there's no guarantee I'll find something. I was a one-man shop, and I did a lot of small jobs without taking time for paperwork."

She sensed that he was starting to waffle. "I'll pay double the going rate regardless of whether or not you're successful. And if you tell me you couldn't find anything, I'll not bother you again."

"You'll pay double?"

"Yes. And I won't question your results."

"You realize I could charge you for twenty, thirty hours, not lift a finger, then tell you I didn't find anything."

"I know that," Margaret said. "But I trust you're not that kind of person. If you were, I don't think my husband would have done business with you."

"One of those, huh? If he was such an upstanding and honorable guy, why is it you don't know what I was working on for him?"

"It was a long time ago, and we were going through a really rough patch. Maybe he thought we wouldn't make it."

"Yeah, I hear you. I didn't know my wife was cheating on me until she walked out and took the dog with her."

They talked for a while longer; he told her if he agreed to take the job, she'd have to pay a retainer up front. She assured him that was no problem. After they discussed timing, he agreed to do it.

"Call me the minute you have something," she said.

"You mean the minute I know whether or not I have something," he replied.

"Yes, either way."

Margaret hung up the telephone and began waiting.

The Discovery

After telephoning to say he'd received Margaret's retainer check, two weeks went by with no further word from Tom Bateman. Jeffrey called twice; once to ask if she wanted to receive a copy of the minutes for the partners' weekly meetings and the second time to ask if she'd given any more thought to his buyout of her shares in McCutcheon & Schoenfeld. Both times she answered no.

There were a number of other calls: the dry cleaner reminding her that Albert's suit had yet to be picked up, a secretary for the library's fundraising campaign asking if she could chair this year's gala, and Josie asking how she was doing.

"I've been worried about you not eating. Since the Portlands moved, I've got Tuesdays and Thursdays free. If I won't be a bother, I'll stop by and fix you a bite of lunch."

"A bother?" Margaret replied. "Why, you couldn't be a bother even if you tried. With Albert gone, you're the brightest spot in my day."

After chatting for a few minutes longer, Josie said she would be there with some homemade oatmeal cookies in about 20 minutes.

When she hung up the telephone, Margaret began mulling over what Josie had said about having Tuesdays and Thursdays free. For as long as she'd known Josie, the woman had worked five days a week and sometimes six. Two weeks after her twin girls were born, she'd returned to work. She wasn't crazy about scrubbing floors and cleaning toilets; her family needed the money. With three kids and a one-legged husband, the job of breadwinner had fallen on Josie.

As she sat there drumming her fingers on the table, a thought began to take shape. Josie's situation wasn't all that different from her mama's. Both women had borne the same burden of responsibility. Margaret could still picture the tears in her mama's eyes the day Aunt Rose came to take her.

"It's for the best," Mama said. *"Aunt Rose will give you all the things I can't."*

That part was true, but Margaret found no happiness in it. It was wrong, terribly wrong for life to be so unfair.

IF YOU NEVER TRY, YOU WILL NEVER SUCCEED.

She'd been unable to change her mama's circumstances, but there was something she could, and would, do for Josie.

That afternoon as they sat at the table with their pimento cheese sandwiches, Margaret asked if Josie was planning to take on another client for Tuesdays and Thursdays.

"Afraid so," she replied. "The family that bought the Portland house has four little ones, so I figured I'd stop there on the way home."

"So you haven't spoken to them yet?"

"I haven't had the chance."

"Good. I need extra help, and now that you're available…"

Josie tilted her head, a suspicious frown tugging her mouth downward. "You need help with what? Nothing here needs doing."

"It most certainly does. Why, I can't even remember the last time that silver tea service was polished, and it's been ages since I've done anything with those back bedrooms."

"That's a lot of hogwash, and you know it. There ain't a speck of tarnish on that tea pot, and we freshened up those guest rooms just this spring."

Sensing that her original plan was not working, Margaret switched strategies.

"The truth is I need a companion. Someone to see that I eat properly and—"

Josie laughed out loud. "Now that's an even bigger bunch of hogwash! You need somebody to take care of you like I need another mouth to feed. What in heaven's name are you up to?"

Margaret tried to remain straight-faced, but a smile broke free. "Okay, the truth is you could use a break, and I could use some company. An arrangement like this works for both of us. I'll pay you the same as the Portlands, and the work will be a whole lot easier."

Josie turned away, looking off into the distance. When she turned back, her dark eyes were misty.

"It's a real sweet offer," she said, "but I can't take it."

"Why not?"

"With no real work to do, it'd be like charity."

"It most certainly is not. It's a kindness that I never got to do for my mama."

"Doing for your mama is different; that's family."

"Family's not just blood relatives," Margaret countered, "it's anybody you care about. Would you deny a woman with no other family the small pleasure of doing something nice for somebody she cares about?"

Josie chuckled. "You may not have a family, but the good Lord sure enough gifted you with a lofty way of thinking."

"Are you saying you'll do it?"

"I'm saying I'll give it a try. All things considered, I suppose that tea service does look like it could use a good shine."

Margaret laughed, and they settled back with a fresh pot of coffee and the oatmeal cookies Josie brought. They were both on their second cup when the doorbell rang. Claiming this was part of her expanded duties, Josie hurried to answer it. A minute later she was back.

"There's a Mr. Tom Bateman asking to see you. Do you want to—"

Before she finished the sentence, Margaret was on her way to the door.

Tom Bateman was waiting in the foyer. He was tall, broad shouldered, and carried a bit of extra padding around his waist. He wore a tweed sports jacket, and his shirt was open at the collar. Unlike what Margaret had pictured, he was extremely good looking and seemed to be in great physical shape.

"I thought you were going to call," she stammered.

"I was, but then I thought better of it. There was a reason why your husband didn't want you to know about this, so before we get into what I was investigating we should talk."

She winced. "Please don't tell me Albert had another family."

"It's nothing of the sort," he said.

The relaxed look of his expression and the way his eyes crinkled at the corners made Margaret think Tom Bateman was someone who smiled often. On the telephone he'd sounded bristly and impatient. Curt almost. She'd imagined him short, bald, and portly; he was none of the three.

Trying to hold back the anxiety clawing its way up her throat, she thanked him for coming and led him into the living room where they sat across from one another. He pulled a thick folder from his briefcase and laid it on the coffee table in front of him.

"You were right, I did a job for your husband back in forty-four, but it wasn't about anything he was involved in. He was looking for information on your family."

Margaret looked at him with wide eyes.

"My family?"

He nodded. "This was over twenty years ago so when you called the name didn't register, but once I pulled the file I remembered it quite well. Most people hired me to check out things like a cheating wife, an unscrupulous business partner, or a runaway kid, but this case was very different and it stuck with me."

"We'd been married over twenty-five years by then. Why in the world would he be checking on my family?"

"It's not what you think. He wasn't looking for background dirt or anything like that. He just wanted to find them. He said you'd lost track of your siblings years earlier, and he wanted to locate them. We agreed that I wouldn't send any reports to the house because he was planning to surprise you. The investigation was making decent headway until I discovered something pretty troubling. When I told him about it, he said to drop the case."

"Drop the case? Why?"

Tom smiled. It was a warm smile, one that came from the inside. In the depth of his eyes, she could see a genuine look of compassion.

"I remember your husband really well. Like you said, he was a good man. He felt that hearing about what I found would only cause you more heartache, so he paid me for my time and told me to forget it. I put the report in the file and hung onto it. I thought there was a chance he'd change his mind and come back wanting to know more, but he never did."

"I haven't seen any of my brothers or my sister for over fifty years," she said. "Mama and Louella were both dead and buried before I married Albert, so I won't be too surprised if some of the others are as well. I lost my husband a month ago. He was the love of my life, and losing him was the most painful thing I've ever experienced. I made it through that; I think I'm strong enough to handle a little more bad news."

He reached into the folder, pulled out a Blair County criminal complaint dated 1910, and handed it to her. "This is about your father."

Margaret's hand trembled as she held the paper and read through the report.

"Martin Hobbs, a union representative for the National Brotherhood of Electrical Workers, has been reported as a missing person. He is suspected of embezzling almost $1,000 in union membership dues entrusted to him. Hobbs was last seen on January 27, 1910. The following day he sent a message that he was sick and would be unable to report for work. He was scheduled to return on Monday but failed to report.

"In an earlier incident which occurred in 1908, Hobbs abandoned his family in West Virginia and took up residence in Pennsylvania. His latest disappearance, we believe, shows a tendency to repeat this behavior pattern. At this time, his wife and children claim to know nothing about his whereabouts. Subsequent to his disappearance, Mrs. Hobbs and the children left Barrettsville and returned to her maternal home in Coal Creek, West Virginia.

"Hobbs also maintained a spousal relationship with a Martha Mae Keller and was residing with her since his transfer to Altoona. While Keller does not deny the relationship, she claims to have no knowledge of Hobbs's prior marital status or the missing funds. Union officials have offered a $100 reward for information leading to the arrest of Hobbs."

When she'd finished reading the report, Margaret sat there feeling the memory of that time come alive again. It had happened a lifetime ago and she thought she'd forgotten it, but here it was as painful and ugly as it was during those terrible years. She'd known about her daddy's mistress and his disappearance; they all did. That's why they left Barrettsville.

She'd also known about the earlier time when he'd left them in Coal Creek, and they'd struggled along until there was nothing left in the money jar. She was only five when he'd disappeared that time and could barely remember him. But she remembered the years that followed. She remembered being hungry and watching her mama cry.

She hadn't known about the missing money.

Pushing back the tears and trying not to feel the ache of it, she looked at Tom and asked, "Was this the only thing you found? What about my brothers or my sister, Nellie?"

"Nothing on Nellie." He opened the folder and read from a page of handwritten notes. "Ben Roland settled in Farstack, Alabama, married a woman named Rebecca Sawyer, and spent twelve years working for the Woodward Iron Company. In October of 1937, he lost his life in the Woodward coal mine explosion. There is no record of them having had children, and there was nothing more on Rebecca Sawyer. You said you already knew about Louella. She never married and died of tuberculosis in 1916. Your brother, Dewey…"

Margaret leaned forward, her heart suddenly racing.

"Dewey joined the army in November 1917, did his basic training in Spartanburg, South Carolina, at Camp Wadsworth and was shipped out to France the following summer. My initial report from the Veterans Bureau stated that he was wounded in France but supposedly treated here in the States. I didn't follow up, because that's when your husband, Albert, said to drop the investigation."

"Dewey. Was he—is he—still alive?"

Tom shrugged. "I honestly don't know. To find out, I would've had to do a much more extensive search of the Veterans Bureau files, which presented a bit of problem since that organization became part of the Veterans Administration about twenty years earlier."

"Was there anything on any of the others—Virgil, Oliver, John Paul? Edward was the baby. Surely you found something on him."

He gave a grimace and shook his head. "I only worked on this for a short time, then your husband—"

"I know," Margaret said sadly. "Told you to drop the investigation."

Tom gave an apologetic nod. "I wish I could tell you something more, but..." As his words trailed off, he stood. "If you like, I'll leave this folder with you. Perhaps you can get someone else to take it from here."

He gathered the sheets of paper, slid them back into the folder, and handed it to Margaret. "Good luck. I hope you do find your family. It's what your husband wanted for you."

As Margaret stepped into the hall to show Tom out, she bumped into Josie who was standing there with a plate of cookies.

"Sorry," she said, "I was coming in to ask if you and your guest would like—"

"Not now," Margaret replied and continued toward the door.

Again, she thanked Tom for coming. They shook hands, and he left. When Margaret turned back, Josie was still standing there with the cookies.

"You're just going to let him leave like that? You're not going to ask him to keep looking for your sister and brothers?"

"He's retired. He doesn't do detective work anymore."

"But you didn't ask."

"I had to practically beg him to look for the file. There's no way he'd—"

"Not if you don't ask. After all these years of worrying about your family, you're gonna let the one person who might have a shot at finding them walk away?"

"I couldn't ask him, not after he's already said—"

"If it's no, it's no. At least you'll have tried. If Elgin or one of my kids was missing, I'd do way more than ask. I'd get down on my knees and beg him to keep looking."

Margaret stood there, her eyes flicking back and forth first through the window at Tom as he moved down the walkway then back to Josie's impassioned expression.

"You've got to do it," Josie pleaded. "You'll hate yourself if you don't."

If you never try, you will never succeed.

A fire sparked in Margaret's eyes. "You're right, I should have—"

Before she'd finished the thought, Josie shoved the plate at Margaret, flung open the door, and darted down the walkway. She was skinny as a stick and lightning fast.

Tom was almost to his car when she hollered out, "Excuse me, sir. Mrs. McCutcheon would like you to come back. She forgot to ask you something."

He grinned. "I thought she might."

Once he was back inside, Margaret hemmed and hawed for several minutes, first claiming she'd forgotten to give him his final check, then asking questions about how he thought one would go about obtaining a detective willing to undertake such a search. After almost 10 minutes, she finally got around to asking if he'd be willing to pick up where he left off.

"Josie thought I should ask you to do it, since you're familiar with the case and you've already done so much work on it. I explained that you were retired, but she suggested it wouldn't be the same as taking on a new case. Just more like finishing up one you'd already started."

"It's been twenty-four years. That's a long time for a missing person case to sit and grow colder. I didn't have a whole lot to go on back then, and with no new leads to follow…"

"I could give you more; tell you things Albert wasn't aware of, like details on my brothers and sisters. That's something to go on."

"You need someone with fresh eyes, a new way of looking at things. I've been retired for five years, and don't have the connections I once had."

"But you've got experience, and Albert trusted you."

He hesitated a moment then grinned. "I'll admit, it's an interesting challenge, but I'm not ready to take on a full-time job. It's too—"

"It doesn't have to be full-time. Work on it when you want; I promise not to hound you. I've waited this long; it won't kill me to wait a bit longer."

"Without much to go on, it could easily be six months, maybe even a year or more. And after all that, you might not know anything more than you know now."

"At least I'll know one more thing," Margaret said. "I'll know I tried."

He smiled and gave a nod. "You've got me on that."

Her face brightened. "So you'll do it?"

"Depends," he said and smiled. "Are you asking, or is that still Josie?"

With her cheeks taking on color, she lifted her eyes and said, "I'm asking."

That afternoon they talked for almost three hours. Tom asked questions and took notes as Margaret told what she could remember. She recalled most of their birthdays but in some cases could not say where her brothers had been when she last heard. After she found herself unable to answer several questions, she shook her head and slumped back in disappointment.

"Seems I don't know that much about Nellie and my brothers after all. If only I could…"

"Give it time," Tom said. "Once your memory starts going back, you'll be surprised at what you come up with."

That night when Margaret drifted off, she was picturing the dirt road that wound its way up the mountain to where the small house sat just beyond the bend in the creek.

1901
Coal Creek, West Virginia

In the Beginning

The year Margaret Rose was born was one Eliza Hobbs would remember forever. Her marriage to Martin was rocky almost from the start, but that summer brought soaring new highs and a low that would forever taint their relationship.

At one time Eliza was considered the prettiest girl not just in Coal Creek but in all of Kanawha County, West Virginia. She had light brown curls, eyes the soft blue of a summer sky, and a smile that drew people to her. Back then she'd had her choice of suitors, but she'd chosen Martin. He was taller than most, broad-shouldered, and didn't have a speck of coal dust clinging to his skin.

"The mines will kill a man before his time," he'd said. "I've got bigger plans."

Eliza knew he spoke the truth, because her daddy had been laid in the ground the year before his 40th birthday.

As they pushed back and forth in her mama's porch swing, Martin told of how he was already apprenticed to a Charleston electrician and in five years would be considered a master electrician himself.

"I'm gonna make it big; really big," he'd said. "A few years from now, when everybody's looking to have electric lights in their house, I'll be riding the gravy train."

He was a smooth-talker who won her over with promises of love and a life finer than anyone in that coal mining town could ever imagine. After painting their future with a rose-colored brush, he'd gone down on one knee and asked her to marry him. A lovestruck woman, Eliza said she'd never wanted anything more in all her life and pressed her lips to his.

A month later, they were married. He took her to Charleston just as promised, but it was a two-room flat on the fourth floor of a building with narrow hallways, strange smells, and the sound of raucous laughter that continued into the wee hours of morning.

While their courtship had been sweet with promise, their marital life was challenging and rough as sandpaper against Eliza's skin. If Martin had a bad day at work, he brought his grievances home with him and inevitably a cross word escalated into a full-blown battle. He'd complain that she was a terrible cook and a poor excuse for a wife. She'd come right back at him, saying the dingy old apartment was not what he'd promised. For a while it seemed as though the marriage was destined to fail.

Eliza missed Coal Creek, the friends she'd known, the people she'd grown up with, and the church she'd attended. In Charleston she found none of that; there was only Martin and the arguments that seemed to go on forever. On two different occasions Eliza packed her bag and said she was going home to Coal Creek, but both times Martin pleaded with her not to go.

"We've gotten off to a rough start," he said, "but we love each other, and we'll get through this. Give it time, Eliza, and it will get better. I swear it will."

In time, her resolve would weaken and she'd grow teary. Then he would lift her into his arms and carry her off to bed.

Oliver was born that first year, and the tiny flat seemed to grow even smaller. With no room for a crib, Eliza emptied a dresser drawer of Martin's work clothes, padded it with soft cloth, and laid their first child in it. Before Oliver outgrew the drawer, she was pregnant again.

In early December, word came that her mama was sick and Eliza was needed at home. By then the apartment felt almost claustrophobic, so she jumped at the chance.

"It won't be forever," she said. "Just until Mama gets on her feet. When you've got time off, you'll come to visit us."

Weary of listening to Oliver cry and Eliza complain about the apartment, Martin readily agreed. He promised to be there for Christmas and early the next morning bundled Eliza and the baby off to the train station. Once they were gone, he no longer felt the constraints of marriage and spent most of his evenings at the tavern.

Despite his promise, he didn't make it home for Christmas nor to welcome in the new year. When he finally did arrive back in Coal Creek, Eliza had already given birth to Ben Roland and buried her mama.

By this time, Martin had grown used to coming and going as he pleased, spending evenings at the tavern, and having no one to answer to. To him, this was the best of both worlds. He could enjoy his freedom and still hold onto Eliza. Instead of stating she no longer had ties to Coal Creek and insisting she return to Charleston, he argued for the opposite.

"Let's keep it this way for a while," he said. "At least until I'm making enough to get a bigger place where there's room for the kids."

It was a lie he told and Eliza eagerly believed. She wanted to be away from Charleston as much as he wanted her to be. In Coal Creek she had friends, and she'd found a peaceful life that was nonexistent elsewhere.

Those first few years, Martin came home every other weekend and at times every weekend. After a week or two apart, they'd fall into each other's arms and make love with the passion of newlyweds. During the two days he was at home not a cross word was spoken, and it seemed as though their arrangement was the answer to a perfect marriage. While there was not enough time for resentment and petty grievances to build up, there was plenty of time for lovemaking.

As the years rolled by, their family became larger. Dewey came along the following year, then Louella, and after her John Paul. With each new baby, Martin grew less tolerant, quicker to anger, and less inclined to make it home on weekends. When he did make it home, he often spent his time back by the smokehouse where he kept several jugs of bootleg whiskey.

Little by little, their relationship soured. He yelled at the children, she complained about him not coming home, they hauled out the old complaints they'd once forgotten, and found reasons to dislike one another. While the children were what made Eliza happy, they were Martin's nemesis. After almost nine years together, she saw him as foul-tempered and belligerent, not at all like the man she thought she'd married.

There were times when she regretted not having stuck to her guns and left him in the early months of their marriage, before Oliver, back when she still had other options. Now with five children and a sixth on the way, she had no alternative but to stay.

⚭

Margaret Rose was born on the day Dewey celebrated his fifth birthday. On March 6th, Eliza felt the onset of labor and sent for the midwife. With this being her sixth baby, it was expected to be an easy delivery. Before lunch the midwife settled in, began massaging Eliza's stomach, and preparing for delivery.

"It won't be long now," she said confidently.

John Paul, born thirteen months earlier, had taken less than an hour to make his entrance into the world, but this baby proved far more stubborn. Eliza labored all that day, and by time the moon crested in the night sky the midwife was frantic. She'd never lost a mother or baby but feared this would be her first. Moments before the clock struck midnight, she roused Oliver, Eliza's eldest.

"Do you know where Doc Perkins lives?" she asked the boy.

He looked at her, rubbed the sleep from his eyes, and nodded. "Down by the bend in—"

"Then get dressed quick. I'm gonna need you to fetch the doc. Your mama's in a bad way."

Before the lad had time to pull on his britches and scoot out the door, the clock chimed. Seconds later Eliza screamed, and Margaret Rose slid into the world. It was March 7th.

The midwife stayed for two days to help out. On the second day, she took Eliza aside and told her that two babies having the same birthday was a sure sign.

"A sign of what?" Eliza asked.

"Unity. Those two babies are joined together the same as if they'd been born twins. The boy will be her protector for as long as they live."

Not given to the belief of such superstitions, Eliza pooh-poohed the thought.

Before the week was out, she knew what the midwife had said was true. While the other children went about their day ignoring the new arrival, Dewey did not. Right from the start, he seemed to take ownership of the new baby. A dozen times a day he peeked inside the cradle, and if the infant so much as whimpered he'd call for Eliza to come and check on her. Once Margaret Rose was fed and diapered, he'd stand there and ease the cradle back and forth until she was sound asleep. Before the baby was two weeks old, he knew how to lift her from the cradle and quiet her crying.

⟡

A week before Margaret Rose was born, the company Martin had been with for 10 years lost the electrical installation contract they'd counted on. Then they laid off nine men and stopped paying for overtime. Martin was one of the few who still had a job, but it meant he was expected to do more work with no extra pay. For six straight weeks he had to work a full day on Saturday and a half-day on Sunday, which put him in a mood blacker than a coal miner's face.

During that time, he wrote just one letter to tell Eliza he was working his ass off and didn't know when he'd have a chance to come home. Instead of asking about her or the new baby, he wrote three paragraphs about how he had half a mind to report the company to the Brotherhood of Electrical Workers Union. He then signed it "Love, Martin" and enclosed money enough for her to buy groceries.

When he finally made it back to Coal Creek, Margaret Rose was over a month old and already starting to smile. Instead of hurrying back to take a peek at his new daughter, he stomped around the kitchen complaining about the unfairness of his situation and how hard he had to work.

Having grown accustomed to the angry outbursts that could come or go in the blink of an eye, Eliza figured he needed a bit of time to simmer down and let go of the anger. While he went on about a lazy-ass boss telling him what to do, she busied herself about the kitchen. Every now and again she gave a nod; it was enough to prove she was listening but not enough to stoke the fire of his anger.

That tirade went on for over an hour before he appeared calm enough where Eliza thought she could talk to him.

"Margaret Rose was born on Dewey's birthday," she said pleasantly. "She's a feisty little thing. Pretty as a picture and has your eyes."

"If this means you're gonna be asking me for more money, you can forget it," Martin snapped. "Without that overtime, I've got nothing more to give."

He walked back to the bedroom, took a quick look inside the cradle, and told Eliza he was going out to the smokehouse.

As he stomped out the door, an ominous shiver crawled up her spine. She could usually sense the depth of his moods, but this time she'd misjudged him. The anger was still there, hidden just below his skin, and waiting to explode.

When Martin returned to the house, the sky was dark, the wind had picked up, and an echo of thunder rolled across the mountain. A storm was coming; Eliza was sure of it. She was uncertain whether it would come from the sky or her husband, but fearing the worst she'd fed the children early and tucked them into bed.

He came through the door red-eyed and wobbly as a new colt, staggered into the kitchen, set a jug of moonshine on the table, and plopped down in a chair. Under most circumstances, Eliza found it easier to give in to him than argue; she'd let him have his way and wait for his mood to change. But she'd seen the ugliness that came with his drinking, and that was the one thing she couldn't tolerate.

"I told you not to bring that in here," she said. "If you've got to drink, do it out by the smokehouse."

Martin narrowed his eyes and glared at her. "You've got no right to tell me what I can or can't do in my own house. I'll drink wherever I damn well please."

"This isn't your house," she said angrily. "It's my mama's."

He slammed his fist against the table so hard the jug bounced off and splattered on the floor then pulled himself up from the chair and stood.

"Like hell it is. I'm the one paying the bills. I'm the one feeding you and these kids. Far as I'm concerned, that means it's my house."

Eliza saw the bits of spittle that flew from his mouth and peppered the table, which only made her more determined.

"Just because you're paying the bills doesn't change the fact that it's still—"

"Yeah, it does. It changes everything. Your mama's dead and in the ground, and you don't have a nickel to your name. Without me, you and these kids got nothing."

"Do you think that's something to be proud of?" Eliza yelled back, her temper flaring as it never had before. "Providing for your family doesn't make you some kind of hero. You're only doing what most men do."

Martin crossed the room in three long strides, grabbed hold of her hair, and yanked her head back. With his face hovering over hers, he screamed a string of threats and obscenities far worse than anything she'd ever heard before. He was still going strong when Dewey ran into the room.

"Mama, come quick. Margaret Rose is breathing funny!"

Not giving up his hold on Eliza, Martin glared at the boy and yelled, "Get out of here!"

Dewey stood motionless for a few seconds, then started toward his daddy with fists flailing.

"Let Mama go!"

In a movement so quick it would forever be a blur in Eliza's mind, Martin released his hold on her, picked up Dewey, and hurled him across the room.

She heard the splintering of bone when he hit the wall. Now freed, she ran to the child and held him to her chest. His arm hung at an odd angle but instead of crying out, he pleaded, "Mama, you've gotta come see about Margaret Rose."

The door slammed. Without looking up, Eliza knew Martin was gone. He was on his way back to the smokehouse.

Wrapping her arm around Dewey's shoulders, she guided him back toward the bedroom. Before crossing the threshold, she heard Margaret Rose struggling. The baby's breath was heavy and labored. It had the raspy sound of something caught in her airway. When Eliza saw the tiny chest rising and falling quickly, she scooped the baby from the cradle and carried her to the kitchen.

Dewey cradled his arm like an afterthought as he followed along. With a worried expression that was way beyond his years, he asked, "Mama, is Margaret Rose gonna be alright?"

"I think so, Dewey, and if she is, it will be because you saved her life."

Eliza never went to bed that night. Once she had a kettle of water steaming atop the stove, she held the baby in her arms and stood rubbing circles across the tiny back. As the sun crested the horizon, the baby's breathing slowed and she dropped off to sleep.

Martin slept in the smokehouse that night, and when he woke from his drunken stupor the reality of what he'd done came at him like a battering ram. He and Eliza had their differences, and they'd butted heads any number of times before but never like that. A few times he'd lost his temper and been overly aggressive with her but not with any of the kids. He could only vaguely remember the altercation with Dewey. He remembered the boy coming at him and the terrible sound of Eliza's scream. Other than that, nothing.

He lowered his face into his hands and started to sob. He didn't need to remember the details to know it was bad. Very bad. The kind of thing for which Eliza would never forgive him.

As much as he enjoyed having the freedom to stay in Charleston and live life on his own terms, he didn't want to lose Eliza. He'd fallen in love with her the first time he'd seen her. Despite their differences, he still loved her. She was to him what the children were to her.

There were times when he thought if she had to choose between him and the children, he would be the loser. He wished it were different. He wished that, like him, she was content to have their life together be just the two of them, but that wasn't Eliza's nature. From the day she'd first discovered herself pregnant with Oliver, she'd taken on the glow of motherhood and even after six kids it had not dulled.

Earlier on there had been times when she'd threatened to leave him, and she might well have done it had he not pleaded for her forgiveness. But now, this thing with Dewey could be enough to have her turn her back on him forever. It was true that she didn't have a cent to her name, but she did have the house and she was still a good-looking woman. The probability was that any number of miners would welcome the chance to move in and play daddy to the kids.

That thought made Martin feel sicker than ever. His stomach rolled, and the whiskey he'd drank regurgitated and spilled from his mouth. His head throbbed, and he couldn't stop himself from sobbing.

It was late afternoon when he finally drew a bucket of water from the well, washed himself, and brushed back his hair. Sooner or later he would have to come to grips with what he'd done, face Eliza, and ask her forgiveness.

He approached the house and stood outside the screen door. She was inside, moving about the kitchen with the baby held to her shoulder. He peered through the screen looking across to the far side of the room but did not see any of the other children.

Speaking through the screen, he said, "Eliza, I'm real sorry for what I did. It was never in my mind to hurt you or the boy. It was the whiskey making me crazy."

She turned away without answering.

"You saying this isn't my house made me feel ashamed, like I haven't done right by you. I'm a man, Eliza, and like any man, I've got a certain amount of pride." He waited for her to respond, and when she didn't he continued. "I know I had too much to drink and got crazy, but that doesn't mean I don't love you; I do. I love you and every one of these kids. Maybe I don't show it as much as I ought, but that doesn't mean it's not in my heart."

She kept her back to him and said nothing.

"Be reasonable, Eliza. You're my wife. Sooner or later you're gonna have to forgive me."

She turned and looked at him with a hatred he'd not seen before.

"I don't have to do anything of the sort. There is no forgiveness for a man who'd break his son's arm."

"Eliza, please. At least try to understand."

She went into the children's bedroom and shut the door.

For the next two days, she didn't speak another word to him. He apologized a dozen or more times, but she looked away as if he weren't there. In the evening she'd leave a plate of food on the stove for him, but neither she nor any of the kids sat with him to eat.

On Monday, when he was supposed to return to his job in Charleston, he remained at home.

"I might get fired for not showing up today, but I can't leave here knowing you feel this way," he said mournfully. "I've done sworn I'd give up drinking and apologized every way I know how. What else can I do?"

"You might try telling your son you're sorry," she said. "I'm used to your moods and the way you go around blaming the world for every bad thing that happens, but he's not. He's a little boy who should be looking up to his daddy instead of being afraid of him. Being upset about work doesn't give you cause to take your anger out on Dewey."

Martin lowered his gaze to the floor as she spoke.

"You hurt him more than you hurt me. He's the one you need to ask for forgiveness."

Realizing the only way he'd get Eliza's forgiveness was to first get Dewey's, Martin talked to the boy before he left for Charleston.

"You gotta believe I didn't mean you any harm," he said. "Your mama and I had words; she said some hurtful things, and I lost my temper. I was wrong and I'm real sorry about it, but I'm your daddy and you gotta forgive me. You can do that, can't you, son?"

Without looking square into father's face, Dewey nodded.

Martin wrapped his arm around the boy's narrow shoulders and gave a genuine smile.

"I'm gonna make it up to you, Dewey; you'll see. Like I told your mama, I'm turning over a new leaf. From here on in, I'm gonna be the kind of daddy you kids deserve. I promise you that. Now let's go tell your mama. She's gonna be real happy about you forgiving me. Yessir, real happy."

The Fragile Forgiveness

After the incident with Dewey, it seemed as though Martin truly had changed for the better. At first, Eliza had her doubts. They'd been through this several times before, and while he'd be on his best behavior for a few weeks, sometimes months, he eventually went back to what she'd come to believe was his true nature.

This time was different. This time it felt as though he actually *wanted* to spend time with the children. He returned to Coal Creek every weekend, and often he brought some little gift for Eliza or one of the children. Although it was a four-mile walk from the train station, he'd come in smiling and calling for the kids. Once they were clustered around him he'd reach into his pocket, pull out a bag of candy, hand it to Eliza, and say, "Look what I brought my best girl." If it wasn't candy for her, it was a few marbles or a whittling knife for one of the boys.

Such a drastic change baffled the children at first, and a thin layer of apprehension hid beneath their smiles. This was especially true of the older boys, Oliver and Ben Roland. Wary though they might have been, they knew enough not to let it show. When their daddy called they came, and no matter what little trinket he'd pull from his pocket they'd carry on as if it were the very thing they'd been wishing for.

Dewey was another story. His resentment ran deep as a river. If he spotted Martin nearing the front gate or caught the sound of his voice, he'd head for the woods behind their back yard and be gone for the remainder of the day. Three Saturdays in a row he missed dinner, and the only thing that kept Martin from taking a switch to him was the plaster cast that still covered the boy's arm. On the few occasions when Martin's mood turned sour, it was almost always because of Dewey. Twice he tried to talk some sense into the boy but came away angrier than before.

"Talking to him is the same as hollering down a well," he said. "A waste of time."

Determined to hold on to this newfound peace at any cost, Eliza massaged the tightness in Martin's back.

"Be patient with him," she said. "He's just a child, and he's frightened. Give him time. He'll get over it."

"He'd better."

Shortly after he left for Charleston, Eliza called Dewey to come sit with her as she pushed back and forth in the swing with Margaret Rose in her lap.

Scrambling onto the swing, he asked, "Can I hold her?"

"Only if you promise to listen to what I have to say."

"I always listen," he replied defensively.

"Not always," she said and slid the baby onto his lap. "When your daddy tried to explain that he felt bad about what happened, you heard but you didn't really listen."

Dewey's smile faded. "What am I 'posed to do? I forgived him."

"No, you only said you forgave him, but that's not the same as forgiving him in here." Eliza touched her finger to his chest. "I know your daddy's got his faults, but he really is trying. Can't you can see that?"

Dewey nodded reluctantly. "I'm trying too."

"Do you think maybe you could try a little bit harder? If you did he'd be in a good mood all the time, and everybody's life would be a whole lot happier. You wouldn't just be doing it for your daddy, you'd be doing it for me and Margaret Rose and us all."

Dewey hesitated. Keeping his eyes on the baby, he mumbled, "Okay."

Two weeks later when Martin returned home and saw Dewey standing with the other boys ready to greet him, he gave a wide-open grin and handed Dewey the peppermint stick that he'd intended to give Eliza.

From that point on, things seemed to get better. On his next visit,

Martin brought Dewey a folding knife that was nicer than what he'd given the older boys. Dewey, in turn, thanked him profusely.

Mimicking what he'd seen his brothers do, he hugged his daddy's neck and said it was precisely the thing he'd been wishing for. Given a quick glance it would appear all was well, but the boy's expression barely managed to hide the resentment simmering beneath his skin.

As it turned out, that summer was the best they'd ever had. Martin's company received a contract to install electric lighting across the south side of Charleston and along the Kanawha River walkway. It was three times larger than the one they'd lost and twice as profitable. Martin was made a job foreman, paid for overtime, and received an override on everything his workers made. With extra money in his pocket and more freedom to come and go as he pleased, he began returning home on Friday evening instead of Saturday. By the time he'd come whistling up the road, Eliza would have the kids fed and ready for bed.

"You can stay up long enough to see what your daddy has in his pocket and ask about his week," she'd say, "but then it's bedtime."

After a bit of wheedling and pleas for more time, they'd gather around their daddy and listen as he told of the week's adventures. Martin made everything sound like a splendid adventure just as he had in the early days of their courtship, and he gloried in the telling of it. Standing and stretching his arms above his head to illustrate the grandeur of it, he told of how his crew wired the Clancy Building, a structure that stood higher than eight houses stacked atop one another.

"Because of my crew," he said proudly, "that building now has electric lights in the hallways and offices up as high as the sixth floor!"

Swayed by the swagger of such a story, Oliver and Ben Roland both declared that being an electrician had to be the best job in the world. Martin looked over to Dewey.

"What about you, Dewey?" he asked. "You think so too?"

Eliza cringed, fearing what the boy might say, but much to her surprise he said exactly what he thought his daddy wanted to hear.

"I sure do." He gave a grin that was almost believable to someone who didn't know him as well as his mama did. "Especially if a man can be the boss of a crew like you, Daddy."

Martin roared with laughter then reached across and tousled the boy's hair.

"Boss Man, that's what the men on the job call me." He tilted his chair back, rested his heels against the rung, and grinned. "Yessir. Being called Boss Man and having a bunch of fellows do as you say makes a man feel mighty good about his self. Mighty good."

Without waiting for any of the kids to ask, he moved on to telling how his crew singlehandedly crisscrossed the city, replacing gas streetlamps with electric lights.

"They're bright as the noonday sun," he said. "Why, a single bulb can light a street from one end to the other."

Later that night when he climbed in bed alongside Eliza, his touch was as gentle as it had been in that first year of marriage, and she gave herself to him willingly. They made love as they had before Oliver was born, and Eliza began to believe he'd gone back to being the man he once was: a man with big dreams. A man who could see promise in the future. In the wee hours of the morning after he'd turned on his side and gone to sleep, she lay awake wondering how it was that such a change had come about.

The two jugs of bootleg whiskey in the smokehouse grew dusty that summer. Instead of drinking, Martin spent afternoons with the older boys. He took them fishing, taught them to shoot a rifle, and even carried a bucket as he and Oliver gathered slack coal for the cookstove. Exhausted from all the activity the kids went to sleep early, crowded in the bed and on floor pallets in a single bedroom. That's when Martin went to Eliza.

It was like the early days of their courtship. While the children slept, Martin and Eliza pushed back and forth in the porch swing or sat beside the creek with the cool mountain stream splashing their ankles. They talked until the night sky was filled with stars; then they made love. He undressed her slowly, savoring each moment, and laughed when she turned her face from him.

"I'm embarrassed that you should see me this way," she said shyly.

"I'm your husband," he replied. "It's permissible."

"Permissible perhaps, but not seemly."

He laughed again and, despite her objections, pushed his tongue inside her mouth and lifted her onto the bed.

The second week of August, a blanket of heat settled over the mountain and the air became so thick it was hard to breathe. On a day when it was possible to raise a sweat just sitting, Martin made the four-mile walk from the train station and came in looking like he'd been caught in a rainstorm. There was no smile that day, and whatever he'd carried home in his pocket stayed there. He gave Eliza a quick peck on the cheek and said he'd be back by the smokehouse.

Fearing the worst, she replied, "Supper's almost ready; why don't you eat first?"

With an air of impatience pulling at his face, he mopped a rivulet of sweat from his forehead and glared at her. "If I wanted to eat, I'd have said so."

She was going to suggest a cool drink from the well, but before she had the chance he slammed the screen door and disappeared. Since there was nothing much she could do about Martin's mood, Eliza fed the children supper, tucked them into bed, then sat on the front porch to await his return.

The sky went from purple to black, and the night sounds of the mountain grew louder as they rolled across the ridge. The plaintive cry of a mountain lion hung in the air; then came a flutter of wings and the crack of a branch. A tear rolled down Eliza's cheek, and for what could have been the thousandth time she whispered a prayer that he wouldn't come in drunk.

"Not this time," she said, her words breaking with her sobs. "Not when everything is going so well. Please...not tonight of all nights."

Her prayer went unanswered, and as the hours inched by they took with them whatever hope she'd had that he would be sober. Too many times she'd sat here and waited. Too many times she'd wished for it to be different. Too many times she'd watched her hopes wither and die. Now she knew what to expect. Martin would drink his fill, then stumble through the door and fall heavy upon the bed. Or upon her.

She watched the moon drift across the sky, and when it started its descent she stood and went inside. There was very little time, an hour, maybe two, before the baby would wake and cry to be fed. She sat on the side of the bed for a moment. Then, without changing into her nightdress, she fell back and lowered her head onto the pillow.

Weary but unable to sleep she lay there, and before long she heard the sound of Martin's work boots lumbering across the porch. There was a thump followed by cussing. The thought of him coming at her as he had in the past churned in her stomach.

Not now, she prayed. *Please, not now.*

Closing her eyes, she pretended to be asleep. Eliza caught the smell of whiskey before she felt the weight of him fall onto the bed. Moments later he turned on his side and grabbed her breast.

"Wake up, wife," he mumbled, his words slurred.

She didn't need to hear the words to know what he wanted. It had happened countless times before. She'd expected it then but not now. She thought they'd moved past all that ugliness and moved on to a more loving relationship. Found a measure of happiness. As a huge weight of sorrow settled in her chest, her eyes grew watery then overflowed. Tears rolled down her cheeks and dropped silently onto the pillow.

Feigning sleep did not dissuade him. When he was like this, he didn't care whether she was awake or asleep. He'd take what he wanted then roll onto his back and sleep.

He was fumbling with the buttons on her dress when she heard the baby cry. At first it was just a whimper; then it became a wail. She pushed his hand aside.

"I've got to see to Margaret Rose. I'll be right back."

Apparently too drunk to argue, he rolled onto his back.

"Shut her up fast," he said, "I'm..." He mumbled a few less understandable words and began to snore.

On Saturday Martin slept until mid-afternoon. Anticipating that he'd be in a foul mood and nursing a hangover, Eliza sent the eldest three to visit Rita Miller's boys.

"Mention that you can stay the night if Rita doesn't mind having you," she told Oliver.

She'd seen it as a way to keep the pot from boiling over; give Martin the peace and quiet he'd be looking for and hope he'd wake in a better mood. The rainstorm that rolled through just after dawn brought a breeze that made the heat seem tolerable. Martin woke in a somewhat better mood and decided it was a good day for fishing.

"Fix me a bite to eat, and fetch the boys," he told Eliza.

"They're not here. I sent them to the Millers so you could get some sleep."

For a moment he just looked at her with his brows knotted together and his chin set hard as a rock.

"You sent them away when I'm home?" he said, his voice bristling with anger.

"I thought you'd want—"

"I don't give a damn what you think! They're my kids. When I'm home, I expect them to be here."

"John Paul and Louella are here. They'd love to spend time with their daddy. I could fix a picnic basket, and we could take them down by the creek to—"

"Are you deaf? I said I was in the mood to go fishing! There's no fish in the damn creek."

Still trying to salvage the day, Eliza offered to go get the boys if Martin would keep an eye on the little ones while she was gone.

"Don't bother. If they don't care enough to be here when their daddy's home, I'm sure as hell not gonna chase after them."

There was nothing Eliza could do to placate him, and the tension that rippled through the air grew greater by the minute. Each time she suggested something, he countered with a snide remark or a jibe so hurtful that it left marks on the inside of her skin.

"It's been a wonderful summer," she said. "Please don't ruin it now."

He glared at her. "Me? It's not me. You're the one."

They went back and forth for hours. When the sun began to set, he said he was leaving to catch the late train back to Charleston. As she stood at the door watching him go, the tears came again.

"There was something I wanted to tell you," she whispered mournfully. "Something I thought you'd be happy about."

By then, he'd vanished into the darkness of the road.

The Summer of Discontent

The heat wave that blanketed the mountain in August hung on throughout most of September, and Martin remained in Charleston the entire time.

In the fourth month of carrying a new baby, Eliza felt the heat more than most. Her breath came in fluttering gasps, and she suffered dizzy spells that left her so woozy she held onto a chair or table to keep from toppling over. In a condition such as this, there was little she could do when the leaves of the corn rolled inward and the tomato plants started to droop.

A blistering sun baked the ground into a dry crust, and they went for weeks on end without a drop of rain. The week before school started, she and the boys harvested the last of the crops and she canned and stored what she could. When she placed the turnips in the dugout that served as a root cellar, a fear of the oncoming winter settled in her heart.

By then, the money Martin left in the jar had dwindled to almost nothing. She spent the last of it to buy flour, lard, and molasses. Along with eggs from the chickens and the food she'd stored, this had to keep them going until he came home.

In late September a billow of dark clouds settled over the mountain, and Eliza grew hopeful that a storm would at long last rid them of the unbearable heat. For two days she stood on the porch watching the sky and praying for rain. She could hear thunder echoing along the hollow and see lightning in the distance, but her prayers went unanswered.

The sweltering heat continued for another two days before the sky finally broke open. Once the rain began it came in torrents, rushing down the side of the mountain, flooding the fields, and causing the creek to overflow. It rained for a full day and night before it stopped. Then the temperature plummeted.

With the onset of cooler weather, Eliza felt certain Martin would come home. She had yet to tell him of the baby that would be arriving in the middle of the winter, and such news could wait no longer. Her breasts had already grown to double their size, and she'd had to loosen the waistband of her skirt. Before long there would be no hiding the fact that she was with child, whether she told people or not. Just last week, Arlette Doty eyed the way her dress was stretched tight across her breasts and asked if she was expecting another little one.

Eliza didn't want Martin to hear about it that way. He was the baby's father; he deserved to hear the good news from her, not neighbors or the children. She'd wanted to tell him the last time he was home, but he'd been in a black mood and she'd decided to wait. What difference would a week or two make? she'd thought. She never imagined it would be two months.

The Friday after the heat wave broke, Eliza had the kids fed, bathed, and ready for bed before dark. Figuring Martin would be anxious to see them after such a lengthy absence, she allowed them to stay up well past bedtime. The hours came and went and long after they were all asleep in their beds, she sat on the porch and waited. When the moon rose high in the sky, the chill of night settled around her. A tiny voice in the back of her mind whispered that he wasn't coming but she ignored it, pulled a shawl around her shoulders, and continued to wait.

He didn't make it that weekend or the next, and her heart began to feel heavy as a stone. She went from day to day wondering where he was, if he'd been hurt, and why he didn't send some word of when he'd be back. When the fear in her chest swelled to the size of a watermelon, she sent a letter asking him to come home. She said the family missed him and explained that the money he'd left in the jar had run out. She didn't mention anything about the baby, because it was news she wanted to deliver personally.

The following weekend he came home late in the afternoon on Saturday, not on Friday evening as he had in the summer. In the months he'd been gone he'd gained some weight, grown a mustache, and changed in a way Eliza couldn't quite put her finger on. He wasn't in a bad mood, but neither was he interested in seeing the kids.

"The boys don't realize you're home," she said. "They're out back. I'll call them in."

He shrugged. "Don't bother. I'll see them before I leave tonight."

"You're leaving tonight? Why so soon?"

Shifting his weight from one side to the other, Martin pushed back in the chair and absently glanced off, not at anything specific but looking away from Eliza.

"We've been real busy on the job. I need some time to rest up and get ready for work."

"You haven't been home for two months. I figured you'd at least stay until Sunday."

"Well, I'm not. There's things I've gotta do in Charleston."

"On Sunday? You don't work on Sunday so why—"

"Stop complaining, Eliza. You said to come home because you needed money. I came; isn't that good enough?"

"Yes, we do need money, but it's more than that. I wanted you here because you're the children's daddy. They need you to spend time with them, teach them things. The boys are getting older, they need—"

His eyes narrowed. "Why is it always about what they need? Do you ever think about what *I* need? I've gotta work; if I don't, nobody eats."

Eliza saw the color rising in his face and became worried that this visit would turn out to be like the last one.

Not now; please, God, not now.

"I know how hard you work," she said, forcing the sound of sweetness into her words. "I may not always say something, but the children and I appreciate it more than you know."

Pulling her mouth into a smile, she crossed the room and lowered her face to his. She'd intended to kiss him full on the mouth the way he liked, but he jerked his head to one side and she ended up brushing her lips across his cheek. The way it happened struck her as odd, but there was no way of knowing whether or not his move was intentional. For a moment she thought she'd caught the scent of something different on his skin, but she pushed it aside and continued. What she had in mind was far more important; she had to tell him about the baby.

Still keeping her tone pleasant, she said, "Maybe if you could find a way to spend more time with the boys, you could train them to be helpers and take some of the burden—"

"Lord God, Eliza, are you out of your mind? Oliver's the oldest, and he's barely turned nine. Coal miners might send their kids to work at such an age, but I'm not a miner, I'm an electrician. My job is important, kids can't possibly—"

"Right now, they can't, but in time..."

When a cloud of ugliness settled on Martin's face, she left the remainder of what she was thinking unsaid. With a weary sigh, she dropped down in the chair on the far side of the table and they sat in silence for several minutes. She knew when he was in such an obstinate mood, the only way to get around him was to agree with whatever he said. Pressured by the need to tell him about the baby, she decided to do just that.

"Perhaps it's unfair to expect a man as busy as you are to be traveling back and forth on the train all the time. Working as many hours as you do, I can understand why you'd need time to rest up, and with this summer having been so hot..."

As she continued the anger on Martin's face faded, and a thought she hadn't considered before came to her.

"It might be easier on everyone if the children and I were living in Charleston. There's no reason why we couldn't move so we'd all be together. I'm willing to—"

"No. Absolutely not. I can't afford a bigger place, and the apartment I've got is too small. You said so yourself. We were crowded when the only one we had was Oliver. With six kids it would be—"

"Seven," Eliza corrected. "In the winter, it will be seven."

She waited, thinking he'd show some emotion or say something, but he didn't. He just sat there looking shell-shocked, the color gone from his face and his mouth hanging open. A full minute rolled by.

"Seven? You're telling me there's another one on the way?"

She nodded and tried giving him a playful smile. "I suppose with us spending all those evenings together and it being so romantic—"

"Romantic, my ass! What in God's name were you thinking?"

"I wasn't *thinking* anything. It just happened."

He stood and started pacing the kitchen floor. "Do you know how much pressure this puts on me? I've got a full-time job to take care of, and with you asking me to come home every other weekend—"

Her eyes followed him as he walked from one end of the room to the other.

"I'm not asking you to do anything," she said. "I don't love Charleston, but I'm willing to take the children and move back there. You're making more money now, and with what you'd save on train fare we could get a bigger place."

"You are not coming to Charleston!" he shouted. "I'm busy working and don't want you and this pack of kids hounding me."

His words sliced through Eliza's heart like a straight-edge razor. Her eyes filled with tears.

"What do you mean 'hounding you'? I'm your wife. These children are your family. Yes, we depend on you, but that doesn't mean—"

"I'm sorry," he said, his tone still gruff. "I didn't mean it to sound the way it did, but there's no place for you in Charleston. I'm busy working, and when I'm not working I've got union meetings and other things going on."

Eliza looked up, hoping to see a glimmer of truth in his words, but there seemed to be none. His expression told nothing. Whatever the truth was, he'd hidden it behind the flimsy veil of excuses.

It was as if an invisible wall had suddenly sprung up between them. With nothing more to say to one another, she sat in silence as he continued to pace across the kitchen. For several minutes the only sound was the thump of his boots striking the wooden floor; then Margaret Rose woke and started crying.

"I've got to see to the baby," Eliza said. "She's been sleeping for a few hours, so she's probably wet and hungry."

Martin gave a nod of acknowledgement and said nothing.

⸎

After Eliza changed the baby's diaper, she nursed her and sat in the rocking chair, creaking back and forth. She half-expected Martin would be gone when she returned to the kitchen, but he was still there at the table with a glass of whiskey in his hand. She glanced around and didn't see the jug so maybe he was just having a nip to take the edge off, as he sometimes said.

He tipped the glass to his mouth, placed it on the table, and gave a nod, indicating she should sit across from him. Eliza did so, wondering whether his stony expression was one of remorse or anger. In an effort to break through the uncomfortable silence, she said, "Sorry, I didn't mean to run off like that, but once she starts crying—"

"Us having all these kids, that's something we need to talk about."

"Margaret Rose is still a baby. A year from now she'll be on solid food and—"

"And there'll be another one coming right behind her," he said sharply. "Then what? Do you plan to spend your whole life taking care of babies? What about me? What about the attention a wife is supposed to show her husband? If you keep having babies, we're never gonna be free of responsibility."

"Having a family isn't just a responsibility, it's a reason to be happy. If you'd only—"

"I'm not like you, Eliza. Having all these kids doesn't make me happy. The truth is I don't want any more. I put up with you having the first six because that's what you wanted, but now it's time for you to start considering what I want."

There was a tone to his words that Eliza had never heard before. With her heart thumping hard against her chest, she asked, "And exactly what is it you want, Martin?"

"I want you to get rid of this baby."

The blood in her veins ran cold, and for a moment Eliza thought her heart had stopped.

"I realize this is something you probably don't want to do," he continued speaking in a hard-edged emotionless tone, "but if you love me the way a wife is supposed to love her husband, you'll do it."

"Loving you has nothing to do with this, Martin! I'm five months along. It's too late to start wondering whether or not you want another baby."

"I'm not wondering, Eliza. I'm saying for certain I do not want this baby."

"You should have thought of that earlier this summer when you were climbing on top of me night after night."

His expression did not change one iota. His brows still hooded his eyes; his jaw rigid as ever.

"I'm your husband. That's my right."

"Right?" she echoed. "Funny, I never saw it that way. I always believed it was an act of love." She pulled a deep breath but didn't soften her expression. "Regardless of what you call it, if you do it often enough you can expect that sooner or later you'll have a baby."

"Not necessarily," he replied. "If a woman finds herself in a family way, there are ways to take care of it."

"My God, Martin, surely you're not suggesting…"

"Don't carry on like it's the most god-awful thing you've ever heard of, Eliza. There are women in Charleston who do it all the time. They use a brew made out of things like pennyroyal and rosemary. You drink it down, and a day or two later the baby's gone, the same as if it came about naturally."

She hung her head. He could have asked for most anything and she would have done it for him, but this? Never. She covered her face with her hands and began to sob. From somewhere outside she heard the sharp trill of a bird and beneath that the laughter of the boys at play, but inside there was only the sound of Martin's ragged breathing and the shattering of her heart.

"I can't," she said.

"You can," he replied. "It's just a question of whether or not you love me enough to actually do it." He slid his chair back and stood. "I think it's better if I leave now, Eliza. I'll give you time to think about how this is gonna be good for us, and when I come back we can talk some more."

She couldn't bear to look at him, but as she sat there sobbing she heard the door slam and knew he was gone.

1968
The Search

Remembering

Once Tom Bateman agreed to take the job, he began spending one or two afternoons a week with Margaret. They sat at the dining room table, him with a notepad, her with the lifetime of memories that had begun to surface.

At first there seemed to be very little she could tell him: a few names, how they'd moved from one place to another, and how she'd hated to leave Barrettsville.

"After we'd been back in Coal Creek for a while, I started to see the joy of living in the hollow. When I had to go to Charleston to stay with Aunt Rose, I didn't want to leave."

"Aunt Rose, were you named after her?"

Margaret nodded. "She was Mama's oldest sister. Mama was the baby in her family. Rose was fifteen years older and nowhere near as pretty."

"Were there just the two sisters?"

"Four. No boys, just four sisters. The Palmer Girls, people called them."

Tom jotted down, *Palmer, mother's maiden name.*

It seemed as if each answer led to another question, and little by little Margaret's story began to come together. Faces that had faded over the years took shape and grew more vivid as she told of the boys.

"Oliver was the oldest. He was seven the year I was born." She added up the years in her head and laughed. "Good grief, he'd be seventy-four years old now. I can't imagine him an old man. Before we left Barrettsville, he'd grown taller than Daddy and could carry both me and Virgil on his shoulders. He was strong but not nearly as strong as Ben Roland."

At first it was only the small things she remembered. Some came from her own recollection of the time, but more came from stories that had been handed down. Stories her mama, Oliver, and Ben Roland had carried from Coal Creek to Barrettsville and back again. She told of the summer when her daddy took the boys fishing and almost always came home with candy hidden in his pocket.

"Mama used to tell us Daddy was capable of being a good man, but he'd somehow gotten off track and couldn't seem to find his way back. She claimed early on he'd been as loving as a man could be, but that sure wasn't how us kids saw him. Every last one of us hated him. When he came home, we'd make ourselves scarce so he couldn't find a reason to whack us on the head or take a switch to our legs. When I was a baby, Daddy threw Dewey across the room and broke his arm. Mama claimed it was an accident, that Daddy just wasn't himself and never meant for such a thing to happen, but Dewey didn't believe it for one minute."

Tom listened attentively, never interrupting as the memories unspooled, saving his questions for when she finished. After she'd told how her mama played the piano with the children gathered around, he asked what kind of songs they sang.

"Mostly church songs," Margaret answered. "*Amazing Grace, The Old Rugged Cross, Abide with Me*... Most of them I've forgotten."

She laughed as she told of how Louella, who was only three years older than her, sat on their mama's lap singing louder than anyone. Tom wrote, *Check church records.*

That's how he worked. He'd listen to a stretched-out story full of memories and turn it into a single fact. A clue perhaps or a place to start. His questions never came across as probing. They were almost always tied to something Margaret remembered and served to trigger an even deeper memory.

When Margaret ran dry of what she had to tell, she prodded Tom into talking about himself. She asked why a man with only a scattering of gray hairs and barely a line on his face would be looking to retire so early.

At first, he simply shrugged and said, "Burned out, I suppose." But as the days turned into weeks, they developed a friendship and he confided in her about how he'd lost confidence in his ability to judge people after his wife left him.

"I signed the divorce papers, and before the ink was dry she married the guy she'd been having an affair with. They'd been seeing each other for two years. Imagine, it was right under my nose, and I never once suspected. I was stupid," he said and shook his head. "Just plain stupid."

"Not stupid," Margaret said kindly. "Blind maybe. When you fall in love with the wrong person, you make excuses for their faults. You keep believing they're that person you fell in love with, and you don't let yourself see the way they've changed. Mama did the same thing. She saw Daddy as the man she fell in love with, and right up until the end she thought that once he'd sewn his wild oats he'd settle down and go back to being that man. Of course, he never did. Once an apple gets rotten, it's never gonna turn sweet again."

When a meeting didn't bring out anything of importance, they often spoke about their personal lives. She told him how she and Albert had once planned to have a family and how that dream had slipped away as the years rolled by.

Tom never pushed her beyond what she was ready to talk about, and Margaret was glad for that. On days when she'd spoken about something too troubling to forget, the thought of it followed her to bed and came back in the dark of night. In her dreams she could see the small house set back from the road, feel the dampness of the woods where weeds and wild saplings grew, and smell the smoke of the coal stove. Twice she woke in a cold sweat, reaching for Louella or Nellie.

On nights such as that Margaret found it impossible to sleep, so she'd climb from the bed and stand looking out the window. The carpet of grass that stretched across the yard, with hydrangeas and bachelor buttons bordering the side and magnolia trees in the distance, always comforted her. She'd tilt her head back, gaze at the stars scattered across the sky, and breathe a sigh of relief, realizing that she was in Georgia, safe in the house that Albert built for her.

Standing at the window and waiting for her heartbeat to slow, she'd think back on her childhood. She called to mind the good things: the sound of her mama's voice; the plinking of the old piano; playing tag with Virgil and Dewey; Louella's breath warm against her cheek as they whispered secrets beneath the covers. For every sweet memory, though, there was another that was bitter and too painful to keep.

She could still remember the feeling of hunger and found herself wondering if she should go to the kitchen for some cookies or a piece of cake. She could have done that easily enough, because in this house there was always plenty, but she knew it wouldn't take away the hunger. That returned when she allowed herself to start remembering.

She couldn't help but worry that the others still felt it—the older boys or Virgil, younger than her by a year. More than 50 years had gone by, and she'd not heard from even one of them. But neither had she gone in search of them.

Why? Was there still a secret to keep hidden, or was the pain of remembering just too much to bear?

✺

Josie now came every day. Most mornings Margaret had the coffee made before she arrived, so they sat at the kitchen table and talked. Between the two of them, they were never at a loss for words. They talked about the war in Vietnam, the upcoming presidential election, and how they laughed at *I Dream of Jeannie*, but most of all they talked about their families. Josie complained that her teenage girls wore skirts that were far too short and picked at their food like birds. From time to time Margaret talked about how much she missed Albert, but more often it was about her childhood in West Virginia.

One afternoon when gray skies cast a covering of gloom over everything and the rain seemed relentless, Josie asked Margaret if she'd ever had chicken with homemade dumplings.

"Not since I was a little girl," Margaret said. "I never made it because Albert didn't care for dumplings, but I sure did love Mama's chicken and dumplings. It was something she made for special occasions." She talked of how they seldom had a chicken for the pot and used most any kind of wild bird they could get.

"Even crow," she said and laughed.

That afternoon she and Josie worked side by side, talking about a dozen different things as they mixed the buttermilk biscuits and dropped them into the bubbling broth. Once it was finished, they sat at the kitchen table and ate together.

Josie was unusually quiet for a while. When a second helping of dumplings was gone from her plate, she said, "You know, I can't help but overhear some of what you've been telling that Mr. Bateman."

The corners of Margaret's mouth tilted upward. "I doubt any of it is news. I've already told you most of those stories."

Apprehension tugged at Josie's face. "Yes, but you've told me a lot more than you've told him. The tale about your mama playing the piano and everybody singing along was nice, but you didn't say anything about how she had to sell it to buy food."

"No, I didn't," Margaret replied glumly. "I guess I don't talk about it because it was such a terrible time." As her thoughts drifted back to that year, she felt the muscle in the back of her neck tighten. "Mama selling the piano wasn't the worst of it. By then, Daddy had disappeared to God-knows-where, Oliver and Ben Roland were gone, and the rest of us didn't know from one day to the next what would happen. Mama was sick a lot and worried that the little bit of money she had left wasn't going to carry us through another winter." There was a lengthy pause. "That's the year I was sent to Aunt Rose."

"Just for the winter, right?"

Margaret turned her eyes toward the window. The rain was heavy now, coming in sheets, just as it had that day. Remembering caused her to feel the sting of it all over again.

"No, it was forever. Aunt Rose's husband was dead and she had no children, so she needed someone to help out with the chores."

Josie leaned in. "You left Coal Creek and went to live with her?"

As she sat watching the rain, Margaret nodded. "It was what Mama wanted. She thought I'd have a better life, but I didn't. I missed her, my brothers and sisters, and I hated Aunt Rose. I hated her because she looked down on me and the people I loved. That first day she took me to the department store, bought me three new outfits, and threw away the flowered dress I wore to her house. It wasn't befitting my new station in life, she said. I loved that dress because Mama made it for me, so later on I fished it out of the trash bin and hid it under my mattress. Knowing it was there made me believe someday I could go back home."

"Did you?"

"No. Mama died a year before Aunt Rose, so I got a job, rented a furnished room, and stayed in Charleston."

"What about the rest of the family? Were any of the other kids sent away?"

"Eventually we all were. Ben Roland and Oliver left of their own accord the year we moved back from Barrettsville. They went to Wheeling to work for a glass manufacturing company. Ben Roland worked there for a while but didn't stay. Once he left I don't think anyone knew where he was, not even Mama."

"Don't you think you need to tell Mr. Bateman this? You're only telling him the good stuff, about your mama playing the piano and your daddy taking kids fishing. He needs to know about you kids being sent away, otherwise he's never gonna find your family."

Margaret didn't agree or disagree that afternoon, but for the remainder of the day she thought about what Josie said. That night, as she stood at the window watching puffs of rain come and go, she began to remember the things she'd spent years trying to forget.

On Friday when she and Tom Bateman sat at the dining room table, she told him everything she remembered. She talked about Oliver working in Wheeling, West Virginia. Before he joined the army, Dewey worked for a couple of newspapers, first in Charleston, then in Columbus, Ohio. She didn't know the name of either newspaper but remembered he ran a printing press for a time. Nellie remained in West Virginia but might have left Coal Creek in 1915 or 1916 to live with a family in Huntington. Margaret couldn't remember ever hearing their name.

As she unspooled the memories, Tom scratched page after page of notes. He wrote the names of towns and families. Bracketed to the side was an approximation of dates according to what Margaret remembered.

She knew very little about John Paul, only that he was a year older than her, loved the woods as if he were born there, and was deaf in his right ear. At first, she was going to say the deafness had come about because of a fall from a tree. Then she decided to tell the truth.

"It happened when we lived in Barrettsville," she said. "Daddy cuffed John Paul on the side of the head, and he howled like he'd been murdered. He kept crying for the longest time, and finally Daddy said if he didn't stop carrying on he was gonna whack him on the other ear. John Paul finally stopped crying, but after that you could stand next to him and scream into his right ear, and he wouldn't hear you."

"What about the other two?" Tom asked. "Virgil, and the youngest boy. Edward, wasn't it?"

"Yes, Edward. He was a number of years younger than the rest of us, so he remained at home with Mama and Louella for a while. I don't know what happened to him after that."

"And Virgil, you have any thoughts on him?"

"Virgil was always a puzzle. For me and for everybody. He was closed-mouthed and quiet. Skinny as a stick. He could be sitting at the dinner table, and unless you looked directly at him you wouldn't know he was there. Daddy picked on Virgil all the time. No matter what that boy did, he never got a single word of praise for it. You didn't have to be a genius to know that sooner or later something was going to happen. Not long after I went to live with Aunt Rose, he supposedly walked down off the mountain and that was the last anybody saw of him."

"But he was still a kid, wasn't he?"

Margaret nodded. "Yes, he might've been nine or ten. A few days after he disappeared, Aunt Rose said Mrs. Welty claimed she'd seen him down by the train station. I didn't put much stock in anything Mrs. Welty said, because she was one of those women who likes to hear herself talk. Nobody really knew where Virgil went, and to the best of my knowledge he was never heard from again."

"After your mother and Louella passed on, did you or anyone else ever go back to the house in Coal Creek?"

"I didn't, and I don't think anyone else did but I can't be sure. Given the hard times we went through there, I imagine they felt as I did: it was a place better forgotten."

Tom sat there fingering his chin for a minute or so as he wrote, *House?*

"This hollow you've been talking about, does it have a name?"

"Not a proper name. It was just called Coal Creek."

When he asked for directions, Margaret stopped talking for a moment. As much as she wanted to find everybody, or even a single somebody, she didn't want to revisit the misery of the past.

"It's a fair distance outside of Charleston," she said reluctantly. "Take Campbell's Creek Road until you come to a sign that says Split Rock Mine. Then turn and follow that dirt road up the mountain. When the creek bends to the left, the road forks. Stay to the right, and about a mile up that road is where the house is. But I doubt anyone up there will remember us. You're more than likely wasting your time."

He wrote *Campbell's Creek Road* in the notebook, circled it, then closed the book and slid it into his briefcase.

"We won't know whether it's a waste of time unless I check it out," he said and grinned. "I'll call when I have something."

A feeling of apprehension had already settled in Margaret's stomach, but she couldn't say whether she was more afraid of what he would find or what he wouldn't.

On the Road

When the alarm clock buzzed at 5 am, Tom reached over and hit the snooze button. He wasn't a morning person, never had been, and another 15 minutes wasn't going to make a whole lot of difference. He'd considered flying and nixed the idea. To get where he was going he'd need a car anyway, so driving made sense.

The trip was over 500 miles, mostly highway. With a little luck, he'd make it before dark and have time to look around before checking into a motel. Over the weekend, he'd studied the road atlas and mapped out a route for hitting Coal Creek first, then Charleston, and, depending on what he came up with, possibly continuing on to Huntington. Then he'd cross over into Ohio, check out the Columbus newspapers, and after that the glass manufacturers in Wheeling.

When the alarm buzzed the second time, he silenced it and climbed out of bed. As much as he disliked mornings, he was anxious to get going. There was something about this case that made him feel good about working again.

It reminded him of the Blakely case. Homer Blakely left the dinner table saying he had to use the bathroom then vanished. The family waited dessert for over an hour thinking he might be a bit constipated. His granddaughter went to check on him and discovered him gone. After a week of searching, Tom found the old guy doing what he'd done as a young man: playing the ponies at Pimlico.

Cases like that had a feel-good resolution, and Tom thought the same could be true about this one. On the up side, he had more information than he'd had back in '44; on the down side, the age of the case was troubling. It was 24 years older than it was back then.

After a quick shower and a cup of instant coffee, Tom was on the road. He didn't really care for the instant stuff because it left a bitter taste in his mouth but hadn't wanted to waste time brewing a pot. He took the back roads across Polk County, stopped once to grab a container of fresh-brewed coffee and a buttered roll, and continued until he hit the interstate. Making a left onto I-75, he headed north.

The first hour flew by—the traffic was light, and he made good time—but once the coffee and roll were gone, the drive began to get monotonous. There were few distractions on the road, stretches without a single billboard, and only a handful of rest stops. Tom snapped on the radio, but this was mountainous country and the reception was terrible. He twisted the dial for a while, hoping to find something—country music, gospel, news, even a weather report would have been welcome—but the only thing he got was static. Eventually he gave up, snapped the radio off, and reached across the seat to pull the notebook from his briefcase. With one eye on the road and the other scanning his notes, he went back to thinking about the case.

He'd spent a lot of time with Margaret and had a good background on the Hobbs family; that was going to be helpful. Even though she'd said going back to Coal Creek could be a waste of time, he had a hunch he'd get lucky. People remembered things and they talked, especially if there was some sort of scandal attached to the story. A father who'd abandoned his family not once but twice was definitely fodder for gossip. His thought was that he'd come across a neighbor or friend who knew something.

As he drove, he began thinking over what he knew about each of the brothers. Oliver was born in 1894, taller than average, and strong. He'd be 74 years old now. Probably too old to still be working, but if he'd stayed with the glass manufacturing company and retired around 1959, it was feasible he was now collecting some kind of retirement benefit. A flicker of hope made Tom smile. Then he remembered how Margaret had described her older brother. He didn't sound like a stay-in-one-job kind of person. He'd traveled with the family from Barrettsville back to Coal Creek and then immediately left home. Him and Ben Roland both—why?

Ben Roland, a life tragically cut short. Back in 1944 Tom had known only that the family came from a coal mining town, so he'd taken a chance and searched the membership of the United Mine Workers Union. He'd checked all the brothers' names, but Ben Roland was the only match. He was listed as deceased. He'd been married to a Rebecca Sawyer. Tom subconsciously added her to his search list. Meeting Ben Roland's wife would be a nice surprise for Margaret.

Shortly past noon, he crossed into Tennessee. Since he'd never been to Chattanooga, he decided to stop there for lunch. He saw the sign: Chattanooga keep left, I-75 North; keep right toward Knoxville. He veered right and kept going. He'd never been to Knoxville either.

He expected Knoxville to be another half-hour or 45 minutes, but he hit a six-mile stretch of construction and the traffic bottlenecked. It slowed to a crawl for 20 minutes, and his stomach started grumbling. He'd been hungry before he reached Chattanooga. Now he was ravenous. A few miles past Athens, he spotted a sign saying Knoxville was another 50 miles. He pulled off at the next exit, wolfed down a quick burger, grabbed a Coke and two candy bars, then got back on the road. He could do without seeing Knoxville, at least this time around.

Just past Knoxville he took Route 40, merged onto I-85, and continued north. With a full stomach and few distractions, he went back to thinking about the Hobbs family. Margaret had given him a place to start with Nellie. If she'd lived in Huntington as a young girl, there was a reasonable chance that she'd married and settled down there. Once he got to Huntington, his first stop would be the city clerk's office. Hopefully, he'd find her name in the marriage records and not death certificates.

John Paul was more of a challenge. The only thing he had to go on there was that the boy was deaf in his right ear and loved nature. No last known address other than Coal Creek. If at some point in time he'd consulted an ear doctor or purchased a hearing aid, Tom had a chance of finding him. The chance was slim, though, considering how little money the family had and how much a specialized doctor would have cost.

When Tom finally got to the end of Sullivan County, he left

Tennessee and passed into Virginia. Virgil was the most troubling of all the brothers. No matter how many times Tom tried to imagine a scenario that would establish an obscure path for him to follow, he circled back to the same question: How did a 10-year-old boy with no skills and no money leave home on his own?

Something was wrong; didn't jibe. Was it possible he did have money? The $1000 that disappeared with Martin Hobbs was still unaccounted for.

Tom yawned and rolled his neck. Sitting behind the wheel for such a long stretch was both tedious and tiring. Beautiful as the countryside was, he'd had his fill of seeing nothing but trees. In time I-85 became Route 119, and he wouldn't have realized he was in Kentucky were it not for a small sign at the side of the road. The view remained the same: blacktop bordered by more trees. Once he got to West Virginia, he started looking for a place to stop for dinner. By then the highway had narrowed and turned into a two-lane mountain road that took him through Logan where he left 119.

He'd planned to finish the drive to Charleston after dinner, but once he'd downed a king-size prime rib and two beers, he felt too tired to drive. Checking into the Sleep E-Z motel, he asked for a wake-up call at 7 am. It was an hour's drive to Charleston. He could be there by eight and in Coal Creek by nine. He'd watch TV for an hour or two, then get a good night's sleep and start fresh.

⁂

As he drove the next day, Tom wasn't sure what to expect when he turned off of Campbell's Creek Drive onto the unmarked road. Margaret had described the area to him, but the last time she'd seen the place was over 50 years ago. Given that much time a lot could change, but from the looks of things nothing had.

The Split Rock Coal Mine sign was there just as she'd said. The turnoff, graveled for about 100 yards, quickly turned to a dirt road rocky, badly rutted, and only wide enough for a single car. With the Buick bouncing up and down as it was, Tom thought for sure the car would bust a spring before he made it out of the hollow.

Margaret said the bend in the creek was about two miles up from

Campbell's Creek Road, but to Tom it seemed longer. When he finally came to where the road forked, he kept to the right and started looking for houses. There were very few, most of them set back from the road and partially hidden by overgrown brush. A half-mile later, he spotted what looked like a driveway and a house with smoke curling up from the chimney. He pulled in, stopped partway down the drive, then got out and headed for the house.

The girl who answered the door was wearing overalls and an oversized tee shirt. He could tell she was young, in her 20s maybe, but her expression looked old and tired. She looked at him without saying anything, so he spoke first.

"Sorry for disturbing you; I hope I'm not interrupting your breakfast."

"You ain't."

Since she obviously wasn't much on small talk, he cut to the chase. "I'm trying to locate members of a family that lived a little further up the hollow a while back. Their name was Hobbs. They had six boys and three girls. The daddy was—"

"You from the government?" She eyed him suspiciously.

"No, ma'am, I'm not. I'm a friend trying to help Margaret Hobbs find her missing brothers and a sister named Nellie."

"What's she want 'em for?"

Not prepared for such a question, Tom could only hope the truth would work.

"She's come into a fair bit of money and wants to share it with the rest of her family."

"Lucky them." The girl grinned, turned, and hollered back, "Mama, you know a family livin' up here, name a' Hobbs?"

An old woman hobbled out from the back room and said, "Who's askin'?"

Tom explained a second time that he was a friend trying to help Margaret Rose find her missing brothers. "After she got married and moved to Georgia, the family apparently lost touch with one another."

The old woman hiked her mouth up on one side and sneered. "More 'n likely it was intentional. Their daddy was the meanest man I ever set eyes on. The devil himself would've left town to be rid of him."

"Did you know the family?"

"Used to. Most of 'em moved away, but Louella stayed 'til their mama died. Her and me went to school together, except she quit in the ninth grade on account a' her mama being sick."

"Was it just the two of them?"

"Then it was. Earlier on some of the boys was still home."

"Do you know where any of the brothers went after they left here?"

She shook her head. "Not really. The littlest one, Edward, I think his name was, he got sent off to the same family what took his sister. I don't remember her name."

"Nellie?"

"That sounds about right."

Having caught sight of a toddler with his bare bottom hanging out, the old woman turned and yelled, "Darleen! Come get a diaper on this young'un!"

When it looked like she was about to go after the boy, Tom quickly said, "I've just got one or two more questions, if you don't mind."

"Make it quick, 'cause I'm busy." She turned and screamed for Darleen again.

"When Louella stopped going to school to take care of her mama, was John Paul still living here then?"

She wrinkled her brow and look at him with a puzzled expression. "John Paul? Was he the oldest boy?"

"No, that was Oliver. John Paul was just a year younger than Louella."

"Oh, right. He was sure enough a strange one. He didn't live with them but used to come and go all the time; be here for two, three days, then disappear for weeks on end. He was real good with a rifle. Could shoot the eye out of a squirrel sitting on the far side of the yard. That last year he'd come in the dark of night, hang a piece of meat in the smokehouse, and be gone before anybody knew he'd been there."

"You know where he stayed the rest of the time?"

"No idea," she said and shook her head. "At one time he was sweet on Francine Swift. She was in his class at school. They didn't get married or anything, but she might know what became of him."

"Do you know where I can find Francine?"

"Last house, far end of the holler. Brice her name is now."

Before Tom could thank the woman for her time, she turned and screamed, "Dammit, Darleen, I'm sick a' telling you…"

He smiled, gave a polite nod, and turned toward the car then turned back.

"Wait, just one more question. Did you or anybody else you know ever see Virgil again?"

"He's the one what run off when he was just a young'un, right?"

"Yes, Margaret said he was only nine or ten years old when—"

The woman reached down, snatched the half-naked toddler into her arms, and yelled for Darleen.

"Far as I know, nobody ever saw that boy again," she said as she pushed the door shut with her thigh.

Before Tom did a three-point turn, pulled out of the drive and headed further up the hollow, he grabbed his notebook and wrote, *Francine Brice? Was John Paul a hunter? Edward sent to Huntington?*

The Hobbs House

As Tom moved along the hollow, he stopped at three more houses. The story was the same at all three; the older folks remembered the Hobbs family living here but couldn't say why the kids left home or where they'd gone. They remembered Eliza Hobbs as a pleasant woman with more than her share of troubles and Martin as little more than a shadow who turned up every so often. No one could say when Martin stopped returning home or exactly when each of the children left. They knew only that they were there and then gone.

Most claimed Eliza died of consumption, but Caldonia Markey insisted it was a broken heart. The woman was 92 years old, blind in one eye and barely able to stand, so at first Tom was skeptical about such a story. As they continued to talk, he discovered Caldonia's mind was sharp as a tack despite the toll the years had taken on her body.

"Eliza loved Martin and those kids," she said, "and for while they did okay, but that man had a heart black as night. You just knew sooner or later he was gonna be trouble." She gave a weary sigh and shook her head. "God didn't intend a man to live separate from his wife. I told Eliza that but she stuck up for him, saying he had to stay in Charleston because he had this big important job. Me and her were close because our houses was one down from each other, and I always felt free to speak my mind with Eliza."

"Did she confide in you? Maybe say why—"

Caldonia leaned in and motioned for him to do the same. Once she made sure no one else was listening, she whispered, "It was because of the devil weed Martin brought back from Charleston."

"Devil weed?"

She waved her hand downward, indicating he should keep his voice low. "This ain't a thing other people need to hear." She again glanced over her shoulder to make sure no one was listening. "When Eliza was carrying Virgil—I don't recollect whether he was her sixth or seventh— anyway, Martin came home with a packet of poisonous devil weed he'd gotten from some whore in Charleston. He told Eliza to brew it into a tea and drink it down, but she wouldn't do it."

"You think he was trying to poison her?"

"No, in his own selfish way, I think he loved Eliza. He swore that stuff wasn't gonna hurt her none; it would just get rid of the baby."

"And she wanted to have the baby, right?"

"Of course, she did. I told you, she loved those young'uns, every last one of them, even the ones that came later."

"What do you mean, the ones that came later?"

Caldonia wrinkled her brow and glared at him as though this were something he should've understood. "Later, after Martin stopped sending her money and started whoring around in Charleston. Arrogant as they come, he was. He'd stay in Charleston and send enough to keep them from starving to death, then after six or eight months went by he'd come struttin' up the road and climb into bed with Eliza like it was his God-given right."

"Couldn't she divorce him? Or take him to court and make him pay to support her and the kids?"

Caldonia gave a cackle and looked around to make sure no one had heard her.

"Women didn't do that back in our day. If you had enough backbone you maybe stood up to your man, but Eliza couldn't do that."

"Because she loved him?"

"She loved him early on. Not later. But where was she gonna go with seven or eight young'uns hanging to her skirt?"

"According to what I've heard, Eliza moved the family to Pennsylvania so they could be with their daddy, so they must have reconciled at some point."

"It was on account a' that man from the Masons. Martin didn't want no part…"

Her words trailed off as a heavyset woman entered the room and crossed over to where they were sitting. With a saccharine sweetness, Caldonia turned to her.

"This here's my daughter-in-law, Rowena. Her and Edgar take real good care a' me." She gave the woman a pinched smile. "Don't you, honey?"

Rowena lowered herself onto the sofa. "Yes, indeed, Mama Markey, we sure do."

Once Rowena sat, Caldonia turned back to Tom.

"As I was saying, Eliza Hobbs was a neighbor but that was some time ago. I don't know much about her family and nothing that could be of help to you." With that pinched smile now stuck to her face, she looked back and said, "Rowena, honey, I'm feelin' real parched. Would you fetch me a drink of water?"

Not looking any too happy about it, Rowena pushed herself up from the sofa with a grunt and headed back toward the kitchen.

As soon as she was out of the room, Caldonia's voice dropped to a whisper.

"I can't say no more now. That woman's the biggest gossip what ever walked the earth, and I ain't gonna give her the pleasure a' knowing me and Eliza's business."

"If I came back at another—"

Caldonia cut in when she saw Rowena coming through the doorway. "It's been real nice visiting with you, Mister Bateman; real nice." The pasted-on smile was back.

Tom stood and bent to kiss the wrinkled cheek.

"I'll be back," he whispered and headed for the door.

When he left the Markey house, Tom continued up the hollow. Caldonia had said the Hobbs house was the next up from hers, but when he came to it the house was barely standing. The back of the building was completely gone, as were the front door and most of the windows. He eased the car off of the road and onto the edge of the property. The ground was heavily weeded in some spots and bare in others. He grabbed his camera, climbed out of the car, and started toward the house, uncertain of what he was looking for but hoping to find something.

Scrambling over what was once a front porch, he stepped inside. Although the stench of smoke was gone, he could tell the place had been destroyed by fire. Broken furniture and pieces of blackened timber were everywhere. A sofa in what must have been the living room was untouched by the fire but covered with soot. The small table beside it had toppled to the floor, its leg broken. It was odd how one thing could remain intact while the thing beside it was destroyed.

Moving through the charred rubbish, Tom made his way toward the back. While the walls were gone and only a few sticks of furniture remained, he could tell there had been two bedrooms. Margaret had said there were nine children, but the house was tiny. Two bedrooms, a living room, and a kitchen. That was it. Had all nine children lived here with their parents?

Tom stood for several moments, studying the small world the Hobbs family had called home and wondering how they'd managed to survive. With the walls down, he could see the well, the top covered with boards but still standing. Further back was what looked like a shack, probably the smokehouse Margaret mentioned; to the side of that, an outhouse.

Nine children in a house with no running water and apparently no electricity. Was that why they'd left here and gone to Pennsylvania? If so, why did they come back?

Tom snapped several pictures, first of the wooded back lot and the badly damaged bedrooms. Returning to the front of the house, he grabbed a shot of the living room. He was getting ready to leave when he caught sight of an oval picture frame left hanging on the wall. Covered with soot he hadn't noticed it earlier, but now it drew him to it.

The glass was so blackened he couldn't tell whether the photo inside had been damaged. Pulling a handkerchief from his pocket, he cleaned a round spot in the center of the glass and revealed the edge of a woman's smile. As he widened the circle, the portrait of a couple wearing turn-of-the-century clothing came into view. There was something about the woman's face that reminded him of Margaret, but the woman in the picture was young, not yet 20 he guessed.

Parents? An older sister?

He tucked the picture under his arm, clicked another shot of the living room and a few more outside the house, and returned to his car.

Tom's last visit was to Francine Brice, and any hopes he'd had of her knowing where to find John Paul were quickly dashed. When he told her one of the neighbors suggested that earlier on she'd been friendly with one of the Hobbs boys, she folded her arms across her chest.

"It was Rosalie Henderson, wasn't it?"

"I didn't actually get the name," Tom said apologetically. "But I thought—"

"Well, you thought wrong, mister. I don't know what kind of trash Rosalie told about me, but I assure you not a word of it is true. John Paul was only interested in the woods and nothing else."

"She was talking about back when you were in school—"

"That was over fifty years ago. I ain't heard from Johnny Hobbs since then. Now git on out of here, and don't be spreading Rosalie's trash talk around town!"

With that, she stepped back inside and slammed the door.

The road ended just beyond the Brice house, so Tom slid behind the wheel and started back down the mountain. He slowed to a crawl when he passed what was left of the Hobbs place. Dwarfed by the forest of Virginia pines and sycamores surrounding it, the house looked small and sad. It was hard to believe a woman like Margaret had grown up there and harder still to believe Eliza Hobbs had raised nine children in those four tiny rooms.

Tom found himself thinking about Eliza and wondering what her life had been like. He tried to envision the house as it might have been back then with childish laughter echoing through the trees and pots of flowers sitting on the front porch, but he couldn't do it. There was a bone-deep sadness in that house, one that had been there before the fire. He'd felt it the moment he lifted that picture from the wall.

His thoughts drifted back to the picture. The man with his hair slicked back and nose pointed straight ahead, the woman with eyes lifted and face angled toward him. Tom was all but certain that woman was Eliza Hobbs. The picture, taken at a time when she was young and so obviously in love, seemed to promise a lifetime of happiness, and yet something had gone terribly wrong.

As he moved on and left the house behind, Tom felt a certain sadness clinging to him. Perhaps it was nothing more than bits of soot stuck to his skin or the gloom of the mountain, but it had somehow changed things. This was no longer just a case to be solved; it now felt more like a commitment to Margaret.

When he reached the end of the road and left the graveled patch to pull back onto Campbell's Creek Drive, he knew the hollow with its natural beauty and obvious poverty was a different kind of world. It was the kind of place where people lived and died without ever stepping foot off the mountain. They held fast to their secrets, but he was as determined as these strong-backed, tight-lipped people. Tomorrow he would visit the city clerk's office in Charleston, and after his work there was done he would return and talk with Caldonia Markey again. She had something more to say, and he was beginning to believe it was a key to unlocking this mystery.

1901
West Virginia

Defying the Devil

After Martin's impossible request about what to do with the baby she was carrying and the bitter way they'd parted, Eliza feared it could be months before Martin returned, but the following Saturday he came whistling up the hollow as if there'd never been a cross word between them.

At the time she was in the kitchen, holding Margaret Rose to her breast. She looked up with an apprehensive smile.

"Had I known you were coming, I would have fed the baby earlier."

"No need to rush," he said, then crossed the room, kissed her lightly on the cheek, and whispered that he'd brought something for her. Pulling a paper bag from his pocket, he placed it on the top shelf next to the money jar.

"I'll leave this up here so none of the kids get into it. You can see to it later."

Believing he'd brought a bag of candy to make amends for the ugliness of the previous weekend, she pushed her anger aside and asked if he was planning to stay the night.

"Of course. If need be, I can stay through Monday."

Eliza heard what she wanted to hear. He'd come home to spend a long weekend with his family. What she didn't hear was the undercurrent of deception floating beneath his words.

It was late October, the time of year when days were warm and pleasant but darkness came early and with it a chill that settled into her bones. Carrying this child was different than the others; Eliza wasn't sleeping well, and she felt the cold as never before. There was a shawl around her shoulders from morning till night, even on days when the sun was hot enough to warm the floorboards of the front porch. That afternoon she complained about the crack on the side of the house that leaked cold air into the bedroom, and Martin said he'd fix it.

"Today?" she asked, her eyes wide and a smile tugging at the corner of her mouth.

He gave a nod and called for Oliver to come and lend a hand.

Normally he hated doing repairs, so Eliza saw this as a sign that he was reaching out, trying to make things right between them. If he was willing to try, she would also.

With Martin coming home so soon, she sensed there was a possibility all the anger and bitterness was now behind them, forgotten or forgiven. Today she could see a shadow of the man he'd been earlier that summer, and while there was no assurance this behavior would continue she had reason to be hopeful. Earlier that month, Eliza had preserved most of the fruit they'd harvested. She'd been fearful there might not be enough to see them through the winter, but with Martin making such an obvious show of trying she wanted to make this weekend special.

Selecting the best of the apples still in the basket, she peeled and sliced them, took a bag of flour from the shelf, and began mixing the dough for her pie crust. As she sprinkled water into the floury mix and worked it into dough, she found herself remembering how it felt to have the kind of happiness they'd shared back then. A warmth that she hadn't felt for several months settled inside of her, and as she slid the pie into the oven she realized she no longer needed the shawl.

Martin returned to the house as she was setting out the plates for supper. He spotted the pie sitting atop the stove and grinned.

"Apple pie, my favorite."

There were evenings when supper was a frenzied affair, when a too-hot stove caused the biscuits to burn, the baby started screaming, or one of the kids toppled a glass of milk, but none of those things happened that night. Margaret Rose was asleep in her crib, and the boys were full of questions as Martin told of his latest job installing lights along the river walkway. The minute supper was over, Martin looked over at Eliza and gave a wink then told the kids to go to bed.

"Your mama and I need some time alone," he said.

Oliver grumbled for a few seconds, but when Martin lifted his arm and pointed toward the bedroom that was the end of it.

Warmed by her memories of the summer evenings when they'd sat together on the porch or walked down by the creek, Eliza suggested they sit outside to have coffee and pie.

"I'll take a piece of that pie," Martin said, "but don't bother with coffee." He gave her a sly grin then added, "Fix yourself a cup of that tea I brought, then come sit beside me."

"Tea? You brought me tea, not candy?"

"It's something special. I think you're gonna like it."

"Tea? You spent money to buy tea when you know I make my own?"

She took the paper bag from the shelf, opened it, then held it to her nose and sniffed. It had a strong odor, mint-like and sharp with hints of citrus and evergreen.

"What kind of tea is this?"

"It's a mix. I don't know that it has a name. The girl said—"

"What girl?" Eliza reached for her shawl and pulled it around her shoulders.

"The girl that sold it to me. Good Lord, Eliza, I bring you a gift and instead of appreciating it, you start questioning me like—"

"This doesn't smell like any tea I know of."

She tipped the bag and sprinkled some of the mix into the palm of her hand. At first the dried leaves appeared to be brown. When she lifted her hand for a closer look, she could see the tiny tinge of purple pennyroyal and twigs of what most likely was rosemary.

As she stood holding the deadly mix in her hand, she felt the world around her crumble. Her heart slammed against her chest, she felt the baby move, and tears filled her eyes. When she spoke, her voice crackled with bitterness.

"This isn't tea. It's the poison that causes a woman to lose her baby, isn't it?"

Martin folded his arms across his chest. "Don't act like I'm some kind of monster, Eliza. I'm just trying to see you do what needs to be done."

"You're trying to kill our baby."

"We don't need another kid. I told you how I feel."

"Killing this child is the same as killing any of the others—Oliver, Ben Roland, Dewey—"

"Don't put that on me, Eliza. You're the one what wanted all them babies. I didn't. I was happy with it being just you and me. I should've spoke up then, but I cared about you enough to let you have your way. Now it's time you let me have my way."

"My way, your way, what kind of nonsense is that? We're not arguing over who gets the last slice of pie, Martin, we're talking about a baby. A new life God saw fit to give me."

Martin looked at her with his jaw set hard as a rock.

"God didn't put that baby inside of you, Eliza, I did, and since I'm the one who gave it to you, I got the right to take it away!"

"Over my dead body," she said and turned her back to him.

For several minutes there was a stark silence with nothing more than bits of anger bristling through the air. Then Martin came and touched her shoulder.

"Try to see it my way," he pleaded. "We've already got six kids, and every time I turn around one of them needs new shoes or something. I'm already working my ass off so you'll have money enough to raise them. If you keep having babies year after year, how am I supposed to afford it?"

"We'll find a way. I can make do with less. The boys are big enough to help with—"

"That's not the answer. If you want me coming home on weekends, then I gotta give up working overtime and the only way I can afford to do that is if you stop having babies."

"Going forward we'll be more careful. We can plan—"

"That's not good enough. We've already got six. I don't want any more. If you love me, Eliza, you'll listen to what I'm saying and get rid of this baby."

Hearing the finality in his words, she picked up the paper bag, refolded the top, and held it out to him.

"Take this back. I won't need it. I love you, Martin, but not more than I love this baby. If I can find room in my heart to love both you and our children, I don't understand why you can't."

He took the bag from her and put it back on the top shelf.

"That's staying here, 'cause I'm giving you time to reconsider. After you think about it for a while, I believe you'll come to see I'm right."

She didn't answer or turn to face him.

"Look away if you want, Eliza, but the truth is you and the kids need me. You know damn well you do. This might be your mama's house, but that ain't gonna feed the kids or put shoes on their feet."

He took his jacket from the hook and pulled it on.

"I'm leaving now 'cause we got nothing more to say to each other, but when I come back I'm gonna be expecting you to tell me this baby is gone."

Eliza heard the door open then close, and she knew he was gone.

⬯⬯⬯

The next morning Eliza woke with her head aching and her heart heavy. She had a sickening premonition that this time Martin would not be back. They'd said some unforgivable things to one another, and he'd left before the sky was fully dark.

Shortly after Oliver and Ben Roland left for school, Eliza heard a knock. Before she could get up from the chair to answer, the door slid open and Caldonia Markey poked her head inside.

"You okay?" she asked.

"Martin's not here, so come on in."

"This morning I made sweet biscuits. With you feeling so poorly, I figured these might…" As she drew closer and saw Eliza's face, she stopped. "Lord God, honey, what's wrong?"

"It's nothing. I just had a bad night; didn't get much sleep."

"It's more than that. Your face is swollen, and your eyes look like the devil poked a stick in 'em." Caldonia leaned in, studying Eliza. "You and Martin have a tussle?"

She gave a reluctant nod. "It was terrible. I'm afraid he may never come back."

Caldonia squatted down beside her and hugged her shoulders. "Why in the world would you think—"

"He as much as said so." Lowering her face into her hands, Eliza started to sob. "I love Martin, but what he wants is impossible. He's asking me to choose between him and this baby. I would do almost anything for him but not…this."

She stood and took the paper bag from the shelf, her hand trembling as she showed it to Caldonia, and explained it was a brew meant to rid a woman of the child inside of her. Caldonia lifted the bag to her nose, sniffed it, and looked up as if she'd seen a ghost.

"This here's devil weed."

"Martin said it was a tea that wouldn't harm me. Supposedly it causes a woman to lose a baby, same as if it came about naturally."

"Call it what you will, but that don't change nothing. This here's devil weed. It will for sure kill the baby and maybe you too."

"But Martin said—"

"Makes no difference what he said. This is the same stuff that killed that pretty little Walker girl."

"Bernice Walker? She died of influenza didn't—"

Caldonia was already shaking her head. "Devil weed, that's what killed her. Poor girl got herself in a family way. When her beau ran off, she took this stuff figuring she'd get rid of the baby and nobody'd be the wiser. She lost the baby that same night, then up and died two days later."

Eliza sat down, her mouth hanging open.

"Devil weed's poison as poison can be," Caldonia said. "You need to get rid of it."

The two women had been friends for many years, but Eliza had never before spoken of her darkest secrets. She'd never told of the times she could catch the scent of another woman's perfume on Martin's skin or how he'd been so adamant about them not moving to Charleston. She'd spoken of the good nights when they walked by the creek or sat side by side on the front porch but never of the nights when he came to her with the smell of whiskey souring his breath and ridden her like a horse.

Now Caldonia listened and remained silent until Eliza had finished. Taking her friend's hand in hers, she said, "Get rid of that stuff, right now. A man like him will see you take it one way or another. If he can't get you to take it willingly, he'll trick you into it—hide it in your food, drop it into a bucket of well water, or God knows what. If you die, what do you reckon will happen to these babies?"

Eliza's heart stopped for a second. She didn't have to wonder what would happen to the children; she knew. Martin didn't love them as she did. He barely tolerated them. Before she was cold in her grave, they'd be abandoned. Left behind to starve or dropped off at an orphanage. As that thought rose into her throat, it took away whatever words she might have spoken and left only tears.

Caldonia pulled a handkerchief from her pocket and handed it to Eliza. "Crying ain't gonna fix nothing. What you got to do is get rid of that stuff."

"I've already asked Martin to take it back to wherever it came from, but he refused. He said he expected me to take it."

"You can't trust him to do it. You have to do it yourself. Take that bag out into the woods and burn it. Once the devil weed is nothing but ashes, it can't hurt nobody."

Later that morning while the younger children napped and the older ones had not yet returned from school, the two women carried the bag deep into the woods and took a match to it. They stood downwind of the fire, waiting and watching until the smoldering embers died away and the only thing that remained was a tiny pile of ash. Before they started for home, Eliza stomped on the ash and ground it into the dirt. As the toe of her boot burrowed into that last bit of ash, she knew she'd buried something more than the devil weed. She'd buried the last remaining bit of love she'd had for Martin.

The Onset of Winter

In the days that followed, Eliza began to accept that Martin might not return for a very long time. Perhaps never. He was a willful man who clung to his anger the way a mother does her child. Although she was hopeful he would send money at the end of the month, she knew there was a very real possibility he would not. Taking the last few dollars from the jar, she tucked them into a small pouch and hung it behind the headboard of her bed. The pouch would remain there to be used only for the direst emergency.

With the swell of fear in her chest growing greater by the day, she began to prepare for the coming winter. In the cold grey light of morning, she climbed from her bed, lit the stove, and set to work. On the worst days, when the dampness of the mountain settled in her bones and her heart ached with thoughts that were as fragile as a dandelion fluff, she pushed past the queasiness in her stomach and gathered kindling or carved the carcass of a squirrel into thin strips of meat to hang in the smokehouse. On good days, when she could push fear and thoughts of Martin to the back of her mind, she took pride in the way Oliver and Ben Roland worked alongside of her, and she grew strong enough to chop wood or hold the shotgun to her shoulder and take down a jackrabbit or wild turkey. Twice she sent Oliver to ask the postmaster if she'd received an envelope from Charleston, and both times he came back empty-handed.

On the third Friday of November Eliza woke to a covering of snow on the ground, the first of the season. To the children it meant a day of snowballs and tumbling down the hill, but to her it was a sign that the worst of winter would soon be upon them. She had a small amount of meat hanging in the smokehouse, but the molasses was gone. The flour, now down to the bottom of the bag, would be emptied out in three, possibly four days. And perhaps most frightening of all, they were down to only six shotgun shells.

That night, after the children had exhausted themselves playing in the snow and trundled off to bed, she sat at the table and penned a letter to Martin. In it she spoke of her need for help and how much the children missed him. She said that although his last visit had ended on such a bitter note, she believed as a father and husband he needed to know how very bleak their situation had become. She explained that the money was gone and they did not have food enough for another month, then confessed that she hadn't used the tea he'd brought, saying it was not because she loved him less than the children but because she believed it sinful to destroy a baby the Lord had seen fit to give them. She pleaded for his understanding and swore if he could find it in his heart to accept this child, she would not ask for one penny more than he'd given her in the past.

Although we are husband and wife, I have no wish to foster undue hardships on you, she wrote, *and ask only that you provide for our family's barest necessities. If the weather is too harsh and you are unable to make it home, Mr. Barnes at the company store has agreed to grant us credit providing he receives a guarantee that you will be responsible for the purchases. If you would kindly send him a letter to that effect, I assure you we will buy only enough to see us through the winter.*

After she had run dry of words, she signed the letter, *Your loving and dutiful wife, Eliza.* She sat for a while looking at the letter and wondering if there was something more she could have said, a word or a sentence that would soften his heart, but in the end she could think of nothing. She folded the sheet of paper, slid it into an envelope, and addressed it to Martin at the apartment they'd once shared.

On Monday morning she would give Oliver two pennies to buy a stamp and send him off to mail the letter. Leaving the envelope on the kitchen table, she turned down the lamp and climbed into bed.

Martin almost never returned home when the weather was inclement, so hearing him on Saturday morning startled her. She was sitting on the sofa with Margret Rose at her breast when the door opened.

"Eliza," he yelled, "I'm home."

A sense of relief swept over her as she answered, "In here."

Seconds later, he was standing in the doorway with a grin.

"I saw the medicine I gave you is gone."

"Let me explain…"

"No need," he said. He bent and kissed her cheek. "You did as I asked, and that's good enough." Lowering himself onto the sofa alongside of her, he patted her knee. "I appreciate what you did, especially since I know it wasn't to your liking. Now what's done is done, and we've no need to talk about it again."

Pulling a bag of peppermint candy from his pocket, he handed it to her.

"For you," he said, "and I put some extra in the money jar so you can buy cloth for a new dress."

Eliza choked back the burn of resentment rising in her throat and forced a smile to her face. He was happy believing the baby was dead, and for that she hated him. Hated him as she had never hated anyone before. The money truly would be a godsend; it meant the children would not go hungry, and they would have shoes to wear when snow fell and ice crusted the ground. In time he would learn the truth, but for now she would say nothing and let him take pleasure from this terrible lie.

She thanked him for his gift and asked how long he was planning to stay.

"Just for the day," he said. "I have to take the evening train back."

Have to or want to? she wondered.

He didn't offer excuses as he usually did, so she held back her thoughts and didn't ask for any. She wanted not to care, not to feel the ache that came with his callous indifference, but it was impossible. With him sitting so close, the memory of what they'd once meant to one another was still there. It sat side by side with her hatred of a man who could kill his own child. Were she able, she would pluck the recollection of that happiness from her heart and be done with it forever, but love was not something she could so easily cast aside. Seeing him again weakened her resolve. For now the best she could do was push those memories to the back of her mind and think only of how she would feed and care for the children.

He squeezed her knee and said he'd like a bite to eat before he started back.

"When you're finished with the baby, you can fix me something."

Suddenly remembering the envelope on the kitchen table, her heart quickened.

"I'm finished now." She eased Margaret Rose from her breast, ignoring the baby's squeals of protest. Quickly buttoning her shirtwaist, she suggested he visit with the boys while she prepared dinner. "They're outside, in the back yard."

When he stood and turned toward the kitchen, she brushed by him, keeping her body between him and the kitchen table.

"Go," she said and waved him off. "Enjoy some time with the boys."

Not having had her fill, Margaret Rose grew fussy and started squirming to get free. If it weren't for the envelope, Eliza would have set her on the floor and let her crawl around the room, but right now she couldn't. Her body was the only thing blocking Martin's view of the table.

He eyed her with a puzzled expression. "Ain't she wanting to get down?"

"I suppose so," Eliza replied with a laugh. She turned and lowered the baby to the floor with one arm as she reached with the other, grabbed the envelope, and slid it into the pocket of her apron. Seconds later, Margaret Rose started screeching with her arms reaching up.

"What's she fussing about now?" Martin asked.

"She just wants to be picked up again."

Martin shook his head and turned toward the door. "Damned if I understand why any woman wants a bunch of babies."

Once he was gone from sight, Eliza pulled the letter from her pocket, dropped it into the belly of the stove, and watched as it disappeared in a burst of flames.

The remainder of the afternoon was good. Martin became the center of attention, and the children oohed and aahed at his stories. He grinned as he jumped from one tale to the next, and he always had another one to tell. He talked about the tall poles carrying telephone wires across the city, steamboats chugging up and down the river, and rows of shops that offered everything from ready-made clothes to silk chairs so fancy a person wouldn't dare sit in them.

"That's flat out crazy," Oliver said. "Why would anybody buy a chair they can't sit in?"

Martin laughed. "I can't say why they do it, but they do. If you don't believe me, ask your mama. She lived in Charleston when you were first born and seen it herself."

Oliver glanced over. "Is that true, Mama?"

"It sure enough is. Of course, a lot of years have gone by since I was in Charleston, but from what I hear tell it's just as your daddy says."

As Eliza listened to his stories, it reminded her of when they were courting, when they sat together on the front porch swing and he filled her head with similar tales. As her mind drifted back to those thoughts, she found herself wishing times like this could go on forever, that they could recapture the magic they once had and he wouldn't leave. It was the life she wanted but it wasn't the life she had, and before the sky turned dark Martin stood and said he had to get going.

"So soon?" She'd hoped the sweetness of the day would entice him to prolong his visit, maybe stay the night.

He gave an exasperated huff. "I already said I've got to be back in town tonight."

In the flicker of an eyelash, he could go from being one person to another and it always left her feeling as though he'd slammed a door in her face. Times like this, she loved and hated him in equal measures.

"Will you be coming home for Christmas?"

He shrugged. "Maybe, maybe not. Depends on how busy I am."

"The boys would love to see you, and so would I."

"I know, I know. But don't start harping on me. If I ain't too busy, I'll come. That's the best I can promise."

Inside her head she screamed, *If you truly love me, you'll find a way to be here,* but she gave a nod and said nothing.

He brushed a kiss across her cheek and started toward the road. After he'd taken several steps, he turned back, flashed a smile, and waved.

She smiled back and whispered, "Bye."

It was only one small word, but it carried a million splintered pieces of her heart.

The Charleston Visit

Eliza had never intended to lie to Martin about the baby. He'd created the lie himself when he saw the pennyroyal tea gone from the shelf and assumed she'd taken it. True, she'd not corrected him, but she planned to send a letter telling the truth and explaining that she simply didn't want to spoil his visit with unpleasantries. As the weeks rolled by, that letter became increasingly difficult to write. On three different occasions she sat at the table with a pen in her hand but couldn't get beyond the first few lines saying she hoped he was well and the children missed him.

November became December, more snow fell, and the letter was never written. After a while, she decided it was unnecessary. The next time he came home, he'd recognize the obvious truth.

But he didn't come home, and on Christmas Eve she and the children rode to church in Caldonia and Jeb's wagon. Afterward Caldonia insisted they come for Christmas dinner. For weeks Eliza had been dreading the thought of Christmas without Martin, but it turned out to be one of the nicest she'd had in years.

That Christmas there was only one gift in the Hobbs household, and it didn't come from Martin. It was a wooden sled that Jeb made for the kids. It had a rope handle and was big enough to carry two kids at a time.

The happiness of Christmas stayed with Eliza well into the new year, but by the second week of January she began to worry again. It had been over four months since Martin's last visit, and he almost never stayed away that long. She again considered writing the letter, only now with the baby coming soon the thought of it was twice as intimidating.

Not knowing whether such a long absence was because of work or if he had found reason to be angry, she started to fear he'd somehow learned of her condition. Perhaps on the way back to Charleston he'd remembered how her breasts were swollen and the waistband of her skirt left unbuttoned. Whether he might have figured it out himself or run into a neighbor who mentioned it, one thing was certain. If he did know, he'd be infuriated thinking she'd made a fool of him.

The more Eliza mulled it over, the more she became convinced Martin had discovered that she'd not killed the baby. On previous occasions when he'd not returned home for an extended length of time, he'd sent a letter offering some sort of excuse: the weather was bad, work was busy, there were union meetings. He'd also sent money. This time there was nothing, not even for Christmas.

Months ago a letter from her might have sufficed, made it seem less like a deception and more like a simple misunderstanding. Now it was too late for that. She had to go there, see him face to face, and explain how things had gotten out of hand. She'd say the fault was all hers, then massage his shoulders and trace kisses along the back of his neck the way she'd done last summer. When it was just the two of them, he was always in a more relaxed mood. If he was more relaxed, it stood to reason he'd be more understanding. She'd explain how his happiness was all she'd wanted, which was why she hadn't had the heart to correct the misconception. As Eliza rolled the idea over and over in her mind, it grew stronger and more absolute. Believing this was the right way to mend their broken marriage, she began formulating a plan.

The money jar was down to a handful of coins, but she still had the few dollars hidden in the pouch behind the bed. It was enough for a train ticket into Charleston. She could ask Caldonia to take the children for a day or two, wear the dress Martin bought her when they were first married, and go to his apartment and stay the night.

That evening after the children were asleep, she pulled the blue dress from the closet to check if it had wrinkles in need of an iron. One look at the dress, and her heart fell. The waist was tiny. Now, almost nine months along with her stomach the size of a ripe pumpkin, she wouldn't be able to close the buttons. The gathers that once fell softly from the waist would be stretched tight across her stomach and make her condition all the more obvious. If he was already angry about the baby, thrusting the situation in his face was not going to help.

Eliza gave a disheartened sigh and dropped down on the side of the bed. Long into the night she thought about it, trying to come up with another plan. She considered going back to the idea of a letter and thought of a dozen different ways to phrase her words, but not one of them seemed right.

The first rays of light were edging the horizon when she finally decided to stick with her original idea. The plan was still good, only her timing was off. She'd wait and go after the baby was born. Seeing her look as she did when they lived in Charleston with her waist tucked in and cheeks rouged would soften his heart. She was all but certain of it.

There were only a few coins left in the jar, but she could make do. She'd dole out smaller portions to make the food last, substitute acorn meal for flour, roast pine nuts when the meat ran out, and hold back on using the shotgun.

One month, maybe two at the most. Surely, she could do it. It was not a terribly long time.

⊂◯⊃

The baby was born before the end of January. It was a boy, and Eliza named him Virgil after a granddaddy Martin had once spoken of fondly.

With this baby there was no midwife. When the labor pains began, Oliver ran to the Markey place and told Caldonia it was time. She followed him back to the house, brought Virgil into the world, and stayed for three days.

During the afternoons, when the oldest boys were still in school and the younger children napping, the two women talked. Eliza told Caldonia of Martin's last trip home and how it had been five months since that visit.

"With Martin that ain't necessarily a bad thing," Caldonia said and laughed. "Long as he provides for his family and—"

"That was the last I heard from him. Since then I haven't gotten so much as a postcard."

A look of surprise swept across Caldonia's face. "What you talking about? He been sending you money, ain't he?"

Eliza shook her head. "Afraid not. I can't say for sure, but I think it's because he's angry with me." She told how she'd allowed Martin to believe she'd taken the pennyroyal tea and lost the baby. "My suspicion is that he has somehow learned the truth and feels I tricked him."

"That don't give him cause to—"

"Martin doesn't need cause. If he thinks he's right, he does whatever he has a mind to and the world be damned."

"Then we got to show him he's wrong."

Eliza reached out and took Caldonia's hand in hers. "Not we. Me. As soon as I'm strong enough, I'm going to go see him in Charleston and…"

She went through her plan, telling how she'd held onto enough money for a train ticket and was counting on Caldonia to watch the children.

"It'll only be for a day or two."

"They can stay as long as need be," Caldonia replied. "The boys can bunk in with mine, and I'll take Margaret Rose and Luella in bed with me. Isaac's cradle might need to be cleaned up a bit, but it will do just fine for Virgil."

"I know taking care of seven kids is a lot to ask but—"

"Shoot, it ain't nothing at all. My two will be glad for the company."

A swell of gratitude rose in Eliza's throat, and when she whispered, "Thank you," the words of her mama came back to her.

When you've got a burden bigger than you can carry, God will send somebody to help carry it.

Caldonia was her somebody.

⌾⋙⊛⋘⌾

Once the blue dress no longer strained at the seams, Eliza was ready for her trip. She would go on a Saturday and arrive in the afternoon. If Martin was working a half-day he'd be back at the apartment, and if he was working a full day she wouldn't have long to wait.

Saturday morning, she was awake before dawn. A fluttery feeling settled in her chest and caused her heart to race. Whether it was nervousness over what the day would bring or the thought of once again being with Martin, she wasn't sure. She knew only that it was pushing her forward in a way that seemed exciting. Although there were plenty of times she hated Martin, she also still loved him and today that love warmed her heart and caused her toes to tingle.

Humming happily, Eliza took her corset from the drawer, laced it loosely, and pulled it around her body. With the front buckles and snaps closed, she reached to the back and tugged the laces until it was snug around her waist. After binding her breasts with strips of muslin to keep milk from leaking onto the bodice, she slid the dress over her head.

There was something special about the dress, something more than just the lace collar and ribbon trim. It brought back sweet memories and made her feel she was capable of changing things. A shiver of anticipation slid down her spine, and she smiled. Today was going to be a good day; she was all but certain of it.

At 10:30 when Jeb arrived to take her to the train station, she was ready and waiting. As she shooed the children out of the house and into the wagon, he gave her a broad grin.

"You look mighty pretty, Eliza; mighty pretty."

"Thank you," she said and blushed. It had been a long time since she'd had such a compliment.

When they stopped at his house to drop off the children, Eliza kissed each one and handed the baby to Caldonia.

"Virgil had a good feeding this morning, so it'll hold him for a while. When he gets hungry, give him sugar water mixed with a bit of cow's milk. He might not like it, but it'll tide him over until tomorrow. I'll be returning on the 2:25 train."

It was less than 10 miles from Coal Creek to Charleston, but the train took nearly two hours. It doubled back on itself, stopped at every junction, then crossed over the Kanawha River and traveled along the western bank. After what to Eliza seemed an endless journey, it finally crossed back over the river and chugged into the Charleston station.

The station was on the southwest side of Charleston, the apartment on the northeast side. It cost five cents to take the trolley, but with having to cross the river she had no choice.

Choosing a seat by an open window, she watched as the trolley passed through town. So much had changed since she'd lived here, but she thought of Martin's stories and tried to pick out things he'd mentioned: fancy shops, streetlamps on almost every corner, buildings taller than a person could imagine. She was lost in thought when the trolley passed Jackson Street. Realizing she'd missed her stop, she scrambled to her feet, pulled the buzzer, and climbed down from the trolley. Turning south, she walked back toward Maxwell. Once she rounded the corner and saw the small apartment building, she had the distinct feeling that nothing here had changed.

As Eliza made her way through the dim hallway and up the four flights of stairs, she knew keeping the family in Coal Creek had been the right decision. This was no place for children. Martin had been right in telling her not to move to Charleston. At the time she'd wondered if he had ulterior motives, but now she could see he'd been thinking only of them.

Hurrying up the last few steps, she pulled an old key from her purse and tried to slide it into the lock. It didn't fit. She fumbled with it for a moment and then knocked. There was movement inside, and she smiled at the thought of seeing him again.

When the door finally swung open, a tall redhead with scarlet lips stood there. Suddenly Eliza couldn't breathe. Her knees started to buckle, and she braced herself against the doorframe.

In little more than a whisper, she said, "I'm looking for Martin Hobbs. Does he live here?"

"Yeah. But he ain't here now."

Before Eliza could ask the woman's name, things began to swirl about her: the smell of the building, the dark stairwell, the anxiety of the trip, fear, anticipation. Her knees gave way. As she started to fall, the woman reached out to grab hold of her.

"You okay?"

Eliza tried to answer, but her words were nothing more than a stutter.

"Come inside and sit a spell." The woman wrapped her arm around Eliza and led her into the living room. "It's this damned hallway. It'd make anybody sick. Stinks to high heaven, and there ain't a breath of air to be had."

As she sat, Eliza recognized the sofa. It was the one she'd sat on years earlier. A bit more faded and worn in spots but the same.

The woman introduced herself as Bess Redstone. "Rest a minute while I get you a drink of water."

Still too dumbfounded to do anything else, Eliza gave a nod and sat as Bess scurried off.

She returned with the water, handed it to Eliza, and waited as she took the first few sips. Once the glass was empty and Eliza had started breathing steady, Bess said, "So, you wanna tell me who you are and what you want with Martin?"

With unsteady words, Eliza explained that she was Martin's wife and hadn't heard from him in five months.

"He doesn't return home often, but with it being this long and him not sending any money I had no way of knowing if he was dead or alive."

"That bastard." Bess dropped down in the chair opposite Eliza. "He told me he'd been married, but you was dead and his three boys were living with his sister."

Dead? Three boys?

Eliza suddenly recalled the hatred she'd felt when Martin had been happy thinking she'd let the baby die. That hate swelled in her chest and pushed aside the love she still had.

"We have seven children, not three. The baby, Virgil, was born two months ago, and as you can see I'm not dead, but we might all be if he doesn't start sending us enough money to live."

She continued, naming each child, saying when they'd been born, and telling of the struggle they'd gone through with no money, no food, and no shells for the shotgun. Bess leaned forward, listening as Eliza spoke, giving an occasional nod as if the story was one that was all too familiar. When she heard how nine-year-old Oliver had used their last three shells to shoot a jackrabbit so the family wouldn't go hungry, she left the chair, came to sit beside Eliza, and covered Eliza's hand with her own.

"I may not look it now, but I know what it's like to go hungry. I remember nights when I thought I'd die of starvation before morning."

Eliza looked at Bess with wide eyes. "When was that?"

"A long time ago. I was eight, Pauline was twelve. She's my sister. After Mama and Daddy died, it was just the two of us."

"Alone? Who took care of you?"

"Nobody. We took care of ourselves."

"But how—"

"Did whatever odd jobs we could find, begged for handouts, stole stuff. Slept in hallways. It ain't something I'm proud of, but when you're hungry you do what you gotta do to get by."

"That's terrible," Eliza said. "No child should have to live like that."

"Yes, I know."

The two women talked for a long while, Bess telling of the life she'd known as a child and Eliza telling how things had fallen apart between her and Martin. As they sat there, an understanding emerged.

"I stole and done plenty of other bad things in my life, but I ain't never been a homewrecker," Bess said. "Your troubles with Martin ain't of my doing."

"I don't fault you. He's a man who—"

"Martin and me, we been together less than four months. The truth is, he don't mean nothing to me and I don't mean nothing to him."

"I'm glad of that. Glad for you and for me." Eliza took a deep breath and looked around the painfully familiar room then back to Bess. "Martin's a lot of things, some good, maybe some bad, but the one thing I can't deny is that he's the father of our children, and having a daddy part of the time is better than having none at all."

"I sure as hell can't argue with that."

With those thoughts still hanging in the air, they sat in silence for a few moments.

"So, what are you gonna do now?" Bess asked.

"I don't have a choice. I've got to stay and ask Martin for money. Right now, I don't even have enough for train fare home."

"Maybe there's another way," Bess said. She gave a mischievous smile as she explained about a loose floorboard in the closet where Martin kept a roll of bills. "He thinks I don't know, but I seen him getting money out for his poker game. If a man's got money enough for poker, then he damn well ought to be feeding his kids."

"I can't take that money without asking. He'd be furious." A hint of hesitation dangled at the end of Eliza's words.

"How's he gonna know? I ain't gonna tell him, and he ain't gonna know you been here."

Another flicker of hesitation drifted by before Eliza spoke. "Then he'll blame you."

"Martin thinks I don't know about the money, so I ain't worried."

"He's no dummy. He'll figure it out, and when he does there's no telling what he'll do."

"I ain't scared a' no man." Bess lifted the hem of her skirt, showed a hunting knife stuck in the side of her boot, and grinned. "Pauline got beat up pretty bad by a man she trusted, and I ain't never forgot it."

A look of apprehension tugged at Eliza's face. "That knife won't be enough to protect you if Martin gets really mad. I've seen how he can be. Before you've got time to think about it, he'll have that knife out of your hands and at your throat. Once he discovers that money missing, you won't want to be around."

"I been thinking a' leaving anyway. Pauline's got a place over by the railroad station. I can stay with her."

Eliza sat for a moment longer mulling it over; there was something very right and something very wrong about such a plan but try as she may, she couldn't decide which was which. Then she thought about the children waiting at home and gave a nod. "I'd be truly grateful to have the money."

Bess flew into the bedroom like an excited squirrel and returned moments later with a handful of folded bills. Stuffing it into Eliza's palm, she said, "Take this and get out of here before he comes home."

"I don't know how I can ever thank you."

"Don't waste time trying. Just promise me you'll never let your kids have to fend for themselves on the streets."

"I promise," Eliza said.

◌⟊◌

Gertrude Sloan was sitting beside the window when Eliza left the building. Catching sight of Eliza, she stood, rapped on the glass, and called out, but Eliza hurried away, apparently not seeing or hearing the call. Gertrude dropped back into her chair with a thump of disappointment.

"Ah, well. Maybe next time."

If there was one thing Gertrude could not abide, it was seeing the brazen hussies that paraded in and out of Martin's Hobbs's apartment. Hopefully having Eliza back would put a stop to it.

1968
The Search Continues

Charleston

On Tuesday, Tom Bateman was standing in front of the historic city hall building before it opened. As soon as the guard unlocked the doors, he crossed the lobby and headed for the records department of the city clerk's office. Clara Goodman was on duty that morning, and she was in no mood for nonsense. When Tom said he was looking to find any or all death certificates for people bearing the last name of Hobbs, she glared at him and said he was out of his blooming mind.

"Half the people in Kanawha County are named Hobbs, and I hope you ain't expecting me to pull—"

Tom leaned forward, his elbow propped on the counter. "Really? Half?"

She laughed. "Well, maybe not half, but there's a lot. Too many for me to be going through if you don't even know the whole name."

"Okay then, how about if I give you a couple of names and you check those out?"

"A couple is two."

He'd planned to check all the names, but with Clara giving him a hard time he had to narrow it down. He already knew Eliza, Louella, and Ben Roland were dead, so he wouldn't use up his resources on them. Caldonia had said that both Nellie and Edward were sent to live with a family in Huntington, and Virgil had walked away and disappeared.

There was still the possibility that Oliver, Dewey, or John Paul had either returned to the area or settled here.

"Look for Oliver Hobbs, Dewey Hobbs, or John Paul Hobbs, okay?"

"I said two; that's three."

"Yeah, but they're all from the same family."

She spit out a huff of annoyance and asked, "You got the district or year on these deaths?"

"Afraid not. It would probably be sometime after 1918, possibly in or around Coal Creek."

She shook her head and rolled her eyes. "You can stand here and wait, or come back in an hour."

"Think I'll grab a cup of coffee and come back in an hour. Can I bring you something?"

"Huh? Bring me what?"

"I'm going down to the luncheonette. Can I bring you back something? Coffee, an egg sandwich, a pastry?"

She gave a genuine smile for the first time. "Yeah, that'd be real nice. Coffee and maybe one or two of them French cruller things."

Tom winked at her and returned the smile. As he headed down Virginia Street toward the luncheonette, he was wearing a grin. It felt good to know that despite his five years of retirement, he hadn't forgotten the tricks of the trade.

On his second trip that day to City Hall, Tom visited the Kanawha County Health Department and the Motor Vehicle Bureau and saw Clara Goodman in the city clerk's office again. He now knew that none of the missing Hobbs siblings had died, gotten married or divorced, owned a car, or held a driver's license in Kanawha County.

He also knew that someone in the Hobbs family had requested a new birth certificate for Virgil, and they'd changed his name from Hobbs to Palmer. According to the record Eliza Hobbs submitted the initial request, but the document was picked up and signed for by Martin Hobbs. The processing stamp was dated August 17, 1913.

This struck Tom as strange since according to Margaret and the National Brotherhood of Electrical Workers, Martin disappeared in January 1910. Tom asked himself why a man with a reward out for his arrest would come home to West Virginia to pick up a new birth certificate for the son he'd cared nothing about.

Before the day was out, he was beginning to understand how Margaret lost track of her family. It seemed as though one by one they'd all disappeared without a trace.

That night Tom sat in his hotel room going through his notes. He'd spent a lot of time at City Hall but come away with very little. He'd eliminated a number of possibilities, but the only new facts he had were the precise dates of Eliza and Louella's deaths and Virgil's change of name. There was no Virgil Palmer listed in any of the area telephone books, no driver's license with that name, and no marriage certificate, so just knowing the name wouldn't be all that helpful unless he had a fix on where Virgil had settled.

Tom kept coming back to the fact that Virgil was only nine or ten when someone had changed his name and apparently helped him to disappear. Nothing about this made sense, and he simply didn't believe Martin was the one to claim the new birth certificate.

He circled the dates of Eliza and Louella's deaths. Tomorrow he'd try the library. Maybe there'd been an obituary in the newspaper, and maybe, just maybe, it listed the surviving kin.

He set the notepad on the nightstand, snapped on the television, and watched the end of *N.Y.P.D.* The show was half over when he tuned in so the plot seemed disjointed, but it didn't matter because his thoughts were elsewhere.

At the Charleston library, he got lucky. The librarian was a chatty woman who seemed eager to help. She said her name was Annie McDonnell and told him the library had microfiche files for the *Charleston Daily Mail* going back 75 years plus a historical records reference section.

As she led him toward the small room in the back, she whispered, "Our collection is quite extensive. Anything you want to know about Charleston, you'll find in here."

Tom thanked her and said he was looking for information on a family who'd lived in Coal Creek. She smiled and momentarily forgot her hushed voice.

"I grew up in Coal Creek," she said. "My daddy was a coal miner."

"Any chance you remember a family named Hobbs?"

"That's a pretty common name around here. In grade school we had three or four of them. A girl in my class was named Hobbs, but I don't recall her first name."

"Louella, Margaret, Nellie. Any of those names ring a bell?"

"Margaret. I think that's it. She had a brother one grade back from us."

"That'd be Virgil. You remember anything about him?"

"Only that he was a skinny little kid who got picked on a lot."

The historical reference room had shelves lining both walls, study tables in the center of the room, and a microfiche viewing area in the back. She started to set up the machine. "Okay, you've got the *Charleston Daily Mail*. What years were you looking for?"

"Nineteen-fifteen, sixteen, and seventeen. The obituaries."

"Back that far it's not sorted by section. You'll have to scan the pages. You looking for an obit on that kid—Virgil, you said his name was?"

"Not him. His mama and older sister. Why?"

"It's just that I know there's nothing on Virgil. He left town way before that and he's never been back, at least not to my knowledge."

"So you remember when he left?"

"Everybody remembers. It was quite the scandal. He was in maybe the third or fourth grade when it happened. He walked from Coal Creek to Charleston, then disappeared for good. I doubt a kid that age could get anywhere on his own. It's likely his brother came and got him."

"Which brother?"

"The older one; the one who was always protecting him at school."

"Oliver?"

She shrugged. "Can't say. He was a big kid, red hair, a boxy build."

Tom pulled a small note pad from his pocket and jotted down, *Oliver, red hair?*

After five hours of searching through the microfiche files, Tom had nothing. What he had learned was that the Coal Creek area seemed to be one where people were born, lived, and died without ever moving away. In a tight-knit community like that, he was certain somebody knew something. The question was who? And what did they know?

That afternoon he drove back to Coal Creek and went directly to the Markey house where he'd met Caldonia. When he rapped on the door, it was the daughter-in-law, Rowena, who answered.

"Sorry," she said. "Mama Markey's feeling poorly and not up to company."

"This won't take but a few minutes," Tom said. "Last time I was here, Caldonia mentioned that she'd like to chat with me again."

"Yeah, well, maybe she was just being polite." Rowena stood with her arm braced against the door frame and her body blocking the entrance. "She might've been more up to it that day. If you wanna tell me what this is all about, I can maybe see if she's up to talking."

Tom thought back on the way Caldonia had made a decided effort to keep whatever she knew from Rowena.

"I'd be happy to do that," he said, "but the information I'm looking for goes back to way before your time. Likely as not, you weren't even born yet."

The antagonistic look on her face softened. "What makes you think that?"

"Well, look at you. You're what, in your early forties?"

She laughed. "Don't I wish!"

"So listen, you think maybe I could chat with Caldonia for a few minutes? You could sit in, maybe see if what we're talking about rings a bell."

The suspicion was back. "Nope. Mama Markey's napping, and I'm not gonna disturb her."

"I could wait."

Rowena was already shaking her head. "No telling how long she'll sleep."

Tom could see he was getting nowhere. "Okay then, maybe I'll stop back tomorrow, see how she's doing."

"Suit yourself," Rowena said, "but I ain't promising nothing."

When Tom pulled out onto the dirt road and headed back to Charleston he'd already decided to come back, but to get to Caldonia he needed to find a way around Rowena.

Finding the Past

On his way back to the hotel, Tom stopped at the Thirsty Bear Tavern, had a beer and a club sandwich, and hurried back to his room. He settled at the desk and studied the spread of notes laid out in front of him. This case was like trying to put together a jigsaw puzzle without knowing what the final picture was supposed to look like. Most people left a paper trail as they traveled through life but not the Hobbs siblings. They were here then gone. People remembered them, but that's where it ended. The only trail they'd left behind was one of piecemeal memories.

The few facts he had been able to find only served to raise more questions. Did Martin Hobbs come back after his supposed disappearance just to collect the papers for Virgil's name change? Or did someone else, pretending to be Martin, sign for the papers? Who? Why? And then there was the question of Nellie and Edward, apparently shipped off to some nameless family in Huntington. Were they adopted? Did they also have new names? Was it possible the new family had requested their school records?

Tom penciled in a reminder to check the Coal Creek school.

He'd planned to make a quick stop in Coal Creek the next morning and then start for Huntington. Now he was rethinking it. A nagging in the back of his mind kept arguing there was more to be found in Coal Creek from the people, particularly Caldonia Markey. She'd seen the story through from start to end. She and Eliza had been close, best friends from what Tom could gather. Chances were she knew a lot more than what she'd said, but the question was whether or not she'd be willing to share it with him. He circled Caldonia's name, put a question mark beside it, and sat there thinking.

After 15 minutes, he picked up the telephone, told the operator he wanted to place a long-distance call to Heatherwood, Georgia, and gave her Margaret's number.

⟡

Margaret answered so quickly it was almost as if she'd been sitting there, waiting for the telephone to ring.

"I wish I had better news," Tom said, "but so far all I've gotten are bits and pieces of information; nothing concrete." He asked if there had ever been any mention of Martin returning to Coal Creek after they'd come back from Barrettsville.

"Not that I know of," Margaret replied. "Once we left Barrettsville, no one ever heard from Daddy again."

Then Tom asked about the red-haired brother.

She laughed. "That was Ben Roland. He was the only redhead. Oliver used to tease him, saying he was adopted. He wasn't, but it used to drive him crazy when Oliver said that."

"Was Virgil close with Ben Roland?"

"Closer than he was with anybody else. Most of the time he just wanted to be off by himself, but if he had any kind of problem Ben Roland was the one he'd turn to."

Tom explained Virgil's name change from Hobbs to Palmer and how a man claiming to be Martin Hobbs had signed for the document. "Any chance that was Ben Roland?"

"It could have been. He was about seventeen the year Virgil disappeared and big enough to pass for a full-grown man."

Tom told her about his visit to Coal Creek.

"Apparently, there was a fire in your family's house. The back of it is completely gone. I did a walk-through to see if there was anything that could be salvaged, but the only thing I came up with was a photograph. It was on the wall in what looks to have been the living room. The glass wasn't broken, so the picture is in fairly good shape. Judging by the way the man and woman were dressed, I figured it was your parents."

As he spoke, Margaret closed her eyes and saw the grainy photograph. It was one of the few things her mama had taken to Barrettsville and brought back with them. She pictured the brown sofa where she'd sat side by side with her mama and the piano that sat pushed up against the far wall before her mama sold it.

"We called that room the parlor," she said. "I remember that picture. It was Mama and Daddy's wedding photo."

"Your smile is a lot like hers," Tom said. "While I was there, I talked to a number of families living along the hollow. Most only had sketchy memories of your family and couldn't say what had happened to Nellie or the boys. The one exception was Caldonia Mar—"

Margaret gasped. "Aunt Caldonia's still alive?"

"You remember her?"

"Of course I do; she was like a second mother to me. To all of us. She and Mama were like sisters." Margaret paused a moment letting her thoughts roll back over the hundreds of times her mama had said, *If anything happens to me, you and your brothers go to Caldonia. She and Jeb will...*

"Uncle Jeb. What about Jeb?" she asked. "Is he still alive?"

"As far as I could tell, it was just Caldonia, her son, and daughter-in-law."

"Oh." The disappointment in Margaret's voice was obvious.

"Caldonia told me Nellie and Edward went to the same family in Huntington, but she didn't say the name. I think she knows but isn't telling. My bet is Eliza told her to keep certain things a secret, and that's what she's doing."

Margaret gave a soft chuckle. "I wouldn't be the least bit surprised. There's nothing she and Mama wouldn't have done for one another."

"That would explain it, because when Rowena came into the room she just stopped talking, and—"

"Rowena?"

"Her daughter-in-law. I got the impression there's a bit of hostility there, and Caldonia doesn't want Rowena knowing any of what she called Eliza's secrets."

"What secrets?"

"There wasn't time enough to find out. I went back today, but Rowena wouldn't let me in. Claimed her mother-in-law was napping. Maybe if you could talk to her…"

"Great idea. Caldonia will remember me, I'm positive of it. I could telephone her and—"

"I think she'd be a lot more forthcoming if you spoke with her face to face."

All of a sudden, Margaret's enthusiasm was gone. "That may be, but I don't see how—"

"Fly down tomorrow. I'll meet you in Charleston, and we'll drive out together."

A lengthy silence followed.

"Margaret, are you still there?"

"I'm here, but I'm not sure I want to go back to Coal Creek. The last time was for Louella's burial, and I'm afraid that…"

"Afraid? What is there to be afraid of? There's been a lot of changes in those years; not in Coal Creek but in you. Back then you were a young girl with no family and an uncertain future. Now you're a woman taking control of your life. Coming back to Coal Creek can't hurt you, Margaret. It can only help you."

Tom was about to say seeing Coal Creek again might make her realize how lucky she was to have left the place, but before he had the chance she spoke.

"Thank you. That may not have been meant as a compliment, but to me it was." She drew a long breath. "Albert and I never talked of Coal Creek. He knew how devastated I was when Mama sent me to live with Aunt Rose, so he tried to protect me from any memory of the past. He did it because he loved me, and I can't fault him for that. But memories come bundled together, the good with the bad. It's sad to say, but in shielding me from the bad memories, he robbed me of the good ones. The memories of people like Caldonia and Jeb."

"Is that a yes?"

She laughed. "It's definitely a yes."

They spent the next two hours with telephone calls to check airline schedules and make plans. The morning flight was full so Margaret was booked on the afternoon flight, which didn't land at Kanawha Airport until 6:37 pm.

"That's probably too late for us to start out to the Markey place," he said. "We'll grab dinner, then head back to the hotel. I'd like to get an early start the next morning so we're there before Caldonia takes her afternoon nap."

"Hotel?" Margaret said nervously.

"Yes, I'm staying at the Daniel Boone. I figure it's more convenient if we're in the same hotel, so I reserved a room for you."

"My own room. That's good."

"Hold on there," Tom said with a laugh. "You didn't think…"

"Of course I didn't. Not for a minute."

⌒◡⋇◡⌒

When Margaret hung up the telephone, an excitement she hadn't felt in years began to swell in her chest. She could feel the blood racing through her veins and her heart growing lighter. Seeing Caldonia again was something she'd never imagined possible. Caldonia was not blood family, but she was family all the same.

Thinking of family made her remember Josie. Margaret snatched up the telephone and dialed Josie's number. After three rings, Josie answered and Margaret spoke with excitement about the plan that had come together to go back to Coal Creek.

"I figured Mr. Bateman would find something," Josie said.

"I don't know what he has yet," Margaret said, trying to fight the smile that kept tugging at her mouth. "We have to remember, he said he only has bits and pieces so far."

"If anyone is gonna find your family, he'll be the one to do it."

They talked for a few more moments with Josie promising to check on the house while Margaret was gone. When she hung up the telephone, she couldn't fight her smile anymore.

From the very start Margaret had believed in Tom Bateman; believed he would find her family. Now she could almost feel it happening. How foolish it had been to wait so many years, to fear a place that she'd once called home. As she pulled the overnight bag from the back of the closet and began to pack, she imagined a family reunion, a huge party with everyone together again, happy and laughing, agreeing that it had been foolish to have ever allowed themselves to drift apart. In the center of the group would be Caldonia, big-bosomed and welcoming as she'd been so many years ago.

She tried to picture her brothers as they'd be now, older but somehow the same. Dewey, with his dimpled chin and deep-set eyes; Oliver, standing a head taller than the others; John Paul, white-haired but with the same boyish grin; and Virgil, a shadowy figure standing off from the others. Nellie and Edward were impossible to picture. They'd been so very young when she'd left Coal Creek. Nellie's blonde curls were easy to remember, but try as she might she couldn't recall if her sister's eyes were blue or brown. The same was true of Edward. He'd been a toddler when she'd last seen him; two, maybe, or three.

She took her grey tweed suit from the closet; then she remembered the flowered apron Caldonia always wore and decided against the tweed. *Too formal.* Replacing the suit, she opted for a rose-colored sweater set and tan slacks.

It had been years since Margaret had traveled anywhere, and now she was feeling uncertain about what to bring or not bring. Tom mentioned dinner so she'd need a dress and shoes, plus a few more changes in case she stayed to visit with Caldonia. Once any and all dress situations were covered, she realized the overnight bag was way too small. Replacing that she considered the weekender but that also seemed too tight, so she ended up with the full-size suitcase, which, after an extra pair of shoes was added, had to be squeezed shut.

When Margaret finally crawled into bed, a thousand thoughts crowded into her mind. Although Tom had only spoken of Caldonia, the feeling that she was about to be reunited with her brothers had already taken root.

Lying there in the darkness, she wondered if she would recognize each of the boys on sight and if they would recognize her. When she left home, she'd been a girl with coltish legs and no bosom. She'd had a narrow face that over time had grown rounder. Her body was now fuller, her hair darker and streaked with silver. Margaret tried to call up the image of her younger self, but it proved impossible. That girl was gone forever, replaced by a woman who resembled her mama.

A narrow ribbon of moonlight slipped through the blind and fell across the floor. In the dim light, Margaret could see the cluster of photographs sitting atop the dresser. Without looking at them, she knew what each frame held. The largest one was Albert dressed in a dark suit and giving the camera his lofty lawyer smile. The one beside it held the two of them together at a country club dance. The heart-shaped frame was a souvenir from their 25th anniversary dinner.

So many wonderful times, and all of them were now gone. Albert would never get to meet her family, never know the woman who was like a mother or the brothers who jostled and teased one another. He'd never experience the haunting beauty of that wooded hollow, hear the call of a night bird, or taste the icy cold water drawn up from the well.

A sigh rolled up from her chest, the sound of it mournful and hollow.

"Oh, Albert, we wasted all those years. If only you had believed I was strong enough to accept the truth. We could have been a family. It was never the truth that pained me. It was the terrible not knowing."

The Road Home

The loudspeaker crackled, and the stewardess's voice filled the cabin.

"Ladies and gentlemen, welcome to Charleston, West Virginia. Please remain seated until the plane has arrived at the gate."

For 50 years Margaret swore she'd never return to Coal Creek. Yet here she was, not just returning but looking forward to it. Excited at the prospect of seeing Caldonia again. As she started down the walkway, she spotted Tom Bateman waiting at the gate. He waved then moved through the crowd and pulled her into a welcoming hug.

"Good trip?" he said and smiled.

Margaret returned his smile and gave a nod. They'd been working together for nine weeks and in that time, they'd become friends. The kind of friends who could tell each other anything and were never at a loss for words.

After a quick stop at baggage claim, they got into the car and headed for the city. Once they left the highway, Margaret saw a Charleston far different than what she'd known. Glass-fronted office buildings stood in places where there had been rows of ramshackle tenements. The trolleys were gone replaced by shiny new buses, and cars were parked end to end along both sides of the street. When she left, Charleston was a fairly large town. Now it was a city that could probably rival Atlanta.

She counted five different department stores on Capitol Street alone, and there were shops of every size and shape.

"I'm amazed at how the town has changed," she said.

"If you want, later on we can take a drive and look around. But first let's get you checked in at the hotel, put your bag in the room, and find a place for dinner. Okay?"

"Perfect. I skipped lunch this afternoon; now I'm hungry enough to eat a horse."

Tom grinned. "There's a nice little tavern down the street from the hotel but no horse on the menu. Think you can make do with a burger or steak?"

Margaret laughed and said a steak sounded wonderful.

After stopping at the hotel, they settled in a back booth at the tavern where it would be quieter and they could talk.

"Wine or cocktail?" Tom asked.

"It's been a while since I've had a cocktail, so tonight I'll stick with wine. I don't want to fall asleep in the middle of dinner."

"We're having steak, so is a red okay?" He studied the wine list and asked if she'd prefer a pinot noir or the somewhat milder merlot.

"Easy choice. Pinot is one of my favorites."

"Mine also." He waved the waitress over and ordered a bottle.

When she brought the wine, she also brought a small bucket of peanuts and set it on the table alongside an empty bucket for the shells. As Tom was talking about the drive to Coal Creek, Margaret took a peanut, broke it open, and popped it into her mouth.

"These are delicious," she said, "like you get at a baseball game or the circus." She took a few more and pushed the bucket toward Tom. "Try one."

He did and nodded in agreement. "They are like ball game peanuts." He segued into the time he and five friends went to see an Atlanta Braves game.

"Food is half the fun of being there," he said. "Just like you can't enjoy a circus without a bag of peanuts, you can't go to a ball game without having a hot dog."

"Or a fall festival without a jelly apple," Margaret added.

They both laughed, and before long they were talking about all the places and foods they hoped to experience one day.

"New York City in December," Margaret said. "I'd like to see the Rockefeller Center Christmas tree lighting, then buy a bag of roasted chestnuts from a street vendor and walk down Fifth Avenue looking at the department store windows."

Tom had a number of things on his list: lobsters in Maine, cheesesteak in Philadelphia, and vinegar fries on the Atlantic City boardwalk.

When the waitress came to ask if they were ready to order, Margaret shook her head. "Give us a little more time."

Tom poured them each a second glass of wine, and as the minutes slipped away they continued to talk.

"It's been a while since I went to dinner with a friend," she said. "I hope I'm not rambling on like a doddering old fool."

"You? Never," Tom said and grinned. "I'm enjoying this as much as you are. Getting back to work was the best thing I've done in years, and I have you to thank for it. When I came to your house that first day, I was kind of hoping you'd ask me to work the case."

"But you made a point of saying you were retired."

"So I did," he said and laughed. "I actually was until I pulled that file out. Thinking about all those unanswered questions made me realize how much I missed working."

When they finally ordered it was almost 9 pm, and a guitarist was setting up in the corner opposite them. They finished the bottle of wine with dinner, then ordered dessert and coffee. As they sat there talking about nothing in particular, Margaret found herself humming along with the guitarist. He played country music, easy songs that seemed vaguely familiar. When they finally left the restaurant after midnight and strolled back to the hotel, she was humming *King of the Road* and trying to remember the lyrics.

They said good night and parted in the hotel hallway. Tom headed for his room, and Margaret to hers. At the last second, he called to her and looked back with a grin.

"Don't forget, eight o'clock tomorrow morning. In the lobby."

She nodded, and a yawn slid out. "I'll be there."

The lack of sleep from the night before and the excitement of the trip finally caught up with Margaret and the moment her head hit the pillow, she was fast asleep.

When she woke, sunlight was glinting through a broken slat in the venetian blind and the telephone was ringing.

"Hello," she answered sleepily.

"It's eight-fifteen; are you ready to leave?"

Margaret bolted up. "Almost. Give me fifteen minutes."

Moving around the room like a tornado, she showered, dressed, ran a comb through her hair, slicked on a bit of mascara and a dab of lipstick, and was out the door. Tom was waiting alongside the elevator. When she stepped off, he handed her a container of coffee.

"Overslept, didn't you?" he said.

"Yes," she admitted sheepishly.

The traffic was slow leaving the city, but once they got on the highway it started to move. Before they turned onto Campbell's Creek Drive, Tom asked if she remembered Rowena.

"Not really," she said. "The name sounds familiar, but I can't say from where."

"My concern is that she could refuse to let us see Caldonia or stand there like a watchdog so Caldonia can't tell us what we need to know." Tom explained how on his previous visit, Caldonia changed the subject whenever her daughter-in-law was within hearing distance. "Apparently, Eliza trusted her enough to share something she didn't want anyone else to know. Now Caldonia's protecting that secret."

"But it's been fifty years," Margaret said with a frown, "and Mama's been gone for so long. Why would she still want to keep the secret?"

"Maybe she sees it as being a good friend. Maybe there's something more to it."

"You think she knows where my sister and brothers are?"

Tom shrugged. "Maybe, maybe not. Whatever happened took place over fifty years ago. People don't necessarily stay in the same place. They move around, change jobs, get married, any number of things. She may not know where they are now, but I'll bet she knows enough to point us in the right direction."

The thought of once again being with her sister and brothers caused Margaret's heart to skip over a few beats. "Aunt Caldonia will tell me what she knows, I'm positive of it."

"I think so too," Tom said, "if we can get Rowena to let us in the house."

Before they could come up with a feasible plan, he was turning into the graveled drive that led to the road up the hollow.

Margaret sat silent for several minutes as the car bumped and bounced along the dirt road. She rolled down the window, sniffed the air, and peered up at the towering sycamores and Virginia pines, listening for familiar sounds. When she spied the first few houses, she knew nothing on the mountain had changed.

The memory of the years after their return from Barrettsville swept through her mind, painful as ever. She'd thought time had dulled the ache of it, but it hadn't. Her stomach rumbled and a bitter taste rose in her throat, a reminder of the coffee she'd had earlier.

"It's all still the same," she said. "Beautiful but cruel."

"Cruel? In what way?"

"Men disappear or die digging coal out of the mountain, and women like my mama are left trying to scrape enough food out of the ground to feed their family."

"Your father never worked as a coal miner, did he?"

"No, but he was one of those who disappeared."

Nothing more was said until they pulled into the drive beside the Markey house.

"Look familiar?"

She nodded, climbed out of the car, and walked toward the back side of the house.

"Wait a minute, where are you—"

She glanced back, held her finger to her lips, and motioned for him to follow. When he was close enough to hear, she whispered, "The pathway that ran from our house to Caldonia's is still here, and that barrel is actually a kid-sized door Jeb made for us. It leads to the kitchen, and there's no lock on it. Once I'm inside, I know Aunt Caldonia will talk to me."

Tom's eyes went wide. "That's the craziest idea I've ever heard! You don't know what these people will do. If they catch you crawling through that back door, they're liable to shoot first and ask questions later."

"Not if you go to the front door and keep Rowena busy for a while. Once Aunt Caldonia knows it's me, she won't let anybody do anything."

Tom tried arguing that it was way too risky, but Margaret's mind was made up. She started toward the barrel then turned and motioned for him to move around to the front door. At that point there was nothing he could do but comply.

Knocking on the door far louder than was necessary, he called out, "Hello? Anyone home?" Trying to give Margaret enough time to crawl through the pint-sized door and reach Caldonia, he knocked a second time even though he'd already heard footsteps. This time he struck the door with a fist rather than his knuckles.

At first, the heavy footsteps sounded like Rowena's. Tom heard a man yell something, and the door swung open. Rowena stood there, hands on hips, with a scowl.

"What's wrong with you, banging on the door like that?"

"Sorry," Tom said, "I didn't realize it was that loud. I thought—"

"Not loud?" Rowena took a step closer to him. "You was banging on that door so hard it woke Edgar! Edgar and half the corpses in the hollow!"

"I said I'm sorry. I didn't realize there was a baby—"

"Chowder-head," she grumbled and rolled her eyes. "Edgar's my husband. He's been working the night shift, and sleeping ain't easy when—"

A bald man half her size came up behind her. "Rowena, you got a problem here?"

She turned to him, her voice softer. "No problem, Edgar, honey. Go back to sleep. This guy's here to see your mama." Glancing back at Tom, she said, "You are here to see Mother Markey, aren't you?"

"Yes, I have a few more questions."

Edgar elbowed Rowena out of his way and stepped in front of her. "What kind of questions you got for Mama?"

"I thought maybe you or your mama could help me out. I'm looking for a few members of the Hobbs family. They lived one house up from here, the place that had a fire—"

He was interrupted by the sound of breaking glass and a scream.

"Mama!"

Edgar took off running toward the kitchen. Rowena and Tom were right behind him.

Caldonia's Secret

A broken bowl lay on the kitchen floor with splatters of sausage gravy everywhere. Seemingly unfazed by the mishap, Caldonia stood there hanging onto Margaret's arm and smiling like it was Christmas morning.

Edgar was first through the kitchen door. "What happened here, Mama?"

Caldonia grinned. "One a' my lost lambs has done been found."

Rowena pushed past Tom, slipping and sliding in the gravy. She charged across the room and pulled up in front of Margaret.

"Who the hell are you? How'd you get in here?"

Margaret backed up a few inches and started to explain. "We lived just up the—"

"You don't owe her no explanation," Caldonia said and squeezed Margaret's arm. "I guess Rowena done forgot her company manners." Looking across at Edgar, she said, "You remember Margaret Rose, don't you?"

He gaped at Margaret for a moment, mouth hanging open.

"Well, I'll be... I wouldn't have known you if I fell over you. What's it been, thirty, forty years?"

"Try fifty," Margaret said and laughed.

Circling around most of the spilled gravy, Edgar crossed the room, hugged Margaret, and kissed her cheek, which seemed to irate Rowena all the more. Giving him a look that could kill, she said, "Is somebody gonna tell me what's going on?"

"Margaret's a Hobbs. They lived up the road a piece." He turned to Margaret and asked, "You come through the barrel?"

When she nodded, he laughed. "Ain't nobody used it for—"

"Over fifty years." Margaret introduced Tom and explained that he was helping to look for her sister and brothers.

Caldonia listened and gave an understanding nod. "Your mama figured sooner or later one of you kids was gonna come looking to find the others. She told me, 'Caldonia, when that happens, you help them if you can.'" With her arm still hooked onto Margaret's, she said, "Come, let's sit in the parlor while Rowena cleans up this mess." Halfway across the room she glanced back at her daughter-in-law. "Whip up a bit more of that sausage gravy will you honey? We ought to offer our guests breakfast."

With her face turning color and her right eye blinking like a firefly Rowena looked to Edgar, but by then he was following behind the others.

In the parlor Caldonia sat in the armchair padded with extra cushions, and Margaret scooted a straight chair close to her. Tom and Edgar took the sofa across from them. As soon as everyone was settled, Caldonia started asking about Margaret's life. Where had she gone after Aunt Rose died? Had she married? Were there any children?

One by one Margaret answered the questions, and when asked if she'd been happy she answered yes.

"I regret that we never had children, but Albert was a loving husband and we had a good marriage."

A bittersweet smile tugged at Caldonia's mouth. "Knowing that would've made your mama happy. She wanted all you kids to have a good marriage and a happy life."

"Is that what she told you?"

Caldonia nodded. "A hundred or more times."

They talked for a while longer then she hollered back, asking if the gravy was ready. When Rowena answered yes, Caldonia looked over at Tom and grinned. "Mr. Bateman, you look like a city boy; you ever had sausage gravy and biscuits for breakfast?"

"Not that I can recall," Tom said.

"Well, then, you are in for one fine treat. Ain't nothing like it. Why, Margaret Rose could easily put down three or four helpings when she was just a little bitty thing."

Pushing herself up from the chair, Caldonia headed back to the kitchen. Tom and Margaret followed along but Edgar left, saying he needed to get some sleep.

Although Margaret had a million questions, she held back on them and allowed herself to enjoy the time with Caldonia. Gathered around the table, they talked of the old days. The good times when there was food on the table, the Christmases they'd shared, and the summer Martin came home every weekend with surprises in his pocket.

"You might not remember that," Caldonia said. "You was just a bitty thing then, but the older boys, they'd remember. Dewey never had no love for your daddy, but he told me that summer it was different."

Leaning into the conversation, Margaret asked, "When did you talk to Dewey?"

"A real long time ago," she said and shook her head. "My memory ain't what it used to be, but I reckon it was a year or so after that first war when he was still walking with a cane."

Margaret's heart suddenly felt lighter than it had in years. Thousands of times she'd thought of Dewey and cried, always wondering, never knowing, and too afraid of the answer to go in search of it. Now here it was.

"Dewey's alive," she said, her voice quavering.

"He was then. I can't say if—"

"Did he say where he was living, or what line of work he was in?" Tom asked.

"He's a doctor or leastwise was gonna be. He was learning from a fella he worked with in the army." Caldonia pushed her plate back. "This chair's hard on my bones. We gotta move back to the parlor." She looked over to Tom and gave a wink. "Mr. Bateman, you wanna come give me a hand?"

Tom helped her up from the chair and offered his arm.

As they were leaving the room, she turned back and said, "Rowena, honey, after you finish cleaning up in here, I'd like you to come join us."

Rowena said she'd be sure to do that, and Caldonia turned away with a smug smile. Once they were beyond earshot, she leaned toward Margaret and whispered, "She won't come 'cause she thinks I want her to. That woman don't like me any more than I do her, but she puts up with me cause she figures I won't be around much longer."

"Oh, I doubt that's true, Aunt Caldonia. Why would anyone—"

"It's true enough," Caldonia said. "But I keep on living just to annoy her."

Once they'd settled in the parlor, Caldonia spoke more freely. She said the last time she'd seen Dewey he was living in a town not far from Huntington. "I think it was Greystone. Something like that anyway."

Margaret's heart rose into her throat. "Huntington? Nellie was sent to live with a family in Huntington, did you know that?"

"Course I did. When your mama got sick, she talked to Pastor Dale and he fixed it up. The Hunters are good people what couldn't have kids a' their own. That's why your mama let them take Nellie and Edward. It about broke her heart to see those last two babies go, but she figured it was for the best cause she was sickly and couldn't protect them no more."

Tom wrote the name *Hunter* in his notebook. "Protect them from what?"

Caldonia glanced over her shoulder, then looked back to Tom and whispered, "Finding out about the thing in Barrettsville."

"What thing in Barrettsville?" Margaret asked.

"The one with your daddy."

"Daddy ran off and left us. I don't see how—"

"Margaret Rose, you know I'd give you anything I've got, but that story ain't mine to tell. Your mama had her reasons for not wanting the rest of you kids to know."

Margaret looked more puzzled than ever. "The rest of us…does that mean one of us does know what happened?"

Caldonia nodded. "Ben Roland, of course, and Oliver, and poor little Virgil."

It made sense that Oliver and Ben Roland knew what happened because they were the oldest, but Virgil was a year younger than her.

"Are you sure you've got that right? Mama didn't even know where Virgil was. He ran off and changed his name."

The old woman's wrinkled face softened into a smile. "Your mama knew exactly where Virgil was. Long as she was alive, she knew where every one of you kids was. You might think your mama sent you away because she didn't love you, but it was the opposite. She loved you so much, she wasn't willing to lay her troubles at your feet."

"What troubles?"

"That's something you're gonna have to ask Ben Roland or Oliver."

"I would if I could. Tom has yet to locate Oliver, and Ben Roland's been dead for thirty years, killed in a mine explosion in Alabama."

Caldonia sat there shaking her head for a moment. "What about Virgil, was he working the same mine?"

"Did Eliza send Virgil to Alabama to be with Ben Roland?" Tom asked.

"She sure did," Caldonia said. "Most folks figured the boy ran off, but Eliza's the one who changed Virgil's name and gave him train fare."

"He was just a kid; why the name change?"

A wistful smile settled on Caldonia's face. "Virgil hated being a Hobbs. He knew his daddy never wanted him and said he'd be happier if he wasn't saddled with the name to remind him of it. Eliza was worried the name would be like a stone around his neck, so she told him he could change it if he'd a mind to. In fact, Jeb was the one who picked up his new birth certificate, but down at the city clerk's office he gave your daddy's name instead of his own."

She paused a moment, then shook her head and chuckled. "Virgil was a skinny little kid but independent as they come. He'd decided to go through life on his own terms, and Eliza figured that was a good thing."

"Why Palmer?" Tom asked.

"It was Eliza's name before she married Martin, so she told Virgil to take it, 'cause then he'd remember he had a mama who loved him with all her heart."

Margaret pulled a handkerchief from her bag and dabbed her eyes. "How could I have been so blind? How could I not have known these things about my own family?"

Caldonia reached across and placed a bony hand on Margaret's arm. "Honey, you wasn't blind; you was just a little girl growing up. Your mama didn't want you knowing these awful things. That's why she sent you to live with your Aunt Rose."

"Living with Aunt Rose was nothing like living with Mama."

"Your mama knew that. Being separated from you pained her worse than it did you. There were times when the hurt of you being gone felt like a knife in her heart. She'd cry for a long while, then wipe her eyes and remind herself that you had food in your belly, clothes on your back, and the hope of a better life."

With sorrow tugging at her face, Caldonia shook her head and looked off as if she was remembering something too private to share. A few seconds later, she heaved a mournful sigh, one that had the sound of something drawn up from the depth of her soul. They sat in silence for several minutes before Caldonia turned to Margaret.

"If you ever start to wonder why your mama did what she did, look in the mirror and see the woman you've become, Margaret Rose. You're smart, pretty, dressed nice, got yourself a home, and had a good marriage. None of them things would a' happened if your mama had kept you here with her. She knew what this life is like, so she sent you away. You might know a lot of loves in your life, but you ain't ever gonna know a love as big as your mama's."

The minutes turned into hours as they sat and talked. Margaret told of her life with Albert, how she'd struggled with the thought of never having children, and how she'd been like a lost soul in the days after his death.

"I was in his office feeling sorry for myself one night when I noticed the paperweight he kept on his desk; it read, 'If you never try, you will never succeed.' He lived by that rule. No matter what, he never stopped trying. Not during the Depression; not when the business had its ups and downs; never. Over the years I'd thought about my sister and brothers a million times, but we'd lost touch with one another and I figured that was that. It was the same as if I had no family, except that I did.

"I sat there thinking about Albert's rule for a long while, and I realized why I didn't know where my family was." Her tone brightened as she glanced at Tom and smiled. "It was because I hadn't tried, really tried, to find them. Finally, I got up enough courage to ask Tom if he'd help me try and find everyone, and he found you. I never dreamed—"

"That I'd still be alive," Caldonia said and gave a cackle that filled the room.

Morning became afternoon, and the sound of thunder could be heard in the distance. Caldonia warned that a storm was coming and said she could always tell by the ache in her bones. When the thunder drew closer and heavy raindrops began to pepper the roof, Margaret scooted her chair closer so as not to miss a word as she listened to Caldonia relay what Eliza had said about Oliver.

"He never came back. Not while your mama was alive and not after. That was how she wanted it, and he did as she told him."

"But why would Mama tell Oliver not to come home?"

"I done said, that ain't my story to tell. You got to ask your brother."

Caldonia said she'd not heard from John Paul either, nor did she know where he might be.

"He'd come and go while your mama was alive; show up one morning, stay a few days, then be gone for weeks. When he was here, he was happy enough to do what had to be done—check there was meat hanging in the smoke house, chop wood, fill the coal bin or whatnot—but after a few days, he'd disappear and you'd wonder if he'd ever be back again. Eliza always said he felt most at home when he roaming through the woods."

"Did he keep coming after Mama was gone?"

"While Louella was still alive he did, but she never once saw him. She'd wake up in the morning and find a bunch of wood stacked by the door or the coal bucket filled and know he'd been there. After she died the house sat empty, and far as I know he never came back."

It rained all afternoon. As they huddled close with the crack of thunder sounding overhead, Caldonia told tales from a time when Margaret was too young to remember.

"You were two the summer Jeb built the barrel door. Your mama had gone to Charleston and came home with a fistful of your daddy's money. She was worried he'd find out, come back in a rage, and do something to hurt one of her babies. Jeb built that secret door and didn't put a lock on it so if there was trouble you kids could come hide over here."

"Was there ever any trouble?"

Caldonia pulled a deep breath and leaned back into her pillows. "Just that one time, but you young'uns mostly used that door to come bothering me for cookies." She looked down at the gnarled hands in her lap and shook her head. "Lordy, how I miss those days. Having Eliza to talk with, you kids running in and out all the time…"

When the sky began to turn dusky, the rain finally let up and Tom said they had to be going. Margaret stood, then bent and kissed Caldonia's cheek.

"I'll be back, Aunt Caldonia, I promise. I'll write to tell you how our search is going, and I'll send pictures. Before you know it, I'll be here for another visit. If we're lucky, I might be bringing more of the family."

Caldonia said she needed to stand up and motioned for Tom to come give her a hand. When he bent to lift her, she leaned in and whispered something in his ear. He grinned, gave a nod, and said, "Yes, ma'am, I'll be sure to do that."

When they pulled out onto the dirt road, Margaret asked if they had time enough to stop by her family's house.

"I know you said it was pretty badly damaged by a fire, but I'd like to see it one more time."

"Once it gets dark, driving down a mountain road I'm not familiar with could prove a bit tricky. How about staying over another night, and we'll come back tomorrow?"

"That's a great idea," Margaret said. "We can pick up a box of cookies at that nice bakery, then stop by Aunt Caldonia's and bring them to her."

She moved into saying that since they hadn't had time for a drive around Charleston the night before, it might be something they'd want to do tonight. With one thought following another, they'd turned onto Campbell's Creek Drive before she remembered to ask what Caldonia had whispered to Tom.

He laughed and didn't answer right away.

"Come on. What was it?"

"She said next time you come back, I should come with you."

Margaret was at a loss as to what to say after that.

Moving Forward

That evening the weather turned cooler, and the threat of rain lingered in the air. Margaret freshened her lipstick, pulled on a raincoat, and met Tom in the lobby of the hotel.

"Would you rather take a drive around the city or explore on foot?" he asked.

"We've been sitting all day," Margaret said. "Let's walk."

They left the hotel, crossed over to Capitol Street, and turned toward the river. Starting out, they talked mostly of what the day had brought: the name Nellie might now be using, a place to search for Virgil, and, best of all, news of Dewey.

"He's a doctor." Margaret eyes sparkled when she spoke of him. "It's what he always dreamt of doing. When we were in Barrettsville, he said he was going to save up for college. He had a box in his dresser drawer and every time he got a dime for mowing somebody's grass or doing an odd job, the money went straight into that box. After a whole summer of saving, I don't think he had more than two dollars when we moved back to Coal Creek."

One story led to another. Spending the day with Caldonia had opened a treasure chest of memories, some good, some not so. Before now, it had been too painful to look back, painful because she could see only the past without anything to look forward to.

Now it was different. Tom had opened up the roads leading to her sister and brothers. Today he'd taken her to see the woman who'd been like a mother. Tomorrow he'd find Nellie and after that Dewey.

"When you leave Charleston, are you going to Huntington?" she asked.

Tom nodded. "It's not that long a drive; fifty or sixty miles maybe."

"Would it be an imposition if I came along?"

"Not at all," he said and smiled. "I was planning to ask if you wanted to come, but you beat me to the punch."

They walked until they came to the river. Margaret stood looking up at the old streetlights. She remembered so few things about her daddy. There were no father-daughter moments, no memory of him hoisting her onto his shoulders, kissing her good night, or walking hand in hand. There was only the memory of him boasting that he'd installed those streetlights.

One of the lamps flickered on and off. Another was dim as a candle. Margaret thought them rather like her father: unreliable.

Beyond the street was the Kanawha River, silent and dark. It was the dividing line between Charleston and South Charleston. Margaret knew South Charleston all too well. It was where she'd lived with Aunt Rose. Those years she could remember easily enough but had no desire to do so.

She turned to Tom. "Let's start back. I'm getting hungry."

Earlier on they'd strolled along at a leisurely pace, chatting as they walked, stopping to peek into the shop windows, admiring the potted plants and brick walkway. Now they quickened their step and moved with purpose. A dense mist was already in the air, and rain seemed imminent. Halfway down Capitol Street, the sky broke open and they ducked into a doorway. They'd planned to go to the steakhouse on Carter Street, but with the weather as it was they'd be soaked by the time they got there.

Tom looked around, spied a small restaurant called Mario's, and pointed to it. "If you're okay with Italian, let's stop there."

She gave an eager nod. "Italian's great."

Sandwiched in between the bank and a flower shop, the restaurant seemed nothing special on the outside but inside it was charming. Mahogany-paneled walls surrounded tables with white tablecloths and candles, and the savory aroma of freshly baked bread, crushed olives, and herbs floated toward them.

Margaret drew in a deep breath as she looked around. "Oh my, this is lovely." She slid out of her raincoat and handed it to Tom. A maître d' took the coat, escorted them to a table in the corner, and pulled back a chair for Margaret.

"Buon appetito," he said and left. Before Margaret had time to gather her thoughts, a waiter was there with a basket of warm bread, a saucer of herbed olive oil, and the wine list.

Throughout dinner the conversation flowed as freely as the wine. She and Tom laughed and talked as if they been friends forever. After the waiter cleared their table, he brought small aperitif glasses and offered them a choice of amaretto or limoncello. They both chose the icy cold limoncello and settled back to talk of the trip to Huntington and make plans.

"I thought we could have an early breakfast and check out of the hotel," Tom said. "We can drive out to Coal Creek, visit your old house, stop to say goodbye to Caldonia, and leave for Huntington from there."

Margaret eyed the near-empty aperitif glass and looked at him with a raised eyebrow. "Just how early is early?"

"Six, six-fifteen."

Her eyes went wide. "In the morning?"

"Only kidding." He let go of the grin he'd been holding back. "I figured maybe nine or ten. There's no real rush. It's the weekend; we won't be able to get into the library or city clerk's office until Monday."

By the time they left the restaurant, the rain had ended and the night had taken on a chill. They hurried along, and as they crossed at the intersection of Capitol and Washington Streets Tom took her arm. Later that night when Margaret was in bed waiting for sleep to come, she thought back on it and remembered how he'd not let go even after they were on the sidewalk. She felt her ears and neck growing warm. It was nothing, but it felt like something.

Annoyed at herself, she turned on her side and went back to picturing Dewey's dimpled chin.

The sky was still dark when Margaret woke. She glanced at the clock and groaned. Too early. Turning on her other side, she closed her eyes and tried to force herself back to sleep. The harder she tried, the more awake she became.

A million thoughts raced through her head, and she hopscotched from one to another. The decision to fly to the place she'd sworn never to return to turned into a happy meeting with Caldonia but brought more questions about why her mama had moved the family back from Barrettsville. The possibility of being reunited with a sister and brothers she hadn't seen in decades was balanced with Caldonia's insistence that Eliza had told Oliver not to come home. Dining out with a man she'd known for a scant three months made her remember Albert and the life she'd built with him in Georgia. Her life was now running at a lightning-fast speed. A strange fluttering rose in her chest, and she found it impossible to determine whether it was nerves or anticipation.

Coming here was the most impetuous thing she'd done in...50 years? Longer maybe. Perhaps ever. Last night she'd telephoned the airline, canceled her return flight reservation, and not bothered to make another one. A two-day trip was one thing, but now she was heading off on a jaunt that could last heaven knew how long.

It was out of character for her; totally out of character. She and Albert had always been such practical people. Every move was planned and budgeted. Once, when she'd complained that there was no spontaneity in their life, he'd said that spontaneity was nothing more than recklessness wearing a different hat.

Was that what she'd believed, or had she simply been swept up in his plans?

When narrow ribbons of light began to thread the horizon, Margaret gave up trying to sleep and sat up in bed. It was barely 7 am; too early to meet Tom. She'd done most of her packing last night, and now here she was with three hours to kill and nothing to do.

She snapped on the television and called room service, saying she'd like coffee and a toasted muffin. Another first. Albert had been staunchly against using room service. Ridiculously expensive, he'd called it, three times the price of eating in the coffee shop. On the few occasions when she'd accompanied him on a business trip, she'd had to dress and go down to the restaurant to get her morning coffee.

The thought of Albert aghast at what he'd most certainly term "frivolous spending" came to mind, and the tiniest smile curled her lips.

As she waited for her breakfast, she continued to think of Albert. It reminded her of how different her life in Georgia was compared to Coal Creek, and she decided to call Josie. Knowing her friend was an early riser, Margaret wanted to catch her before she got started on her day. She turned down the sound on the television, picked up the telephone again, and placed a long-distance call. Within minutes, she and Josie were chattering as if they sat side by side.

"I'm so happy you're making progress," Josie said. "Any idea how long the next part of the trip will take?"

Margaret shook her head even though Josie couldn't see her. "None, but I'm hoping to find everyone—or at least news of everyone—by the time we come home."

There was a lengthy silence, and Margaret wondered if Josie thought it was improper of her to travel with another man so soon after Albert's passing.

"Tom's such a gentleman," she said, not sure how to bring up the topic.

"I've no doubt about that," Josie said with a chuckle. "I only asked because Mr. Schoenfeld called the house while I was there checking on things."

The corners of Margaret's mouth turned down. "Oh? And what did he say?"

"He didn't say anything particular to me, but I know what he wanted."

Albert's shares in the firm, Margaret thought. She huffed in annoyance. "If he calls again, you tell him I'll give him an answer when I'm good and ready."

"And you want me to say it exactly like that?"

The thought of sweet Josie telling off anyone made Margaret laugh. "No, I suppose not. Just let him know I understand his concerns and will get back to him when I can."

They talked for a few more minutes; then a knock sounded at the door of Margaret's room and she said a quick goodbye.

The coffee arrived steaming hot in a small silver pot; the muffin covered with a cloth napkin was still warm. On the tray there was a small pitcher of thick, rich cream and tiny bowls of butter and jam. Plumping the pillows and placing them behind her, Margaret lifted the tray onto her lap and sat watching the news as she enjoyed her first-ever breakfast in bed.

She was waiting in the lobby when Tom stepped off of the elevator.

"Well, now, isn't this a nice surprise," he said and smiled. "After last night, I thought I'd be the one waiting for you."

She returned the smile. "Actually, I was up early. I had coffee and a muffin in my room."

"That's nice." Tom slung his duffle bag over his shoulder and grabbed the oversize suitcase sitting beside her. "Let's check out and look for a place to eat, okay?"

"Sounds perfect," she said as she felt the excitement swell in her chest. This time she recognized it for what it was: her newfound independence.

After a drive around town, they settled at the Pancake Palace and both ordered the Sunday Special. The stack of pancakes came with sliced strawberries, sausage patties, three different syrups, and a biscuit.

Margaret looked at the heavily-laden plate and thought, *I'll never be able to eat all that,* but she did. When they were finished, they lingered over a second cup of coffee.

It was after 1 pm when they turned into the gravel drive and started up the hollow. Passing by Caldonia's house, they continued on and pulled into the pathway that ran alongside the place she'd long ago called home. The wild elderberry bushes and mountain laurel were so overgrown that from the road the house was almost hidden. When it came into view, she gave a gasp. Tom had warned her it had been destroyed by fire, but she still wasn't prepared for the sight of it.

Easing the car door open, she stepped out, stood looking at the place for a minute, and started toward it. Tom was right behind her.

"Are you sure you want to do this? I've gone through the house, and there's nothing here. Absolutely nothing."

Margaret slowed her step but didn't turn. "That's what Mama tried to tell me all those years ago. There's nothing here now, and maybe there never was." She stepped inside and closed her eyes so she could envision things as they once were.

"I'm home, Mama," she said in a soulful whisper. "I've come to tell you I understand why you sent me away. I know how much you loved me, how much you loved all of us. Caldonia knew it all along, but I didn't. None of us did. I'm going to fix that, Mama. I'll find them, all of them, and we'll be a family, the kind of family you wanted."

When she opened her eyes, Tom was standing beside her.

"I was worried you might fall through the floor. I didn't mean to intrude."

She pushed the sorrow she was feeling aside and smiled. "You're not an intrusion. You're the reason I'm here."

They walked through what was left of the house together as she shared her memories of how the boys had slept in the back bedroom and the girls shared a bed with their mama.

"When Daddy came home, we'd all pile into one room. We'd argue about who got the bed and who slept on the floor pallets until Oliver came up with a system for us to take turns. When the weather was nice the older boys sometimes slept in the smokehouse and that gave us more space. Daddy wasn't home all that often before Barrettsville, and afterward he never came home again. I believe by then Mama had stopped expecting he might, because she rarely mentioned his name."

"This is such a small house. Did you ever imagine you'd be living in a place as large as where you are now?"

Margaret laughed. "Not in my wildest dreams."

As they were returning to the car, she stopped and looked back. The house was barely standing now. When it crumbled and fell to the ground in a year or two, that would be the end of it. In 1912, she'd left here carrying the bad memories and regret that had burdened her heart all these years. Now she was leaving them behind. The good memories would remain in her heart forever, and the bad ones would be buried beneath the house.

They made one last stop before they left Coal Creek. They brought Caldonia the box of cookies they'd bought and stayed for a little over an hour. When Rowena said her mother-in-law had been up too long and needed to take a rest, Margaret could see the truth in her words. There were dark circles beneath Caldonia's eyes, and she seemed frailer than she had been the day before.

"We've got to be going anyway," she said and kissed Caldonia's cheek. "As soon as I find everybody, we're going to have a family reunion. If you're feeling up to it you can come, and if not I'll write and tell you all about it. I'll send pictures—"

Caldonia cut in to say she'd be looking forward to it; she motioned Tom to lean down.

"You make sure Margaret Rose has that party, you hear?" she whispered. "I'm expecting the Lord to call me home pretty soon, but I'm gonna be looking down and keeping an eye out."

Tom smiled and said he'd most certainly do that.

A short while later, they pulled onto the highway and headed west toward Charleston. When Charleston disappeared in the rear-view mirror, Tom said they still had about two hours of driving and asked if Margaret wanted to stop for a snack.

"No thanks," she said. "I'm still full from breakfast."

As they picked up speed and drew closer to Huntington, she couldn't help but wonder if Caldonia would still be there when they returned. It seemed that with each bit of happiness life doled out, there was an equal amount of sorrow.

1902

The Hidden Path

When Eliza left Martin's apartment with the money, her heart was in her throat. Luckily she'd caught a trolley right away, but at the train station there was a two-hour wait for the 6:37 to Coal Creek. The waiting room was empty except for a small group of businessmen smoking cigars and talking boisterously. Eliza crossed the room and sat behind them. From there she could watch the door but hopefully avoid being seen. As the minutes slid by she grew increasingly nervous, and a frightening picture of Martin coming after his money rose in her mind.

The men departed shortly after six, so Eliza left the waiting room and stood on the platform despite the chill that had settled in the air. The 6:37 chugged into the station on time, and she hurried aboard. The sky was dark when the train left Charleston and darker still when it arrived in Coal Creek.

She'd hoped to find someone with a buggy or wagon at the station, someone willing to give her a ride up the hollow, but there was no one. Even the stationmaster's booth was dark. With no alternative, she set out on foot. It was a long walk made harder by darkness. In the pitch black of night, the mountain seemed bigger, the sounds louder, with danger hiding around every bend.

At the mouth of the hollow where the oaks were only starting to bud, the quarter moon provided a bit of light. Higher up the mountain, the towering Virginia pines made the road so dark a person could no longer see their hand before their face. Eliza's movements were slow and cautionary. With the small bag clutched to her chest and the cold night air pressing against her skin, she moved one foot in front of the other and with each step prayed that her boot would find solid ground. When the screech of an owl cut through the air, she startled, lost her footing, and fell. Quickly scrambling to her feet she continued, her breath coming in shallow little puffs and her heart thudding against her ribs. She was nearing Caldonia's house when she heard something moving through the brush.

"Please, God," she prayed, "not a mountain lion."

Legs trembling and threatening to collapse beneath her, she quickened her step. Moments later, there was the shriek of a small animal. A bobcat with what looked like a rabbit in its mouth darted past her and disappeared into the woods.

By the time Eliza reached the Markey place, she was chilled to the bone and soaked through with nervous perspiration. Pounding her fist against the door, she hollered for Caldonia or Jeb. Moments later a lamp was lit, and she saw a figure moving toward her.

When the door opened, Caldonia was standing there. "What on earth happened?"

The tears Eliza had been holding back suddenly broke free, and she fell into her friend's arms.

"I'm afraid," she said through her sobs, "afraid I've done something terrible."

"Now, now." Caldonia pulled Eliza close, patting her back. "Things always seem terrible in the dark of night. Come morning, it'll look different." With an arm wrapped around Eliza, she walked her back to the kitchen and settled her in a chair. She stoked the fire and set a kettle on to boil. Once the water was bubbling, she brewed a mug of motherwort tea and set it in front of Eliza.

"Drink this to calm your nerves. Then we can talk about what's troubling you."

As Eliza sipped the tea, she told of everything that had taken place. For the first time since she'd hurried away from the apartment, she opened the bag and counted the money. Ninety-six dollars.

Caldonia looked at the stack of bills and shook her head. "That's a powerful lot of money. How you figuring Martin came by it?"

Eliza shrugged. "No idea. That woman, Bess, said it was his poker money. You think maybe he won it?"

"It's possible, I suppose. 'Cept if a man come by that money honestly, he wouldn't have no need of hiding it 'neath the floor."

Eliza thought about it for a moment and nodded. "No matter where that money came from, Martin is going to be furious when he finds it gone. Bess said she was leaving, and with her gone he might figure out I took it and come looking for me."

"Not if he don't know you been there."

"There's no way he could know. Nobody saw me, and Bess won't say anything."

"True," Caldonia replied, but her eyebrows were pinched and her face twisted into a worried-looking frown.

The next day, without any discussion, Jeb started clearing a backwoods path from the Hobbs house to theirs. The path started behind a clump of elderberry bushes that grew wild in the Hobbs's backyard and was all but invisible. A stranger wouldn't have known it was there unless they knew to look for it. As soon as the path was finished, he began work on a child-sized back door that from the outside looked like an old barrel.

Before spring turned into summer, the Hobbs children knew exactly what to do if trouble erupted. The youngest, Margaret and Virgil, were too young to see to themselves, but the older ones were taught to care for them. Margaret Rose was already walking, yet Dewey was told to snatch her up and carry her to the pathway. Ben Roland was responsible for Virgil, and Oliver was to count heads and make sure everybody was there.

"But, Mama," Oliver said, "what about you?"

"Don't worry, I can take care of myself." She said Martin loved her and would never do anything to cause her harm, but even as the words came from her mouth she questioned the truth of them.

That spring Jeb and Caldonia began watching over Eliza and the children as if they were their own. On Sundays they all rode to church in Jeb's wagon, and if a storm came through Jeb would come tapping on the window to ask if they were okay. Once it was warm enough to begin planting, he brought his horse and plow and turned a strip of ground large enough for a decent-size cornfield. Oliver, nearing nine that summer, was stretched out like a string bean, so both he and Ben Roland worked alongside Eliza as she sowed the corn, planted tomatoes, pole beans, and turnips.

The weather that summer was the best anyone in Coal Creek could remember. It was neither too hot nor too wet. The sun shone full in the afternoon, warming the ground but not drying it. The right amount of rain fell, and everything grew. The sprouts in the cornfield showed sooner than expected and before the month was out stood as tall as Oliver. That year it seemed as if Mother Nature was trying to make up for the hardships she'd caused the year before. With such a bounty, Eliza began canning in early August.

The money she brought from Charleston remained hidden in the pouch behind the bed. From time to time she took out a dollar or two to buy seed or supplies, but every penny was spent judiciously.

Although she never spoke about the fear that had settled in her bones, it was always there. At night when the wind whistled through the tree tops and the cry of a bird could be heard for miles, she'd lie in bed listening for the sound of Martin's boots coming from the road. When the fear felt as though it would suffocate her, she began keeping the shotgun alongside her bed and an extra box of shells hidden in the drawer.

⁓◦✿◦⁓

On the Monday after Eliza's visit to Charleston, Bess disappeared. She was sleeping when Martin left for work that morning, but when he returned later in the evening she was gone. On the kitchen counter there was a note saying her cousin in Philadelphia had taken ill and she needed to be by the poor woman's side.

Martin was annoyed by her sudden disappearance but far from frantic. Women like Bess were easy enough to come by. Sure, he'd enjoyed her company, but he'd never really thought of it as more than a bit of fun so there was no love lost.

That same evening he shaved, pulled on a fresh shirt, and went to the Wolf's Head Tavern where he met Martha Mae Keller. When he offered to buy her a beer, she said she preferred champagne. Martin laughed, told her she was his kind of woman, and ordered a bottle.

Moving from the bar to a small table, they spent the evening together and more than once he felt the toe of her shoe slide along the inside of his leg. He thought for sure he was in for a good time, but at the end of the night when he invited her back to his place she smiled and said maybe another night.

He leaned closer, breathed heavily into her ear, and whispered, "I'm gonna make sure there is one."

When Martin returned to the apartment that night, he could still smell her perfume and feel the touch of her hand on his thigh. No doubt about it, Martha Mae Keller was his kind of woman.

For the next three nights, they met at the Wolf's Head and spent the evening together. While Martha Mae certainly seemed enamored by him, she held off going back to his apartment and it was driving Martin insane. By Thursday he was determined to have her, no matter the cost. He explained that he had a poker game on Friday night and asked if on Saturday evening she'd like to dine at the Red Door Inn, then return to his apartment to spend the night.

Martha Mae smiled, knowing the Red Door was a place frequented by Charleston's elite. She answered yes and ran her tongue along the edge of his lower lip.

On Friday Martin was feeling pretty damn good about himself as he started getting ready for the poker game and went to the closet for some extra cash. He kneeled, pulled up the floor board, and stared down at the empty hole. For a moment, he sat there feeling flabbergasted. Then it hit him.

Bess!

"Son of a bitch!" he screamed.

For the next hour, he stomped from the living room to the bedroom and then back cussing a blue streak and yelling about how he'd find Bess and take it out of her hide. But as the minutes ticked by and the time for the poker game grew closer, he realized he had just one option: to show up, play with the $14 he had in his pocket, and hope to God he won.

Martin had a cockiness that was hard to deny, and when he showed up at the game he was the same as always.

"You boys ready for an ass-whipping?" he said and laughed.

Tony came back at him saying they'd see who was going to do the ass-whipping. "I'm feeling lucky tonight."

Martin was a shrewd player; he knew when to raise the stakes and when to fold. For a while, the game went back and forth. He folded on a few hands and took a nice pot on some others. When Pete announced the last hand Martin was up by only six bucks, which wasn't enough for what he was planning with Martha Mae.

On the first round of betting, Ed was the only one to fold.

"I've got nothing," he said and tossed his cards on the table.

Then they started the draw. Pete took two cards, and everybody else took three. Martin, who was last in line, wanted just one.

When a player drew just one card, it was generally because they were holding a money hand. Figuring Martin had the game in the bag, five guys folded. Then it was just Pete, Martin, and Big Mike.

Big Mike tossed a five-dollar bill on the table and raised the ante. Pete eyed his cards, shook his head, and folded. With a bit of a smirk, Martin matched Big Mike's bet and raised him ten.

Big Mike glared across the table. "Ten? Ain't we got a five-buck limit?"

"Not on the last hand," Pete said.

Big Mike took off his glasses, rubbed his eyes, and replaced the glasses. He studied his cards for a few moments and laid them on the table. "I'm out. That's too rich for my blood."

Martin tossed his cards on the table and reached for the pot.

Still miffed at the outcome, Big Mike reached across the table and picked up Martin's cards.

"What'd you have?" He looked at the cards, and his face blossomed into the color of a summer strawberry. "Two pair, that's it? You raised me ten with twos and sixes?"

"Not my fault you chickened out."

"I was holding three Jacks. That beats the crap out of your lousy two pairs!"

"Yeah, if you matched my bet and called. But you didn't."

Mike looked across to Pete. "Can you believe this?"

Pete shrugged. "He bluffed, and you fell for it. Nothing wrong with that."

Still wearing that smug smile, Martin said he hoped there were no hard feelings. To show his heart was in the right place, he bought a round of drinks for the table.

That night he won 26 bucks plus the 14 he'd come with. He was back in the money and ready for Saturday night.

After their dinner at the Red Door Inn, Martha Mae and Martin became a regular item. She'd see him three or four times a week; they'd meet for dinner in restaurants with soft lighting and starched tablecloths, then go back to his apartment. She pleased him in ways no one else ever had and always left him wanting more. A dozen or more times he suggested she move in with him, but each time she shook her head and said she wasn't ready. On nights when she stayed over, she'd be fast asleep in the morning when he left for work and gone when he got home.

After a while, Martin no longer thought about Eliza and the kids. He pushed the guilt he felt from his mind and went about the business of living. On the rare occasion when he'd remember Eliza, he'd tell himself the whole thing was her fault. He'd never wanted all those kids; that was her doing. If she'd listened to what he wanted and done as he'd asked... Martin could come up with a dozen different ways to rationalize his behavior, but in time he found he no longer needed to.

That summer he lived as he'd never lived before. When he wasn't with Martha Mae, he was either playing poker or going from one tavern to the next asking about Bess and claiming she'd stolen his money and run off. At the Rusty Nail, the bartender said it didn't sound like the Bess he knew.

The same thing happened in a half-dozen other places, but that didn't dissuade Martin. He continued to search all summer and well into September. When he wasn't with Martha Mae, the apartment was little more than a stopping off place. He left early in the morning and seldom returned before midnight.

On the Tuesday afternoon he encountered Gertrude Sloan, he'd sprained his leg and was limping home to get a decent night's rest. She was in front of the building, sitting on the steps, spread out so there was no way to avoid her.

She scowled at him. "Well, look what the cat drug in."

Trying to move past her was impossible. She was smack in the middle of the stoop with grocery sacks on both sides.

"Excuse me," Martin said, making it obvious he wanted to pass.

Gertrude was an obstinate old woman set in her ways. If she liked you, all was well and good. If she didn't, she let it be known. Moving slower than a snail and complaining as she went, she started to gather her groceries and accidently knocked over the bag of apples. She gave Martin a squint-eyed look as the apples rolled down the steps.

"I see you got another of those hussies coming and going. When I saw your sweet missus here, I thought for sure you was gonna straighten yourself out, but no, that ain't—"

Martin stepped back. "Eliza? You saw Eliza here?"

She gave a nod. "Your missus is a good woman, too good for the likes of—"

Martin grabbed Gertrude by the shoulders. "When? When did you see Eliza here?"

She wrested herself free. "Let go of me! I got nothing to say to you."

"Please, Mrs. Sloan. You want me to get back together with Eliza, don't you? Before I can do that, I gotta know when she was here."

Gertrude eyed him suspiciously for a moment. "A few months back, before the red-haired one moved out."

Martin stood there looking dumfounded for a moment. "Eliza was here, in this building, a few months ago?"

"Ain't that what I said?"

"Yes, but it's strange I didn't see her."

"You wasn't here." With her face pinched into a frown, Gertrude looked down her nose at him. "Could be she saw that redhead hussy and decided she'd had enough of your cavorting."

"Well, I'll be damned!" Martin kicked one of Gertrude's apples clear across the street, stepped over the rest of her stuff, and hurried upstairs.

He poured himself a stiff drink and dropped down on the sofa. She'd played him for a fool, a damn fool. He'd wasted months looking for Bess when, without a doubt, it was Eliza who took the money.

Martin's Return

For the remainder of that week, Martin could think of nothing else. He'd picture Eliza laughing at how she'd outfoxed him and lose focus on whatever else he was doing. On Wednesday, Jim Murray asked for a screwdriver and Martin handed him a hammer. Then after they'd spent the day wiring the third floor of the Slocum building, it had to be redone because somewhere along the line Martin had put in the wrong connector.

Even his relationship with Martha Mae was thrown off. On Thursday when they went to dinner at the Regency Room, he talked of nothing but how Eliza had stolen his money. He didn't notice when Martha Mae yawned twice during dinner.

Finally she said, "Instead of just talking about it, why don't you do something?"

"Do what? Tell the police?"

She nodded and said she was in the mood for dessert. "Pudding maybe or one of those little petit four things."

Martin claimed no policeman would arrest Eliza. Thinking back on the pennyroyal incident, he said, "She's too clever. She makes you think sugar wouldn't melt in her mouth, but the truth is she's hell bent on having her way."

Again, Martha Mae yawned. "Then find another way to make her give the money back."

That night Martha Mae did not return to the apartment with Martin. She said she was weary of listening to him complain about Eliza.

"Are you a man or mouse?" she asked. "If somebody steals something of yours, it's up to you to get it back."

Having Martha Mae talk to him in such a way made Martin angrier. Up until now he'd felt a tad guilty about not sending Eliza money, but no more. If she wanted trouble, then she would get it. He knew where she was, and he knew where she kept the money.

As the moon climbed higher in the sky and began to fade, he stood at the window thinking of what he was going to do. In between the bursts of anger, he found moments when he could remember how they'd once loved one another. When those thoughts came he forced them away, reminding himself that she'd come like a thief in the night and taken money that rightfully belonged to him. She could have asked for what she needed, but she didn't. Instead she'd waltzed in and taken it all. Martha Mae was right. He needed to do something about it.

It was nearly 5 am when Martin reached the point where he could no longer keep his eyes open. He threw himself across the bed, fell into a deep sleep, and didn't wake until after 10.

He arrived on the jobsite a full three hours after they'd started, bleary-eyed and half-awake. Before an hour had gone by, he made three different blunders. When he dropped a terminal connector and had to climb down the ladder to retrieve it, Charlie Crane, the job foreman, hollered, "Get your head out of your ass, Hobbs, and watch what you're doing!"

Fifteen minutes later, Martin crossed wires and blew out the line they were working on; that was when Charlie came over with blood in his eyes.

"What the hell is wrong with you?" he yelled, sticking his nose in Martin's face.

"Sorry," Martin mumbled. "I didn't sleep so good last night. I got a problem with—"

"Your problems are not my problems. You're done for the day. Go home, and don't come back until you're ready to stop screwing around and do some work."

This was the first time Martin had been called out in front of his crew, and it made him feel like a piece of crap. Worse than a piece of crap. To be sent home like a misbehaving child added insult to injury. He narrowed his eyes, glared at the foreman, then stomped off hollering he didn't know whether he'd bother coming back.

"Suit yourself," Charlie shouted.

Tired as he was, when Martin left the jobsite he didn't go home. Instead, he headed over to the train station and bought a round-trip ticket to Coal Creek.

He had to wait the better part of an hour, but once the 12:10 pulled in he climbed aboard and before the train had left the station was asleep. Nodded off as he was, he missed his stop and had to get off at Becker's Hollow. Still too weary to make the five-mile hike on foot, he paid a wagon driver a dollar to take him home.

⚬※⚬

Throughout the summer, Eliza had half-expected Martin to show up looking for his money. On a good day she could rationalize he had no reason to suspect her, but on a bad day she'd remember how he could fly into a rage over something of little significance. At those times, the fear in her chest would grow heavy as a stone.

In the early months she'd been diligent about bolting the door at night, keeping the children close at hand, and making certain the shotgun was always loaded. After the leaves began to turn and school reopened, she grew comfortable with the thought that her fears were unfounded. On a Friday afternoon, before Oliver, Ben Roland, and Dewey had returned from school, she heard a wagon rumble up the road but paid it no mind and continued changing Virgil's diaper.

Moments later she heard the sound of boots thundering across the front porch, and her heart stopped. The front door banged open, and Martin came in hollering her name. There was no time to gather the children and get away; this was it. She shoved Virgil in the cradle, pulled the covers over him, and turned toward the kitchen.

Martin stood in the kitchen, the empty money jar in his hand, his face scarlet and his features so distorted she barely recognized him.

"Where's my money?" he screamed.

"What money?" she said timidly.

"You know damn well what money!" He hurled the empty jar at her, and she ducked.

The jar crashed against the wall, sending shards of glass across the room.

"I have no idea what you're talking ab—"

"Don't give me that innocent shit!" He crossed the room in three long strides and grabbed her by the shoulders. "I want the ninety-six dollars you took from my apartment!"

Her heart hammered against her ribs as she struggled to stay calm. "I didn't take your money, Martin, I swear I didn't."

He leaned in, his nose touching hers, his breath acrid. "Don't lie to me! You were there. Mrs. Sloan saw you."

He knows.

Every nerve in her body suddenly felt raw and exposed. The thought of the three little ones playing in the back yard flashed through her mind. She had to trust that Bess hadn't given up their secret.

Summoning enough courage to respond, she said, "You're right, I was at the apartment. I came to tell you we needed you at home, to say—"

"Liar!" He screamed and shook her with such force that her head snapped back and hit the wall.

A sharp crack sounded, and Eliza felt the pain ricochet through her body. Tears flooded her eyes, and she gave a gut-wrenching groan.

"You saw I wasn't there, so you stole my money and left! That's the truth, ain't it?"

The boys will be home from school soon. If he kills me, what will he do to them?

Powered by a force greater than her own, she jerked her knee into his stomach and wrenched herself free. She'd caught him off guard, and before he snapped back the shotgun was in her hand. She aimed at his chest.

"Back up, Martin, or I'll put a bullet in you."

He gave a cynical laugh. "You ain't got courage enough to shoot a man, Eliza, you—"

She brought the shotgun to her shoulder and eyed him down its sights. "If you don't stop and hear me out, I will shoot you, Martin. So help me God, I will."

For several seconds, he stood as if he were trying to take measure of whether or not she'd actually pull the trigger. Finally he backed away. "Okay, Eliza, I'm listening. Say what you got to say."

Eliza had never been a good liar. Once she'd tried lying to her daddy, and he'd seen through it before she'd finished the tale. Now she had to make it believable and lie as if her life depended on it, because in truth it did.

"Yes, I went to the apartment," she said, "but not to steal anything. I wanted to tell you the kids and I missed you. I planned to say how sorry I was for the misunderstanding we'd had and beg your forgiveness. I was going to stay the weekend but come to find out you've got a woman living with you."

He stood there, arms folded across his chest and jaw clenched tighter than a bear trap. "What makes you think I'm gonna believe that bullshit?"

Eliza held her breath and tried the only ploy she could come up with. "If you don't believe me, Martin, search the house. See what you find."

"I just might do that," he said and started looking around the room.

Caldonia was the only one who knew about the pouch hanging behind the headboard of the bed. Eliza had told no one else, not even the boys. It wasn't visible from under the bed. The only way to find it was either move the bed or stick a finger between the posts, feel for the string, and fish it up. Eliza's hands were smaller than Martin's and her fingers thinner; she could reach through the narrow slot between the posts. She hoped he couldn't.

She felt as if her heart would explode as she watched him go from room to room, pulling open drawers, looking behind things, feeling across the top shelf of the closet. Following along behind him, she kept a tight grip on the shotgun but lowered the barrel so it was no longer pointed at his chest. He tossed things aside, slammed the dresser drawer, then squatted and looked beneath the bed.

"That money's here," he grumbled. "I know it's here."

"Think about it, Martin, if I had all that money, don't you think I would have bought myself a new dress or a lantern to replace the one with a broken shade?"

He stood and turned to look at her. "I can't say what you'd do, Eliza. Having you point that gun at me and threaten to shoot makes me wonder if I ever really knew you."

"I feel the same about you," she said somberly.

After he'd spent a good hour searching the place, he dropped down in the kitchen chair. Hunched over with his hands on his knees, he sat shaking his head. The violence was gone from him, replaced by a look of weariness.

"I just don't get it," he said. "If you didn't take that money, who did?"

"How would I know, Martin? I know almost nothing of your life in Charleston."

Eliza set the shotgun aside and sat across from him. They sat in silence for several minutes.

"You said you was gonna beg my forgiveness—for what?"

She took a deep breath, felt for the gun beside her chair, then spoke, her words gentle but not overly conciliatory.

"We'd not seen one another for almost five months, and I knew you left here thinking I'd used that tea you brought home but I didn't. I couldn't find it in my heart to kill our baby. I never meant to deceive you, but—"

He lifted his head, wide-eyed. "You had the baby?"

She nodded. "A boy. Virgil."

Without a word, he turned away and sat there shaking his head. Several seconds inched by before he said, "You went and had that baby knowing I was against it. Did you even once stop to think about how you're gonna feed all these kids you got?"

Eliza's eyes narrowed. "These aren't *my* kids, Martin. They're *our* kids. You're their daddy, and you're supposed to provide for them. You said ninety-six dollars was stolen out of the apartment. Well, think about this: if you'd sent us just one quarter of that money, we wouldn't have gone hungry that winter."

"You never wrote to tell me you needed money. If you had, I would've—"

"Really?" She stood, picked up the gun, walked to the far side of the room, and turned to him. "This is the first time you've been home in a year, and not once did you send money. Did I really have to tell you we needed something to live on?"

They went back and forth for a while. He kept claiming that if he'd known of the situation he'd have made more of an effort to help out; she stood firm on the thought he should have known. In time the baby woke, and Louella came in saying she was hungry.

Martin gave Louella a forced smile, but when Eliza picked up Virgil and carried him back to the kitchen Martin looked away and said he had to be leaving.

"The boys will be coming home from school shortly," Eliza said. "Do you want to stay and visit with them?"

Without letting his eyes meet hers, he shook his head. "This ain't a good day. I'll come back, maybe in a week or two."

As he started down the road leading out of the hollow, Eliza wondered if she would ever see him again. Once he'd disappeared around the bend, a strange new emptiness settled into her heart.

Later that night, when the children were sleeping and the only sounds to be heard were the forlorn cries of the mountain, Eliza sat on the front porch with a wool shawl pulled tight around her shoulders. As the wind rattled through the trees, she thought back on a time when she loved Martin and he loved her and of how they'd sworn to spend the rest of their life together. When they'd stood at the altar and made that promise, she never dreamed that one day she'd point a gun at his chest and threaten to shoot.

Would she have done it? Maybe; maybe not. There was a fine line between love and hate, and sometimes it was impossible to know which side of the line you were standing on.

A rustling sound came from the elderberry bushes, and a squirrel scampered off. She thought about the possibility that Martin might never return and questioned whether or not she could make it alone. Right now, they were fine. It had been a bountiful summer, and she still had most of the money Bess had given her. But after that money was gone, what then? With seven children, she had nowhere else to go. At least here they had a house to live in.

Remembering how she'd told Bess that half a daddy was better than none, she wondered if that might be the answer. Eliza didn't know if she and Martin would ever love one another again, but he would forever be the children's daddy. Maybe that was enough. Maybe they could go back to the way it was when he came home once or twice a month.

With the anger now behind them, they could try to start over. To show good faith, she'd ask for a very modest amount and make no demands on his time.

The longer she thought about it, the more convinced Eliza became that she could make it work. She remained there until the wee hours of the morning, thinking through the letter she would write. When she finally stood and went inside, dawn was threading the horizon.

Returning to Charleston

It was suppertime when Martin arrived back in Charleston. On the train, he'd thought about stopping by to see Martha Mae but decided against it. With Martha Mae he had to be at the top of his game, and right now he wasn't feeling that way.

Seeing Eliza again had been troubling, especially when she pointed the shotgun at him and threatened to pull the trigger. Knowing Eliza as he had in the past, he would have laughed at the thought but not today. There was a different look in her eyes. And she hadn't asked him to stay over; that was another bothersome thing. She'd said he could stay for a visit with the boys. Visit. A man should be free to do more than *visit* his own wife and kids.

Instead of going back to the apartment or the Wolf's Head Tavern where he'd risk running into Martha Mae, he stopped at O'Leary's Saloon, ordered a beer, and stood at the bar thinking. Maybe he would return to Coal Creek next week or the week after. He needed to show Eliza he was man enough to do the deciding about when to see her and the kids. With what he'd won playing poker, he could easily afford to toss a 10-dollar bill on the table and say, "Buy yourself a new dress." Better yet, he'd bring her a new lamp to replace the broken one. That'd make her eyes pop. With electric lights going in all over Charleston, oil lamps were dirt cheap now. For 50 cents or less, he could play the hero.

He chuckled at the thought, drained his glass, and ordered a refill. He didn't have to ask to stay there whenever he wanted to. All he had to do was show up and wait for her to do the asking.

⊙⟩∮⟨⊙

When Martin went to dinner with Martha Mae Saturday night, he told her he'd straightened things out with Eliza. While he hadn't gotten his money back, he was now able to figure out who'd taken it.

"So what's that mean to me?" she asked.

"Nothing," he said. "We're good, same as always."

The week went by with no further mention of Eliza or Coal Creek. On Friday, as they were walking home from the Regency, he said he was going back to Coal Creek for the weekend.

She stopped walking and turned to him. "Why?"

"I been thinking I ought to visit the kids. Last week I didn't get to see the boys."

Hanging onto his arm she looked up, her eyes woeful and her lip pushed out in an obvious pout. "You can do that anytime, but this Sunday the Burlew Opera House has a show with Jimmie Hodges, and Maureen said it was—"

"I done said what I'm gonna do. That show can wait until next week."

They walked the rest of the way in silence. When they got back to his apartment, Martha Mae said she was feeling headachy and any lovemaking was going to have to wait until he got back from visiting the kids. The following morning Martin stopped at Lowenstein's, bought a hobnail glass oil lamp, and headed for the train station. He'd already made up his mind to stay the night, regardless of what Eliza had to say.

⊙⟩∮⟨⊙

When Eliza heard Martin's footsteps on the porch, her body tensed. Him returning this soon could only mean trouble. Before she had time to set the baby down, get the shotgun, or pull a knife from the cupboard drawer, he was standing in front of her.

She sucked in a breath and tried to sound less terrified than she felt.

"I'm surprised to see you back so soon."

"Why? I said I'd be back to see the boys."

"Yes, but…"

Eliza was on the verge of saying how him promising to do a thing didn't mean he'd actually do it when she noticed the way the corner of his mouth was curled. He looked like a man pleased with himself. A man in a good mood. The muscles in her back relaxed ever so slightly, and she gave a tentative smile.

"If I'd known you were coming, I'd have made an apple pie."

"I ain't in no hurry. You still got time to make one." He ignored Virgil and asked where the kids were.

"The little ones are playing out back, but you might have to call for Oliver and Ben Roland." She stood and set Virgil on the floor. "We had a fair bit of wind last night and it tore loose a bunch of branches, so they're gathering kindling." She gave what she hoped would seem a loving smile. "They've missed seeing you, so once they hear your whistle they'll know you're home and come running."

"If they're looking to find out what I got in my pocket, they'd better." He set the bundle he was carrying on the counter and came toward Eliza.

He took hold of her shoulders, and a flicker of fear swept through her. It came and went in less than a heartbeat, but in that split second she flinched. She felt it, but there was no way of knowing whether he did.

He stood with his face hovering over hers, his hands locked onto her.

"You're glad to see me, ain't you, Eliza?"

The question took her aback, and she suddenly felt a need to convince herself as well as him.

"Of course, I am, Martin. How could you possibly think otherwise?" Her words were more pronounced than they needed to be and spoken loud enough to drown out the hammering of her heart. "We may have had our differences, but you're still my husband."

"That I am," he said and pressed his mouth to hers in a way she'd not known before.

The feeling was foreign to Eliza and not one she found pleasant. He carried the smell of another woman on his skin and the taste of tobacco on his lips. A sliver of time slid by, and as it did she decided she would do whatever was necessary to keep their family together. When he pushed his tongue inside her mouth and grabbed hold of her breast, she didn't slap him away as she had done before.

"Later," she whispered, easing back his hand.

For a moment he seemed stunned; then a laugh rolled up from his chest, and he stepped back.

"Okay, later."

That afternoon it seemed as if time had doubled back on itself, and barring the stiffness of Eliza's smile it was as it had been two summers ago. While the boys gathered kindling, Martin chopped the larger branches and stacked logs. Before the thunderstorm rolled through, there were three crates of dry kindling on the back porch and the woodpile was a foot higher than it had been. Shaking the rain from their jackets, they hurried inside and Martin gave all six of the older kids a peppermint stick including Margaret Rose who was not yet two and had to be watched so the candy didn't get stuck in her throat.

After handing out the peppermint sticks, he turned to Eliza. "I brought you a present too, and I believe it's something you've been wanting." He retrieved the package he'd carried in earlier and handed it to her.

Presents were a rarity in the Hobbs house, so it seemed like Christmas morning as the children crowded around to watch Eliza peel back the brown wrapping paper and reveal the milk white glass lamp decorated with tiny rosebuds.

Louella touched the lamp with her tiny finger. "I ain't never seen a lamp with flowers."

"That's cause you ain't never been to Charleston," Martin said. "There ain't nothing you can't find in Charleston if you set your mind to it."

"It truly is a beautiful lamp," Eliza said. She looked up Martin and smiled. "Thank you for thinking of it."

Moments like this, her resolve weakened. Over the years he'd filled her heart with shards of anger and slights too painful to forget, but in between those things she could still find a few good memories. Times when she once again saw the young man who'd won her heart. The man she'd married.

Later on when they gathered at the supper table, Martin spoke of all he'd done in the year he'd been away. As he told of joining the Masonic lodge and how he'd sworn a solemn vow of secrecy regarding the rites and ceremonies of the order, the boys sat and listened with wide-eyed wonder.

"You can't tell nobody?" Oliver asked. "Not even us?"

"Nobody," Martin repeated. "Once you enter the meeting hall, everything's secret."

Ben Roland gave a skeptical-looking grin. "Who's gonna know if you told us?"

"See, that's the thing about being a Mason; it's all on the honor system. You don't do it, because you done swore you won't do it." He went on to tell how he'd started out as an apprentice and already moved up to journeyman. "By year-end I'm gonna be a Master Mason. What do you think about that?"

Ben Roland's eyes lit up, and a smile stretched the full width of his face. "I wanna be in the secret club too, Daddy. Can I join?"

Martin reared back in his chair and gave a hearty laugh. "Before you join, you gotta do a lot of growing up. Then you gotta get a job and know somebody. The Masons ain't just a secret club, they're a brotherhood, and they don't let some nobody in. You gotta have a buddy who's willing to introduce you, and you gotta prove yourself before you can be a Mason."

"Prove myself how?"

"Lots of ways. You can be real good at your job, help people who are needy, work for a charity…" Martin went on to tell how he'd spent two whole days fixing the lights in Sisters of Mercy Hospital and not taken a dime for it.

Eliza listened as Ben Roland peppered Martin with a dozen or more questions about what kind of job he would need and how old he had to be before he could join. When he finally ran out of questions, she asked what had prompted Martin's decision to become a Mason. A sly grin tugged at the corner of his mouth.

"Connections," he said. "Me and the other brothers, we're like this." He held up his hand and twisted two fingers together. "Brother Martin, that's what they call me. You got them kinda connections, you're gonna get better jobs and make more money. Jimmy Wilkes already said he's gonna get me in as a district rep with the union."

After they finished eating, Eliza cleared the dishes away and carried Virgil off to bed. The other children remained at the table, caught up in the various tales of Martin's adventures. Before long Margaret Rose's eyelids got heavy, and she climbed into Dewey's lap. A short while later John Paul fell asleep in his chair, and Eliza said it was way past the hour when all children should be in bed.

By the time she climbed into bed alongside of Martin, a strange feeling had settled in her chest. Whether it was love, hate, or a mix of the two she couldn't say. When he moved closer and slid his hand inside her nightgown, she pushed him off.

"Don't..." she whispered and turned away.

Grabbing her shoulder, he turned her back to face him.

"What now, Eliza?" he said with an air of impatience. "I thought we was done playing this game."

"It's no game, Martin. You've made it perfectly clear you don't want any more children, and I don't want to risk it."

Sounding a bit bewildered, he said, "That's it?"

"That's it," she replied, even though she couldn't say if that truly was the reason or there was something more. "If I were to get in a family way again—"

He dropped back onto the pillow with an angry huff. "There's things you can do, ways a woman can keep from having babies if she—"

"I won't do it, Martin. I'm not going to drink that pennyroyal tea, not ever."

"I ain't talking about that; there's other ways."

He said he'd heard of a lady's wash that cleaned a woman out so she didn't end up with a baby. As he spoke, he moved closer and touched his hand to her cheek. Tracing his finger down the side of her neck and across her shoulder, he whispered of how he had to have her and how he'd been a fool to stay away so long.

"It'll be different this time," he said.

Without taking notice of the tears in her eyes, he climbed atop her.

1968

Huntington

It was after 6 pm when Margaret and Tom checked into the Hotel Prichard on the corner of Sixth and Ninth Street in downtown Huntington. Moments after Tom pulled up in front of the 13-story red brick building, a bellman loaded their luggage onto a brass cart and wheeled it through the marble-floored lobby.

"Oh my," Margaret whispered, "this is much fancier than I'd expected."

Tom gave an almost imperceptible shrug and grinned. "The manager at the Daniel Boone recommended it."

As she stood waiting for Tom to check them in, Margaret noticed him having a rather long discussion with the clerk behind the desk. She moved up behind him.

"That's not what I asked for," Tom said. "You'll have to find something else."

"What's wrong?" she asked.

"They assumed because we were traveling together, we wanted adjoining rooms." Tom turned back to the clerk. "Surely you've got something else. The same floor maybe but not—"

Noticing the harried look on the clerk's face, Margaret leaned toward Tom and whispered, "Adjoining rooms are fine with me, but if you're concerned I'll try to take advantage of you…"

Tom sputtered a laugh, then turned back to the clerk. "Since my traveling partner has promised to control herself, we'll go ahead and take the adjoining rooms."

At 7:30 they met in the hotel lobby, had Manhattans in the cocktail lounge, and dined in the hotel restaurant. Tom asked if she was up for another Manhattan or would rather switch to wine. She opted for wine, and he ordered a bottle of pinot noir. When the wine arrived at the table, it was accompanied by a small plate of hors d'oeuvres. As they passed the appetizers back and forth to one another, Margaret asked how they would approach the search for Nellie, Edward, and Dewey.

"With tomorrow being Sunday, we'll have a slow start," Tom said. "I can't access the records bureau or library until Monday, so I thought I'd start out with the old smile-and-dial method."

Margaret eyed him quizzically. "Meaning what?"

"Well, I've checked the telephone directory; there's seventeen Hunters and four Hobbs listed here in Cabell County. If none of those work out, I'll branch out to the surrounding counties. I'm also going to try and find the town of Greystone. Caldonia claimed it was not far from Huntington, but I've checked. It's not in Cabell County."

She laughed. "That's how I started looking for you. Before I came across your card, I was calling every Bateman in the telephone directory."

"Sometimes it works; sometimes not. I'm feeling pretty positive, because thanks to Caldonia we've got a lot to go on."

One word led to another, and before long they were sharing stories of their lives and things that had nothing to do with the search for her family. Tom spoke of how as a young man he'd lived in New York City and shared an apartment with three other young men. He'd attended the City College of New York to study criminal justice and spent nine years working for the district attorney's office before he'd moved to Georgia and set up his own practice.

She in turn talked about how Aunt Rose had been her primary training ground for life as a married woman.

"Every Tuesday and Thursday she instructed me on what she called 'the things a lady should know.'" Margaret laughed. "I hated all that properness then, but later on when I started dating Albert I was glad I'd learned it."

Long after she'd climbed into bed and turned out the light, she lay there reliving the conversations of the evening. As she thought about Aunt Rose and her weekly lessons, a fondness Margaret had never felt before crept into her heart. She wondered if she'd ever told Albert the story of those lessons; she couldn't remember doing so.

On Sunday morning at breakfast, Tom pulled out a notepad with the list of names he planned to call and slid the tablet across the table to Margaret.

"We can make short work of this if we split it up. You take the first part of the list, and I'll take the rest. If we don't come up with something here, we'll try the surrounding counties."

Margaret agreed, and without lingering over another coffee they headed back to the room. Since it made sense for them to be within speaking distance of one another in case questions arose, they unlocked the doors between the two rooms and left them standing open. Tearing off the first page of the note pad, he handed it to Margaret.

"Start with these listings for Hobbs." He explained how she was to introduce herself, apologize for interrupting their day, say what she was looking for, and then ask questions. "People can be a bit wary of a stranger on the telephone. If you make them feel comfortable before you jump into asking questions, they're less likely to hang up on you."

Her first call was rather awkward, and after she'd gone through all the things Tom instructed her to do she got stuck talking to Homer Hobbs for well over a half hour. In what she had to assume was an effort to be helpful, he went into the most minute detail explaining how his grandfather had come over from Scotland, settled in Kentucky, raised nine children, and now had 17 grandchildren, none of them a Nellie or Edward.

"We've got a Millie," he said, "but that's as close as we come."

When she finally hung up the telephone, Tom was standing in the doorway laughing. "If you let yourself get caught up in that kind of conversation, this is going to take forever."

"But you said I should make them feel comfortable before—"

"Comfortable, yes, but you don't have to be the best of friends." He asked if she'd like to sit in on a few of his calls to get the hang of it, and she followed him back to his room.

As he ran through the next three phone calls, Margaret sat and listened. He had a warm way of speaking with people, friendly but also efficient. He spent five or six minutes on a call, got the answers he was looking for, and moved on to the next listing.

Twenty minutes later, she returned to her own room and finished telephoning the Hobbs listings. Those calls were considerably faster but no more productive.

By noon they'd called every name on the list and knew nothing more than when they'd started. Of the 21 numbers Tom had, seven were no answers, one was temporarily disconnected, and 13 claimed no knowledge of a Nellie or Edward Hunter or Hobbs. The yellow pages were equally disappointing with no listing for a Doctor Hobbs or Virgil Palmer.

Setting names of the no-answers aside for later in the evening, Tom said, "That's it for Cabell County."

He pushed back from the desk and went to the lobby in search of directories for the surrounding counties. A bellhop who looked like little more than a boy scrounged through a closet and handed him three directories: Mason County, Putnam County, and Lincoln County.

"That's it?" Tom said.

The kid nodded. "That's all there is. Go north of Huntington, and you're in Ohio."

"Thanks." Tom started toward the elevator, then turned back. "You ever heard of a town called Greystone?"

The kid shook his head.

"What about Ohio? Is there a Greystone over in Ohio?"

Again, the kid shook his head. "Not that I know of."

With disappointment slumping his shoulders, Tom said, "Thanks anyway," and headed for the elevator.

Back in the room, he and Margaret spread the directories across the desk and started searching for a Hunter or Hobbs connection. They found 32 potential names in Mason County, 23 in Putnam, and only seven in Lincoln County. With Tom being the faster of the two, he took the Mason and Lincoln directories and handed Putnam to Margaret.

She'd finished calling the handful of Hobbs and was halfway through Putnam County's Hunters when she hit upon Millard Hunter. After she'd explained how she was looking for some long-lost relatives, she asked if there was an Edward or Nellie in his family.

"Yes, there's a Nellie, but—"

Margaret jumped up from the chair and waved to get Tom's attention. He spotted her and hurried over. As she was talking, he mouthed, *You found Nellie?*

She nodded. "So you have got a Nellie? A Nellie Hunter?"

"Yes, but—"

"Was she born in Coal Creek, West Virginia? Was she adopted? Was her name Hobbs before—"

"Hold on," the man exclaimed. "I've been trying to tell you, our Nellie is only three years old. She was born right here in Huntington. I'm sorry to disappoint you, but she's not the one you're looking for."

"What about her mama or grandma? Could be she was named after—"

"She wasn't. It was after my brother, Nelson. He died at Dunkirk."

"I'm sorry about your brother," she said in a contrite way. "I don't suppose your mama…"

He answered no without waiting for the rest of the question. Margaret hung up the telephone and dropped into the chair.

"We're never going to find them," she said wearily. "You've gone to all this trouble for nothing."

"Think that way, and you'll never make detective." The hint of a smile curled the corner of Tom's mouth. "This business is fraught with blind alleys and wrong turns, but if you don't check them all out you might miss the one thing that leads to what you're looking for."

"I suppose."

"It's been a long day, and you need a break. How about we get out of here? We can go for a walk, maybe see a movie, and have some dinner."

"Don't you think we should keep going? At least finish these lists?"

"Nope." He stuck a notepad in the directory to mark her place and flipped the cover closed. "When you get discouraged, the best thing to do is walk away and come back the next day when you're feeling better. You'd be surprised at how a fresh start can change the way you see things. Maybe open up possibilities you hadn't seen the day before."

Margaret gave him a wry smile. "Sounds very Pollyanna."

He laughed at her expression. "It is, but it also happens to be true."

They walked for a while then headed for the Keith-Albee Theatre to see *Funny Girl*. By the time they went to dinner, Margaret was feeling much more positive about everything. They were still talking about the movie when they returned to the hotel. As they moved toward the elevator, the bellboy called out to Tom.

"Excuse me, sir." He scuttled across the lobby to catch up to them. "I've been thinking about that town you were looking for."

Tom stopped and turned to the boy. "You mean Greystone?"

"Yeah, that's it. You sure you don't mean Grayson? There's a Grayson over in Kentucky."

Tom glanced at Margaret. "Caldonia said it was in West Virginia, didn't she?"

"She said nearby. I'm not sure."

"Grayson's not far," the bellboy said. "Twenty-five or thirty miles, maybe. Just across the border."

"Do you have a Kentucky telephone directory?" Tom asked.

The boy shook his head. "Sorry, no. I can have the manager order one or they might have one down at the drugstore."

"Thanks." Tom smiled at Margaret and gave a wink. "Let's go find a phone book."

Moving with a quick and purposeful step, they hurried out onto Ninth Street and headed for the drugstore.

In the rear of the store, past the ice cream freezer, behind a display of hairspray, combs, and brushes, there were three telephone booths. Next to them, a medal stand that held eight swing-out directories and a shelf to write on. With Margaret looking over his shoulder, Tom checked the directories and found three for West Virginia, three for Ohio, and two for Kentucky, Boyd County and Carter County.

Grabbing the Carter County directory, he flipped through the first few pages in the front of the book and ran his finger along the list of towns. He found Grayson and turned to the residential section. There he found two listings for Hobbs, neither of them with the first name of Dewey. After jotting the names and numbers for Herbert and Edna

Hobbs in his notebook, he flipped back to the yellow pages and checked under doctors, medical offices, clinics, and surgeons. Nothing. No Doctor Hobbs, Dewey or otherwise.

On the chance Dewey could have moved to a neighboring town, he pulled out the Boyd County directory. Under residential listings, he found one listing: Louise N. Hobbs.

Looking over his shoulder, he asked, "Was Nellie's first name Louise?"

Margaret shook her head.

Believing anything was worth a try, he added Louise's phone number to his list and turned to the yellow pages. There he hit pay dirt with a listing for Doctor Oliver D. Hobbs in Ashland. Looking up with a grin, he said, "I think I found something."

Although she'd never before thought of it that way, Margaret counted up the years and came to the realization that Dewey could easily have a son old enough to be a doctor. Her heart began to flutter and beat against the walls of her chest like a bird struggling to fly free. A sigh weighted with equal measures of happiness and sorrow rose from her throat.

"It's sad that I've missed so much of Dewey's life; now here he is with a son who's a doctor."

"Hold on, it's way too early to be thinking that," Tom said. "I don't want you to be disappointed. Remember, this is a long shot. This doctor is not in Grayson, and Oliver is a common enough name that he could be anybody."

Margaret smiled. "He's not. He's Dewey's son, I'm certain of it."

That night she found it impossible to fall asleep. Long after she'd turned out the light and climbed into bed, she lay there calling up the memories of Dewey. Flickers of the street lights below danced across the ceiling as she pictured what the next day would bring: the two of them, brother and sister, sitting side by side, Dewey's hair now turned silver, but the dimple in his chin as adorable as ever. She'd tell him of Albert and how he'd built a thriving law firm from nothing, and she'd listen as he told her of what he'd done in his life. The war, his marriage, children, the pathway that had led him to becoming a doctor. She wanted to hear it all, every last word, all the everyday parts of his life and all the special moments she'd missed out on knowing.

Dewey would know where to find Nellie and Edward, and once the four of them were together it would be a grand day of sharing memories and catching up. Together they'd figure out the secret of why they left Barrettsville and why their mama sent them all away. Margaret would insist Tom come along. She'd say, "If it were not for Tom, I would have never found you." Then they'd welcome him into the fold as if he were another brother.

Margaret closed her eyes and tried to force herself to sleep, but it was useless. How could she expect to sleep when tomorrow was going to be the grandest day of her life?

Lost Memories

On Monday morning Margaret rapped on Tom's door at 15 minutes before 8 am. When it swung open, he stood there dressed but shoeless.

"You're early."

"I'm anxious to get started," she said with a sheepish grin.

"We've got plenty of time. The library and records departments won't be open until nine, and I doubt the good doctor will be there much earlier than that."

She followed him back into the room and stood waiting while he pulled on his shoes and grabbed a jacket. They stopped at the hotel coffee shop for breakfast, and when he ordered sunny-side-up eggs and ham, she frowned and said, "Just coffee for me."

Once the food was delivered, he insisted she at least have a piece of toast. She nibbled at the edge of it and set it back on his plate.

"I can't eat," she said, then moved on to telling of how Dewey had the rare ability to make everything sound more exciting. "When he talked about where he'd go or what he'd do, you simply had to believe him. He said he was going to be a doctor, and now he even has a son who's followed in his footsteps."

Eying her with pinched brows, Tom warned, "I think you're jumping the gun. We don't know for sure this doctor is Dewey's son. We don't even know if he's related. Remember, this is only a lead. It may turn out to be something, or it may not."

"Oh, it's something; I'm positive of it. Oliver's my brother's boy. Don't you get it? Oliver D. Hobbs. Oliver was our oldest brother's name, and the D is obviously for Dewey."

The band of furrows across Tom's forehead grew deeper. He shook his head and gave an apprehensive sigh. "I just hope you're not in for a huge disappointment."

She assured him that she could handle whatever happened, but the look of concern remained on Tom's face.

They left the hotel, drove north, and crossed over the Ohio River. The river, like the Kanawha, separated one place from another, and today it was running fast just as the Kanawha had been on that last afternoon she'd spent with Dewey. As they turned onto the Scenic Byway and headed west, she spoke of that afternoon.

"It was windy that day and the river was choppy, but it didn't bother us. We just sat there on the riverbank, eating our sandwiches and sharing a bottle of Coca-Cola. Dewey said he was dead set on being a doctor, and that's why he'd joined the army." The memory came into view, and a small chuckle rose from her chest. "When he asked what I was going to do with my life, I said marry a rich man and move as far away from Charleston as I can possibly get."

"And did you?" Tom asked.

She laughed again. "Not really. We left Charleston, but Albert was just starting out so we struggled by on a law clerk's salary for years. I'd been so boastful about how I was going to marry for money, but in the end I did just what Mama did. I married for love."

The memory of her mother was one weighted with sadness and for a while she sat silently, watching the endless thickets of trees fly by as they continued west. In time the river turned, taking a more northerly direction. The road swerved with it. When they exited the byway and made a left onto Twelfth Street to go back across the Ohio, she gave a lingering sigh.

"Albert was a good man. Nothing like my daddy. Mama used to tell us Daddy was different when she married him. Supposedly he was loving and fun to be with. One time I asked her what made him change. She said the devil took his soul, but Dewey said the devil had nothing to do with it. He claimed it was that Martha Mae Daddy lived with."

The Twelfth Street bridge ran across the Ohio River and into Kentucky. Two blocks later they turned left onto Winchester Avenue and parked in front of the small brick building. With Tom leading the way, they crossed the lobby and entered the doctor's office.

The nurse behind the desk peered over her glasses. "Can I help you?"

Margaret spoke first. "We'd like to see Dr. Hobbs."

"The doctor is at the hospital and not expected until after eleven. Did you have an appointment?"

"Not really, but I think Dr. Oliver Dewey Hobbs will be glad to see me. We're family."

The nurse removed her glasses and set them aside. With her eyes narrowed and her nose twitching suspiciously, she eyed Margaret. "And your name is…?"

"Margaret Rose McCutcheon. I lost touch with my family years ago, so Oliver has never met me. I'm his aunt. His daddy's sister."

The nurse's jaw stiffened, and her lips became a tight line. "I don't know what you're up to, but I suggest you leave before I call—"

Tom jumped in with an introduction and handed her a business card.

"I hope you can forgive Mrs. McCutcheon's enthusiasm," he said. "She's very excited, because this is the first lead we've had." He went on to explain how they'd been searching for Margaret's family and were told that her brother, Dewey, had become a doctor. "Since Oliver was their oldest brother's name, Margaret jumped to the conclusion that Dr. Hobbs was Dewey's son. If we're mistaken, we apologize." He gave an unassuming smile.

Looking only at Tom, the nurse's expression softened. "Oh. Well. I can't say if he's related or not, but Dr. Hobbs's middle name is David not Dewey."

"But what about his daddy?" Margaret asked. "Was his name Dewey?"

The nurse glared at Margaret and turned back to Tom. "My under-standing is that Dr. Hobbs did take over the practice from his father, but that was before my time so I don't know the given name of the first Dr. Hobbs."

Margaret tugged on Tom's arm. "Let's wait and talk to Oliver when he comes in."

"I'd prefer you didn't," the nurse said pointedly. "The doctor has patients straight through until three-thirty. I can fit you in then if you wish."

Jumping in before Margaret had a chance to argue, Tom said that would be fine and they left the office.

Margaret settled into the car with her chin lowered onto her chest. "I'm disappointed."

"Why? We've got a lot more now than when we started. We can use our time to go to the public library. I've got a feeling we'll find out everything we need to know about the first Dr. Hobbs there."

At the Boyd County Public Library, they settled into the microfiche reading room and started going through copies of the *Daily Independent* dating as far back as 1920. The library only had one microfiche reader, so they took turns peering into the lens and browsing through pages of the newspaper. Tom took the first shift.

Page by page he rolled through stories of Billy Sunday and Scott Fitzgerald, banner headlines about women now being able to vote, and Herbert Hoover's prediction of a greater than ever economy. In between the articles were advertisements for Viceroy cigarettes, Baby Ruth candy bars, Lysol, and contrived-looking apparatuses that promised to break a child of thumb-sucking. After two hours of searching, he slid aside and let Margaret take over.

"Look for articles relevant to the medical field," he said. "You never know where we'll find something."

Margaret went through 1935 then moved onto 1936. She was halfway through August when she spotted the photograph of Dewey standing in front of the red brick building. He looked the same as she remembered. His face was a bit more squared, his shoulders slightly rounded, but his smile and the dimple in his chin were exactly as she'd pictured them.

For a few moments she sat there saying nothing, allowing the image to be forever ingrained in her mind. With a grin that stretched the full width of her face, she gave a yelp and told Tom she'd found what they'd been looking for.

The article spoke of how Dewey Hobbs, injured at the battle of Argonne, had served as a medical aide in France then returned to America, obtained his medical degree from Johns Hopkins University, and interned under the tutelage of Dr. Robert Somme. The article gave no home address but said the newly-established offices of Dr. Dewey Hobbs would be located on Winchester Avenue.

Margaret looked up at Tom hopefully. "Don't you think this means Oliver Hobbs has to be my brother's son?"

Tom smiled. "It certainly seems so."

Margaret glanced at her watch: 1:30. "Maybe if we go back early…"

Tom shook his head. "Absolutely not."

They found a luncheonette at the far end of Central Avenue and settled into a booth.

There were times in Margaret's life when she'd wanted time to slow down, when she'd wanted a moment to last longer or a special day to go on forever. Now when she wanted it to hurry along, the minutes crept by like an old man with a heavy sack on his back.

After what seemed like an almost endless wait it was 3:30, and they were back in Dr. Hobbs's reception room. A man who Margaret could have easily mistaken for Dewey was waiting for them.

"I understand you're my dad's sister," he said and smiled. "Maggie, isn't it?"

Maggie. No one but Dewey called her that. He'd remembered, remembered and told his son.

Oliver was older than Dewey had been when she'd last seen him, but the look she remembered was there. The crooked smile, the lock of hair falling carelessly onto his forehead, the dimpled chin. Her heart swelled, and the tears she'd held back for so many years filled her eyes. Reaching out, she took his hand in hers.

"You look a lot like your dad."

He laughed. "So I've been told."

Tom stepped forward, introduced himself, and explained how they'd been searching for Margaret's siblings. They shook hands, and Oliver invited them back into his office. As they walked back, Oliver asked if she'd seen Aunt Nell or Uncle Edward.

"Not yet," Margaret said. "Dewey and I were the closest. I thought once I found him, he could help me locate the others."

"I'm not sure how much help Dad will be, but I can give you the addresses for Aunt Nell and Uncle Edward. They live not far from here in Huntington. Uncle Edward is a lawyer, happily married, no children. Aunt Nell married Kevin Fisher and they have four girls, each lovelier than the other…"

Oliver's office was small, but it had a welcoming feel. The high-backed chair had worn spots on the arms, and on the mahogany desk sat a pile of folders and an assortment of family pictures. Bookcases lined the wall behind him, and in front of the desk were two plush leather chairs.

"Have a seat." He motioned to the chairs and asked if they would like a cold drink.

"I can't wait to see your dad," Margaret said. "How is he doing?"

Oliver picked up one of the framed photographs on the desk and handed it to her. "This one was taken three years ago. It's Mom and Dad with my sister, Maggie, and me."

"Maggie?"

"Named after you," Oliver said and smiled.

Margaret took the photograph from him and studied it. At first glance, Dewey looked as she might have expected: the dimple and his hair turned silver. Yet something was different. His smile was flat without mischief or happiness in it. She set the picture back on the desk.

"Your sister is beautiful, and it's a lovely photograph," she said, "but your dad doesn't seem to be smiling. Is he sick?"

"Not sick in the traditional sense." Oliver took a deep breath and leaned forward with his hands folded in front of him. "Dad's health is good, but his memory is failing. Sometimes he remembers things, and other times he doesn't. He often speaks of the past, so I'm hopeful he'll remember who you are."

Margaret sat stunned for a moment. "Everybody forgets things; isn't that just part of getting older? Last week I forgot where I put my car keys and—"

"It's worse than that. Sometimes Dad forgets what year it is or who Aunt Nell is or where he lives." Oliver's eyes were filled with sadness and a heartbreaking acceptance of what was. Margaret could see his pain was greater even than hers.

The crushing guilt of having wasted so many years settled in her chest. She should have searched for Dewey and the others long ago. Now she didn't know if she was courageous enough to face the brother who was her soulmate and have him turn away. Could she live with him not knowing who she was? To be together and have him not remember all they'd meant to one another? Which would be more painful, to know she'd come this far and turned away or accept that what was once a forever thread had somehow been broken? If Dewey had forgotten everything, how would she find the rest of the family?

Jagged-edged fragments of her heart broke away and tore at her throat as she spoke.

"I'd still like to see my brother. Will you tell me where he is?"

Oliver smiled. "I had a feeling you might say that. When I heard you were here, I called Mom. She and Dad are coming to dinner at our house this evening, and we'd love to have you join us." He scribbled the address on a note paper and handed it to her. "Would six o'clock be okay?"

Margaret nodded and thanked him for the invitation. Leaving the office, she leaned heavily on Tom's arm. "I waited all these years, and now it may be too late."

"People don't forget someone they've truly loved, Margaret. When you see Dewey, I believe he'll remember."

She sniffed back the sob rising in her throat. "And what if he doesn't?"

"Then you'll remember for him. You'll tell him the same stories you've told me. By sharing those memories, you might give him back some of what he's lost."

The Visit

Oliver's house was on the cul-de-sac at the far end of a quiet street. It was a white colonial with a wide front porch and a long driveway. A Mercury station wagon with wood paneling on the sides was parked in the drive. Tom pulled in behind it and parked.

"Do you think that's Dewey's car?" Margaret asked nervously.

"Could be; it looks like an older model." He leaned over and patted her hand. "Relax, Maggie. Don't worry about what might be lost. Think about what might be found."

Margaret raised an eyebrow. "Maggie?"

He clicked off the ignition and turned with a mischievous grin. "Uh-huh. It suits you better. I've always thought Margaret was too stuffy a name for woman like you."

"A woman like me?" She laughed and shook her head.

From the moment they stepped onto the front porch, Margaret felt the warmth inside the house. Through the sheer curtains she saw shadows of people moving around in the softly lit room and heard the sound of pleasant conversation. Words flowed with an easy rhythm.

When the echo of the door chime came from inside, her hand trembled and a scattering of petals fell from the bouquet she'd brought.

She hadn't thought to ask Oliver's wife's name or that of his mother, and when the door opened she stood speechless. Tom stepped forward with a smile and greeted the woman who answered.

"Thanks for having us tonight. I'm Tom Bateman, and this is Maggie, Dewey's sister."

The woman reached out and hugged Margaret and then Tom. "I'm Claudia, Oliver's wife." She pushed back the door and gestured for them to come in. "Oliver's told his dad you were going to be here tonight, and I think he's looking forward to it. I know Mama Hobbs is."

She moved through the foyer into the living room. Margaret recognized Dewey the moment she stepped into the room. He was sitting on the sofa, and beside him sat a woman with a soft round face and eyes the blue of a cloudless summer sky.

"Mama Hobbs, this is Dad's sister, Maggie, and her friend, Tom."

"Please, call me Ellen," the woman said. "Dewey has spoken of you so often, I feel as though I already know you." Leaning toward Dewey, she said, "Sweetheart, do you remember your sister, Maggie?"

Dewey gave a slight nod, but his expression didn't change. Neither smiling nor frowning, he had the look of a man whose thoughts were a million miles away. Margaret hesitated for a few moments then crossed the room and kneeled beside him.

"Dewey, it's me, Maggie. We have the same birthday, remember?"

He glanced at her, bobbed his head, and looked away. He didn't remember. He didn't even know who she was, not really. All those years she'd believed if they ever found one another, a wave of happiness would sweep over them and wash away the missing time. Now here they were together, and the only thing she could feel was the terrible ache of losing him all over again.

Ellen lifted Dewey's hand from hers and stood. "You two haven't seen one another in such a long time. Come and sit by your brother. You have a lot to talk about, and I really should help Claudia in the kitchen."

Margaret sat next to Dewey, slid her arm through his, and leaned ever so lightly on his shoulder. If she only had this one evening with him, she was determined to make it something he could remember. Instead of asking what he remembered, she began to reminisce about the memorable moments she'd held on to.

"I loved that big old house in Barrettsville," she began. "I remember how we used to sneak out to chase fireflies and that girl from across the street—Mary Ellen, I think her name was—the minute she saw you out there, she'd come running over. Oh my gosh, she had such a crush on you!"

As she spoke a soft chuff came from Dewey, and the corner of his lip curled ever so slightly.

Segueing into a tale of her life with Albert, she said sadly they'd never had children. "He was just starting out, and we were barely scraping by. Then we left Charleston and moved to Georgia. I didn't know where you were, so I left word with Mrs. Mulroney at the boarding house. I said if you came by to give you my new address. I guess you didn't come back to Charleston because…"

Dewey patted her hand. "She died."

"Mrs. Mulroney died? When?"

He stayed quiet for several seconds. "Before the end."

"She died before the end of the war?"

He nodded.

"That's why you never got in touch with me."

A short while later, Claudia called them to dinner. Margaret sat next to Dewey with Tom and Ellen directly across from them. The more they talked, the more Dewey remembered. It was mostly the early years in Coal Creek and Barrettsville. He remembered very little about his time in the army but could easily recall the Markeys' barrel door and laughed when Margaret said she'd crawled through it a few days earlier.

"I scared Aunt Caldonia out of her wits when I pushed the inside flap open and came in." She laughed as she described how the bowl of sausage gravy had splattered all over the room. "Aunt Caldonia's the one who told me you'd become a doctor. She said someone you'd met in France helped you get started."

Margaret noticed how Ellen never took her eyes off of Dewey. When he looked puzzled or bewildered, she'd jump in with some clue to jolt his memory. At the mention of the doctor in France, Dewey frowned in thought.

"Yes," Ellen said, "it was Dr. Somme. He's since passed on. Dewey was in the medical transport team at the Battle of Liege. When Robert was injured Dewey carried him back to the field hospital, which saved his life." She smiled across at Dewey. "Sweetheart, you remember

Robert, don't you? You were working together when we met."

He gave an obligatory nod.

There were times when Dewey would join in the conversation and laugh along with everyone else and other times when she could see he was lost in his own thoughts. Ellen helped him remember the later years, and Margaret helped him remember the early days. Making a choice not to upset him with the harder times, she stuck to the good things and the times worth remembering.

Shortly after ten, Ellen said she and Dewey had to be leaving. She hugged Margaret as if they were lifelong friends and pressed a folded notepaper into her palm.

"Here's our telephone number and address. Come and spend the day with us tomorrow."

"We'd love to, if you're sure we won't be an inconvenience."

"Inconvenience?" Ellen laughed. "Why, it would be a blessing. Dewey and I have both enjoyed this evening more than you can possibly know."

"Me too." Margaret leaned in and brushed a kiss across her new sister-in-law's cheek.

Before she and Tom left a few minutes later, Oliver thanked them for coming and said he hadn't seen his dad this happy in months.

"If you can stay in the area until Saturday, Claudia and I would like to have a family cookout in the backyard."

Margaret looked at Tom; when he nodded, she said they'd be delighted to come.

"Good. I'll invite Aunt Nell and her brood, Uncle Edward and Alice, and Maggie's family. We'll do it in the afternoon because Dad is better earlier in the day, especially if there's a crowd. At night, when he's tired, he finds it harder to follow the conversations and gets frustrated."

There was almost no traffic at night, and as they drove back across the Ohio River Margaret could hear the sound of rushing water and see what seemed like a million stars twinkling overhead. It was as perfect a night as she'd ever known. Nothing about this trip had been as she'd originally envisioned, yet she couldn't have wished for anything better. With a great swell of gratitude rising in her chest, she turned to Tom.

"I have so very much to thank you for." She blinked back the tears that threatened to overflow her eyes. "You've not only found my family; you've changed my life."

Tom was silent for a moment; she heard him draw in a deep breath before stretching across the seat and touching her shoulder.

"You've changed mine also, Maggie," he said.

Later on, after she'd turned out the lights and gone to bed, she thought back on that moment and replayed his words. Tom usually had a casual, almost mischievous way of keeping the mood light, but when he'd spoken those words his voice had been filled with a great depth of sincerity. They'd grown close, no doubt about it, but Margaret wasn't sure she was ready for anything other than friendship. Tomorrow she would find a way to make it clear to him they were friends and nothing more.

◌⟋⟍⟋⟍◌

In the days that followed, Margaret visited Dewey every day. She and Tom would have breakfast at the hotel and then head over to Ashland. They'd arrive before ten and spend the afternoon talking about whatever came to mind. From time to time Dewey forgot her name or Tom's, but whatever he forgot Ellen remembered.

Margaret skipped over the painful things—times when there'd been little to eat or no coal for the stove—and focused on the sweet memories. She told stories of barefoot summers when the sun baked the mountain, afternoons wading through the cool water of the creek, the big house in Barrettsville with its huge front porch and creaky staircase, the songs they'd sung at church, Caldonia's endless supply of cookies, and the sled Jeb made for them.

One afternoon, after they'd talked of the train ride back to Coal Creek, Margaret asked if Dewey knew why they'd left Barrettsville.

"Caldonia told me something happened, and it had to do with Daddy."

Dewey looked past her to where the window faced out onto the side yard. The question hung in the air for several seconds before he shrugged.

"I think I've forgotten."

Whenever he looked confused or weary, Ellen was there with a thought or comment that moved past the awkwardness of the moment.

"It was probably not worth remembering," she said. "An insignificant family squabble, no doubt."

She and Dewey told stories of how they'd met and when he'd opened his own practice in the red brick building.

"Oliver was born that same year," she said. "He's named for your older brother."

"I thought so, but why David?"

"David's my brother, younger than me by two years. The year after we had Oliver, our daughter came along."

"We call her Maggie," Dewey said. "She's Margaret Rose, like you."

As they went back and forth piecing together the various stories of their time apart, Margaret felt a newfound happiness. For so many years she'd worried about Dewey; wondered where he was and whether or not he had a good life. Now she knew. He and Ellen were perfectly matched, and the love they felt for one another was obvious. Yes, his memory was failing and someday the recollection of everything they'd shared would be gone. But for now, he was happy. Time gave no promises, and with life being as fragile as it was Margaret was starting to believe that the present was the most important time of all.

In the evening when she and Tom returned to Huntington, they walked along the river, explored the city, and dined together. They discovered a little out-of-the-way pub with crispy French fries and juicy hamburgers and a pizzeria they returned to twice. As they strolled along, Margaret found herself enjoying Tom's company more than she cared to admit even to herself.

❦

On Saturday morning, Margaret was awake before dawn. She'd spoken to both Nellie and Edward during the week, but this would be her first time seeing them in person. The excitement of it was fluttering through her like a flock of butterflies.

As it turned out they'd both been adopted by a family named Hudson not Hunter, so Caldonia had been right about some things and wrong about others. Margaret would be going back to visit Caldonia sometime soon, but she already knew she'd not mention the error. What Caldonia had given them was enough to find Dewey, and that in itself was a huge blessing.

Margaret and Tom were the first to arrive at Oliver's house.

"Oh dear," she said as Claudia opened the door. "I hope we're not too terribly early."

Claudia laughed. "You're family. When family shows up early, we just put them to work." She led Margaret into the kitchen and handed her a stack of plates to carry out back where Oliver was setting up the tables. Tom offered to lend a hand with the furniture and disappeared out the door.

For the next hour, Margaret worked alongside Claudia in the kitchen. She mixed mayonnaise into the potato salad, arranged sprigs of parsley around the edge of the cheese platter, and helped to frost the cupcakes. When the doorbell chimed, Claudia smiled and said Margaret should get it.

"It's probably Maggie. She's been dying to meet you."

Maggie, eight months pregnant and walking sway-backed, came with her husband and a shaggy dog named Spike. Nellie and her family arrived moments later with Edward and his wife not far behind. Dewey and Ellen were last to arrive. By then the back yard was abuzz with conversations floating back and forth.

Margaret didn't recognize Nellie immediately. They were sisters who'd once slept in the same bed, but time had darkened Nellie's hair to a blond that could easily be called brown. Later, when Nellie's girls were busy playing a ring toss game, Margaret caught the sound of high-pitched laugher and turned around.

It was a sound she remembered. The laughter came from the second youngest, the one with hair as gold as Nellie's once was and a cascade of curls tumbling down her back. Margaret smiled. The child was a spitting image of the little sister she remembered.

Edward was an even greater surprise. He looked more like their daddy than the toddler she'd known.

"Do you remember anything about Coal Creek?" she asked.

He laughed. "Not really. The few memories I do have probably came from stories Mom and Dad told about going to Coal Creek and bringing me home to live with them."

"Mom and Dad?"

He laughed again, this time a hint of blush colored his cheeks.

"The Hudsons," he explained. "We grew up calling them Mom and Dad."

"I'm glad you had a happy childhood," she replied as inside she grieved for the terrible loss their mother must have felt. "You know, Mama loved you too. She loved all of us. Loved us enough to send us away. There's no love bigger than that."

"That's what Mom told us," Edward replied. "She said our birth mama was as beautiful as Nell and the most loving woman she'd ever met."

"That was the truth," Margaret said and smiled.

Shortly after the sun started its descent, they gathered at a table piled high with homemade salads and platters of meat. She sat with Tom at her side and Dewey directly across. As they laughed and talked, passing salt shakers and baskets of biscuits from one hand to the next, she looked at the long row of faces. Fourteen in all; 15 if she included Tom.

This was what family felt like. The warmth of it filled her heart and satisfied her soul in a way she'd never before known. For all those years she'd put her own dreams aside and let Albert make the decisions, but he'd been wrong. They'd never needed a bigger house or more money in the bank. What they'd needed was a family. She'd given up on having it the first time around but never again, she vowed. Never again.

They remained in Huntington for another three days, and the day before they left Margaret told Ellen they'd be going to Wheeling.

"Oliver was working for a glass manufacturer there. Tom believes we'll be able to track him down."

"Oh, wouldn't that be wonderful. Please give us a call and let us know how you make out. Wheeling is not terribly far, and I'm certain Dewey would love to see him."

Margaret promised she would stay in touch. As Tom pulled out of the driveway, she turned just in time to see Dewey step out onto the porch and wave goodbye. Her eyes grew misty, and tears clouded her vision. She knew there would come a day when he would no longer remember her, but the memory of this time was engraved on her heart and she would remember for him.

1903

A Fragile Happiness

Having Eliza threaten to shoot him and turn away after they'd climbed into bed aroused Martin. It was a side of her he hadn't experienced before, a challenge that got his blood pumping. After that first weekend he wanted more, but he sure as hell didn't want more kids. Martha Mae used the Marvel Whirling Spray Ladies Syringe to prevent unwanted babies. Eliza would just have to do the same.

Before he returned for a second visit, he stopped in at the pharmacy and purchased one. Handing her the box, he said, "You can't possibly have no objection to using this, Eliza. It says in black and white this ain't nothing but a wash to keep your insides clean."

Looking rather skeptical, she asked where he'd gotten it.

"The pharmacy. See for yourself, the name's right there on the box. It's easy. All you gotta do is squirt your insides after we done something, and that's the end of us worrying about more kids."

As she sat there reading through the directions, he said, "I ain't taking no for an answer. I said I don't want no more kids, but you're my wife, Eliza, and I got rights."

In the end she agreed to using it, and he started visiting twice a month. He'd show up with a few sticks of candy for the kids and a little something for Eliza and later leave Coal Creek feeling like a homecoming hero. He was hard-pressed to say which he enjoyed most: the kids oohing and aahing when he told of all he was doing in Charleston or having Eliza capitulate to his ever-increasing urges.

Although Martin enjoyed Eliza and the kids, he was not about to give up Martha Mae. She had talents no man could walk away from, and having both women was something for a man to brag about. It didn't take a whole lot to satisfy Eliza, but from time to time Martha Mae got testy about him going back to Coal Creek. When that happened, he'd buy her a new pin or bracelet and promise to take her to some show she wanted to see.

"There ain't nothing between me and Eliza," he'd say, "but I gotta go there to see them boys. They're my kids."

She'd fold her arms and pull her lips into a pout. "Seems to me you could just send a few dollars and be done with it."

"Sounds like somebody is a bit jealous," he'd say and turn away with a smug grin.

As far as Martin was concerned, Lady Luck was permanently perched on his shoulder. Week after week he left the poker game with a pocket full of money, and on the few occasions when he lost he'd make double the next time. With everything going his way, Martin could pretty much afford to do whatever he wanted.

That winter he became a Master Mason, and Jimmy Wilkes came through with the union rep spot. There wasn't a great deal of money in being a rep, but the perks were good and it was a sure-fire way to move up the ladder. If he made it to union boss, he could be sitting on his duff and barking out orders instead of climbing lampposts and crawling across rafters. Getting to that level meant a lot of schmoozing with his uppity-up brothers at the Masonic Lodge, which was no problem.

◦◦◦

Eliza wasn't certain what to think when Martin started coming home every other week. The night he gave her the Ladies Syringe she wondered what kind of trickery he was up to, but after nearly three months of having him show up as regular as clockwork she'd come to believe this odd relationship was something that might last.

It wasn't the kind of love they'd had for one another in the early days, but she found comfort in having a daddy for the children and something in the money jar. She didn't love Martin anymore, but then, how could she? There was always the taste of tobacco on his lips and the smell of another woman on his skin.

His lovemaking had changed too; he'd become animalistic in bed, rough, demanding things they'd never done before. "Turn this way or that," he'd say, "bend over; arch your back." At times he'd ask for something she couldn't bring herself to do, and he'd leave her with fingerprints on her arm or thigh.

That side of Martin was offset by the way he came home in a happy mood and often with a bit of candy for the kids or something for her. She watched the children gather around him and listen to the tales he spun, tales of life in Charleston, the marvel of electricity, and how he'd risen through the ranks of both the union and the Knights of the Masonic Lodge. She reminded herself that she'd do whatever she had to do, because it was for the good of the children.

Even after they settled into the routine of him returning home every other week she remained wary, always on edge, anticipating the moment when the tide would turn. Each time he came for a visit, he left $10 in the money jar. It was enough for her to afford a bit extra—cloth to make Louella a dress, shoes for Oliver, a doll for Margaret Rose—but she never bought any of those things. She bought only what they needed and hid whatever was left in the sack behind the bed.

"There's no way of knowing how long this will last," she told Caldonia, "and I've got to be prepared for whatever might come."

The week before Christmas, Martin came for a visit and told the children he'd been made a third-degree Master Mason. He showed them the gold-plated pin he'd received.

"This didn't come easy," he said, "but when the committee heard I was working two jobs so my family could live out here in the country instead of being crowded into a city apartment, they said I truly was worthy."

Oliver looked at him skeptically. "I thought you was just an electrician."

"*Just* an electrician? I'll have you know being an electrician is one of the best jobs a man can get these days. But that ain't all I do. I help out the union as well. I'm just a rep now, but before long your daddy's gonna be a union bigwig."

"What's a bigwig?" Dewey asked.

Martin bumped out his chest and grinned. "It's a man who don't have to dirty his hands with working no more. A boss. A bigshot."

The kids had a dozen different questions, and Martin answered them all. Eliza noticed how he even seemed to take pleasure in doing so. She waited until it was well past their bedtime and said for them to put their pajamas on.

"Hold on a minute," Martin said and motioned for everyone to sit. He waited until they were all back in their seats with their eyes fixed on him. "Next week's Christmas, but with all this work I gotta do I ain't gonna be home. That don't mean you ain't getting no presents." He reached into his pocket, pulled out a fold of bills, and proceeded to hand each of the children a dollar. "Your mama's gonna take you to the company store, and you can pick out whatever you want."

Ben Roland stared at the bill. "For real? We can keep this?"

Martin reared back in his chair and laughed uproariously. "For real. And if anybody wants to know where you got all that money, you tell 'em it's from your daddy."

Louella looked at Virgil sitting in Eliza's lap and back to Martin. "What about Virgil, Daddy? He didn't get no dollar."

"He ain't deserving of one." Martin turned to Eliza. "I'm leaving some extra in the jar for you to get yourself a present too."

"Thank you, Martin," she said.

There was no further mention of Virgil. There were some issues Martin might be willing to give on; this was not one of them. To him the baby was a battle he'd lost, and he was not a forgiving man. She knew he would forever carry a grudge against the child.

Later that night as she tucked the baby into the cradle, she whispered a vow that only she could hear.

"Don't worry, Virgil. I'll love you twice as much to make up for the love your daddy doesn't have."

That first year, Eliza went from month to month worrying that each time Martin left money in the jar it would be the last. She bought nothing for herself and very little the children didn't absolutely have to have. Every spare penny was saved and hidden away in the sack.

In the summer she planted a garden generous enough to carry them through the winter, and by fall the pantry shelves were stacked high with jars of apples, beans, tomatoes, and corn. She was ready for whatever happened, but nothing did. Martin continued to return to Coal Creek every other week, and he left money in the jar each time he came. That Christmas he again gave each of the children a dollar and excluded Virgil. By then Virgil was almost two and knew to stay clear of his daddy. On the weekends when Martin did come home, Virgil would crawl under the bed, put his thumb in his mouth, and fall asleep. The first time it happened, Eliza was out of her mind with fear that he'd fallen off a cliff or drowned in the creek. She and the older boys searched for an hour before they discovered his hiding place.

For the better part of two years, everything went along smoothly. On occasion Eliza worried about Virgil wandering off to one place or another, but that was about the worst of it until the fall of 1905. In August Eliza missed her monthly, but she attributed it to the work she'd been doing in the garden. They'd planted half again what they did the previous year and she'd spent endless hours in the blistering sun, her back aching, and her legs so weary she could barely stand. The three boys helped, but with the eldest of them only 11 they couldn't be expected to carry a man's load.

The one person she could not look to for help was Martin; he'd made it known from the start that he was not the least bit interested in farm work.

"I work all week," he'd said. "When I come here, I expect to enjoy myself. I don't know why you want to garden anyway. I bring home more than enough for food. If you want to garden, do it when I'm not around."

She missed her monthly again in September and blamed it on the stress of getting the food preserved and stored.

After all the work we've put in this summer, I can't just stand by and let it spoil.

In October, the days turned cool and five of the children went off to school. With only the youngest two, Margaret Rose and Virgil, at home, she was free to sit in the rocker and relax. By then her breasts were swollen, and even the slightest whiff of tomato made her feel nauseous.

Impossible, she thought. She'd used the Marvel Whirling Spray religiously. The minute Martin climbed off of her, she'd hurry to the outhouse with that syringe and wince as the frigid solution swished through her insides. On a good night it was uncomfortable and on a bad night downright painful, especially in the dead of winter when the icy swirl rattled her bones.

Before the first snowfall, her waist had grown thick and soon there would be no denying the new life inside her. Given how Martin felt about Virgil, Eliza cringed at the mere thought of telling him. Each time he came to visit she steeled herself, fearful he might guess the truth by the look of her body. To have him discover it that way would be the worst yet. Eliza had to tell him, but as the weeks flew by she simply couldn't find the courage to do so.

In the deepest, darkest part of her heart she knew that once he found out, this fragile happiness they'd found would be gone forever. He'd tell her to get rid of the baby, and when she refused he'd walk away just as he'd done before or do something even worse. Turn violent, harm her or one of the children. There was no way she could let that happen.

The second week of December, Martin said he had a number of things to take care of in Charleston and wouldn't be back again until the first of the year. That's when she decided the best way to tell him would be with a letter.

After they made love that night, she claimed she was going to the outhouse to do her lady wash. Instead of the syringe, she took a pencil and sheaf of writing paper. While he slept, she penned a five-page letter telling him of the baby coming and explaining how it was through no fault of her own. She swore that she'd been diligent in her use of the spray, but it had somehow failed them. On the last page she wrote that since they'd been so happy together the past two years, she was praying he could find it in his heart to forgive her and love this child. She signed it, *Eliza, your eternally devoted wife.*

She folded the letter into an envelope, addressed it *Martin, my love*, returned to the house, and tucked it into a kitchen drawer.

The next evening as he was preparing to leave, she slid the envelope into his coat pocket. He would no doubt be angry when he discovered it, but with a month before he was due back again he had time to cool down and see things more rationally. Perhaps; perhaps not.

As she watched him walk down the pathway and turn onto the road, her heart felt heavy as a stone. Martin wasn't just her husband; he was the children's father. Standing there on the porch with the wind so cold it froze the teardrops on her cheek, she prayed this would not be the last time she or the children ever saw him.

Finding the Letter

Arriving back in Charleston, Martin decided to stop at the Wolf's Head Inn. A whiskey or two would be a pleasurable end to what he'd considered a good weekend. Barely through the door, he spotted Martha Mae sitting at a table with her friend, Maureen, and a well-dressed man who looked old enough to be her daddy.

"Well, I'll be damned," Martin grumbled and crossed the room to where they sat.

Standing over Martha Mae with the look of fire in his eyes, he locked his arms across his chest. "What in the hell do you call this?"

She glanced up at him and turned back to her companions. "Maureen, I believe you've already met Martin." Turning her attention to the silver-haired man, she said, "John, this is Martin Hobbs, a friend of mine."

"A pleasure." John gave Martin a nod and asked if he'd like to join them.

"You bet I do," Martin snapped. Grabbing a chair from the far side of the table, he carried it around and pushed in next to Martha Mae. Leaning toward her he spoke in a loud whisper.

"Is this what you do when I go to spend a day or two with my kids?"

"I was bored. Did you expect me to sit home and twiddle my thumbs?"

"I was gone one night. You couldn't wait one night?"

Martha Mae laughed. "Now look at who's getting jealous."

A few choice comments went back and forth before she finally told him John Daley was Maureen's beau.

"They're newly engaged and invited me out for a glass of port to celebrate."

"Oh. Well then." He stumbled through an awkward apology and ordered another round of drinks to help celebrate the occasion.

Before her glass was empty, he took hold of Martha Mae's arm and said it was time for them to be leaving. As soon as they were out the door, he wrapped his arm around her waist and pulled her into the shadow of the building.

"Damn, I missed you." He pressed his body to hers and ran kisses along the edge of her jaw. "Let's go back to my apartment."

"It's kind of late, and I'm a bit tired."

"Don't worry, I know just what will perk you up." He brought his mouth to hers and parted her lips with his tongue.

She pulled back ever so slightly, but that made Martin want her all the more. She was the kind of woman who knew how to drive a man crazy. He kissed her again and pinned her against the building.

"Martha Mae, I've gotta have you tonight. Either you come home with me, or I'll—"

"You'll what?" she teased.

"I will do something that will likely get us arrested." He smacked her on the bottom, snaked his arm around her waist, and edged her down the street toward his building. While they were still in the hallway, he shrugged off his coat. Once inside the apartment, he tossed the coat on the sofa and began tugging at her shirtwaist.

"Take it easy," she said and pushed him off. "I'm in no hurry. Pour us a few sips of whiskey, and wait until I get undressed properly." She dropped onto the sofa and bent to unbuckle her shoes. That's when she spotted the envelope that had fallen from his coat pocket.

"What's this?" she said and picked it up. She glanced at the envelope. "Martin my love? Who's this from?"

From the cupboard where he was pouring the whiskey, he glanced over his shoulder and asked. "Who is what from?"

"This!" She tore the envelope open and started reading.

"I have no idea what you're talking about."

As she scanned the pages, he crossed the room and held out the glass of whiskey he'd poured for her. Without looking up from the letter, she batted his hand away and sent the glass sailing across the room. Whiskey flew across the rug, and the glass rolled until it hit the wall.

"Nice," he snapped. "Real nice. You wanna tell me what's wrong?"

"This is what's wrong!" She stood up from the sofa, shook the letter in his face, and began reading Eliza's words in a mocking voice bristling with rage.

"My dearest husband, it is with a heavy heart that I write this letter…"

Martin stood there looking bewildered. "What in God's name is that? Where'd it come from?"

"It's a letter from your wife. I'm guessing it fell out of your coat pocket."

Martin snatched it from her hand. "I've never even seen this."

"Obviously. But I'll save you the chore of reading it; she's expecting another baby!"

A feeling of panic shot across Martin's chest, and his throat tightened. "That's impossible. I never—"

"Oh, yes, you did! And it's been going on for quite some time, according to this letter. I should have suspected something ages ago. When I think of all the weekends you were away and I sat waiting…" She pressed her hand to her forehead and moaned. "I'm a fool; a naive fool. When you asked me about how I prevented having kids, I thought your only concern was for me."

"It was, Martha Mae, I swear it was."

"Liar! You told her about the Marvel Whirling Spray. You bought one and gave it to her. She says so right here in the letter."

Martin felt the walls of the room closing in on him, and beads of perspiration rolled down his back. "She's lying. I didn't do that. I swear I didn't."

"Really? Then why would she say it? How would she even know about it?" She shoved him with such force that he stumbled backward and fell onto the sofa. Leaning over him with her nose just inches above his face, she screamed, "You're a liar, Martin! A liar and a cheat!"

He looked up wide-eyed. "Martha Mae, please. None of this is true, not one word. At least let me tell my side of the story before you start calling me a liar."

She stepped back and turned away. "Nothing you can say will change things."

Martin's heart raced, and his head pounded like the inside of a kettle drum. Desperately trying to collect his thoughts and piece together a story that sounded plausible, he scrubbed his hand across his chin. "This is Eliza's doing. I said it before, she's clever. Tricky as the day is long. She probably knows I been seeing you and is trying to put an end to it."

Martha Mae looked at him slant-eyed. "How would Eliza know about us?"

"Same way she found out about Bess. You remember I told you how she came here, chased poor Bess away, and stole my money?"

"You said you weren't sure what happened."

"At first I wasn't. But Mrs. Sloan told me she'd seen Eliza snooping around, and that's when I put two and two together and figured it out. I'm thinking she came back again, found out about you, then did this to get even with me and break us apart."

"This letter doesn't sound like a woman who's trying to get even. It sounds like someone who's scared."

Struggling to find an out, Martin latched on to the idea. "Maybe that's it. If she's been with somebody else and got herself in a family way, she'd be worried about what people will say. That's why she's looking to lay the blame on me."

Martha Mae gave a weary sigh and rolled her eyes. "Somebody else, huh?"

He nodded. "It's sure not me. I spend time with the kids when I'm there, that's it."

"You don't sleep with her?"

"Nope. I sleep on the sofa."

She turned away and stood looking out the window. "I don't believe you, Martin. I want to, but I don't."

"It's the truth, I swear. Tell me what I can do to prove it."

Keeping her back to him, she shrugged. "There's nothing you can do. This letter says you're the father of the baby, and you say you're not. Who am I to believe?"

"*Me*, Martha Mae. Believe me. You know how much I love you. I'd never cheat on you. Never." He came up behind her and put his hand on her shoulder. "Tell me what I can do to make this right, and I'll do it. I'll do anything."

She shook his hand loose from her shoulder, stepped away, and turned to face him. "Nothing can change what has already happened, but I will tell you this: if you ever, and I do mean *ever*, return to Coal Creek, that will be the end of us."

The image of Eliza and the kids flashed through his mind.

"What about the kids? I'm their daddy. Don't you think I ought to see them from time to time? What if I went less often?"

"I said *ever*, and I mean *ever*. If you want to see the children, send train fare and have them visit you here in Charleston."

Her face was as unyielding as that of a sphinx. Martin toyed with the idea of arguing that the children were too young to ride the train, but her expression made him push the thought aside and agree to her terms.

Martha Mae did not stay at the apartment that night. She tore the letter into tiny shreds, tossed it into the trash basket, and demanded Martin walk her back to her own place. At the doorstep he tried to kiss her but she turned away, saying it was going to take some time for her to forgive him and move past the betrayal she'd suffered.

"I'll wait," he said. "As long as it takes, I'll wait."

⊙⟩≋⟨⊙

In the weeks that followed, Martin gave a great deal of thought to the potential pitfalls of what he'd agreed to. Not going back to Coal Creek would work for a while, but Eliza was no fool. Sooner or later she'd come to Charleston looking for him. She'd done it before; what was to stop her from doing it again? Even though he couldn't say how it happened, he didn't doubt she was carrying another baby.

Since he hadn't had a chance to read the letter for himself and thought it unwise to even mention the subject to Martha Mae, he had no idea of when the baby was to be born or what Eliza might be planning to do. A thousand *What ifs* ran through his mind. The worst of all possibilities would be having the two women meet. If that happened, every lie he'd ever told would come to light. He'd only mentioned the three older boys to Martha Mae. What would she do if she found out there were seven kids with an eighth on the way? And if she asked where

Eliza got the Marvel Whirling Spray, Eliza would answer honestly. Then what?

Night and day Martin worried about the disasters that could happen. He started looking over his shoulder whenever he took Martha Mae to dinner and got jumpy as a cat if he heard footsteps hurrying along the hallway. Before long his poker game began to suffer, and he could no longer count on coming home with money in his pocket.

In early January, he and Martha Mae attended Maureen's wedding and came back to the apartment afterward. She was in the mood for lovemaking, but try as he may Martin couldn't make it happen.

That's when he decided to disappear. Other men had done it. He could too. He'd move somewhere else. Get an apartment on the far side of town or, better yet, go north or west. The idea took root in his mind that night, and before a week had gone by it was larger than life.

At the next Masonic Lodge meeting, Martin made sure to sit beside Jimmy Wilkes. As soon as they'd concluded the business of the day, he turned to Jimmy and struck up a conversation.

"I feel like I'm in a rut and need a change," he said. "Have you heard of any job openings up around Sissonville or maybe over in St. Albans?"

Jimmy thought for a moment then shook his head. "Nothing around here. I got a great one that's three hundred and fifty, maybe four hundred miles north of here."

"Where's it at?"

"Altoona. The company I'm with is expanding into Pennsylvania, and they're looking for somebody to head up the team. The money's great, and you'd be running the show. I was gonna look into it myself, but the wife said she didn't want to move up there."

"That wouldn't be a problem for me," Martin said. "Think you could put a word in, maybe get me an interview?"

"Yeah, no problem."

Before the January snow was gone from the ground, Martin was on a train headed for Altoona. Martha Mae was at his side.

A Child is Born

Eliza waited for an answer to her letter, but none came. She expected Martin to be angry about them having another baby but trusted that in time he would get over it, push aside the anger, and return home.

He'll come in January, she told herself, but he didn't.

The beginning of 1906 was bitter cold and seemed to drag on forever. Then in February the snow was twice what it normally was. Even though she knew he was not one to brave such weather, she listened for the sound of his boot steps on the porch.

The baby was due in April, but with no money coming in Eliza had begun to worry about expenses.

"I've no need of a midwife," she told Caldonia. "This is my eighth. I can manage on my own."

Caldonia eyed her apprehensively. "All the same, I'd feel better if—"

Eliza shook her head. "Six dollars is already gone from the sack, and I've no certainty of when we might get more. I've got to make what I have last."

Later that afternoon, Caldonia pulled Oliver aside.

"Never mind what your mama says. When she's ready to bring this child into the world, you come and fetch me."

In early March, on a day that was icy and threatening more snow, Eliza's back began to ache and she feared this was not a good sign.

She carried in two good-size logs, banked the fire in the oven, fed the children, and paced back and forth across the kitchen.

"Is it time, Mama?" Oliver asked.

Eliza shook her head. "It's too early. This might be nothing more than a touch of indigestion. Louella can stay with me, but you and Ben Roland should take the others into the bedroom. Read them a story, or get them interested in playing some kind of game."

Oliver nodded. He was not yet 12 but had the worried look of an old man stretched across his face. "Should I fetch Aunt Caldonia?"

"Not yet. I'm just having a hard day. Now do as I say; keep a close eye on Margaret Rose and Virgil."

After he'd herded the children into the bedroom, Oliver returned every few minutes, poked his head into the kitchen, and asked how she was doing. Waving him off, Eliza claimed there was nothing to worry about. The expression on Oliver's face didn't change. He looked at Louella and said, "When it's time for Mama to have the baby, you've gotta tell me."

"I ain't never done this before. How am I gonna know when it's time?"

Oliver made a decision, slipped out the door, and headed for the pathway to the Markey house. When he pushed back the barrel and crawled into Caldonia's kitchen, he looked like a frightened squirrel.

She turned from the stove and smiled at him. "Land sakes, what's gotten into you?"

"Mama says it's too early for the baby," he wheezed, "but she looks like—"

Grabbing a jacket from the hook and not bothering about a scarf, Caldonia followed Oliver back to the house, matching him step for step as they hurried along. When they got there, Eliza had stopped pacing. She was hunched over, holding onto the chair, her face now scarlet and drenched in a slick of sweat.

Caldonia grabbed her by the arm and led her toward the bedroom. "Don't tell me it's too early. This baby is coming whether you're ready or not." Over her shoulder, she told Oliver to set three kettles of water on the stove and fetch an armful of dry logs.

"Get that fire burning hot, then gather up some towels and clean rags."

Lowering Eliza into the bed, she asked, "How long you been having pains?"

"Since yesterday, but—" Her muscles tensed, and her head rolled back as the pain slammed into her back. "It's not like the other times, and I thought…"

A look of concern creased Caldonia's brow. "That baby should've been here by now. Let's see if I can figure out what's going on."

She lifted the gown and began inching her fingers across Eliza's stomach. Starting low, she worked her way up, moving first to the right, then back again, feeling with her fingers, smoothing her palm across a spot, then moving her fingers along pressing ever so slightly. When another round of birthing pains came, she held her ear to Eliza's stomach and cupped her hands atop the bump she'd felt.

Once the pain ended, she sat up. "The baby's breech. Its head is right here." She touched her hand to the spot just below Eliza's breastbone.

Eliza's eyes were wide with fear. "Dear God. What do we…"

Giving Eliza's thigh a comforting pat, Caldonia said, "Don't you worry none. We're gonna turn this little bugger around and get him moving." She hollered for Ben Roland and told him to take a bucket, go down to the creek, and gather as many chunks of ice as he could find.

"Send Oliver," Eliza said with a groan. "He's…"

"Ben Roland can do it," Caldonia replied. "I want Oliver here in case…" Her words fell away as Eliza stiffened in pain yet again.

When Ben Roland returned with the bucket of ice, Caldonia wrapped several large chunks in a wet rag and placed it on the spot where she'd felt the baby's head.

Eliza shivered. "Oooh…that's too…"

"It's cold, I know. It's gotta be," Caldonia said. "This little devil has settled in warm and cozy. If his head starts feeling cold, he might look to move."

Eliza sucked in a long breath and winced as another birthing pain took hold of her. They came often now; too often.

"Caldonia," she whispered, "if something happens to me, tell Martin—"

"Ain't nothing going to happen to you. And the only thing I'm gonna tell Martin Hobbs is that he should've had his no-good ass here to welcome this baby into the world."

Before Eliza could answer, she felt her stomach push hard to the right.

"Glory be." Caldonia grinned. "It looks like this little fella is turning himself around."

Almost two hours passed before the baby's head was where Caldonia wanted it. When the biggest pain yet came, she told Eliza to bear down hard. Moments later, Nellie Hobbs was born.

Spring came late that year but summer followed close behind, and as the days grew long Eliza began to realize that Martin would not be back anytime soon. Perhaps never. Nellie's birth had been difficult. It left her body drained and unable to do all she'd done the summer before. That year the garden was smaller and more manageable but less bountiful. When the first frost covered the ground, the pantry was less than half full.

Over the past two years Martin had been fairly generous, and Eliza, always fearful that she would one day find the wolf at the door, saved every spare penny. That winter she thanked God for having done so, because it seemed that they were always in need of something. Flour, lard, molasses, lamp oil, the list was endless, and bit by bit the money in her sack dwindled. With the pantry less than half full, it seemed that every week they ran out of something else.

When the year ended, she and Caldonia sat on the front porch looking up at the night sky and talking of what the future might bring.

"Do you believe he'll ever come back?" Caldonia asked.

Eliza shrugged. "It happened before. It could happen again."

"Last time, you went to Charleston looking for him. Do you think you'd do that again?"

"Not yet," Eliza said. "I've got enough money left to tide us over a while longer, and I'd like to give Martin a chance to come home because he loves me and the children."

"What if he doesn't?"

Eliza shrugged again. "I'm sure 1907 can't possibly be as bad as what we've already gone through."

In early February, Ben Roland was shooting at a jackrabbit when the Browning that had been handed down from Eliza's daddy exploded in his hand. It was too dangerous to even think about using the shotgun again, so she spent $28 for a new Winchester and had to take Ben Roland to the doctor three different times. That same month Oliver started limping, and she discovered it was because his big toe was pushed up against the end of his boot. Again, there was no recourse but to spend the money for a new pair of boots, which was another $3.25.

That spring she walked down to the general store and took Louella with her. While Eliza was selecting the thread she needed for mending a dress, Louella explored the shelves and caught sight of a blue satin hair ribbon.

Tugging on her mama's sleeve, she whispered, "This is the most beautiful hair bow I ever seen. Please, can I have it? I won't ask for nothing else ever, I swear."

The ribbon was the color of Louella's eyes. Eliza glanced down at the price. Five cents. For five cents she could buy a box of salt or a small bag of flour. She hesitated for several seconds and shook her head. As Louella put the ribbon back on the shelf without a word of complaint, Eliza saw the sadness in her daughter's eyes.

That night after the children were asleep, Eliza sat alone on the porch. She watched the moon rise higher in the sky, and a great sorrow settled on her shoulders. It was unfair that the children should have to do without even the tiniest pleasures when Martin denied himself nothing.

She thought back on a time when the two of them sat on this same porch and remembered how he'd promised her the world. She'd never asked for the world. She'd asked only that he be a father to their children. A man who would see to it that his daughter had a ribbon for her hair and his sons wore shoes that fit.

A new anger rose inside of her. Before she'd held it back, believing it better for the children. It wasn't better. Not for her; not for any of them. Martin had a responsibility and it was high time he lived up to it, regardless of how he felt about her having another child.

As the last stars faded from the sky, Eliza made her decision. She would go to Charleston while she still had money enough for train fare. She would stand face to face with Martin and demand that he provide for his family. And if he refused, she would follow him to the union hall and shame him in front of his friends.

Whatever she had to do, she would do.

Three days later, Caldonia was babysitting all eight children and Eliza was on the 7:15 train headed to Charleston. Martin never worked on Sunday, so chances were she'd find him at the apartment quite possibly still asleep. If she knocked on the door and he didn't answer, she'd pound on it until he did. And if he had already gone out, she would sit on the front stoop and wait for him to return.

She'd thought of everything, including the possibility that he had another woman living with him. If that were the case, she was prepared to tell him he could do as he wanted as long as he made provisions for their children. The only thing she would not do is leave without some sort of satisfaction.

Anxious to save time, she took the trolley from the train station to Jackson Street and walked across to the apartment building. It had been four years since she'd last been there, and the building seemed different somehow. As she climbed the four flights of stairs she listened for the sound of something familiar, but there was only the tinny whine of a harmonica and a baby's cry.

Standing in front of the door, she took a deep breath, squared her shoulders, and knocked. Voices came from inside, and a woman hollered, "Just a moment." It was as she'd thought; he had someone with him.

Eliza steeled herself for the confrontation. Right off she would tell the woman she'd not come to cause her grief, that her being there was about the children and nothing more.

Seconds later, the door swung open. "What you want?"

For a moment Eliza was too shocked to speak. There was indeed a woman, but she was smaller than a child with a hunched back and a topknot of cottony white hair.

"I'm sorry to bother you," Eliza said. "I'm looking for Martin Hobbs."

The woman shrugged. "I no know."

"Martin Hobbs," Eliza repeated. "He lives here in this apartment."

"He no live here." The woman turned and called, "Berto, come."

A man who was only marginally taller than the woman hobbled to the door. "What is it that you need?"

Eliza felt a rush of fear thicken in her throat. "I'm... I'm...looking for Martin Hobbs. He's supposed to live here."

The old man shook his head. "Not here. We been here a year. Maybe you got the wrong apartment?"

"Maybe," Eliza said and turned away.

She tried to think.

Maybe he got a better apartment. Maybe he's down the block or around the corner.

On the third-floor landing, she stopped and knocked on Gertrude Sloan's door. Gertrude opened the door, and before Eliza could say anything she shook her head.

"You're too late. He moved out."

Her words hit Eliza like the sting of a hornet. "When did this happen? Was it recent? Did he say where he was going?"

Gertrude gave a cynical snort. "Me and him didn't talk much. He didn't like me any more than I did him."

"Would he have told anyone else in the building? The landlord, maybe?"

Gertrude shook her head again. "I doubt it. He moved out owing rent." She watched the way Eliza was leaning over on the door jam. "You okay? You look like you need to sit a spell."

"I'm okay," Eliza replied, even though she wasn't.

When she left the building, Eliza didn't take the trolley and walked back to the train station. As she forced herself to move one foot in front of the other, she came to realize that in the back of her mind she'd always believed sooner or later Martin would return home. During the hard times, she'd held onto that belief and comforted herself with the knowledge that if the situation became desperate she could go to Charleston and find him. Now that last thread of hope was gone.

In an effort to quell the panic rising in her chest, she pictured the children and thought of how she might provide for them. A woman alone had few resources. A woman with eight children had none.

For now they had a house to live in, water to drink, and land to farm. They would not starve. She would teach the children to be strong and independent, and somehow they would survive.

That summer Eliza used most of what she had in the sack to buy seed and shells for the Winchester. Jeb plowed the ground, and before the sun had cleared the horizon Eliza and the three older boys were working in the field. Oliver was 13 that year and strong enough to carry a 50-pound bag of seed on his back without buckling beneath the weight of it.

In late July a rainstorm came up, and they stood on the back porch looking out at the stalks of corn rising from the ground. Alongside the corn were rows of pole beans, squash, and sweet potatoes. As the droplets of rain splashed against the plants, Eliza smiled.

"It's going to be a good year," she told the boys. "We'll have enough to feed ourselves and extra to sell."

The rain continued through the night and well into the next day. There were times when it slowed to a drizzle and Eliza grew hopeful that was the end of it, but it wasn't. On the fourth day the wind picked up, and they heard thunder in the distance. By then the rain was coming in torrents, and the roof had sprung a leak in the bedroom. Oliver volunteered to climb onto the roof and patch the hole, but Eliza shook her head.

"Not until this rain stops," she said and set a bucket beneath the drip.

For two days the thunderstorms continued, at times the rain so heavy the bucket would fill in a matter of minutes. Eliza's heart grew heavy as she stood at the window and watched.

"Lord God, I hope this stops soon," she said. "The crops can't take much more."

At 3:00 that afternoon, the sky turned a sickly shade of green and there was the roar of a train in the distance.

"Tornado!" Eliza screamed.

Snatching Nellie from the floor and herding the little ones playing nearby, she screamed for Oliver and the others to come quickly. As they hurried out to the root cellar the wind stilled, and Oliver suggested maybe they'd seen the last of the storm.

"We haven't," she said as she lifted the door and rushed the children down the steps. Once everyone was inside, she climbed in behind them, pulled the door closed, and slid the latch into place.

She hadn't thought to bring a lamp so the tiny space was pitch-black, cold, and rank with the smell of dampness. There was no room to move about or sit, so they stood shoulder to shoulder waiting for what was to come.

"I'm scared," Margaret Rose cried. "I wanna go in the house."

"Not yet," Eliza replied.

For a few moments, the silence was almost deafening. Then came the terrible roar of wind, the crashing of trees, and a shattering sound that filled Eliza's heart with dread. She told the children to each hold onto each other's hands and spoke the words she'd learned as a child.

"Our Father, who art in Heaven, hallowed be they name..." When the prayer was finished, she asked that He keep them safe and spare their home from what most certainly would be destruction.

There was no way of knowing how long the storm remained overhead. Once the howling ceased and the air grew still, Eliza stayed there in the safety of the root cellar trying to find courage enough to release the latch and venture out. When she finally did she lifted the door, looked up at the sky, and saw a bright sun overhead.

Emerging from the cellar, she was relieved to see the house still standing and devastated to find a good part of the crops lost. A Virginia pine had fallen across the lower half of the cornfield, and much of it was lost. The sweet potatoes were spared but would come in puny, as would the pole beans. At best it would be a pitifully small harvest; certainly not enough to see them through the winter.

For the remainder of the day, they worked at clearing away the debris and shoring up a section of the back porch that had been torn loose. Later that night after the children had gone to sleep, Eliza sat at the kitchen table and wrote two letters. The first was to the Brotherhood of Electrical Workers in Charleston. It told of her predicament and asked if they could provide a recent address for Martin Hobbs.

The second was to the Masonic Lodge. In this one she said the family had fallen on hard times and would very much appreciate any assistance they might be able to provide. She explained the devastation of the tornado.

My husband was extremely proud of being a Mason and often spoke of the good works you do, she wrote, *so I am praying that you take this into account and help us.*

She signed both letters *Mrs. Martin Hobbs.*

⊂⊃⊛⊂⊃

On August 24th, Eliza received a response from the Electrical Workers Union. The typed letter was brief and to the point. It stated that Martin Hobbs was no longer a member of Local 466 in Charleston and went on to say that at present it was not known whether or not he was affiliated with another local. The letter was signed "Charles E. Waterson."

A week later a loud rumble sounded from the road, and when Eliza looked out there was an automobile parked in the front yard. She'd seen automobiles in the streets of Charleston, but to the best of her knowledge there had never been one in Coal Creek. A man in a dark suit climbed out of the car just as she stepped down from the porch.

"Mrs. Hobbs?" he said.

When she nodded, he went on to say he was Edward Wolff from the Brotherhood of Masons and had come in response to her letter. Oliver and Ben Roland stood to the side goggling at the car as if it were a thing not to be believed. Wolff motioned them over.

"Fetch the boxes in the back seat and carry them inside." Turning back to Eliza, he said, "I would have been here yesterday, but I had a devil of a time figuring out exactly where your home was and there were no telephone listings for Coal Creek in the Charleston directory."

She laughed. "That's because there are no telephones in Coal Creek."

He followed her back inside the house, and they settled at the kitchen table.

"We were terribly sorry to hear of your family's difficulties," he said. "Has Brother Martin fallen ill?"

"Not that I know of," Eliza replied. "He simply disappeared."

A look of concern tugged at Wolff's face. "Have you reported this to the police?"

"No, but I've tried to find him. I went to his apartment in Charleston and discovered him gone. No one could say why or to where. I wrote to the union, but they too know nothing." She handed him the letter she'd received from Charles Waterson.

"It's strange an electrician of his caliber would walk away from such a well-paying industry. Unless… Do you think Martin may have been the victim of foul play?"

Eliza hesitated, wondering if the Masons would also abandon her once they learned Martin had done so. Wolff struck her as a man who would be more offended by a lie than an ugly truth. He had a kind face and compassion in his eyes.

"I doubt it was anything like that," she said. "I think he has simply chosen to walk away from his family."

"Walk away? For no reason?"

"I'm afraid so." She told the whole story of how Martin had railed at the thought of another baby, how she'd found Bess at his apartment, and how she'd slid a letter in his pocket to tell him she was expecting another child and then never heard from him again.

"That was a year ago last November before Nellie was born."

"Eight children?" Turning his head one way and then the other, he examined the place. "Isn't this house rather small for a family of such a size?"

"I suppose it is, but it's home so we make do. This was my parents' house so it costs us nothing to live here, which right now is a godsend."

He stretched his arm across the table and patted her hand. "Mrs. Hobbs, you've had to endure more hardships than necessary. Our lodge will be happy to provide assistance for your family until your husband is found."

Eliza smiled. "I thank you from the bottom of my heart, Mr. Wolff, but I don't know that you'll be able to find Martin. I've tried every—"

"Trust me, Mrs. Hobbs, unless your husband has left the country, we will find him." He stood and reached for her hand. "These cartons contain foodstuffs and a small amount of money to tide you over. I will be in touch once we know something more."

For the first time in many months, Eliza felt a flutter of hope in her heart.

Edward Wolff

On the drive back to Charleston, Wolff couldn't stop thinking about Eliza Hobbs and her eight children crowded into that tiny house and struggling to stay afloat. She appeared to be a good woman with a warm smile and a gentle disposition. Her children were in need of proper clothing perhaps but they were well-mannered and obliging. The little one was just over a year old and already a heartbreaker. What could induce a man to leave a family such as that?

Wolff pictured Hobbs, always freshly shaven with his hair slicked back and the scent of cologne about him. He didn't seem a man who was hurting for money. He was an electrician, and there was no shortage of work in that field. Had he been injured? Was he unable to work? If that were the case, wouldn't he have turned to his Brothers at the lodge for help?

Wolff thought about that for a while, then remembered Eddie Beckerman. The man had been a proud Mason before he gambled his money away and ended up penniless. Beckerman had not turned to the Brothers for help. Instead he'd abandoned his family. Six months later he drowned himself in the Kanawha River.

It was unlikely Hobbs would follow Beckerman's pathway. He was too cocky, too sure of himself. Confident there had to be another cause, Wolff spent a week mulling the reasons why a man like Hobbs would disappear.

After he'd considered all possibilities, he came to two conclusions: Hobbs was either a crook or a cad.

At the next meeting Wolff sought out Jimmy Wilkes.

"I haven't seen Brother Hobbs at a meeting for quite some time. I hope he's not ill."

"He's not ill, just lucky." Wilkes laughed. "He moved. Got a great job in Altoona."

"Moved, did he? Altoona, Pennsylvania?"

Wilkes nodded. "I would've taken that job myself, but the wife didn't want to leave Charleston."

"Just as well," Wolff said and smiled. "We would have missed having you with us. I'm headed up north in a few weeks. Maybe I'll stop in and say hello to Brother Hobbs. Do you recall the name of his company?"

"Beamer. Beamer Electric. If you see Martin, tell him I said hi."

"I will," Wolff said with a determined nod. "I certainly will."

The next morning Wolff telephoned Carson and Edwards Investigations.

"I'd like you to look into a man living in your area," he said. "The fellow's name is Martin Hobbs, he's an electrician by trade, and the last I heard he was employed by Beamer Electric in Altoona."

"What do you want to know about him?" Carson asked.

"Everything. Where he lives, his salary, his general lifestyle. I want to know where he goes and who he spends his time with." He went on to explain that Hobbs had moved off under rather suspicious circumstances and asked how long such an investigation would take.

"If he's still at Beamer, it'll be quick; a month, maybe less."

In the weeks that followed, Wolff did more than wait. He spent one afternoon at the Electricians Union Hall and discovered that Hobbs was indeed not only a member of good standing but a union rep for Local 914 in Altoona. He also visited the apartment building where Hobbs had lived. Although Gertrude Sloan knew little about Hobbs's life outside of the building she knew plenty about what went on inside, and she was more than willing to talk.

The more Wolff learned about Martin Hobbs, the more he disliked him. When Carson's report arrived in late September, it was nine pages long and quite detailed. It told of how Hobbs had a fine house, lived with his wife, Martha Mae, employed a part-time housekeeper, and dined out frequently. He'd included a detailed description of the house and Martha Mae. Wolff studied the report thoroughly and decided to take action. One week later, he was on a train headed for Pennsylvania.

It was mid-morning when Wolff arrived in Altoona. The trip had been long and tedious, but he'd spent the time thinking of when and how to approach Hobbs. Although he'd originally planned to go directly to Beamer, he'd since thought better of it. Beamer, the union, and the Masons were going to be three of his bargaining chips. From the train station, he went to the hotel, freshened up, and took a short nap. At 5 pm he left the hotel, took a taxi to Hobbs's house, and rapped on the door.

A woman in fine clothing answered. He smiled and tipped his hat.

"You must be Martha Mae. I've been looking forward to meeting you." Without waiting for an invitation, he brushed by her and moved into the foyer. "I assume Martin will be arriving home soon."

She stood there looking bewildered for a moment. "Yes, he'll be home soon. Was he expecting you?"

"I'm afraid not." He introduced himself as Edward Wolff, a fellow Mason from the Charleston lodge.

"Oh. Well then. You want to wait?" She gave a nod toward the front parlor and gestured for him to come along. Once he'd settled in the club chair, she asked if he'd like a drink.

"A glass of water, please, or lemonade if you have it."

"We've got lemonade or whiskey if you want."

"Lemonade will do just fine. Brother Hobbs and I have business to talk over, and I don't want my brain to get fuzzy."

She disappeared into the kitchen and returned with two drinks, a lemonade for him, a whiskey for her.

"I don't mind my brain getting fuzzy," she said and laughed. "It feels good."

"Yes, I suppose it does." He'd said it in a sarcastic way, but she seemed not to notice. "While we're waiting, why don't you tell me a bit about you and Martin? Have the two of you been married long?"

She shook her head. "Not really. We met back in Charleston. We were seeing each other for a while, and he had that crummy apartment;

then all of sudden he got this great job offer. That's when he said, 'We need a fresh start, Martha Mae, so we're going to Altoona, and you're gonna be my new wife.' We got married here." She leaned forward and in a conspiratorial way whispered, "He was married once before, but it didn't work out so well."

An hour ambled by before Martin made it home, and by the time he did Martha Mae had already told Wolff all about what a wonderful life they had there.

"It's way better than it was in Charleston," she'd said.

Seeing Edward Wolff sitting in his living room gave Martin a start. With a forced smile, he said, "Brother Wolff, what a pleasant surprise. Are you in Pennsylvania on business?"

"Actually, I'm here to speak with you."

Martin nodded to Martha Mae as he sat down. "Honey, why don't you wait in the—"

"I'd rather she stay. She needs to hear this."

"This sounds bad," Martin said with a nervous laugh. "Have I forgotten to take care of something at the lodge?"

"No, what you've forgotten to take care of is your wife and eight children in Coal Creek."

"Eight?!" Martha Mae screeched. "You told me you had three boys!"

Ignoring her, Martin jumped to his feet and glared at Wolff. "That's none of your business. You've got one hell of a nerve even coming here. Get out and don't—"

"You're wrong. It *is* my business because your wife came to us looking for assistance when the family didn't have food enough—"

Martin's face turned scarlet. "I said get out! I'm not interested in—"

"You'd better get interested pretty damn quick, otherwise I go to Beamer and the union," Wolff interrupted, his expression as stony as the rock of Gibraltar. "I can assure you, they'll be very interested in what I have to say. When I'm finished, you can pretty much kiss your job and your union position goodbye."

Martha Mae stared at Martin as if she wanted to run a knife through his heart.

Martin shook his head with disgust. "So what is it you want, Wolff? You want me to say I'm sorry? Well, I'm not. I spent a lot of years supporting her and those kids. It was time I did something for myself."

"Losing your job and your union position isn't the worst of it, Hobbs. You could also end up spending the next ten years in jail."

"For leaving my wife? That doesn't mean—"

"You disgust me, Hobbs, but that's not enough to put you in jail. Bigamy, however is. You didn't bother to divorce Eliza Hobbs before you married the charming Martha Mae here in Pennsylvania. That makes you a bigamist. The penalty for bigamy is ten years, so unless you're looking to—"

"Gimme a break, Wolff. I had a chance to better my life, and I took it. Is that such a terrible crime? You'd do the exact same as me if you had the chance."

Wolff shook his head. "No, Hobbs, I wouldn't. That's the difference in us."

Martin folded his arms across his chest and looked up at the ceiling. "Spare me the sermon. Just tell me what you want."

Wolff sat there for several seconds saying nothing. He leaned forward, his fingers tented, and his eyes fixed on Martin's face. "You miss the point. This isn't about what I want. It's about getting your wife and children what they deserve."

"Okay, you win. I'll start sending them something every month. Twenty bucks maybe. You good with that?"

"No. If you want to stay out of jail and keep your job, I expect you to bring your family here to Pennsylvania, find a house with an appropriate number of bedrooms, pay for their support, and see your children a couple times a month."

Martha Mae jumped up. "Oh no, you don't! Under no circumstances do I want them here!"

Shoving her back onto the sofa, Martin said, "Stay out of it."

"No, I won't! Do what you want about the kids, but she's not coming here!"

"Shut up, Martha Mae." He turned back to Wolff. "What you're suggesting is impossible. I can't afford it. I don't make enough—"

"Save your breath," Wolff said. "I know exactly how much you make, what you paid for this house, how much you've got in the bank, what you rake in as a union rep, and—"

"What'd you do, have me investigated?"

"Of course. Do you think I'd make the trip without knowing I've got enough leverage to force you into doing what any respectable man should do?"

A look of defeat settled on Martin's face, and he scrubbed his hand across his forehead. "This is going to kill me. I'll be working my ass off for next to nothing. What about if I could see my way clear to send her forty bucks a month? Would that—"

"No, it would not. You either agree to what I'm suggesting tonight, or tomorrow I start talking to the folks at Beamer. Even if you're lucky enough to avoid jail time, you'll be blackballed in the industry."

Martin shook his head and dropped down on the sofa. "You're not giving me much wiggle room here."

"I'm being far more generous with you than you were with Eliza and the children."

They spent another hour arguing over one thing and another, but in the end Wolff refused to budge. Once he'd laid out exactly what he was expecting Hobbs to do, he added that he had a man in town who would be keeping an eye on him to make sure he followed through.

"And don't even think about skipping out the way you did last time, because before you make it to the next town I'll have the authorities on you."

As Wolff started down the walkway, he heard Martha Mae screaming at Martin. Justly deserved, he thought and turned toward town.

1968

Wheeling, West Virginia

On the morning they were to leave Huntington, Margaret and Tom planned to have breakfast at the hotel. They agreed to meet at 8:30 in the coffee shop. Arriving on the dot, Margaret slid into a booth where she could keep an eye on the door.

"Just coffee for now," she told the waitress. "I'm meeting someone and will wait for him."

After finishing the first cup, she ordered a second and knew right away that was a mistake. She was already feeling a bit anxious, and the extra caffeine was making her even jumpier. Tom was almost always there before her, and he'd never been this late. She knew for certain she hadn't missed him, because she'd had her eyes glued to the door and had watched any number of people come and go. Pushing her cup to the side, she glanced at her watch and held it to her ear to make sure it was still ticking.

She waited until 9:15 then flagged the waitress and asked for her bill. Something was drastically wrong, she could feel it. She'd already checked out so she couldn't go through the connecting doors of their rooms, but she could bang on the main door to his room. If he didn't answer, she'd have the maid unlock it. As a scenario of the worst that could happen ran through her head, she prayed he was okay and not sick, not lying face down on the floor. Although she'd had nothing more than coffee, she left two dollar bills on the table, gathered her things, and headed for the exit. Before she was halfway there he came hurrying in, his face flushed and a grin tugging at the corners of his mouth.

"Where have you been?" she asked angrily. "I've been worried sick."

"You were worried about me?"

"Well, of course I was! With all the driving you've had to do, I thought…oh, never mind. Why on earth did you leave me siting here all this time?"

"Sorry about that. I had to pick something up before we left, and the drugstore didn't open until nine." He handed her the packet he was carrying. "I thought you might enjoy looking at these on the drive to Wheeling."

"Are these the pictures you've been taking?"

"Yep. When we find Oliver, I know you'll want to tell him of your visit with Dewey and Caldonia. Now you can also show him the photos."

She noticed that he'd said "when" not "if" they found Oliver, and whatever irritation she'd felt earlier vanished.

"Thank you. That was so very thoughtful."

Once they slid back into the booth, she decided the caffeine wasn't bothering her after all and ordered another coffee. Lingering over breakfast to look through the pictures a third and then fourth time, they didn't get on the road until almost noon.

"According to the map, Wheeling is pretty far north up in that spike of West Virginia," Tom said. "I figure we've got about two hundred and fifty, maybe three hundred miles of driving. We can do a longer day on the road or stop somewhere. What's your preference?"

Thinking back on how she'd fretted in the coffee shop, Margaret replied, "Stop somewhere. I don't want to worry myself sick about all this driving being too much for you."

Tom laughed out loud. "You've got nothing to worry about, Maggie. I feel more energized than I've been in a decade, and I'm enjoying every minute of this trip. Stopping on the way and exploring a new town, well, now, that will just make it all the sweeter."

They drove until 3:30 and stopped in Parkersburg.

"I've heard this is a pretty interesting town," Tom said, slowing down. "It's old; has a fort that dates back to the Civil War."

With no reservations or pre-arranged plans, they drove around town for almost an hour passing narrow buildings standing side by side like sisters, antebellum houses that were the gracefully aging grand dames of their era, and a church so beautiful it took Margaret's breath away. On the corner of Fourth and Market, she spotted a red brick building with peaked roofs and a turret standing tall above everything.

"Look," she said and waggled a finger at the building. "That's a hotel."

"Want to give it a try?" Tom asked.

She nodded. "Absolutely. It looks so old and interesting."

This time when they registered, they asked for adjoining rooms. Since there was no searching to be done in Parkersburg, they spent the last hour of daylight walking through Julia-Ann Square and turned down Avery Street. When they crossed over Eighth, Margaret hooked her arm through Tom's without giving it a second thought.

He looked down at her and smiled. "It's nice doing spur-of-the-moment things like this. I've done a lot of traveling but usually flew in, took care of business, then flew out without taking time to look around."

"Didn't you feel you were missing out on something?"

"Not until now."

They stopped there on the street and exchanged a meaningful glance. After a moment, Margaret's cheeks flushed and she looked away. She heard Tom chuckle and debated about pulling her arm away but at the last minute decided against it and kept it there until they stopped for a drink at a tiny tavern tucked back from the street.

◠◟◉◞◠

The next morning, Margaret eagerly agreed when Tom suggested they take another drive through town and find a spot for breakfast. After they'd traveled the full length of Market Street and taken another spin around Julia-Ann Square, they turned onto 14th Street and parked in front of a little restaurant called Ada's Lunch. Sitting at the counter, Tom asked what was good. The blue-eyed woman behind the counter smiled.

"Everything," she said, "Lyn Skaggs is the cook." She laughed then added, "He's also my husband."

They lingered over a second and then third cup of coffee as Ada told them how the Biennerhassett family had settled here and built a grand estate on an island in the Ohio River.

"It's a shame you're not staying longer," she said. "There's a lot to do and see here."

"Maybe next time," Margaret said, although she knew there wouldn't be a next time. The thing about having this kind of fun was that once it was over, a person had to forget it and move on.

After leaving Ada's, they drove straight through to Wheeling and checked in at the McLure House Hotel. Just as they'd done in Huntington they scanned the telephone directory, and while there was no listing for Oliver Hobbs they did get the number and address of the Superior Glass Manufacturing Company on the outskirts of town.

"We'll drive out there tomorrow morning," Tom said. "A phone call would be quicker, but people are more responsive when you're talking to them in person."

❧

At the Superior Glass Company, they found that Oliver had worked there for 47 years and retired as a plant manager in 1957. The young man behind the desk looked up from the file folder and gave Margaret a polite nod.

"I didn't know Mr. Hobbs personally, but I believe he was very well thought of."

Margaret smiled. "That's nice to hear. I'll be sure to let him know. We couldn't get a listing for him from the telephone directory. Do you have his address?"

The man blinked and leafed through the file a second time. "We only keep files on retirees who are still eligible for benefits. After Mr. Hobbs passed away, we closed the file."

Margaret's face fell. "Oliver's dead?"

The man removed his glasses and pinched the bridge of his nose. "I'm terribly sorry. I assumed you knew."

Tom stepped in. "We understand. Can you tell me what year the file was closed?"

"Nineteen sixty-three," he said and sat there blinking.

Taking her elbow, Tom steered Margaret toward the door.

"Come on, Maggie, let's find Oliver's family," he said softly. "You'll want to meet them."

Their next stop was the public library. Since they knew the year, it took less than a half-hour of scanning the back issues of the *Wheeling News Register* for Tom to find the obituary. It said, "Oliver Hobbs (1894-1963) passed away peacefully at home and was survived by his wife, Lois Jean Hobbs; his daughter, Jolyn Carter Carroll; son-in-law, Walter Carter Carroll; and two grandsons." The obituary went on to mention Oliver's work at the glass manufacturing company and even included a few quotes from coworkers. The man behind the desk had been right; Oliver was well thought of indeed.

Although it was a bittersweet compensation for not being able to see Oliver, Margaret spoke to Jolyn on the telephone that afternoon.

"I don't know if your daddy ever talked about his family," she said. "Oliver was my big brother. I'm his sister, Margaret Rose."

"Of course, Dad talked about all of you. Ben Roland, Dewey, Virgil... He used to tell us about all the wonderful adventures you had living in Coal Creek."

Margaret wondered if the big family secret wasn't such a secret after all. Maybe Oliver had spoken of it openly. If that was the case, would Jolyn know what had happened all those years ago?

"I'm only in town for another day or two," she said. "I'd love to get together. Maybe meet for dinner?"

"Would you mind coming here?" Jolyn asked. "That way Walter and the boys can meet you. After all the tales their granddaddy's told, I know the boys are going to be very excited at the prospect of meeting their great aunt."

Margaret explained that she was traveling with a friend who'd been helping her locate members of the family and said they'd love to come.

When she met the Carroll family Margaret could see nothing of Oliver in his daughter, but Benjamin, the older of Jolyn's two boys, looked exactly as Oliver had at that age. Peter, the younger boy, looked like his mama.

Jolyn had a bright smile, and she laughed easily as she spoke about her dad's stories.

"Why, he had both of my boys asking to go live in Coal Creek so they could fish and hunt and see the corn that grew taller than a man." She gave a wistful sigh. "I never knew how many of Dad's stories were true, but he sure did make it sound like he'd had a wonderful childhood. Well, until the tornado came through."

Margaret was taken aback by that description of their life. "Yes, that tornado was scary for sure. It sounded like a train coming across the mountain, tore trees from the ground, and carried away Mama's favorite rocking chair."

Jolyn nodded. "That's the same way Dad described it. He said after the tornado killed his daddy and destroyed the house, the family broke apart with each of the kids going to stay with a distant relative, neighbor, or friend; wherever there was room. That's when Dad came here. He sometimes sounded sad talking about how everyone was separated. I don't think he ever really got over that part of it, and I couldn't help but wonder if there was something more to the story."

Margaret paused. "He never spoke about Pennsylvania?"

Jolyn shook her head. "Dad never lived in Pennsylvania, at least not to my knowledge."

A light clicked on in Margaret's head. She realized Oliver had kept the secret after all. If that was what he wanted his daughter to believe, she would not say differently.

Giving a lighthearted laugh, she said, "It was something our daddy used to joke about. He worked there for a while and was always saying if we kids didn't behave ourselves, he'd bring us to Pennsylvania and leave us there." She saw the confusion on Tom's face and ignored it. Instead, she asked about Lois, Oliver's wife.

"I lost both parents that same year. When Dad died, Mama gave up on living." Jolyn absently brushed back a strand of hair that had fallen onto her forehead. "We begged her to come and live with us, but she wouldn't do it. Mama loved their old house the same as she loved Dad and couldn't stand to be separated from either of them. The doctor said it was pneumonia, but we knew better." She gave a sad smile. "Mama used to say, 'Marry a man like your daddy, and you'll never regret it.' She certainly never regretted marrying Dad."

"Your mother sounds like a wonderful woman," Margaret said.

"She was. Both my parents were. I was truly blessed to have a mom and dad like those two, and they were blessed to have each other."

As the two women sat sharing stories of the past, Jolyn suggested she bring out her photo albums.

"I've a thousand pictures of Mom and Dad," she said, "and I really think you'd enjoy seeing them."

"I certainly would," Margaret replied.

"I'll leave you ladies to enjoy yourselves," Walter said. "I'd like to show Tom the workshop I built in the basement."

Jolyn laughed. "Don't be fooled by the term workshop. Walter has his radio down there and spends more time listening to ballgames than working."

"Guilty as charged," Walter said with a laugh as they disappeared down the stairs.

After the children went to bed, Margaret and Jolyn sat side by side on the sofa poring over albums filled with pictures capturing the happy moments of their life. Oliver and Lois on their wedding day; the house they'd lived in for over 40 years; Lois, young and pregnant; Oliver holding an infant to his shoulder, his smile brighter than any Margaret could ever remember. As they went from one album to the next she saw Oliver age and Lois grow plumper, but the happiness on their faces never changed. On their 25th anniversary they'd celebrated with a wedding cake and a room full of friends, a very pregnant Jolyn and a young Walter whose hair had not yet thinned standing by their side. Several times Margaret had to brush back tears, but they were tears of happiness. After they finished going through the albums, Jolyn handed Margaret a stack of photos.

"These are some extra copies. I thought you might want to have them."

It was after midnight when they said their goodbyes and left. Once the house was gone from view, Margaret turned to Tom. "Sad as I am to know Oliver's gone, I'm glad to know he had a happy life."

Tom stopped for a red light. "A very happy life, according to his daughter."

She nodded. "What Oliver told her about his coming to Wheeling right after the tornado wasn't true. We did leave home not long after the storm, but we were all still together when we moved to Pennsylvania and we stayed there for two years. Daddy wasn't killed by the tornado. He wasn't even there when it happened."

"I suspected as much. It was nice that you didn't say anything."

Margaret hesitated a few moments before she spoke again.

"There was no reason to. I think Mama would have been proud of Oliver for creating good memories to replace the bad ones. Before I left home, she told me no child should have to carry the burden of bad memories, and I guess Oliver felt the same about what he told his daughter."

The light changed, and Tom pressed down on the accelerator.

"Still, I can't help wondering what secret Oliver felt he had to keep hidden. Do you think we'll ever learn the truth of what happened in Barrettsville?"

He shrugged. "I can't say, Maggie. But we'll keep looking."

Moving On

They stayed in Wheeling for another day, and Margaret spent Saturday afternoon with Jolyn and the children. After lunch they visited the Kruger Street Toy and Train Museum where Margaret enchanted the boys with stories of how she and their granddaddy had once ridden a train just like the toys on display. The mention of a train trip had slipped out, but she covered it gracefully by saying they'd gone from Coal Creek to Charleston and returned the same day.

Jolyn shared more of her dad's stories and Margaret added to them, telling of apples that fell from the tree so sweet you couldn't wait to bite into them and ice-cold lemonade made with well water. When the boys asked for more, she told of the pint-sized barrel door and said it was a playhouse their daddy had built for them.

Peter, the youngest boy's eyes went wide. "Wow, Granddaddy had a real playhouse! Were you allowed to sleep out there at night?"

Jolyn shook her head ever so slightly, and Margaret caught sight of it.

"Good heavens, no," she said. "Our parents knew it was too dangerous for kids to be out all night. Even if you're inside a playhouse, a bear can sneak up and carry you off before you have time to call for your mama."

"We've got a camping tent," Benjamin said. "There's no bears around here, but Mama still won't let us sleep outside unless Daddy stays with us."

"That's because your mama loves you and wants to protect you."

With his little face pulled into a serious expression, Peter nodded. "Was you not allowed 'cause your mama loved you and wanted to protect you from bears?"

Margaret's thoughts jumped back to the day her mama told her she was going to live with Aunt Rose. She'd said, "I'm doing this because I love you and want to protect you from falling into a life such as I've lived." At the time Margaret had not understood. Now she did.

She reached over and smoothed Peter's cowlick into place. "Yes. Our mamas protect us from a lot of things, and while we may not understand their reason at the moment we always know it's because they love us and want us to be happy."

"Well, I'd be happier if I could sleep outside without Daddy," Benjamin said.

Margaret and Jolyn looked at one another and grinned.

When the afternoon was over, Jolyn dropped Margaret off at the hotel. As she watched them drive off, Margaret knew she wanted to see Jolyn and her family again. At first they'd been a sad reminder that Oliver was gone, but after spending time with them she could see they were a living, breathing souvenir of all the good things he'd left behind.

On Sunday morning, before she and Tom checked out of the hotel, Margaret telephoned Josie again. They spoke as if they hadn't seen one another in ages, and if Margaret were truthful with herself it almost felt like she'd stepped back to a different time. Years earlier, when she was less burdened with life, more carefree. How could she not feel that way? With Tom everything seemed so easy. When she was with him she could forget the tough years when she'd thought of nothing but family. She could forget the pain of losing Albert. She could even forget what people back home in Georgia might think if they heard she was traveling around with a man she'd known for such a short time.

Interrupting her thoughts, Josie said, "That Mr. Schoenfeld came by looking for you day before yesterday."

Margaret was taken aback. "Jeffrey came to the house?"

"Uh-huh. I was working in the panty when he rang the doorbell. I said you wasn't here and he asked where you was."

"What did you tell him?"

"I said you was away on family business. That okay?"

Margaret hesitated a moment wondering what Jeffrey would take away from that. "You didn't mention me being with Tom Bateman, did you?"

"Good heavens no. That ain't nobody's business but yours. I knew if you wanted Mr. Schoenfeld to know, you would've told him."

Margaret gave a sigh of relief. "You're right, it is none of his business. He's just trying to make sure I don't sell Albert's interest in the firm to someone else."

Josie laughed. "You don't need to worry about him. Just keep looking for your family. That's what your mama would want you to do."

Margaret took a deep breath and let go of the anxiety she'd started to feel. "You're so right, Josie. So very right."

When she met Tom in the lobby, she didn't mention the telephone call. Instead, she focused on the things she wanted to see in town before they started the long trek to Farstack, Alabama. Now that they'd found everyone else, Tom thought the next move should be to look for Ben Roland's widow.

"She might know where to find Virgil and John Paul," he suggested.

Margaret nodded. With all her heart she hoped that would be the case.

On the far side of town, away from the shops and bustle of Main Street, was a residential area where tricycles and strollers were parked on porches and flowers edged the walkways. They took a leisurely drive through the neighborhood and found the house where Oliver and Lois lived for over forty years, a small cape cod painted white with green shutters at the windows and an oak tree in the side yard. Without stepping inside, Margaret could picture a comfy chair in the living room, Oliver with his long legs stretched out in front of him and Jolyn on his lap as he spun wonderful stories of the childhood that never was. It was a picture she would hold on to for a very long time.

Several blocks from the house was the little church where they'd been married. They passed by just as the service was ending, and as Margaret watched the children frolicking while families chatted with one another, she imagined that was just as it had been when Oliver and his family were part of the congregation. When Tom finally turned toward the highway, she settled back into the seat and gave a wistful sigh.

"Maybe Mama was right in sending us away. It looks like almost all of us have had a better life. I hope the same is true for Virgil and John Paul. I only wish that Louella…"

She turned her face to the window and let the rest of her thought remain unspoken.

The route to Alabama wound along single-lane highways, through towns, and across river roads. Since they'd not gotten on the road until early afternoon, it meant three or four days of driving with few stops in between.

As soon as they left Wheeling and headed west, they were in Ohio. Once on the road with the highway stretched out in front of them, Tom asked if she'd like some music.

"A great idea," Margaret said and switched on the radio. Twisting the dial first one way then the other, she couldn't catch a single station. Every now and again they'd hear a feathered voice or a few bars of a song, but it was mostly static. After ten minutes of trying, she snapped the radio off.

"I guess there's something wrong with it."

"It's not the radio," Tom said. "The reception's poor because we're in the middle of nowhere. It'll be better after we pass Cambridge and get closer to Columbus."

"How far is that?"

"Cambridge is another thirty miles or so, and Columbus is about ninety…"

Tom paused and leaned forward, peering at the dials on the dashboard. With the start of a frown settling on his forehead, he eyed the temperature gauge needle inching up.

"I don't like the looks of this. The motor's too hot."

"What does that mean?" Margaret asked.

"Hopefully nothing. I'll get off at the exit and give the car time to cool down."

Fifty yards from the exit, the red needle began climbing faster and the expression on Tom's face grew more intense. As they neared the end of the ramp, he spotted a small hand-painted sign that read "gas station." The arrow pointed to the right.

Giving a sigh of relief, he said, "We're in luck. They can check the coolant, and we'll be back on the road in no time."

As it turned out, the gas station was over a half mile down the road. In the distance they could see the red neon sign blinking "Open," but when they pulled into the parking lot the station was dark inside. By then the car was puffing steam like a locomotive.

Tom turned the motor off, got out, and tried the door of the gas station. Locked. The cardboard sign stuck to the glass read:

MONDAY THRU SATURDAY 8AM-8PM
SUNDAY 8AM-2PM

Tom checked his watch, and the lines on his forehead grew deeper.

"Hopefully, the engine is just overheated. I'll give it time to cool down."

To Margaret he didn't sound hopeful at all.

He lifted the hood of the car and left it up, the engine still steaming. As he eyed it nervously, he made a feeble attempt at conversation.

"Did you notice what town this is?" he asked.

Margaret shook her head. "I'm not certain it is a town, maybe just a side road?"

Tom nodded apprehensively. "You might be right. Once the car cools down, we can probably make it past Columbus today. We'll look for a hotel in Dayton."

Margaret noticed the stressed look on his face and the way he kept checking the car. Three times he'd said the engine was probably just overheated, but he didn't sound the least bit convincing to her or, apparently, to himself.

"Are we in trouble?" she asked.

He scrubbed his hand across his chin and shrugged. "Not sure. Once the engine is cool enough, I'll check the radiator and the fan belt."

"Good thing you know about things like this. If it were me, I'd have to call a mechanic."

Instead of laughing, Tom pulled a handkerchief from his pocket, reached into the engine, and twisted the radiator cap off. As soon as the burst of steam dissipated, he took a screwdriver from the glove compartment and started poking around. After less than a minute, he stepped back and shook his head.

"Not good. The fan belt's broken."

"Can you fix it?"

"Not without a replacement belt."

For as far as the eye could see, there was nothing except for the general store and two tiny motel cabins directly across the road.

"I doubt they've got a belt," Tom said, "but maybe they can call for a tow truck or put me in touch with the owner of the gas station."

He started across the road, and Margaret hurried to catch up with him.

"Wait a minute," she called, "I don't want to stay here alone. I'll come with you."

The inside of the store looked like it had been there since the turn of the century. The shelves were a jumble of items. For a moment, she felt hopeful they'd have the belt Tom needed.

At the far end of the counter, an old man sat watching a ballgame on television. His back faced them, and the sound was cranked up to the max. Despite the bell on the door, it seemed obvious he hadn't heard them come in. Tom waited for a moment then coughed loudly. When the storekeeper didn't turn, he circled around the counter, came up behind the old man, and called, "Excuse me!"

The old man jumped up, knocked the chair over, and glared at Tom.

"Scare the life out of me, why don'tcha?"

"Sorry. I tried to get your attention, but I guess you didn't hear me."

The old man righted the chair. "What is it you want?"

"I've got a broken fan belt. My car's at the station across the way, and I was wondering if you could call a tow truck."

The old man shook his head. "I could, but Eddie don't tow on Sunday. Not ever."

"Isn't there another towing service?"

"Around here, Eddie's it. He goes fifty miles out, and nobody else comes over here."

"What about the guy who owns the gas station, could you call him? I'll pay whatev—"

"That'd be Eddie."

"Could you at least call and ask? All I need is a fan belt. If Eddie will open the station and give me the belt, I'll pay double and put it on myself."

Again, the old man shook his head. "It'd be a waste of time. On Sunday, Eddie don't bother answering the phone after two o'clock."

Tom pulled in a deep breath, then rolled his head and nervously rubbed the back of his neck. "Any chance you've got a fan belt here?"

"There's a bunch of car stuff on the bottom shelf. I can't say for sure if there's a fan belt or not, but you and the missus are welcome to take a look-see."

"I'm not—" Margaret began, but Tom grabbed her hand and tugged her over to the shelf.

"Don't get into that now. Just help me look for a fan belt."

"What does it look like?"

"A rubber loop this wide." He held up his thumb and forefinger, indicating the size.

After 40 minutes of searching through an assortment of hoses, wiper blades, gas tank caps, visor clips, and Vote for Hubert Humphrey bumper stickers, they admitted defeat and piled everything back on the shelf. By then the old man had finished watching his ball game and turned off the television.

"You find anything?" he asked.

"Afraid not," Tom said. "I guess we'll have to call for a taxi and go into town to get a room for the night."

"There's no town. Cambridge is the closest, and it's a good thirty miles."

"Where is this?"

"Belmont County. This here's farmland that belongs to the county."

Looking more perplexed by the moment, Tom asked, "What about services? Shopping, restaurants, things like that?"

"You gotta go into Cambridge."

"But how do you get into Cambridge?"

"You gotta drive, but seeing as how your car ain't running I guess you'll have to wait 'til Eddie gets here in the morning and fixes it."

"Isn't there any place to stay around here? Any place to get a bite to eat?"

"This is it. You get what you want from the grocery shelf and heat it up on the hotplate in the cabin."

At that point Tom gave up. Turning to Margaret, he said, "Grab something we can have for dinner." As she walked over to the grocery shelf, he pulled out his wallet. "How much for the two cabins?"

"Four dollars, but it's just one cabin. That first one's mine."

Just as he started to say something more, Tom spotted Margaret coming back with an armful of cans and boxes.

"Okay, we'll take it." He handed the old man a 10-dollar bill, then turned and took the packages from Margaret.

"Wait outside," he said. "I'll be right out."

Moments later, he followed her out, the bag of food in one hand and the room key in the other. "Let's take this stuff back to your cabin and get you settled, and then I'll get your suitcase from the car."

Taking note of the weary look on his face, Margaret tried to lift his spirits.

"This isn't all that bad," she said. "We'll rough it tonight and be back on the road tomorrow morning." She told him they'd be picnicking on a gourmet meal of beans, Vienna sausages, saltines, cheese spread, and peanut butter. When his expression didn't change, she smiled. "Don't be such a worry wart. Everything is going to be just fine."

"I hope so," he said glumly. "I certainly hope so."

The cabin had a tiny round table, a double bed, and a long dresser with a small television. The hotplate and everything else they'd need were beside the TV. Tom set the bag of groceries on the end of the dresser, returned to the car, and carried in Margaret's suitcase.

Throughout the evening, he was relatively silent. After they'd snacked on what served as dinner and watched television for a while, Margaret said she was a bit tired and suggested they call it a night. Tom nodded at her and turned toward the door.

He'd hardly spoken a word all evening and not laughed once during *The Smothers Brothers Comedy Hour*. A worried look tugged the corners of his mouth down. Keeping her voice light, Margaret asked, "Just in case I need something, you are in the other cabin, aren't you?"

Tom shook his head wearily. "The storekeeper lives there."

"Then where are you going?"

"I'm gonna sleep in the car. It's no big deal."

"But you didn't—"

"Maggie, I... We've spent a lot of time together, and I didn't want you to think I'm pulling a fast one. So I'll just sleep in the car. Nothing to worry about. I'll be fine."

Before she could say anything more, he was out the door. For a moment she stood wondering if she should go after him, say it was foolish for him to sleep in the car, and tell him to come back. She thought about what he said and how their friendship seemed to get stronger, sweeter, during the days they'd spent together.

Albert's scowling face came to her mind just then.

Already? she could picture him saying. *When I've not yet been gone a year?*

Trying to push the jumble of thoughts from her head, Margaret washed her face, pulled on her cotton nightgown, and climbed into bed. As she lay there in the darkness, she pictured Tom trying to find a way to get comfortable in the cramped confines of the car. She knew such a thing was almost impossible for a man as tall as he was. She was a foot shorter, and even she couldn't stretch out on the back seat. And with a chill in the night air he'd be stiff as a board the next morning.

After almost an hour of tossing and turning, she pulled on her robe and shoes, padded across the road, and peeked into the car. He was sitting behind the wheel, his eyes closed and his head leaned back. She rapped on the window.

Startled, his eyes popped open. He lowered the window. "Is something wrong?"

"Yes. I'm afraid to stay in that cabin by myself. You have to come back. We're adults. Surely we can control ourselves enough to sleep side by side without anything happening."

Tom laughed out loud. "Maggie, you surprise me. Just when I think I've got you figured out, I realize I haven't even scratched the surface."

He climbed out of the car, and they walked back to the cabin arm in arm.

The next morning Tom was at the station when Eddie arrived. An hour later the fan belt had been replaced, and they were back on the road. That day they drove straight through, stopping only once for gas and a quick lunch at the Root Beer stand. As they drove past rolling hills and through small towns, they talked. Although they discussed a dozen different things, neither of them mentioned the night before when Margaret had curled up alongside of him in her sleep and rested her head on his shoulder.

After they passed Columbus, Margaret pulled the Ohio roadmap from the glove compartment and traced the route they were taking. As they passed from one town to another, she'd say, "Darby's just ahead" or "Only a few miles to Midland Creek."

The hours flew by and before the sun sat low on the horizon, they'd arrived in the southwest corner of Ohio.

"Looks like we'll be in Kentucky before noon tomorrow," Tom said with a slight smile.

That night they had dinner at Beefsteak Bob's and stayed at the Starlight Motor Court, which was a vast improvement over the cabin.

Later on, as she lay in bed waiting for sleep to come, she thought back on the night before and how good it had been to feel the warmth of Tom's body next to hers. As anxious as she'd been to hurry from one place to another in search of her family, she was now starting to dread the end of this trip.

The Search for Virgil

On Tuesday morning they talked about stopping in Louisville that night since it was a place neither of them had ever visited, but that day they made every green light, bypassed the construction zones, and not once got caught up in a traffic jam. Before two o'clock, they were on the northern edge of Louisville.

"We're making such good time, it's a shame to stop now," Tom said.

"If we don't stay in Louisville," Margaret reasoned, "there's nothing much between there and Nashville."

They went back and forth discussing the pros and cons of stopping and when they finally decided to continue on, they were well south of Louisville nearing the town of Brooks.

As they drove through towns and long stretches of single-lane highways, Margaret talked about their trip and how she'd never expected it to turn out this way.

"When I met you in Charleston, I thought I'd be there for a day or two then fly home. I never dreamed it would turn into the trip of a lifetime."

Tom glanced across the seat with a smile. "Is that what this has been, Maggie, the trip of a lifetime?"

"Of my lifetime it has," she said. "Albert considered driving trips a waste of time. 'Why spend all those hours on the road when you can hop on a plane and get where you're going in no time?' That's what he'd say." She glanced at Tom and grinned. "You and Albert are two very different people."

A thought flashed through her mind: If she had to choose between the two men, which would it be? She turned her face to the window, annoyed that she would even consider such a preposterous idea. Albert was dead, and Tom was nothing more than a friend. Again, she reminded herself that this whole experience would be over soon, a thing to be enjoyed for a while, then forgotten.

"We're in Tennessee," Tom said, cutting into her thoughts. "If you don't mind, I'd like to keep going. I think we can make Nashville in another hour or two."

Ninety minutes they later they were driving through the streets of Nashville in search of a hotel. When Margaret spotted the black and gold Hermitage awning, she suggested they give it try, and it turned out to the grandest of all the grand hotels she'd experienced.

They had dinner at the hotel that night and while they lingered over Jameson-spiked coffee, Tom suggested they spend Wednesday touring the city and start for Alabama early Thursday morning. She'd said she needed to think about it, but the truth was she didn't need to. She knew she wanted to stay.

On Wednesday they explored the city. They ate hot chicken at a hole-in-the-wall restaurant, visited the Grand Ole Opry, and sat squeezed together in one seat as they listened to undiscovered musicians at the Bluebird Café. That night Margaret went to bed with her heart heavy in her chest. For days she'd not thought of home, only of the adventures ahead of them, the thrill of finding her siblings and, yes, the fun of being with Tom. She'd let herself slide into the comfort of his arm around her shoulder. She'd even allowed him to sleep in her bed, and, worst of all, she'd enjoyed it. It had been wonderful but the places they'd gone and the people they'd seen had never met Albert, so they accepted Tom as her partner. Back in Heatherwood that would not be the case.

Was this to be her way of life? For each thing gained, there was something equally precious lost? She'd lost Albert and found Tom. She'd found Dewey and the others, now she would lose Tom. After Albert was first gone, lying there with only the black nights to bear witness, she'd thought of moving to another town and starting a new life, but even that came with losses. To start over she'd have to leave behind the friends she'd made, the shopkeepers who called her by name, the women in the library group, Josie.

Burying her face in the pillow, she sobbed. She mourned the love she'd lost and the love she was destined to never know.

On Thursday morning they were on the road before 8 am even though Tom figured it to be no more than a five- or six-hour drive. At breakfast that morning, Margaret didn't finish her coffee and had nothing to eat.

"Are you feeling okay?" he asked; she responded with nothing more than a nod.

While the other days had flown by, this one seemed to stretch on forever as they drove in silence. When Tom said there was a road map for Alabama in the glove compartment and asked if she wanted to follow their route, she shook her head.

"We'll get there when we get there," she said.

When they finally arrived in Farstack, he had to practically coax her into going out for dinner. Even then she turned down a glass of wine and dessert. Twice he asked if he'd done something to make her angry or in some way offended her. She said no and blamed her moodiness on an upset stomach, but she saw the doubt in his eyes.

Later that night, when she was tossing and turning in a motel bed that was too soft in some spots and too hard in others, she thought back on something her mama had said not long after they returned to Coal Creek.

For weeks Margaret had been tearful about leaving Barrettsville. That afternoon she was sitting on the porch swing and feeling lower than a stomped-on worm when her mama came out and sat beside her. For a few minutes they sat there, saying nothing, just pushing back and forth together.

Finally her mama said, "I know how unhappy you are, Margaret Rose, but if you spend your days crying over what you've lost, you'll forget the joy of ever having had it. There are kids in Coal Creek who have never even been to Charleston, and you've been all the way to Pennsylvania. You've lived in a beautiful home, discovered all kinds of treasures, ridden on a train. Imagine how lucky you are to have all those memories to hold on to." She'd then turned Margaret's face to hers. "But if you keep crying, you'll become sadder and sadder until one day you won't be able to remember all that happiness you once had."

Thinking back on her mama's words gave Margaret a measure of comfort. It didn't change anything but reminded her that sometimes a memory is all you're destined to keep.

By Friday morning Margaret had decided to turn these last few days into memories worth keeping. There would be time enough for feeling sad once she was back in Heatherwood.

Tom rapped on the door of her room at 8:30.

"Maggie, do you feel up to having breakfast?"

She stepped out looking bright as she had back in Nashville. "Absolutely."

Tom put a hand on her shoulder and gave her an affectionate squeeze. "You look much better today. I was a little worried."

"I guess it was just one of those 24-hour stomach bugs," she said.

They started toward the parking lot.

"The city hall building is at the end of Bueller Street," Tom said. "Let's head in that direction and see if we can find someplace to eat on the way."

Farstack was a small town with only a handful of choices when it came to restaurants. A few blocks from the motel, they found a small cafe with the front door propped open and a scattering of tables out on the sidewalk. Two of the tables were taken; the third was empty.

"Okay if we sit here?" Tom asked.

This was one of the moments Margaret would remember: the sun warm on her back, the smell of coffee and fresh-baked bread in the air, and Tom sitting across from her as they planned out the day.

"We'll start at the city hall building; all the records departments are there. I can check for a driver's license, home ownership, voter registration, and a few other things. I think we'll get a hit on something."

Although they'd spoken of being at the city hall building when the doors opened at 9 am, they lingered over a second and then third cup of coffee. When they left it was 9:45.

It was only a five-minute drive to the city hall building, but when they pulled up and parked on the opposite side of the street they knew something was wrong. Sawhorses blocked the steps, and yellow danger tape stretched from one side of the entrance to the other. Behind the sawhorses was a stanchion sign.

"What the heck..." Tom stepped out of the car and started across the street. Margaret followed along. They stood side by side, reading the sign.

BUILDING CLOSED DUE TO FIRE

Until further notice, please direct all inquiries to the Jefferson County Records Department in Birmingham, AL. Birth and death certificates will be issued by St. John's Hospital. Automobile registration, marriage licenses, and building permits can be obtained through the Jefferson County Clerk's Office.

"Now what?" Margaret asked.

Tom put his hands on his hips and pursed his lips in thought.

"Virgil was still a kid when he came here, so he must have attended school. Let's try the elementary school, see if they've got a record of him. If we strike out there, we can try the high school."

The elementary school was on the corner of Fourth and Grant. The office was the last door at the end of a hallway decorated with childish drawings, colorful posters, and official notices. When they walked in, the secretary at the front desk glanced up.

"Is there something I can help you with?"

Tom stepped over to her desk. "Yes, we're looking for information on a student who would have attended this school in 1913 or '14."

She cocked her head in thought. "Um, I think records that old are at the city clerk's office. Have you checked there?"

"The building's closed because of fire."

She smacked her forehead. "Oh, right. How could I forget about that fire? It was huge; destroyed all the back offices and most of their records storage."

"Oh dear," Margaret said, leaning into the conversation. "Does anyone keep duplicates of those records?"

The secretary laughed. "You're asking the wrong person about that. Samantha Alvarez might know. She's our administrator, and she's been here a lot longer than I have."

"Is she available?"

"She's in her office, but I don't know if she's busy. Hold on, I'll ask."

The secretary picked up the telephone and pressed an intercom button. "Mrs. Alvarez, I have a couple here looking for student records from 1913. Can you spare a minute to talk with them?" She nodded, then hung up the phone. "Okay, it's the door on the right."

As they went to the office, Margaret hoped the woman would be older, someone who was here all those years ago and could remember Virgil as being a good student or a helpful child. The woman who met them was a well-dressed, attractive blond in her early forties; certainly not old enough to remember Virgil. As Samantha Alvarez stood to greet them, Margaret hoped the records from 1913 were stored in a place other than the burned-out city hall building.

Samantha motioned to the two chairs in front of her desk and suggested they take a seat.

"Louise said you're looking for student records that date back to 1913, is that right?"

Tom nodded. "We were at the city hall building earlier and—"

"That fire was terrible." Samantha drew a deep breath and released it. "Two of our volunteer firemen were injured, and before the night was over they had to call in help from Mulga and Fairfield."

"Were the older student records stored in that building?" Tom asked.

Samantha nodded. "Afraid so. You might be able to get some help from the Jefferson County School Board. They keep some records, but I believe it's mostly just student name and address."

Margaret wanted to believe the county records would provide answers but was not overly hopeful. She gave Samantha a polite nod and asked, "Is it possible there's anyone still working here who might remember a kid named Virgil Palmer?"

"Are you talking about the school superintendent who retired last spring?"

Margaret shrugged. "I can't say if they're one and the same. Virgil's my brother. We lost track of each other when he came here. The last I time I saw him was back in 1913. Mama sent Virgil to live with our brother, Ben Roland, and we never saw each other again."

Samantha raised an eyebrow. "And how old was your brother then?"

"Ten. He would have been in the fifth grade, I think."

Samantha scratched a few numbers on a note pad and looked up with a smile. "I think we've found your brother." She went on to explain that a man who was 10 in 1913 would be 65 in 1968, which was the mandatory retirement age for those in the Farstack School System.

"Mr. Palmer retired last spring, but I'll be happy to give you his telephone number and address."

That afternoon, Margaret called the number a dozen or more times, first from a pay phone, then from the telephone in her room at the motel, but there was no answer. She called the school to make certain she had the right information.

"Hold on, I'll check," the secretary said. After several seconds, she was back and repeated the same address and telephone number Margaret had.

Tom suggested driving by the house, but when they did the windows were dark and no one answered the door. Margaret sat back in the car, her chin almost touching her chest in disappointment. Tom touched his hand to hers.

"Tomorrow," he said. "We'll wait and try again tomorrow."

The next morning, Margaret woke early after a poor night's sleep. She paced in her room for hours before starting to call again. By noon, when there was still no answer, Margaret began to get anxious.

"What if something's happened?" she said to Tom over lunch. "What if Virgil's moved? What if I never again find him? I'll never find out what happened to him or John Paul."

"I think you're worrying needlessly," Tom said. "He's probably just away for a few days. I'm certain if we wait—"

"Away where?"

Having no answer for that question, Tom suggested they could drive over to Virgil's house again and ask around. "Maybe check with some of the neighbors, or write a note and drop it through the mail slot."

"Good idea."

Margaret wrote a note, folded it into a Sleep E-Z Motel envelope, and tucked it in her purse.

I've come this far, Virgil, she thought as they climbed back into the car, *and I'm not leaving until I find you.*

1907 – 1910

A New Life

In early December, Edward Wolff visited Eliza Hobbs again.

"I talked with your husband, and apparently this new job came up rather unexpectedly," he said. "Brother Martin wanted to wait until he'd settled in and found a house before he had you join him, and I am pleased to report that has now happened." He handed her an envelope and smiled. "This is a bit of traveling money and railroad tickets for the family. Martin will meet you at the station and get everyone settled in the new house."

Eliza opened the envelope and looked at the tickets. "Barrettsville, Pennsylvania; that sounds like a long way from Coal Creek."

Wolff chuckled. "It certainly is. You'll be on the train for about eighteen hours, so be sure to bring some sandwiches and snacks."

Eliza looked up with tears in her eyes. "You're a good man, Mister Wolff. I don't know how I can ever thank you."

"Knowing that you and the children will be taken care of is thanks enough, Mrs. Hobbs. It's a lucky man who ends the day feeling he's changed someone's life for the better."

As Eliza stood on the front porch and watched Edward Wolff drive away, she realized she would never see him again and a tiny grain of sadness settled in her heart.

"Your wife is a very lucky woman, Mr. Wolff," she said wistfully. Brushing back a tear, she turned away.

⁂

Eliza had two weeks to get ready. Two weeks to gather a lifetime of memories, pack up the things they would take, say goodbye to friends, and tell the children they would never again return to this place.

"It feels strange to be leaving," she told Caldonia. "Strange and frightening."

"You'll do just fine, and having their daddy around will be good for the children."

Eliza's brows were pinched together and her mouth downturned. "I hope so. If it doesn't work out, I don't know what I'd do."

"You'd do the same as you did this time; write Mr. Wolff a letter and ask him to figure a way to bring you back. That house of your mama's ain't going nowhere, and neither am I. We'll be here waiting if you ever decide you want to come home."

"I suppose I could do that," she said, but it wasn't what she was thinking.

In the darkest corner of Eliza's mind, she kept wondering if a man like Martin could actually change. In the early morning, before anyone else was awake and dawn had not yet crawled across the high ridge, she'd stand on the front porch and look out on the land, studying the thicket of elderberry bushes at the far end of the drive, listening for a cock to crow, and breathing in the scent of the mountain. She wanted to remember it all.

This was a place that took more from a woman than it gave back, but it was home. The only home her children had ever known. The only real home she'd ever known.

A million *What ifs* rolled through her mind. What if Martin was not there when they stepped down from the train? What if a week later, or a month later, he left them again? Here she had friends to turn to, but there…

As she darned socks and laundered the clothes they would bring, she tucked away mementos small enough to carry in her pocket: a buttonwood flower, a bit of dried chicory, the drawing made by her first child, the locket her mother had worn. All parts of a past that would be left behind once she climbed aboard that train. The night before they were to leave, she walked from room to room, worrying that she'd forgotten a treasure with special meaning or a cloth doll that would cause the children to cry for home.

While the sky was still dark, she threw the last few lumps of coal into the belly of the stove and stoked the fire. It was a good stove, one that had served them well, and she would miss it. She set a pot of coffee to brew, slid a tray of biscuits into the oven, then began to wake the children.

Oliver's eyes popped open the minute she touched his shoulder.

"Is it time?" he asked. When she said yes, he turned to rouse Ben Roland and Dewey. He was eager for the move and passed his excitement on to the others.

"Imagine being on a train for a whole day and night," he said and gave the trip the sound of an adventure.

A short while after they finished breakfast, she heard Jeb's wagon turning into the drive. The older children hurried out and scrambled into the back of the wagon, excitedly chattering about the adventure ahead. Margaret Rose remained in her chair with her mouth puckered up as if she were ready to burst into tears.

Even though she was six years old and too big to be carried in her mama's arms, Eliza lifted her up.

"What's the matter, baby?" she asked.

Dropping her head onto Eliza's shoulder, Margaret Rose sobbed. "I don't wanna go to Pennsylvania. I wanna stay living here."

"You can't stay here by yourself. Everybody's going to Pennsylvania. All your brothers and sisters. Your daddy got a house that'll be our new home. You and Louella will have a bedroom just for girls, and when Nellie is big enough she can stay in the girls' room too. Won't that be fun?"

Eliza felt the tiny shoulders shrug. "I don't care about no girls' bedroom. If we stay here, I don't gotta be afraid."

"Afraid? Are you afraid of riding on the train?"

Margaret Rose shook her head. "I'm afraid Daddy is gonna be mean, and we're not ever gonna be happy."

Eliza choked back the fear rising in her own throat. "You don't have to worry about that, honey. Daddy wants us to come. He sent us tickets for the train and money to buy bottles of soda pop. He's doing this to make us happy, Margaret Rose, and we will be."

"You swear, Mama?"

Eliza could feel the scorching fear of her words as she spoke them.

"Yes, I swear we'll be happy." She lowered Margaret Rose to the floor. "Now hurry out there and climb up in the wagon. We've got to be leaving."

As she lifted Nellie into her arms and closed the door, she prayed that what she'd said was true.

⁂

The train went from Coal Creek to Charleston and headed south toward Greenbriar. For the first two hours the children were content to be on the move and watch the world go by as the train traveled along the Allegheny Mountain Range, dipping down into the valleys then rising again with the mountains. They passed by countless rivers and streams, forested areas that looked as if no man had ever stepped foot in them, and small towns that seemed to spring up out of nowhere. When the train stopped at Greenbriar, it sat there for the better part of an hour while people with baggage climbed off the train and new people climbed on.

"Where's everybody going?" Oliver asked the conductor.

The conductor grinned. "You ever hear of the Grand Central Hotel?"

Oliver shook his head. "Un-uh."

"Well, that's where all these people are headed. It's a fine hotel, and some say the water there is warm enough to soak in year-round."

"Even in winter?"

The conductor nodded. "Even in winter. I got a picture postcard of the Grand Central Hotel, and when I come through later on I'll bring it by for you to see."

"Can I see too?" Ben Roland asked.

The conductor gave a hearty chuckle and said everybody was welcome to take a peek.

As the afternoon wore on, they crossed into Virginia and the children grew restless.

"There's nothing to see but trees," Louella complained.

Eliza hugged her daughter's shoulders. "If all you see is trees, then you're missing the magic of the forests."

"What magic?"

Eliza tugged the girls closer and began weaving stories about people who lived deep in the woods and could speak the language of animals. She told them about plants that could cure sickness and flowers that bloomed in winter. When they tired of those stories, she fantasized about what it would be like in Barrettsville.

"I imagine a bit like Charleston," she said, "with cobblestone streets and trolleys to carry people from one end of the city to the other. Mr. Wolff said it's a big house with four bedrooms and running water in the kitchen."

"How do we know if them bedrooms got beds?" Ben Roland asked.

Eliza smiled. "Mr. Wolff said the house was furnished. Not fancy but comfortable."

Oliver pressed his lips into a line. "When I see it, that's when I'm gonna believe it."

Eliza felt the same type of apprehension in her heart but held back saying anything. If the kids knew she was fearful, they would be even more so.

After the train passed through Charlottesville it was time for supper, and she opened the basket of food. Each child was given an apple and two biscuits, one with pieces of chicken and ham, the other spread with sweet butter. They passed the jar of lemonade from one to the other, and afterward the children shared the tin of cookies given to them by Aunt Caldonia.

By then the scenery had changed. The forests became tiny towns with railroad stations smaller than a cabin. When the sky grew dark, even the towns disappeared into the blackness. By then Nellie had climbed into Eliza's lap and drifted off.

"You should all try to sleep," she told the others. "If you don't, you'll be too tired to enjoy the day with Daddy or explore the new house."

The girls and the younger children fell asleep almost immediately, but Oliver and Ben Roland insisted they were old enough to stay up all night. Eliza said they could do as they wanted, but before the train stopped at Culpepper they too were fast asleep.

It was late afternoon when they finally arrived in Barrettsville. It was a small station; not as tiny as some they'd passed but nowhere near as large as the one in Philadelphia or Greenbriar. Organizing the children to make sure they had all the bags they'd carried on, she stepped down from the train carrying Nellie. Dewey and Ben Roland came behind her, then the girls, and lastly Oliver hanging onto Virgil and John Paul's hands.

She stood on the platform looking around. The place had the look of a small town, nothing like Coal Creek. Several minutes stretched by before she spotted Martin coming toward them.

He was wearing a dark suit that she didn't remember him having and looked different than when she'd last seen him. She hoped he'd smile or stretch out his arms so the children would run to him, but he did neither of those things. Instead his brows hooded his eyes and his shoulders were squared back, almost as though he were spoiling for a fight.

Determined to make this day of arrival less scary for the children, she forced a smile.

"It's good to see you, Martin," she said.

"Yeah, you too." He glanced at Oliver and Ben Roland. "You boys get those bags and carry them out front. I've got a wagon to take you to the house."

As the boys hurried off with the bags, Eliza moved the others toward the station house. "This afternoon, we'll need to get a few cooking supplies. Is there a general store—"

"Dunning Mercantile is here in the square, and the trolley runs a few blocks from the house. You can take it back and forth."

"Good. Very good." She couldn't help but notice how he spoke as if she were a stranger, as if they'd never lain side by side in a bed or created eight beautiful children together. Trying to push the thought from her heart, she remained silent for a moment then said, "If you want, I can get some apples and make your favorite—"

"I'm not gonna stay. I've gotta get back for work."

"Isn't this where you work?"

He shook his head. "The plant's over in Altoona, and I've gotta be close by. Wolff said you were gonna need a place with four or more bedrooms, and over by me there's nothing much that size."

"Will you come back tonight?"

Again, he shook his head. "It's too far. I'll be back in a few weeks. Two, maybe three."

Eliza nodded and said nothing. It was too soon to judge him. Possibly he really did need to work, that he was in fact a changed man, but already the doubts were there. She missed Caldonia more than ever.

The large gray house was on the far edge of town nine blocks from where the trolley dead-ended and turned back toward the square. All alone at the end of the street, it stood two stories high with black shutters on the windows and a front porch that was as deep as a room. It was as stately as the houses that lined Edgewood Drive in Charleston, but those houses had electricity, maids to sweep the walkway, and gardeners to tend the flowers. This house had none of those things. It was simply big.

As the kids carried the bags to the porch Martin told the wagon driver to wait, because he'd be going back to the train station. He pulled a key from his pocket and handed it to Eliza.

"I think you'll find most everything you need inside, and there's money on the kitchen table. Now you can write to your new friend Wolff and tell him you got what you wanted."

"Martin," she stammered, "I hope you don't think I—"

"Don't bother explaining, Eliza. I've already heard the story."

As she stood there watching the wagon turn and disappear down the street, Eliza felt a chamber of her heart slam shut. It was the last place she'd kept open for Martin, a tiny wedge of space. Now it was forever locked away. Whatever she'd once hoped for was as impossible as snow in July.

There would be no more looking back; no remembering what once was. If Martin was to hate her, then she would leave it be. From this moment forward, she would live only for the love of her children. She stepped onto the porch, slid the key into the lock, and pushed open the door.

She surveyed the furnishings as she and the children went from room to room: overstuffed chairs in the parlor, plump beds in the upstairs rooms, and the kitchen cupboards filled with dishes and tableware as if someone had just walked away and left the house as it was. On the kitchen table there was a huge carton of food with a card wishing them happiness in their new home. It was from Edward Wolff and the Brothers of the Masonic Lodge.

Beside it was an envelope with "Eliza" scrawled across the front. She recognized Martin's handwriting. Inside there were six five-dollar bills, more than he'd ever given her at one time. She smiled and tucked the envelope into the high cupboard. They had a home to live in, and there would now be food on the table. It was enough, and enough was exactly what she had wished for.

In the days that followed, they settled in. The girls took the bedroom with rose-printed wallpaper and a window overlooking the empty lot beside the house. The three older boys moved in one room and John Paul and Virgil in another. In the attic they found a crib, so the boys carried it down and Eliza kept Nellie in her room.

As it turned out, the house was filled with hidden treasures, and one by one the children uncovered them. Dewey found a carton of story books in the attic, and at first Eliza said it was wrong to pilfer through things that quite obviously belonged to someone else. She relented when she saw how old the books were and added only that they should handle them with care.

A trunk covered with a cloth that was weighted with the dust of many years sat in the far corner of the attic. As Oliver shook the dust from the cloth and opened the trunk to peek inside, he sneezed several times. At first it seemed to be mostly dresses, some too small for Louella and too large for Margaret Rose.

"This just looks like old clothes," Oliver said. "Maybe we'd best leave it here."

Ben Roland shook his head. "Un-uh. If we find stuff Mama can use, she'll be happy."

With curiosity tugging at them, the three boys carried the trunk from the attic and set it in the upstairs hallway. Beneath the dresses they found fancy petticoats, baby clothes, and, at the bottom of everything, a packet tied with a blue string. Oliver loosened the ribbon and folded back the square of velvet cloth. Inside was a diary and a handful of letters.

He carried them downstairs and handed them to Eliza.

"I know you said we shouldn't pilfer, Mama, but this book tells about the lady who lived here. I figured it might say why they left all this stuff behind."

Eliza was torn between her guilt at using someone else's belongings and her curiosity to know why they were gone.

"Perhaps I can learn something to help us understand if it's wrong to be using these things." She told him not to remove anything else from the trunk, took the package, and placed it in the cupboard.

Later that night when the children were asleep and the house so quiet she could hear her own heartbeat, she sat at the kitchen table and opened the diary. On the inside of the book the woman had penned her name: Sarah Alice Bligh. The first page was dated July 9, 1852, the day she'd moved into the house, and it told of how she could see nothing but happiness ahead for her and her husband, William.

As Eliza read from page to page, Sarah Alice's life opened up. In the winter of 1853 she gave birth to their first child, a boy, named for her husband and the father she'd left behind in England. It was a lengthy entry talking about how she missed her family and wished they could have been here for the child's birth. After several more entries, she wrote of expecting another baby and praying it would be a girl.

Although the house is lovely and William denies me nothing, the days are long and lonely. Mrs. Riley comes three times a week to clean but goes about her work and is not sociable. A daughter would be the companionship I so desire. Two pages later she announced Abigail Anne's birth, saying she had never seen a more beautiful baby. By then Eliza's eyes had grown weary. She closed the book, folded it back into the square of velvet, and placed it in the cupboard.

The next evening the children were sent to bed early, and Eliza returned to the diary. For several pages Sarah told of the children's growth and her wish that William spent more time at home. In the summer of 1857, she talked of William's growing concern over the political situation. Two pages later she wrote, *A young senator from Illinois has won the presidency, and William is certain war is imminent. I fear that if this happens, he will be foolish enough to enlist.*

That fear was not mentioned again as Sarah spoke only of the children, saying that young Will was the brightest in his class and Abigail more beautiful every day. In August of 1862, on a tear-stained page, she wrote of how William had enlisted in the Union Army and would be commanding a regiment to keep the rebels out of Pennsylvania.

I begged and pleaded, but he is unrelenting in his decision.

After only a few pages, Eliza came to one written in a hand so shaky it was barely legible.

My heart is broken, Sarah wrote, *for I have lost my precious daughter to influenza. If William were here, he might have brought the doctor in time but he was away fighting this blasted war.*

The hour grew late, and tears filled Eliza's eyes but still she was compelled to see the story through to its end. The first light of morning was on the horizon when she finished the last tearstained page that told of William's death at Gettysburg.

I have come to believe this wretched place is cursed. As soon as I can find a ship to carry us, I will take my son and return to England. I will carry only the clothes we wear, for I want no further reminders of this place.

Eliza carried the sadness of Sarah's story in her heart for several days. When Dewey asked if he might give Margaret Rose the doll they'd found in the trunk, she nodded.

"The family who left those things has gone back to their home in England," she said. "They won't be returning."

She made no mention of the war or the deaths that had occurred.

Once Eliza had given her approval, the children carried down all of the boxes from the attic and unearthed more clothes and such treasures as glass marbles, wooden blocks, and cloth dolls. In the basement they discovered a rocking horse in need of repair and a wagon big enough to carry both Nellie and Virgil.

Using the sewing box she found in an upstairs closet, Eliza altered the clothing they'd taken from the trunk. That Christmas, every one of the children had a new outfit. When they attended Sunday services at the church in the square, Eliza could not have been more proud of her family. At first, she'd feared the sorrow Sarah Alice Bligh left behind was part of the house and would be forever woven into the clothes, but it had proven otherwise. This home that Sarah thought wretched was a blessing to Eliza.

Martin's Dilemma

The happiness Martin enjoyed in Altoona took a sharp turn the day Eliza arrived. Martha Mae was unrelenting in her belief that he should have stood up to Edward Wolff and said no when Wolff ordered him to bring Eliza and the children to Pennsylvania. She called him a spineless dog and refused to allow him in her bed.

He, in turn, blamed her for the problem.

"If you hadn't insisted we get married, I wouldn't be in this fix," he said.

"Me?" she screamed and heaved a vase at his head. "You're the one! You told me there was no need for a divorce."

"I never said that! You heard what you wanted to hear."

Martin thought that locating Eliza in a town 80 miles north of Altoona would have been enough to appease Martha Mae, but it wasn't. Even the slightest mention of Eliza, the kids, or the town of Barrettsville set her off, and she'd fly into a rampage that lasted for hours. When he'd had more than enough of listening, he'd say something about regretting that he'd ever met her. Then he'd have to duck to avoid being hit by whatever she'd thrown.

On the day Eliza arrived, he made no mention of it to Martha Mae. He left home early, met the train, brought them to the house, made a quick turnaround, and arrived home at his normal time. He expected

Martha Mae to be ready to go dinner, but she was stretched out on the sofa in her bathrobe with a pillow beneath her head.

"Why aren't you dressed?"

"I'm not going."

"Not going? Why?"

She pulled the pillow from beneath her head, heaved it across the room, and came at him with her fists flying.

"Because you're a liar and a cheat! Did you think I wouldn't find out?"

Martin took hold of her wrists and tried to keep her slapping hands at bay.

"I did what I had to do. I swear, I didn't so much as touch Eliza. I met her at the train station, took her there, dropped everybody off, and came straight home. I didn't even stay long enough to go in the house, and I told her not to expect me back for another two weeks."

"Two weeks?" Martha Mae screeched. She kicked him in the shin.

Martin reached down and rubbed his leg. "Gimme a break. I'm doing my best. What more can I do?"

"You can divorce her, that's what."

He shook his head, gave a bone-weary sigh, and turned away. "Be reasonable. My trying to divorce her would only make things worse. First off, I'd be hard pressed to show cause, and then it's almost certain to come out about us already being married."

Martha Mae took another swing at him and went back to arguing that he should have divorced Eliza years ago.

With alternate bouts of screaming and crying, the fight continued for three days. Finally he bought her a gold bracelet and swore he'd keep his visits to the bare minimum.

"Just enough to keep Wolff from making trouble."

"Forget about him and worry about me. You only go once a month, never stay longer than one hour, and give me advance warning when you're planning a trip."

"The train ride there and back is two hours! Don't you think that's a bit—"

Her glare made him stop.

The thought of being bossed around did not sit well with Martin, and a new kind of anger started to simmer beneath his skin. At work he flew off the handle at the slightest provocation, and at home he grew sullen and moody.

Every time he went to visit the kids, he had to hand Eliza another 30 dollars. In his estimation, there was little appreciation on her part. Sure, she said thank you, but that was it. Back in Coal Creek, he'd given her 10 dollars and she'd welcomed him into her bed. Now they were living high on the hog with his money, and he got nothing.

❦

After Eliza settled in, she found she could be happy in Barrettsville most of the time. The house was at the far end of a street and there were few neighbors, so she missed Caldonia something fierce, but it was a small sacrifice compared to the hardships she'd suffered in Coal Creek. The children kept her busy throughout the day, but at night she missed the sounds of the mountain and the feel of home.

On nights when the loneliness seemed to penetrate her skin and take hold of her heart, she left the lamp burning and sat in bed reading the letters sent to Sarah Alice Bligh. They were letters filled with longing and words of love. William spoke of the seemingly endless march down Pennsylvania, the drenching rain, and worn boots then said he could endure anything knowing he would return to her when the war was over.

Your love warms me in the dead of winter, feeds me when there is little to eat, and will be the wings that carry me home when this terrible business is done. When I close my eyes at night, yours is the face I see. I fear nothing, for you, my darling, make me strong.

Countless times she read that sentence, wishing that it had been meant for her and trying to imagine her husband's hand holding the pen.

After six months, she came to dread Martin's visits. He was always angry and in a foul mood; there was no way of pleasing him. One month she'd baked an apple pie, the one that was his favorite, but he sneered at it, said it wasn't worth 30 dollars, and left without even tasting it. The next month she didn't bother, and he criticized her for not making one.

"I didn't think you cared for it anymore," she said.

"The problem is you never think about anything but these damn kids.

If you cared a rat's ass about me, you'd never have embarrassed me by going to Wolff and begging for help."

She tried to explain about their condition after the tornado came through, but he had little patience for anything she said. In time, she simply gave up trying. He'd come in, slam an envelope down on the kitchen table, spend a few minutes with the kids, and leave. He complained about everything the children did, said, or wore. On the day Margaret Rose wore her dress from the attic, she twirled around in front of him and asked if he liked it. The only thing he could find to say was that it had probably cost him a pretty penny.

Before the year was out, Martin had gone from being surly and unpleasant to downright cruel. He'd think nothing of smacking one of the kids upside the head for being in his way or speaking when they hadn't been spoken to. He was worse with Virgil, and Ben Roland was next in line. Virgil, he'd resented from the day he was born, but Ben Roland had been one of his favorites up until that January.

It was a bitter cold day with snow changing to sleet then back to snow again. The train ran behind schedule, and he'd had to wait an hour for the trolley. By the time he got to the house, he was in a mood blacker than any Eliza had ever seen. He plunked the envelope on the table, walked over to the parlor, and dropped into the overstuffed chair. Seeing Virgil nearby, he called to him.

"You," he said. "Get over here and pull these frozen boots off my feet."

Virgil was not quite six, small for his age, and scared to death of his daddy. Without lifting his eyes, the lad scurried across the room and started tugging on the boots. They were wet, heavy, and crusted with snow, so the boy's small fingers couldn't get a good grip on the first one. No matter how hard he pulled, it didn't budge.

With his patience worn thin, Martin drew his foot back and kicked Virgil in the chest. The boy tumbled halfway across the room. Ben Roland came into the room in time to see what happened.

At 15 he was narrow across his back and shoulders but tall as Martin and strong as an ox. Leaning over, his face inches from his daddy's, he shouted, "Leave him be, Daddy! Pick on somebody your own size!"

Martin bolted up and came at Ben Roland with his fists flying.

When Eliza heard the crash, she came running in. Oliver was right behind her. It took both of them to pull Ben Roland and Martin apart. When they finally did, she turned to Martin.

"Maybe you'd best be leaving."

Instead of turning toward the door, Martin flopped back down in the chair. "I ain't leaving. I decided to stay the night."

"Stay?" Eliza said, her voice wavering. "But what about work? Don't you have to—"

"Don't you dare tell me what to do, Eliza. I'm paying for you and this house, so I'll do as I damn well please."

"I wasn't saying you shouldn't stay. I only thought—"

"You ain't got brains enough to think. Get in the kitchen, and fix me some supper."

A prickly feeling of fear rolled down her spine as Eliza called for the kids to come along and let their daddy get some rest.

Hoping there was a chance Martin might change his mind and return to Altoona that night if supper were over early enough, Eliza hurried things along. A short while later they all gathered at the table, but it was nothing like it had been back in Coal Creek. There was no conversation, no stories told, no adventures shared. There was only the clinking of utensils against plates and the anger that had settled over the room like an ominous storm cloud.

When supper was done, Martin asked if Eliza had any whiskey in the house. She said no, so he stomped off and went back to the parlor. Once he was gone from the room, Eliza turned to the older boys.

"Take your sisters and brothers upstairs, and make sure everyone gets to bed," she whispered.

Oliver's eyebrows twitched. "I'm thinking Ben Roland and me ought to stay with you, Mama. Dewey can take the kids up."

Eliza shook her head. "I'll be fine on my own. Your daddy's just mad at the world; he's not gonna hurt me."

Oliver hesitated, but Eliza waved him off. "Go on. Get everybody into bed, be real quiet, and close your doors."

Taking more time than usual to clear away the table and clean up the kitchen, Eliza waited until she felt certain the kids were asleep. With the kitchen spotless, she squared her shoulders and joined Martin in the parlor with a piece of embroidery. She focused on her stitching, forcing her tone to seem more normal.

"It's been a long time since you've wanted to stay the night. I thought you most likely had another lady friend."

"So what if I do?" Martin snapped. "You made it clear you ain't interested in nothing but having me pay for you to live here."

"That's not true, Martin. I'm your wife; of course I care about you."

He studied her for a few moments. "Then why ain't you showing it?"

"I do in my own way, by making a home for our children and—"

"You know damn well that's not what I'm talking about."

"If you're suggesting I lie with you Martin, I won't do it. You're my husband, and I'd do most anything for you but not that."

"Why the hell not?"

"Because you don't want any more children, and I don't want to bring another unloved child into the world. Nellie is going on three years old, yet you've never once hugged her or said how pretty she is. And with Virgil it's even worse. You treat him like—"

"Don't give me that horseshit!" He stood and began pacing across the room. "There's more to this than what you're saying. I don't know what your game is, but I'll find out soon enough."

"There's nothing more to it. I'm happy being here with the children, and I'm not willing to risk it by going back to the way we once were."

"You've got no say in it. You're my wife, and I can take what I want whenever—"

"No, you can't." She pulled a heavy bladed knife from beneath her embroidery. "You might try, Martin, but I will fight you tooth and nail. You will not walk away unscathed."

His jaw dropped as he looked first at the knife and then at her face. "You are batshit crazy, Eliza. Batshit crazy. If I wanna take that knife away from you, I can do it easy. You know that, don't you?"

She gave a barely perceptible nod. "Yes, I believe you could, but before you do think about what it will cost you. A man with a scarred face is not nearly as pretty as you are."

Martin shook his head. "I never thought I'd live to see the day my own wife would turn against me."

His expression was sorrowful, his words threaded with a melancholy she'd not heard before. "I don't mean it to be hateful Martin, it's just that—"

He smacked the knife out of her hand and sent it sailing across the room.

"Don't you ever try to tell me what I can or can't do!"

Grabbing the front of her dress he yanked her from the chair, threw her to the floor, and kicked her in the ribs. There was the crack of bone. After that she no longer had strength enough to cry out for she could barely breathe. He dropped his pants, lifted her skirt, tore her knickers away, and climbed atop her. The pain was so excruciating that she blacked out.

When she came to, he was gone.

Repercussions

By the time Martin left the house the trolley had stopped running, so he had to walk back to the train station and wait almost three hours for a southbound headed to Altoona. It was near dawn when he arrived home. He'd planned to stretch out on the sofa and catch an hour or two of sleep without waking Martha Mae, but he didn't have to worry about that. She was sitting in the chair waiting for him.

Noticing the half-empty whiskey glass on the table beside her, he knew there was going to be trouble.

"Before you start in on me, you gotta at least let me explain about—"

"You were with her, weren't you?"

"Only to see the kids and bring the money, like always. The trains were off and—"

"Something is always off, isn't it? Nothing is ever your fault. Those eight kids just fell from the sky, and you didn't have a thing to do with it."

"We've been through this about the kids a hundred times. Let's give it a rest and move on."

She bounded out of the chair and stuck her pointy little nose in his face.

"Move on?" she screamed. "You want me to move on and ignore the fact that you're probably screwing her again? Well, you can just forget it.

This time you've gone too far." She went back to the half-empty glass and drained it.

"Martha Mae," he pleaded, "it's five-thirty in the morning. Don't you think it's time to stop drinking and get some sleep?"

"No, I don't. And you don't need to tell me what time it is; I know, because I've been up all night waiting for you!" She hurled the glass at him.

As he stepped aside it narrowly missed his head, slammed against the wall, and sent shards of glass across the room.

"If you'll calm down and listen, I'm trying to tell you—"

"No, what you're trying to do is concoct another phony story to cover your ass!"

"Martha Mae, this was not my fault. I got to the house at four o'clock, gave her the money, and was gone by five. Because of the blasted snow, I had to walk back to the station and wait all night for a train."

"Liar! I checked with the stationmaster. He said the last train left Barrettsville at eleven o'clock and there wouldn't be another until four in the morning."

"I was there at six and there was no train, I swear."

"Liar!"

This time she picked up a porcelain clock and threw it. The clock slammed into his shoulder, sprung apart, and dropped to the floor.

The fighting continued for almost two hours, and Martin had little choice but to repeat his story. After a while, Martha Mae's words began to sound like nothing more than an annoying drone in his ear. He knew if he could stick it out, she'd eventually grow weary enough to fall asleep. After she polished off another drink and told him this was far from over, she finally gave in to her exhaustion.

Once she was sound asleep in the chair, he telephoned the office saying he was sick and told them he wouldn't be coming in today. He then stretched out on the sofa to get some sleep. It would be a lot easier to reason with Martha Mae when she wasn't drinking.

Just before noon, she dumped a bucket of water over his head. Sputtering, he jumped up, blinking in shock at the chill. She was standing there with the bucket in her hand and that same black-eyed anger in her face.

"I'm giving you a chance to tell the whole story. Are you ready to tell me the truth of what happened last night?"

"I told you the whole story," he said, still groggy.

"And if I were to take the train to Barrettsville and have a talk with Eliza myself, she'd back you up?"

"You can ask her anything you want, but she's a liar," he said defensively. "She's always been a liar. She threatened me, said if I didn't give her more money she'd claim I raped her, but I didn't touch her. I swear I didn't."

"Then why didn't you get back to the train station until after eleven?"

He grimaced. "I know I stayed longer than I should have, but it was only because I was waiting for my boots to dry out. All I did was visit with the kids. She asked me to stay for supper, and I said no."

"If you weren't having anything to do with her, why'd she ask you to stay for supper?"

"I dunno. Maybe she was thinking we could be a family again, but it wasn't because of anything I did."

Her face scrunched into fury. "I don't believe she threatened you."

"Think what you want, but I'm telling the truth."

"No, you're not. You lie even when the truth is in your favor. You're a born liar. A liar and a cheat. But this time, you've made a big mistake. Unlike your precious Eliza, I'm not about to sit and wait while you chase around and have your fun elsewhere. I'm tired of your lies."

He groaned and dropped back down onto the wet sofa. Shaking his head he asked, "How long am I gonna have to listen to this?"

"Not long. I'm through, Martin. I've said all I've got to say. Get out. Your suitcase is by the door."

"Whoa, hold on there. This is my house, and if anybody leaves it's gonna be you."

"Wrong. It *was* your house. Now it's mine. You're leaving, because if you don't I'm gonna tell everything, including how you skim money off the men's union dues and how you married poor little innocent me knowing you were still married to Eliza."

"You think anybody's gonna believe a woman like you?"

"They will if Brother Wolff and I are telling the same story."

Martin lowered his face into hands, sat there for a few moments, then looked up at her with a weary expression. "After all I've done for you, you'd do that to me, Martha Mae?"

She nodded. "Absolutely. Because I know if I don't do it to you, sooner or later you'll do it to me, the same as you did it to Eliza."

When Martin finally left the house, it was late afternoon. At first, he'd planned to get a room in town, give Martha Mae a few days to cool down, and then try to patch things up. As he walked, a new thought came to him.

Maybe he was better off without her. Life was never easy with Martha Mae; yes, she knew how to make him happy, but women looking for a good time were a dime a dozen. He didn't have to put up with her crap.

He could start over. Find a new town, a new woman, a new life. He'd disappeared once; he could do it again. He wouldn't make the same mistakes this time. He'd use a different name and steer clear of the Masons. He could walk away and be rid of Martha Mae, Eliza, and the kids in one fell swoop.

A plan began to settle in his mind. That night he'd collect the men's union dues and pocket the money. It would be more than enough for a fresh start. By the time everyone went back to work on Monday, he'd be long gone.

Although Martin was pleased with the plan, he felt a certain sadness about leaving Martha Mae behind. She'd been the best thing in his life so far. Of course, he wouldn't have had to do any of this if it weren't for Eliza. She was the one who ruined his life. It was her fault. Her and those damn kids. Maybe he'd pay her one last visit before he left. Yeah, one last visit to take back the money he'd given her.

He left his suitcase in the bin at the train station and made the rounds, collecting union dues for the district. It took all evening but netted him a nice $942. He still had time to catch the 10:30 train to Barrettsville.

⁕

When Eliza came to, she was lying on the living room floor with her knickers beside her in shreds. She couldn't remember everything, but she remembered enough to know what had happened. The pain in her side was excruciating and worse yet when she tried to move. Crawling across the floor, she moved over to where she could hold onto the sofa and pull herself up. The pain was bad enough to cry out, but she didn't. The shame of what Martin had done would be a thousand times worse if the children were to find out.

Bracing herself against the furniture, the walls, and then the staircase rail, she made her way upstairs, got into her nightdress, and fell into the bed. She lay there too exhausted to move and too devastated to sleep. When she heard Oliver in the hallway, she called out to him.

"I'm not feeling well this morning. Could you see to breakfast? There's biscuits and—"

"What's wrong, Mama?"

"I fell on the staircase last night. I'll be okay once I rest up."

"My room's right by the staircase; if you fell, looks like I'd have heard it."

"It was late. You were asleep."

"I would've heard…" He hesitated. "Before or after Daddy left?"

"After, long after. I know what you're thinking, Oliver, but it wasn't your daddy. He left shortly after you went to bed."

"If it's all the same to you, me and Ben Roland are gonna be keeping an eye out today. You want me to send for the doctor?"

"It's not necessary. Just a pain in my side. No need to go spending money on the doctor. I'll be fine once I get some rest."

Oliver said he'd see to breakfast. As he turned away she caught the look on his face and knew he hadn't believed her.

Eliza hardly ever took to her bed; even after the children were born, she was up the next day. This time it was impossible. With the pain too great to move, she could do nothing but lie there, comforted by the attention the children showered upon her.

All day they were in and out of her room, asking if she wanted tea, a warm poultice, or an ice pack. If it wasn't one thing, it was another. Louella prepared both dinner and supper while the older boys kept watch over the house, checking the rooms, making sure the downstairs door was locked.

At various times throughout the afternoon, the tears would come. She'd pledged her life to Martin, borne eight of his babies. They'd laughed together, shared the same bed, and even in the most trying times she'd not complained or turned against him. She knew now life with him was and always had been an impossibility. She'd tried to make a silk purse from a sow's ear and failed miserably.

She thought of the Winchester they'd brought from Coal Creek. There'd been no need for it here, and it had remained in the back corner of the closet. Tomorrow she would take it out and have it at her side when he came again.

The hour grew late, and she could finally rest easy knowing the younger ones had been fed and put to bed. Eliza leaned back into the pillows and fell fast asleep. It was a troubled sleep with pain picking at her side and dreams thundering through her head.

A door slammed, and she heard the thud of heavy boots.

"Get the hell out of my way!"

"No," she heard Virgil say, his reedy voice thin but defiant. "We don't want you here no more."

A high-pitched scream followed and then a crash. Oliver's voice came next, angry, shouting something she couldn't make out. Footsteps on the staircase, the thud of flesh against flesh, the crack of bone.

She pushed herself up and climbed from the bed, hanging onto the table and then leaning against the wall. She moved slowly; too slowly. Pushing through the pain, she staggered into the hallway.

Just then, a shot rang out.

"No!" she screamed and crumpled to the floor.

Oliver ran back up the stairs and lifted his mama to her feet. "Are you okay?"

When she nodded, he turned to Ben Roland and took the rifle away from him.

"I told you not to use this unless it was necessary," he said.

Ben Roland didn't step back or flinch. "After seeing what he did to Virgil, it looked pretty necessary to me," he answered.

On the downstairs landing, Virgil looked up with a grin. "We did it! We saved Mama, didn't we?"

Oliver nodded, his face grim, as he looked at Martin's lifeless body lying on the staircase.

"Yeah, Virgil, we did it," he said. His words were heavy with the sound of sorrow.

Louella and Margaret Rose came from their room to see what was going on, and Eliza shooed them back to bed. A horrifying thing had happened, and it was tragic enough to have three of her boys be part of it. She would not permit the other children to bear witness.

Once she assured herself the younger ones wouldn't come out of their rooms, Eliza checked Martin. Just as she feared, he was dead.

"Dear God," she murmured, "how on earth did this happen?"

Ben Roland ducked his head. "I'm sorry, Mama, I didn't mean it to come to this, but when I heard Virgil scream…"

"That rifle was in the downstairs closet. How'd you get hold of it?"

"We took it out earlier today. You told Oliver you hurt yourself when you fell, but we knew better. We figured mean as Daddy can be, he might come back, so we set up a watch. Ollie was downstairs, and I was up here listening."

She glanced at Oliver. "Is this true? You set a trap for your daddy?"

"It wasn't a trap, Mama, just a plan to keep you and the little kids safe."

"And you included Virgil?"

"He wasn't supposed to be here," Ben Roland said defensively. "He got out of bed and came looking for me."

"How'd your daddy get in the house?"

Oliver shrugged. "I think he had a key. I didn't hear nothing until the door slammed and we heard him stomping up the stairs. Virgil grabbed onto him and started screaming. When I started up the stairs after Daddy, he threw Virgil down on the landing and came after me. That's when Ben Roland shot him."

"It's my fault," Ben Roland said. "I'm the one what shot him, and I'll take the blame."

"You're not taking the blame for this," Oliver said. "It was both of us."

Panic swelled in Eliza's chest. Perhaps if it were another time or different circumstances she might have reacted differently, but still angered by the way Martin had shamed her the decision came easily.

"Your daddy has caused this family grief enough," she said. "Neither of you boys are going to take the blame for anything. We'll clean up this mess and pretend it never happened."

Oliver furrowed his brow in thought. "If we're gonna pretend it never happened, we've got to get rid of Daddy's body."

Each of her children had their own gift. Ben Roland was stronger and a dead-on shot, but Oliver was the more practical one, the one to reason things through and search for a sensible solution.

Eliza grimaced, partly because of her pain, more so because of the hard truth Oliver had spoken. "And put it where?" she asked.

"I'll worry about that Mama." Oliver took hold of her arm and helped her over to the bannister. "Lean on me, and I'll help you down the stairs so you can sit."

They went down the steps, slowly, one at a time. With each step she felt the sharp pain shoot through her rib cage, but alongside the pain was the love that swelled inside her heart. They were a family, and they would remain so. For as long as she lived, she would deny the events of this night and protect her boys just as they had protected her.

While the sky was still black, the two oldest boys slipped out the back door of the house pulling the wagon they'd found in the basement. The cargo in the wagon was covered by a blanket. They made their way through the woods and back streets until they reached the west branch of the Susquehanna River where they unloaded their cargo and watched as the current pulled it under and carried it off.

It was early morning when they got home. No one had seen them coming or going.

Despite the pain of what she guessed to be a broken rib, Eliza had managed to scrub the staircase and clean the gun. She set it back in the closet where it had been since they arrived and would remain until they left the house. Louella helped with breakfast that morning, and when the little ones asked about what happened, Eliza said only that Virgil had gotten out of bed and stumbled down the stairs.

"Nothing to worry about," she said, but she knew the sorrow of that night would remain in her heart. It would be with her for every hour of every day for as long as she lived.

◯◐◍◑◯

In the weeks that followed, a union man and the police came around investigating Martin's disappearance. Eliza shrugged and said she had nothing to tell them.

"The last time I saw him was that Thursday of the snowstorm. He brought me money for the kids, stayed for supper, then left. I haven't heard from him since."

"Strange how a man can just up and disappear," the young officer said.

"Not all that strange," Eliza said. She told him how Martin had disappeared when they were living in West Virginia and how the Masons had tracked him down and pressured him into supporting the children. "My guess is that he got tired of supporting them and decided to disappear again."

"Disgraceful," the officer said, his face pinched with a look of disapproval. "A man who'd do a thing like that ought to be shot."

Eliza gave a solemn nod. "Yes, I suppose he should."

1968

The Tragic Secret

As they pulled into the drive of Virgil's house Margaret studied the look of the place, trying to decide whether it appeared as though the owner was simply away for a few days or had packed up and left town. It was impossible to tell. As soon as the ignition was switched off, she jumped out of the car and hurried to the door. Tom followed along behind her.

After she'd knocked on Virgil's door several times, she slid the envelope with the note she'd written through the mail slot and suggested Tom check the back yard. As he circled around, she stepped over the azalea bushes, stood on her toes, and peered in the front window. She heard the sound of a car door open and close but figured it to be one of the neighbors. Not bothering to investigate, she shaded her eyes and pressed her nose to the glass.

"Hey! What the devil are you doing back there?"

Margaret turned so quickly she almost fell into the bushes. "You startled me!"

"I'm sorry about that! Who are you and what are you looking for?"

Margaret climbed across the bushes, brushing away the leaves stuck to her slacks as she came toward the man.

"I'm looking for my bro—"

Her mouth dropped open. After so many years, she'd wondered if she would recognize him but she did. He was older, his hair more silver than brown, but his eyes were the same, as was the way he stood with his head jutted forward and tilted ever so slightly.

"Virgil?"

He nodded. "Yes, what can I do for you?"

She felt the tears rising up in her eyes. "It's me, Margaret Rose."

"Well, I'll be..." He stood there looking stunned for a moment, then reached out and wrapped her in his arms. "I never in a million years thought..."

The tearful reunion was followed by a round of introductions and hours of catching up. Margaret introduced Tom as a friend who was helping her to find everyone. With a fond glance his way, she said, "I could never have done it without him."

She told Virgil of their visit to Coal Creek and pulled the packet of photos from her purse and passed them around. "Aunt Caldonia's still alive, and the barrel door is still there. I actually crawled through it and scared the life out of her."

Virgil and his wife, Jean, both laughed. Jean was bright-eyed and funny, a petite woman who somehow made Virgil seem taller than he was. Margaret liked her easy laugh and the way she jumped in as Virgil told stories of how they met, dated for a year, and then got married.

"I was still living with Ben Roland," he said. "He was best man at our wedding."

For a long while they talked about Ben Roland and his wife, Rebecca, and how they'd taken Virgil into their home and treated him like a son.

"Ben Roland was only eight years older than me," Virgil said, "but he was always my protector; even before Barrettsville but more so after." His eyes grew teary as he told about the day of the mine accident and the agony of waiting to learn whether Ben Roland was one of the few men that made it out.

"Mama was right to never allow any of us to work the mines," he said. "It's a life harder than you can imagine. When I was in high school, I watched Ben Roland come home night after night with an aching back and the coal dust so deep in his skin that it didn't come out no matter how many times he'd wash his hands."

"Did he ever talk about quitting?"

Virgil shook his head. "Rebecca and I both asked him to, and he used to say 'Maybe someday.' At the time, I was working as a teacher and she was waitressing. We could have gotten by even if he made less, so it wasn't just the money."

"Then why did he stay?"

"After Barrettsville he got restless, had to be moving, had to be doing something all the time. He was serious as a preacher. The only one who could get him to laugh was Rebecca, and even for her it wasn't easy."

Margaret frowned at the description of their brother. "That's not how I remember Ben Roland. He was always looking for fun, laughing at everything, playing pranks on people—"

Virgil drew a deep breath. "Working in the mine seemed to be his way of punishing himself."

"Why did he need to punish himself?"

Virgil sat quietly for a moment. Margaret exchanged a glance with Tom and Jean. Tom's face was blank. Jean stared at her hands.

"Was it something to do with what happened in Barrettsville?" Margaret went on.

Shock made his eyes wide. "You know about that?"

"Only that something happened," Margaret said, a tremor in her voice. "Was it bad? Virgil, you have to tell me, was it bad?"

His eyes reflected the grief of remembering.

"Not now," he finally said. "Maybe later."

He moved on to talking about Rebecca and how Ben Roland said marrying her was the best thing he'd done in his entire life.

"I used to tease him and say that I thought bringing me here to live with him was the best thing, but he'd shake his head and say, 'Sorry, kid, you're the second-best.'" Virgil laughed. "Kid, that's what he used to call me. Even after I was grown up and out of college."

"Sounds like the two of you were very close," Tom said.

Virgil nodded. "We were. Ben Roland was like a father to me."

"Where's Rebecca now?" Margaret asked.

"A few years after the accident, she loaded up her car and drove off. Said she couldn't stand living with the sadness of Ben Roland's memory. I didn't hear from her for a long time, and then I got a phone call. She said she was getting married again and asked if we would like to come to the wedding." He looked over at his wife and smiled. "Jeanie and I both went, didn't we, hon?"

She gave a nod. "Yes, we did, and what a wedding it was. Rebecca married a drummer from New Orleans, and all his friends were musicians. We ate shrimp jambalaya, drank Sazeracs, and danced until dawn."

"It was great to see Rebecca happy again," Virgil added. "She asked if it bothered me that she was marrying someone else, and I said absolutely not. I told her she'd mourned Ben Roland long enough, and it was time she started living again."

Margaret thought about the advice. "How long was that after Ben Roland died?"

"Five years. But I would have felt the same whether it was five years, five days, or five months. Rebecca was good to me and good to Ben Roland. She did everything she could to make him happy and loved him until the day he left this earth. A man can't ask for any more than that."

As the afternoon wore on, Margaret spoke about her years with Albert, telling how he'd hired a detective to look for her siblings and then given up the search.

"That's how I met Tom." She glanced at Tom with a smile and talked about the trip to Wheeling in search of Oliver. "Unfortunately, I waited too long. He died five years ago."

"I know. Ben Roland stayed in touch with Oliver after he left the glass company, which meant I was able to talk to Oliver too. We even got word about John Paul at one point."

Margaret's heart pounded, and she clasped her hands. "Did you talk to him? When?"

Virgil shook his head, his excitement dimmed. "No, none of us talked to him, but Oliver got a call once from one of his former classmates who was thinking of moving to Wheeling. He mentioned that someone saw John Paul at the train station in Charleston, and when they asked him where he was headed, he said Canada. He went up there to be a forest ranger, can you believe that?"

Margaret nodded. "I surely can. John Paul always felt more at home in the woods than he did with any of us. Did you ever hear anything more?"

Virgil shook his head. "No, that was the last. I've often wondered if he married or had kids, but there was never any word. I guess he's doing what he likes to do, so we have to believe he's happy."

"Let's hope so. I know Oliver was. We spent time with his daughter, Jolyn, and her family when we were in Wheeling. Did you know Dewey also has a daughter and a son? His son's a doctor and the boy has now taken over Dewey's practice. And, get this, Nellie has four girls, teenagers, no less."

They went back and forth like that, one remembering one thing and the other one something else.

"Do you think all of us being separated the way we were was what Mama really wanted?" Margaret asked at one point.

Virgil shook his head. "It wasn't what she wanted, but after everything that happened it was what she felt she had to do to keep us safe and give us a better life."

When the sky turned dusky, Jean insisted they stay for dinner.

"Nothing fancy," she said and pulled out a box of spaghetti and a bunch of vegetables. She handed Margaret a bag of tomatoes. "You can chop these while I do the onions and peppers."

Sitting there in the kitchen and talking as if they'd known each other forever, Margaret knew before long Jean would be like a sister. She couldn't help but think how foolish she'd been to wait all those years before looking for her siblings. She'd spent decades wishing for a family when all the while she had one. If only she'd looked.

They spent the next three days together, brother and sister, laughing, talking, telling stories, catching up with all the things they'd missed knowing about each other. On the last afternoon, as they sat together in the back yard swing, Virgil said, "I know you want me to tell you what happened in Barrettsville, but it's a hard thing for me to let go of."

"Caldonia said that what happened there affected all of us, but I don't understand why you, Ben Roland, and Oliver were the only ones to know about it."

"Because we were there when it happened. Us and Mama. She made all three of us promise that we'd never breathe a word of it to anybody, especially our sisters and brothers."

"Mama's been dead over fifty years, Virgil, and I doubt she'd want me to go on wondering forever why we were separated."

"I suppose you're right," he said, "but you've got to promise not to tell another soul. Not Tom; not anybody."

"You mean you never told anybody else? Not even Jeanie?"

Virgil nodded. "Especially Jeanie. She loved Ben Roland the same as I did."

The sky had been a clear blue all day, but at that moment a cloud passed overhead and a shadow fell across Virgil's face. In it, Margaret saw the pain of whatever he was about to say. She remembered the small boy who'd been picked on and the big brother who'd defended him, and her heart ached more than she thought possible. She reached across and took his hand in hers.

"Don't tell me if you don't want to. You're my brother, and nothing you say or don't say will change that." She was silent for a long while before she spoke again. "We're family, Virgil. I lost you once, but I'm not going to lose you again. Mama was right in wanting a better life for us, but she was wrong in thinking we'd be better off apart."

"I honestly don't know if she was or wasn't. She thought for sure Martha Mae knew where Daddy was that night and figured if we were scattered around there'd be nobody left but her to blame."

Margaret wanted to ask what blame he was talking about, but she didn't. After a few minutes, Virgil began speaking.

"Do you remember in Barrettsville that night when Mama fell down the steps and broke a couple of her ribs?"

When Margaret sat there looking puzzled, he continued. "It was not long before we came back to Coal Creek; A month or two at most."

Margaret nodded. "Oh, yes, now I do."

"Well, all along, Oliver didn't believe Mama had fallen down the stairs. He thought her being hurt was Daddy's doing. Then that next night, she went around twice to make sure the door and windows were locked. Oliver figured she was scared of something and suspected it was Daddy."

"Why?"

Virgil shrugged. "He'd been in an ugly mood the night before, and everybody knew if he got drunk he was capable of most anything. Anyway, Oliver and Ben Roland decided to keep watch that night to make sure nothing happened to Mama or us younger kids. Since the house was locked up tight, Oliver expected Daddy to come banging on the front door. Nobody knew he had a key, so nobody heard him come in. When he started up the stairs, I was coming down. That's when all hell broke loose."

"What do you mean?"

For a moment Virgil was quiet, almost as though he was picturing how it happened.

"I was in the way; Daddy shoved me, and I started screaming. He pushed me down the steps, and then he saw Oliver coming at him. They fought, and there was a lot of yelling and banging around. I was still dazed from the fall and honestly couldn't say who was getting the best of who. But I did hear the shot. When I looked up, Ben Roland was standing on the upstairs landing with Mama's shotgun in his hand."

Margaret's eyes went wide, and her words grew wobbly. "He...shot Daddy?"

Virgil nodded, then doubled over, covering his face. When he finally spoke again, his voice was thick with emotion.

"Daddy was always so hurtful to me that I'd wished him dead a million or more times, but seeing him there on the staircase with blood all over his face was something I never..."

Margaret moved closer and wrapped her arm around his trembling shoulders. "It was an accident. Wishing somebody dead doesn't mean—"

Lifting his face, he turned to look at her. "I'm not crying for myself, Margaret, I'm crying for Ben Roland. My screaming was what made him fire the gun."

"You don't know that. He was probably just trying to scare—"

Virgil shook his head. "You know Ben Roland could shoot the eye out of an eagle if he wanted to. He shot to kill."

They sat there for a long time, brother and sister wrapped in a blanket of silence, the swing no longer moving. As the sun ducked in and out behind a bank of clouds, Virgil went on to tell how Oliver and Ben Roland put their daddy's body in the wagon, rolled it down to the river, and watched him float away.

"None of us were the same after that. It was as if a piece of us died that night right along with Daddy."

Margaret's eyes grew teary as she listened to Virgil tell of how their mama had sworn all three boys to secrecy. All of a sudden, her constant fearfulness even when they returned to Coal Creek made sense. Although

Virgil never said it outright, Margaret knew if the police did trace Martin to their door their mama would have claimed she was the one responsible for his death.

"Even though Mama told us to never speak of it again, we did when it was just the three of us," Virgil went on. "Sometimes Oliver would say it was his fault for agreeing to let Ben Roland take the shotgun, but most of the time it was Ben Roland blaming himself. I seldom said anything, but God only knows how many times I'd lie away at night thinking if I hadn't screamed like a baby none of that would have happened and we could have gone on living in Barrettsville."

"Didn't you ever think that if you hadn't screamed, Daddy might have come upstairs and shot us all?"

"He couldn't have," Virgil said. "He didn't have a gun."

"You can't say for sure."

"Yes, I can. We were hoping the body wouldn't be identified too quickly, so we emptied out his pockets before the older boys took him to the river. All he had were some keys, a few loose bills, and an envelope full of money."

Margaret drew a deep breath. "I'm sorry."

"For what?"

"Maybe if all of us were around to help share the weight of what you were dealing with…"

Virgil shook his head. "That's not how it works. Guilt is a burden that can only be carried by those who own it. In time, Oliver and I learned to live with ours. Ben Roland never did. He went through life believing he deserved to be punished for what he'd done. I think that's why he worked in the mine. He never complained about it, but Oliver and I knew it was the hell he'd chosen for himself."

They sat and talked until the sun had fallen to the edge of the horizon and Margaret came to realize that although the siblings had been broken apart, each of them had forever carried a piece of the others in their hearts.

That night when Margaret was alone in her room, she prayed. She asked forgiveness for Ben Roland saying he'd suffered enough during his years on earth and had only done what any of them would have done in the same circumstances. She also prayed that one day they would all be together again.

"Everyone," she said. "Oliver, Ben Roland, Mama..."

As she went through the list of names, there was no mention of her daddy.

Return to Heatherwood

On the trip home Tom drove for six hours straight, stopping once to fill the gas tank and for lunch at a roadside stand. It rained for much of the drive, a sad steady drizzle.

"Gloomy day, isn't it?" he said.

Margaret nodded. "Very."

For a while she'd followed their route on the Alabama road map, but as soon as they crossed into Georgia she folded the map and stuck it back in the glove compartment. As they talked about the trip he asked what hotels and sites she'd enjoyed most, but Margaret found herself hard-pressed to give an answer.

She'd loved every minute of the time they'd spent together and on several occasions wished it would go on forever, but it was not going to. In a matter of hours it would be over, and she would have to face the reality of returning home. Home to a house filled with reminders of Albert and friends who just a few months earlier had attended his funeral. They were people who liked and respected Albert. Men who envied his success and women who admired him. More than once one of her friends had commented on how fortunate she was to have such a husband. Natalie Biddle had even suggested she'd trade her Donald for Albert any day of the week. She'd said it in a lighthearted way, but Margaret knew there was more than a grain of truth in what she said.

Just last Christmas, Josie had said Albert was the most generous man she'd ever worked for; one in a million, she'd called him. And in the days following his death, when Margaret was powerless to stop the tears, Josie had listened patiently, nodding her agreement to every good and admirable trait mentioned.

"There will never be another Albert," she said, "but at least you've got your memories."

Memories were not the same as being with someone who made you laugh and feel alive again.

"You seem awfully quiet today," Tom said. "Is something bothering you?

"I'm just sad to see our trip come to an end."

"Just because this trip is over doesn't mean there won't be another one. Next summer maybe we could drive down to see Caldonia."

He said it in an offhanded way, a suggestion, not a plan, and she couldn't bring herself to answer him, so she stared out the window at the rivulets of water flung from the wiper blades.

She could have contented herself with the thought that they'd remain friends, but even that would be impossible. If this were four or five years later, she'd welcome the thought of having Tom in her life but not now. Not when Albert's presence was still so keenly felt. Not when their friends and neighbors were still grasping her hand with that hangdog look and saying if she needed anything, anything at all, to call on them. Regardless of what her heart wanted, she could not bring herself to belittle Albert's memory in such a way.

In Georgia, they rode for miles without speaking. When he finally pulled up in front of the house, Tom carried her bags inside.

"Would you like me to take these upstairs?"

"No, just leave them here. I'll have plenty of time to see to them later on. I'm a little tired."

"Well...okay then. I'm...I'm glad we did this, Maggie. I'll call you soon."

He bent and kissed her cheek, and she closed her eyes to savor it. All too soon, Tom was out the door and down the walk. Margaret watched until the taillights of his car disappeared around the corner and then, struggling to stem the flow of tears, she turned back to face the empty house.

The next morning, Margaret came down and spotted the big suitcase still sitting there at the foot of the stairs. Now she regretted not letting Tom take it upstairs when he'd offered.

As if the thought were a summons, the telephone rang. Margaret answered it, and her heart ached when she heard Tom's voice on the other end.

"If you want, I can stop by and take you to get the last few rolls of film developed, and after that—"

She knew if she didn't do this now, she never would. But as she spoke she could feel her heart breaking into a million little pieces.

"It's probably better if you don't come, Tom. Better for both of us."

"Excuse me?"

"I said I think it's better if we don't see—"

"I heard you the first time, but I'm not sure where this is coming from. I thought we had something special, Maggie."

"We do. Did. You know I care for you, Tom, it's not that."

"Then what is it?"

"Albert. It's been less than six months since he passed away. I can't have people see us together this soon, I just can't."

"Albert?" he repeated. "What does Albert have to do with us?"

"We were married for almost fifty years. Don't you think it would seem disrespectful for me to start dating so soon after—"

"Dating? Is that what you think this is?" He paused. "I thought this was a whole lot more than a casual relationship. I thought we were falling in love. I know I was."

She struggled to hold back the tears. "I felt the same, Tom. And that's why we can't be friends. It would never—"

"I'm not looking to be your friend, Maggie. I want to spend the rest of my life with you."

She twisted the phone cord around her fingers. "I want that too, Tom, but not now. Maybe in a few years."

"Why not now?"

"After Ben Roland died, Rebecca waited five years before remarrying. Shouldn't I show the same respect for—"

"For God's sake, Maggie, Rebecca was in her late thirties. She could afford to wait. We're in our sixties. Neither of us know how many years we've got ahead of us, but however many there are I'd like to spend them together. I don't want to wait around while you pay homage to a man who is dead and buried."

"You make it sound like a foolish formality. It's not. It's what's expected of a widow. If I married you now or next week or next year, don't you think my friends and neighbors who knew and liked Albert would talk?"

"If they were actually friends, they'd celebrate your happiness instead of gossiping about it. If they do choose to talk, let them. Who cares?"

In a voice so small it could barely be heard, Margaret said, "I care."

This time she felt like a canyon too wide and deep to cross had opened between them.

"I'm disappointed in you, Maggie," Tom said, his tone flat, "more disappointed than I ever thought possible. After the experience I had with my ex, I was determined not to let myself get involved with anyone again. Then you came along. Everything about you seemed so sincere, so genuine. I let myself fall in love with you because I believed we truly could find happiness together." He hesitated a moment, drew a deep breath, then let it go. "You used me, Maggie. You used me to get what you wanted. The only difference between you and my ex is that there was no dog for you to take."

"No, Tom, that's not it at all. Please, you have to believe me."

There was a click, then the telephone line went dead.

That night Margaret did not even try to sleep. She waited until after midnight to fold back the coverlet and climb into bed. After only a few minutes, she got up and stood by the window watching the rain.

She reminded herself that she'd known Tom less than six months, and in the beginning he'd been a friend; nothing more. This feeling she had for him was something that had come about while they were on the trip. She had to believe in time it would pass. Once she settled into her old routine, she'd be able to push aside the ache in her heart and move through the day without thinking of him. It wasn't as if they'd been together for 50 years the way she and Albert had.

Trying to comfort herself with her memories, she snapped on the lamp, turned toward the dresser, and straightened the pictures. The silver frame containing the studio head shot of Albert in his dark suit was tarnished in the corners. Funny; she hadn't noticed that before. She made a mental note to remind Josie they'd need to clean it with polish.

Next, she studied the one they'd taken at a country club dance. It wasn't a particularly attractive shot of either of them, and she couldn't imagine why she'd chosen that particular photo to frame. Well, it was time to change it up anyway. With all the pictures she'd brought home from the trip, she'd want to frame a few shots of her siblings. Maybe the group shot from the party at Dewey's house. She smiled thinking back on that night and how Tom had gotten everyone together for a group shot.

"Oh, drat," she said, remembering that the next-door neighbor had insisted he take the photo so Tom would be in the picture. She couldn't use that one, but there were plenty of others.

Figuring she was unable to sleep anyway, she decided to pick out a new photo for the frame. She snapped on the second lamp, grabbed the packet from her bag, and sat in bed shuffling through the photos. Each was a memory to be treasured.

She stopped and lingered over the shot of her and Caldonia. They'd stood on the front porch with the sun on their faces. Tom had taken the shot so he wasn't in that picture, but when Margaret looked closely she could see his shadow in the foreground.

Wondering if perhaps the shadow could be cut out she covered it with her thumb, but that made the picture lopsided. Gathering the photos, she slid them back into the envelope and tucked it into the nightstand drawer. There was no rush. She'd look at them again next week or next month when her mind was clearer.

⁂

Margaret waited two days to call Josie and say she was back.

"If you have time, I could use some company today," she said.

"I can be there in a half-hour," Josie replied. "On the way, I'll stop and pick up some bread, fresh eggs, cream, and—"

"Don't bother shopping. I went to the store yesterday."

"You were home yesterday and didn't call?"

"I unpacked and went through some mail."

"Well, good. I'll make us a nice lunch, and you can tell me all about the trip."

That afternoon as they sat across from one another at the kitchen table, Margaret told of seeing her siblings for the first time in over 50 years and showed the photos.

"It was the trip of a lifetime," she said nostalgically.

One by one, she described those she'd met. Nellie, who was in first grade when Margaret left home, was now the mother of four teenage daughters. Dewey had gone on to enjoy the medical career he'd once dreamed of having. Holding out the group picture they'd taken at the party, she pointed to the younger Dr. Hobbs.

"This is Dewey's son, Oliver. He's taken over the practice now."

Josie held the photo and studied the faces as Margaret filled in the details. When she handed the picture back, she grinned.

"Seems like Mr. Tom Bateman fit in right well."

"Why would you say that?"

Josie leaned over and pointed to the picture. "See this young fella standing next to Mr. Bateman; he's Dewey's boy, right?"

Margaret nodded. "Yes, that's Oliver."

"Well, he's got his arm around Mr. Bateman's shoulder. That ain't something you do unless you're feeling good about somebody."

Squinting at the picture, she smiled. "I'll be darned, I hadn't noticed that before."

"It's not just him. These ladies are looking at Mr. Bateman and laughing like he'd said something funny." She was pointing to Dewey's wife and daughter-in-law.

As Margaret examined their faces, she was swept back to the memory of that evening and smiled.

"They were laughing because Oliver insisted Tom stand in the middle of the group with him. It started out that Tom was the one taking the picture. He claimed it was a family picture, and he didn't belong in it. Then the next-door neighbor came over, and everybody wanted Tom to be in the picture. At first, he was at the far end next to the kids, but Oliver said he should be in the middle." She paused. "Tom said he was better off at the end so that later on we could cut him out if we wanted. That's when Oliver had everybody slide over a space and put Tom in the middle."

He'd also said they had no plans to cut Tom out, but Margaret didn't mention that.

"Sounds like you and Mr. Bateman had yourself one heck of a good time."

"We did," Margaret replied wistfully. "We truly did."

Friends and Neighbors

After several days of moping around the house and wondering if she'd done the right thing, Margaret convinced herself that keeping busy was the key to forgetting Tom. She managed to stall Jeffrey Schoenfeld on the phone yet again when he called about Albert's shares in the firm. Then she called friends she hadn't spoken to in months, scheduled a number of lunch dates, and volunteered to work on the Library Ladies' Pre-K Committee.

On Tuesday when she had lunch with four of the ladies at the country club, she tried to talk about the thrill of reconnecting with her siblings. They listened politely but didn't seem too interested in the details. After the conversation fell silent for the second time in 10 minutes, the other women began gossiping about all the things that had gone on while Margaret was away.

Cassidy Morrison had her nose in a twit because somebody had taken the flowering cactus in the ladies' locker room and moved it from the entrance desk to the window sill.

"Outrageous," she said. "It belongs on the desk. I've a mind to report it to the chairman of the housekeeping committee."

Margaret suggested the move was likely made to provide the plant with more sunlight, but the women agreed with Cassidy that a formal complaint was in order.

After the cactus issue was finally put to bed, Edna Wingate showed off the sapphire ring her husband had given her for her birthday.

"Of course, I picked it out myself," she said. "Millard knows I never like what he buys, so he said, 'Just buy what you want,' and I did." After Edna mentioned the price three times, they switched to talking about how much weight Sara Bentley had gained and the fact that Mary Beth Thompson's new haircut looked like it was done with a lawnmower.

When she returned home that afternoon, Margaret had to take a couple of aspirin and lie down. As she lay there waiting for her headache to subside, she wondered why she'd ever thought those women so entertaining. The next morning, she mentioned the episode to Josie and said she wasn't so sure she wanted to hold onto their country club membership.

"Albert loved it, and we did have some good times there, but I think it's changed."

"Give it time," Josie suggested. "Maybe the ladies just had an off day. You know, the kind where the least little thing gets blown out of proportion. And, don't forget, this is the first time you've gone back to the club alone. That could be making you see things differently."

Margaret gave a dubious-looking shrug. "I guess that's possible."

She was equally disappointed in Irene Duchamp who lived two houses down. They'd been friends forever and had countless good times together, but it now seemed Irene had also changed. It became evident on the Thursday they went to Lili's Boutique. They'd had lunch in town then stopped at Lili's to check out the sale on winter fashions. Irene spotted a blouse she wanted, and when they didn't have her size she acted as put out as a teenager. The poor salesgirl fumbled around and finally came up with a suitable substitute, but Irene continued to harp on the issue even after they'd left the store.

In her mind, Margaret crossed off shopping excursions with Irene.

The one thing she enjoyed was the Ladies Library meetings. She tried to contribute her ideas, but because she missed meetings while she and Tom were away she was behind on everything the group was planning. She enjoyed seeing everyone on the committee again, but that happiness lasted only as long as she was in the library. When she came home, the gloom of missing Tom came back in full force.

Before the month was out, she'd grown tired of socializing and took to staying in all afternoon to watch television or read a book. For a while she tuned in *The Days of Our Lives* and *As the World Turns*, but before long she found the ongoing drama made her even more depressed so she switched the television off.

Having given up soap operas, she began writing letters to her siblings, nieces, and nephews. The letters were often five or six pages long and mostly about the trip and how much she'd enjoyed meeting them. Although she never mentioned Tom by name, an occasional "we" slipped in. It was unavoidable.

In their return letters everyone not only mentioned Tom, but they asked how he was and said to give him their love. Letters such as that left her stumped about how to respond. She could circumvent the question of Tom and write about whatever was happening if there were something new to say, except there wasn't.

At first, she'd written the letters at the kitchen table. After she noticed cookie crumbs stuck to Dewey's envelope, she decided to move into Albert's office. In there it seemed far less likely she'd drift off to thinking about Tom, and it was foolish to let a perfectly good desk go to waste. To make room for her newly-acquired boxes of stationery and the growing collection of novels from the library and the bookstore, she cleared out Albert's desk and the bookcase. The law journals were replaced by books such as *The Agony and the Ecstasy, Portnoy's Complaint,* and *The Time Machine.* Bit by bit, the essence of Albert that at one time had permeated the room disappeared along with the law journals. Only thoughts of Tom remained.

As Thanksgiving neared, the weather went from cool to downright cold. The daylight hours grew shorter, and the nights became longer than ever. Even when she went to bed exhausted, she'd lie there for hours staring up at the ceiling and wondering where Tom was or what he was doing. Over and over, she tried to rid herself of his memory but couldn't. Smack in the middle of counting sheep or saying a prayer, she'd hear the echo of his laugh or feel the weight of his arm across her shoulder.

Along with losing sleep, she lost her appetite and grew thinner by the day. Regardless of what outfit she pulled from the closet, it hung from her shoulders as if it were a size too large.

The only bright spot in her otherwise dreary life was when Josie came. Any cleaning chores she once did were pushed aside. When Josie talked about the tasks she had to get to, Margaret shook her head and claimed it wasn't necessary.

"We can polish the silver next week or the week after," she'd say. "Let's relax today. I've got a letter from Dewey I'd like to read to you."

If it wasn't a letter she was looking to share, it was another reminiscence about the trip. She tried, really tried, to avoid any mention of Tom's name, but he was always there inside her head. In the middle of telling a story about one of her brothers, a smile would appear when she remembered something Tom had said or done. Her stories of Albert, the country club, and neighborhood friends had somehow been forgotten.

A few days before the holiday, Josie invited Margaret to share Thanksgiving with her family.

"It's not real fancy," she said, "but we'd be honored to have you."

Margaret begged off, claiming she'd only put a damper on the festivities.

"Maybe another time," she said.

Josie dropped down in the chair opposite Margaret.

"I doubt there's gonna be another time," she said, "because the likelihood is you're either gonna die of starvation or loneliness before another year comes around."

Margaret gasped. "How can you even suggest such a thing?"

"I can say it 'cause it's true. Ever since you got home, you been moping around here like the world's coming to an end."

"That's because I'm still mourning Albert."

"It ain't Mr. Albert you're mourning, it's Mr. Tom Bateman. When he was coming around, you were laughing and happy. Now you look like you got one foot in the grave."

"Well, it is what it is. Seeing Tom is simply out of the question. It would be disrespectful to Albert's memory. What would people say if I start dating before he's gone a year?"

"Why do you care what they say?"

"Because I'm not one to hang my dirty laundry on the line for folks to gossip about."

"Yours ain't dirty laundry, it's clean laundry that you don't got to be ashamed of airing. You and Mr. Bateman are both single; there's no sin in single folks getting together."

"Under normal circumstances, maybe, but I owe Albert—"

"You don't owe Mr. Albert nothing. You were a good wife to him long as he was alive, and a man can't ask no more than that."

Margaret straightened with surprise. "Why, that's the exact same thing Virgil said about Ben Roland's wife."

Josie laughed. "Maybe if enough people say it, you'll start believing it."

She sat there in thought for a moment. Then, for the first time in weeks, Margaret laughed. That afternoon she was hungry enough to eat a ham sandwich and two peanut butter cookies.

In the days that followed, Margaret found herself thinking hard about Josie's words. If such a thing were true, then did the length of time matter? Who was to say whether it should be five years, five months, or five days? Was time the only measure of love and loyalty, or was there much more to be considered?

She had been a good wife to Albert. She'd lived with an empty spot in her heart simply because he couldn't come to grips with the thought of adoption. She'd given up the joy of a child for him. Wasn't that enough? Was she also expected to give up this one last chance for happiness?

As the answers to those questions became more and more obvious, a great loneliness settled into Margaret's heart. It had the weight of a boulder pressing against her chest. At night as she stood by the window and watched the wind carry off the few remaining leaves, she'd tell herself that dying would be far easier than living with such heartache. Thinking back on their time together, she remembered the warmth of Tom's body lying beside her and the richness of his laughter over all those meals and hours driving. In time she began to wonder if there was a way she could make things right.

She wanted to believe if he loved her three months ago, he loved her still. She'd sent him away, but she'd hadn't stopped loving him. If she hadn't forgotten Tom, wasn't it possible that he also hadn't forgotten her? As the days passed, she allowed that thought to take root. Before long she could feel the boulder becoming the tiniest bit lighter.

The week before Christmas, she sat at what was now her desk and penned a letter to Tom. She opened her heart and allowed all the sorrow and pain she'd felt to spill out onto the paper. She spoke of what a fool she'd been and how she'd come to realize that what they had was true love. Pleading for a second chance, she swore she'd spend the rest of her life trying to make up for the heartache she'd caused and would never disappoint him again. As she dropped the letter into the mailbox, she prayed he'd understand, that he'd see the truth of her words and give their love another chance.

For the next five days she stood at the front window watching the walkway, hoping to see his car pull up in front of the house. She knew when she did, she would go flying out the door to greet him. Right there on the front walkway, where any and all could see, she'd throw her arms around his neck and kiss him full on the mouth. If he telephoned first, she'd tell him to hurry over because she had a lifetime of love to give him.

The days passed slowly. A minute seemed like an hour, and the hours felt endless. It was as if a single day could stretch itself into forever. At first, she reasoned that the mail might be slow, that perhaps he needed an extra day or so to think things over. She even considered that he might be planning to surprise her, show up on Christmas Day and ask if she'd like to accompany him to church.

The one thing she hadn't considered was what she received on Christmas Eve.

Stuffed in between a bunch of greeting cards and the electric bill, Margaret saw the letter she'd sent five days earlier. In a heavy black hand, he'd written "Return to Sender." He'd never even opened the envelope.

Margaret could no longer stem the tears. She cried for hours on end, chiding herself for what she'd done. She'd spent all those years missing her family, yet she'd never gone in search of them. She'd wanted a child, but she'd never pushed Albert into adoption. Now she'd lost Tom because she hadn't had courage enough to believe in their love.

Not once had she had enough backbone to fight for what she wanted. Not once. A woman with no spine got what she deserved.

All her life she'd stood back, content to let the chips fall where they may, but Tom hadn't. He found her family for her. Albert hadn't; he'd built a thriving law firm from scratch.

If you never try, you will never succeed.

On Christmas morning, Margaret woke with a renewed sense of determination. Of course Tom was angry. He had every right to be. He couldn't forgive her, because he hadn't heard what she had to say. Once he understood how truly apologetic she was, he'd be more understanding. The important thing was that she had to talk to him. Explain how she felt, let him know how very much she regretted her stupid decision.

Sitting at the desk with a pad and pencil, she wrote down all the things she needed to say. She read through the list five times and finally decided to stop putting it off. She dialed his number slowly, repeating each digit as she spun the dial around. He answered on the third ring.

"Bateman."

"Hello, Tom. This is Maggie. I need to talk to you, please—"

A click sounded.

"Tom?"

No response.

The sound of desperation rose in her voice. "Tom, are you there?"

A dial tone buzzed.

Her heart felt as though it would explode out of her chest as she redialed the number and sat there listening to it ring over and over. A sense of hopelessness settled into the deepest part of her soul. After 17 rings, she hung up, buried her face in her hands, and sobbed as her heart broke.

1910 – 1917

A Time to Leave

Since the rent had been paid through the end of March, Eliza and the children remained in the Barrettsville house for those two months. While to the eye it appeared nothing had changed, the truth was everything had. Whenever Eliza glanced at the upstairs landing, she could see Ben Roland standing there with the Winchester in his hand. At night she heard the walls whispering echoes of that night. And when she walked through the parlor, her knees went weak and her ribs ached.

She'd suffered two broken ribs in the attack, and they were slow to heal. Once she regained her strength, she told the children it was time they returned to Coal Creek.

"Why can't we just stay? We've been happy here," Oliver asked.

"We can't afford this house without your daddy helping out."

"Me and Ben Roland can both get a job, and you've got Daddy's money that—"

Eliza held her finger to her lips and shushed him. "You're not to speak of that."

No one wanted to leave. Margaret Rose cried and said she'd hoped to stay there for the rest of her life, and Dewey thought it a huge disappointment because for the first time ever he'd made some money toting boxes and mowing lawns. Although Louella was none too happy about moving back to Coal Creek, she agreed not to complain if she could bring the dresses that had been altered to fit.

"If Louella gets to bring her dresses, I wanna bring mine too," Margaret Rose said.

Even though Eliza's intent was to leave the house exactly as they'd found it, the children all had something they'd grown attached to and couldn't bear to leave behind. At first she said no, claiming the treasures of the house had been theirs to use but not to carry off. As the children continued to plead she relented, remembering the words in Sarah Alice Bligh's diary.

I want no further reminders of this place.

"I suppose it'll be okay if each of you takes one thing," she said. "One thing, no more."

Nellie chose the cloth doll she'd carried around ever since Ben Roland had handed it to her. Virgil wanted a handful of marbles and Dewey a magazine called *Robert Merry's Museum*. When John Paul said he was going to bring the big red wagon, Oliver gave a gasp.

"You can't let him do that, Mama."

"I won't," she replied. She explained to John Paul that the wagon was far too big to carry on the train. "You're very good at playing the harmonica. Why not pick that instead?"

He hesitated a moment, then grinned and gave a nod.

"Thank you, Mama," Oliver whispered. Like Ben Roland, he said there was nothing he wanted to bring home with him.

In that last week, Eliza often found herself thinking of Sarah Alice Bligh and wondering if she'd been right in believing the house cursed. Perhaps it was. Perhaps Sarah had left her heartache behind for others to inherit.

On the eve of the day they were to leave, Eliza decided to change the destiny of the house. She wrote a long letter and addressed it "To all those who come to live here." She told of the happy times they'd had as the children explored the attic and basement and discovered the wealth of treasures awaiting them. She spoke of fragrant summer breezes, the wisteria bushes that edged the backyard, and a fireplace that kept the parlor toasty even in the dead of winter. She told of the church in the square and described the shops, then she closed by saying that she, like the previous owner, was returning to the happiness of her childhood home. She folded the letter, left it in the desk drawer, and said a prayer that the walls of this house would no longer whisper of the tragedy that had taken place.

That night Eliza tucked Sarah's diary and the letters into her suitcase. They would go with her to West Virginia. In time, when she had the courage and with Caldonia beside her, she would strike a match to them and watch the last of Sarah Bligh's heartache disappear in a curl of smoke, just as the pennyroyal tea had.

Return to Coal Creek

The train ride back to West Virginia was long and sad. There was none of the happy chatter or eager anticipation that had accompanied them on their trip to Pennsylvania. There was no wondering what awaited them in Coal Creek. They knew.

Eliza reminded the children of things like seeing their friends again and Caldonia's cookies, but nothing cheered them. Looking from one child to another, she saw mouths turned down and shoulders slumped. Gone was the lightheartedness and spirit of adventure that sparkled in them for the past two years.

"I wish we could have stayed in Barrettsville forever," Margaret Rose said glumly. "We're never gonna have another house nice as that one."

Louella nodded. "It was fun to have a girls' room."

Each of the children had their own reason for wanting to stay in Barrettsville. Despite the treasures they carried back, they could find little joy in returning to Coal Creek.

Eliza said little as she sat and gazed absently out the window. She knew they had no alternative but to return to the old house, yet it did not have to be that way forever—at least not for the children. For now, they were together, a family. She would treasure this moment, however brief it might be, and deal with the future when the time came.

Caldonia and Jeb were waiting at the station when the train arrived. Eliza's letter had indicated only that Martin had disappeared again, and they'd be coming home. Caldonia hugged each child as Jeb tossed the suitcases into the back of the wagon. She then turned to Eliza and folded her into an embrace.

"I know you've been through a lot," she whispered, "but you're home now, and when you're ready to talk I'll be here."

As the wagon bounced up the rutted dirt road, Eliza thought of Barrettsville with its shiny green trolley and cobblestone streets. She thought of the girls twirling around in their dresses with lace pinafores and the confectioner's shop where for a dime each child could have a peppermint stick or horehound candy. That was the life she wanted for the children. Living up here in the hollow had been her life, but it was not going to be theirs.

Several weeks passed before Eliza found courage enough to tell Caldonia of all that had happened. By then her stomach had grown round and her breasts were pressed tight against the bosom of her dress.

"In the fall there will be another baby," she said and stumbled through an explanation of the attack, admitting that there was much she didn't remember. It proved even more difficult to tell of the night Martin died. When she spoke of hearing the shot and turning to see Ben Roland with the Winchester, the color left her face and tears filled her eyes.

"No one else knows," she said. "Only you, me, Oliver, Ben Roland, and Virgil. The other children must never know what happened. It has to be that way."

Caldonia nodded and swore she would carry the secret to the grave.

"If there comes a time when one of children questions why things are as they are, they might need to know the truth and if I'm not here…"

Clasping Eliza's hand, Caldonia said, "Don't you worry. If any of the kids ever need anything, I'll be here. We may not be blood family, but we're family all the same."

That summer Eliza sent Edward Wolff a letter. In it she explained how Martin had disappeared again, but she had no wish to find him. She went on to say that Oliver and Ben Roland were growing up quickly and had already spoken of finding work.

Other than digging coal from the mine, there is little for a young man to do here in Coal Creek, she wrote, *and although you have already done so much to help our family, I find I must ask for yet another favor.* She said the boys would be most appreciative if he could give them a word of advice or guidance to assist in their search for employment.

The letter told of how she'd lost her father to the mine and hoped her children would have an opportunity to pursue a better life.

Daddy died in an explosion that came without warning, but I have watched so many others die a slow and lingering death from miner's lung, their backs bent to where they can no longer stand straight, their eyes dimmed from the long hours spend in darkness, and their soul crushed by the bleakness of such a life. There is nothing I want more than to see my children move away from here and turn their backs on this fate.

On the last page, she said the brief time they'd spent in Barrettsville had enabled her and the children to know a life far better than they would ever find in Coal Creek.

Although circumstances did not permit us to remain there, the experience planted a seed of hope in their young hearts, and for that I will be eternally grateful.

She folded the seven-page letter into an envelope and sent it off.

Eliza received a response from Edward Wolff the first week of September. He apologized for the delay in getting back to her and said he had made several inquiries on behalf of the boys.

Alexander Dalworth, a longtime friend of mine and owner of the Superior Glass Company in Wheeling, has agreed to give both Oliver and Ben Roland a try. They will start as apprentices in the manufacturing plant and be given the opportunity for advancement once they have proven themselves capable.

Enclosed were two train tickets, the address of a nearby boarding house, the location of the Superior Glass Company, and the letter of introduction they were to give to Mr. Dalworth.

He closed by saying he thought Eliza a remarkable woman, and that while Martin was no longer welcome at the Masonic Lodge she could continue to call on him for whatever assistance she might need. He signed the letter, "Your admirer and friend, Edward Wolff."

On the day the boys left, Eliza accompanied them to the train station. She kissed them on the cheek, told them to write once they were settled, and stood with tears brimming her eyes as she waved goodbye and watched the train disappearing in the distance. This was what she'd wanted for the boys, for all of her children, and yet it left a hole in her heart.

That October Eliza gave birth to a baby boy and named him Edward for the man who had shown her such great kindness. Over the years she thought of Mr. Wolff often. At times she wished she had married just such a man, but she never sent another letter. She felt it was better that way, for Mr. Wolff was a man she could quite easily fall in love with.

In the years that followed, the Hobbs family led a quiet life. Eliza spent long afternoons sitting on the porch with Edward in her lap, Caldonia by her side, and the children playing in the yard. As she watched them grow and blossom, a new kind of happiness settled in her heart. It was a peacefulness she'd never known with Martin. He'd been a man who sought importance, and yet he'd ignored the people to whom he truly was important. In the end, he'd become a nameless body, swept away by the Susquehanna River, with no one to mourn him or grieve his loss.

At first she'd felt only hatred for him because of what he'd done and the heartache he'd caused, but over time the peacefulness she'd come to know pushed it aside and all that remained was a heartfelt sorrow that he'd never really known the joy of his children.

For months, she'd wrestled with guilt over the money the boys had taken from Martin's pocket, but there was no way she could return it without acknowledging what had happened. Ultimately she came to view it as a stroke of providence, for with it she bought the train tickets back to Coal Creek and saw to the children's needs for well over two years. While there was nothing left over for luxuries, no one went hungry or without shoes.

Dewey was the next to leave home. For nearly a year he'd been helping out at a small newspaper in Charleston. When a pressman left in November of 1912, they offered him the job. Nine months later,

Margaret Rose was sent to live with her elderly aunt in South Charleston. She'd raised quite a row over it and claimed if she was made to go she'd run away from home.

The night before she was to leave, Margaret Rose and her mama sat on the porch pushing back and forth in the swing.

"I realize you don't want to go," Eliza said, "but it's for your own good. Aunt Rose will teach you things I can't. You'll wear nice clothes, go to fancy restaurants, and meet the kind of young men who are worthy of your attention."

"Aunt Rose is terribly cranky, and she's always telling people what to do. If she sees you sitting comfortable in a chair, she pokes her finger in your back and says sit up."

"That's because she wants you to have a backbone that's straight and strong."

"I think it's because she hates me."

Eliza laughed. "Rose doesn't hate you; she loves you. But she remembers what it's like to live up here in the hollow and wants you to have it better."

"There's nothing wrong with living here," Margaret Rose said defensively.

"Do you think it's as nice as when we lived in Barrettsville?"

Margaret Rose pushed back and forth several times then shook her head.

"Wouldn't you like to have a house like that again? To live a place where you can ride the trolley into the square and stop into the confectioner's shop for a hot chocolate or dish of ice cream?"

"Well, sure. But, Mama—"

"No more buts. You're going to live with Aunt Rose, because I want that life for you." She gave a lingering sigh. "If you get homesick and start missing me, I want you to remember one thing."

"What's that, Mama?"

"No matter how much you're missing me, I'm missing you ten times more."

Virgil also left home that year. He was 10, small in stature and relatively thin, but had the reasoning and sensibility of a grown man. Earlier in the year they'd gotten a letter from Ben Roland saying he was now married and living in Alabama, so Virgil took it on himself to write Ben Roland and ask if he could come and live with them.

Mama's changed my name to Palmer, he wrote, *and I'm looking to move someplace where folks don't know I'm a Hobbs.*

By then Eliza's health had begun to deteriorate. The day he left she was feeling poorly and said she wasn't going to be able to make it down to the train station and back.

"I'll get Jeb to go with you," she suggested, but Virgil shook his head, said he knew the way to the station, and didn't need anybody to hold his hand.

Before she could argue the point, he took off walking down the hollow by himself. Mrs. Welby spotted him heading for the railroad station. Figuring a boy his size wouldn't be traveling alone, she started telling people he'd run away.

Once Virgil was gone, only four of the children remained at home with Eliza: Louella, the eldest of the group and the most responsible; John Paul, a year younger but a free spirit who ran through the woods as if he'd been born to nature; Nellie, who some considered the most beautiful of all the children; and Edward, not yet four. A year earlier, Eliza had made plans for Louella to go to Morgantown and live with Nina, the second youngest of the Palmer sisters, but when the time came Louella refused to go. She claimed with Edward still a baby and Eliza too sick to care for him, she was needed at home.

"Next year," she told her mama. "Next year or the year after, I'll go."

The winter of 1914 was bitter cold, and the snow that fell in early November froze before they could clear it from the porch. That entire winter Eliza never left the house, not once. She'd sit by the window and wait, hoping for a letter from one of the children or a visit from Caldonia.

Her cough became far worse, and she lost what little appetite she had. Not even Caldonia's soup could entice her to eat. After only a few sips, she'd set the spoon aside and say she was in need of rest.

Before the trees began to bud, Eliza no longer slept through the night. She'd fall into bed exhausted and wake in the wee hours of morning barely able to breathe. While the sky was still dark, she'd pull a wool shawl around her shoulders and sit on the porch, remembering the sound of the house when it was filled with children. Although the departure of each child caused a piece of her heart to be torn away, it was as she'd planned.

She'd loved Martin, but he'd been right when he accused her of loving the children more than she did him. The children had been her greatest joy in life. It was her love for them that gave her the strength to send them away. She not only loved them more than she'd loved Martin; she also loved them more than she did herself.

That spring when Pastor Dale came to visit, Eliza spoke to him about Nellie.

"She's a beautiful child with a kind heart and I want what's best for her, but my sisters are up in years and I'd be hesitant to send a seven-year-old to any of them."

Pastor Dale nodded. "There's a family in Huntington; friends of my sister. They've got a big home and love to give, but she's been unable to bear children of her own. If you wish I can ask…" There was a certain kindness in his not speaking the actual words.

"I'd rather hoped Nellie would be with other children; brothers or sister, perhaps." Eliza coughed into her handkerchief and folded it over to hide the crimson stain.

"Ruth Hudson is a good woman. I believe she'd make sure Nellie went to a fine school and had friends to play with." He leaned forward. "I know how painful it is to think of something like this, but knowing the Hudsons as I do I believe they would willingly take Edward also so that brother and sister would remain together."

Eliza sat for a moment saying nothing. Tears welled in her eyes.

"If only…" She could not bring herself to speak the thought. A million or more times, she'd sat on the porch and thought of how it might have been if only Martin had loved his children as she did. If only it hadn't snowed that night… If only they could have remained in Barrettsville… There were countless *If onlys* locked inside her heart, but they were like caged butterflies: beautiful, but hopeless.

"There's no need to think of Edward right now," Pastor Dale said. "He's young; keep him with you, and perhaps in a year or two…"

Eliza wondered if she had a year or two but said nothing and nodded.

On a Sunday morning that sparkled with sunlight, a Ford touring car turned onto the dirt road and rumbled up the hollow. When it came to a stop in the Hobbs's drive, the woman was first to get out of the car. Eliza was in the porch swing with Nellie by her side and a wool shawl pulled around her shoulders, despite the warmth of the day.

The woman was young and beautiful with hair the color of Nellie's.

"You must be Ruth Hudson," Eliza said and smiled.

"Yes, I am," Ruth said. Returning the smile, she motioned to the man following behind her. "This is my husband, Willard." She moved close to the swing and squatted so that her face was level with Nellie's. "Pastor Dale told us what a beautiful little girl you are, Nellie, and do you know what I think?"

Nellie shied back, shook her head, and scooted closer to her mama.

"I think you are more beautiful than he said." She moved a bit closer, brought her hand from behind her back, and held out a porcelain doll. "I brought this for you. Do you like dolls?"

Saying nothing, Nellie nodded and reached out for the doll.

"I'm hoping you'll come for a visit at our house. Do you think you'd like that?"

Still pushed up against Eliza, Nellie shrugged.

Ruth had a gentle way. She didn't pull Nellie to her but waited for the child to come on her own. Eliza liked that and as the thought of what a good mother Ruth would make passed through her head, she felt another crack open up in her heart.

A short while later, Louella served glasses of lemonade and they sat talking in the warm sun. Willard was a man with a round face, a pleasant smile, and a quick laugh. He was an accountant, a man who went to work in the morning and came home every night, pleasant looking but not handsome. Eliza found comfort in that; she knew a handsome man could love himself more than his children. Willard would make a good father.

After a while curiosity got the best of Nellie, and she asked Ruth if they had a swing in their yard.

"A brand new one," Ruth said. "Willard put it up just yesterday." She went on to tell of how their house was close enough to go to town every day for an ice cream if they'd a mind to.

Nellie looked at her with a wide-eyed grin. "Every day?"

Ruth nodded and talked of the carnival that would be coming to town in late August. "I've heard there's a man who does magic tricks and candied apples—"

"I never heard of candied apples."

"I've never had one, but supposedly it's a real apple with a crispy candy coating all over the outside. I'd be willing to try one if you would."

Nellie bobbed her head. "I'd for sure try it."

As the sun rose higher in the sky, Edward woke from his nap and came to sit in Eliza's lap. For now, he was content to suck his thumb and watch as Nellie peppered Ruth with questions. When the shiny black car pulled out of the drive, Nellie was sitting in Ruth's lap. She turned with a smile, called out, "Goodbye, Mama," and waved.

Less than six months later, Eliza was confined to her bed with no one but Louella allowed in her room. She'd waited to call the doctor, and when he finally came she was told there was no cure for tuberculosis. He suggested that she keep to her room, rest, and try to eat.

"That will give you as much time as possible."

"Is this contagious?" she asked.

"Very," he replied.

That same day, Eliza sent Edward to stay with Caldonia and penned a letter to Ruth Hudson asking if they would be willing to also take Nellie's baby brother.

Edward is only four, she wrote, *and I am concerned that being taken from the only home he has known will be quite frightening. If you can make a place for him in your home, I believe being with his sister will ease his fear.*

Two days after Eliza received Ruth's reply saying they'd prayed to one day have a son and would treasure Edward as if he were their own, he left with the Hudsons. She wept because she'd not had the chance to say one last goodbye, feel his small hand in hers, or hold him in her arms, but it was as it had to be.

In the months that followed, Eliza begged Louella to go to Morgantown.

"Take John Paul with you," she said. "Your Aunt Nina is getting on in years, and I'm certain she would welcome some help around the house."

Louella looked at her mama with a crooked smile. "Telling John Paul he's got to do anything is laughable. That boy comes and goes as he pleases. He lives in the woods, and that's where he wants to be."

"But I still worry about him," Eliza said sadly.

"You've no cause to worry. He's sixteen years old and knows what he's doing."

Eliza gazed out the window and studied the leafless trees for a few moments. "What about you, Louella? What will you do after—"

"For now I'm staying here to take care of you, and that's that. I can't say what I'll do in the future. Maybe I'll get married, have a houseful of kids, or raise pigs. It's all a long way off, and I'll cross that bridge when I come to it."

She picked up the dogeared copy of *David Copperfield* they'd brought home from Barrettsville and began to read aloud.

"I am born. Whether I shall turn out to be the hero of my own life or whether that station will be held by anybody else, these pages will show. To begin my life…"

When she looked back to Eliza, she had fallen asleep.

Eliza died the first week of March. It was as if her task in life had been to see to the safety of her children. Once her work was done, she passed quietly into the night. Her final request was the children not be called home for her burial.

"I will rest peacefully knowing I have given most of them the start of a good life," she said as she looked at her oldest daughter with tears in her eyes. "With all my heart, Louella, I pray that you too find happiness."

Just as she had asked, the service was a small affair with only a handful of mourners from the church. Pastor Dale, Caldonia, Jeb, and Louella stood at the gravesite for that last goodbye. By then Louella had already begun to see crimson stains in her handkerchief. Without her mama, she had no reason to live.

Less than a year later, she was buried next to Eliza.

1968 – 1969

Chance

After crying for two days straight, Margaret's energy was spent and a new determination took its place.

"If you never try, you will never succeed," she murmured to herself.

She tried calling Tom again, but a mechanical voice clicked on. "The number you have dialed has been temporarily disconnected."

She closed her eyes tight, held to the edge of the desk to brace herself, and forced a stream of slow even breaths.

When she felt steady enough to drive, she climbed into the car and headed for Tom's house. She no longer had a plan for what to say or do when he opened the door; her only thought was to see him still there, to make sure anger hadn't driven him away.

After what seemed an eternity, she turned onto his street. In the distance, she saw his car sitting in the driveway. She let the car roll along slowly but didn't come to a stop. Instead, she turned at the corner, circled the block, came around again a second time, and parked on the opposite side of the street. From where she was, she could watch the house but he couldn't see her car.

She sat there for almost two hours, trying to come up with a plan. If he wouldn't answer her phone calls, then he probably wouldn't answer the door if he saw her standing on the porch. There had to be another way to reach him. A way to show how much she loved him.

She thought back on the last few moments of their time together, on the way he'd reacted when she said it was better they didn't see one another. He'd claimed she reminded him of his ex.

"The only difference is that there is no dog for you to take," he'd said.

Margaret was not there to take. She was there to give. If only he could see that. If only…

A thought came to her, foolish perhaps but worth a try. She turned the key in the ignition and drove off.

She spent the remainder of the afternoon at the Heatherwood Rescue Center. When she left, she was carrying an energetic, face-licking ball of fur. Stopping at the pet shop, she bought a leash and collar and pleaded with the clerk to stamp out a name tag for the pup while she waited.

"It's almost closing time," he said. "Can't this wait until tomorrow?"

She assured him it was a need of great significance and waited while he ran the tag through the machine. On one side it said Chance; on the other side was Tom's name and address. It was growing late, and there was something else to do before she returned to Tom's house. As she clicked the tag onto the pup's new collar, she looked back to the pet shop clerk.

"I know it's late and I hate to bother you further, but you could you also print out an address label for me? The same as the tag. Oh, and I'm going to need a box big enough for him."

The clerk eyed her apprehensively. "You're not planning to ship the dog, are you? Because—"

Margaret laughed. "Heavens, no. I'm going to hand deliver him."

"Then why the shipping label and box?"

"It's for someone special, and I don't want him to know where the package is from until he opens it."

The clerk shrugged. "Your call, but this dog is too active to stay in there for very long."

"Hopefully, he won't have to."

As the clerk was printing out a label, she penned a few words on a small piece of notepaper. The letter she'd written to him before Christmas had been lengthy with flowery statements about love, forgiveness, and forever. This note was only a few words. The answer could only be a yes or no, nothing in between. She rolled the note into a tight cylinder and tied it to the dog's collar.

On the drive back to Tom's, the dog rode in the front seat beside her. He was all over the place, sniffing at everything, climbing in and out of her lap, stretching himself up to offer more kisses.

"Good boy," she said with a quick pat on his head. Tom might be able to ignore her, but there was no way he was going to ignore this little fella. The one thing Margaret knew about dogs was that they made you love them whether you wanted to or not.

When they turned onto the block, she slowed and parked several houses back. It was far enough that he wouldn't see the car even when he stepped out onto the porch. *If* he even did come out onto the porch. If he spotted her, odds were he'd ignore both her and the box she was planning to leave.

Pulling the cardboard box from the backseat, she lifted Chance into it, whispered a reassuring promise that he wouldn't be there long, and started down the street with the box in her arms. She crossed over before she got to the house and came up along the side. There were lights in the back of the house but none in the front, which was most likely the living room. Good; she'd have the cover of darkness. Tiptoeing onto the porch, she sat the box square in front of the door, folded the top into place, rang the doorbell, and ran.

She just about made it to the side of the house when the porch light clicked on. Ducking behind a hedge of overgrown wisteria, she squatted down and peered through the bushes. With the light on, she could see him and for one frightening moment her heart stopped.

That brief glimpse of his face brought a sweeping surge of all that she felt for him. She didn't just love him; she loved him with all her heart. The things she'd written in her letter were not only flowery words. They were the truth of what she felt.

He'd done more than just make her fall in love with him. He'd changed her. He'd given her the courage to fight for what she wanted. Even if he turned her away this time, she would not give up. She would continue to fight for him, because he was worth fighting for.

She watched as he lifted the box into his arms and turned back inside.

Tom carried the box inside and snapped off the porch light. Thinking it was another potted plant from his Aunt Mathilda, he sat the box on the living room floor and started to walk away. Then he heard something move. Turning back, he lifted the lid and saw a long-eared, sad-eyed puppy looking up.

He smiled, and the pup's white-tipped tail started wagging. Before he had time to consider who the dog was from, the pup was out of the box and scampering around the room.

Tom dropped down and sat on the floor. The puppy, a mix of brown, black, and white splatters, saw this as an invitation and jumped on him, scrambling over his legs, climbing up his chest, licking his hands, face, and neck. Tom laughed as he hadn't laughed in months.

"Where on earth did you come from?"

He checked the top of the box. No return address. Nothing but his name and address. As the pup settled in his lap, Tom spotted the tag.

"Ah, so you've got a name. Chance." When Tom turned the tag over to read the back side, he saw the note tied to the pup's collar. "What's this?"

He unrolled the small slip of paper.

I've given you a Chance. Won't you please give me one? The note was signed with a scrawled M.

Maggie.

The memory of how much he loved her came roaring back, and he smacked his hand against his forehead. He'd spent the past three months trying to forget her. Now this. Why?

It was something he hadn't expected. She'd made her position quite clear the last time they spoke, and he'd hung up the telephone angry, hurt, and disappointed. On Christmas Eve she'd telephoned but he'd hung up, fearing she'd say something about how they could still be friends. He didn't want to hear that, and it didn't help to hear how sorry she was to have misled him. He'd thought that was the end of it, but now…

The anger that had been festering inside of him for months softened ever so slightly. As he stood, the tiniest trace of a smile tugged the corner of his mouth. He opened the door and stepped out onto the porch.

"Maggie, are you out here?"

"Yes," she answered hesitantly.

"Do you want to come in so we can talk?"

She stepped from behind the bushes and looked up at him. "More than I've ever wanted anything."

He motioned for her to come and pulled the door back. She looked beautiful. Thinner than he remembered but just as lovely. As she came toward him, she smiled. Determined to not make a fool of himself again, he gave a cool half-smile in return.

Before she was halfway through the door, she said, "I am so, so sorry, Tom. I know I've made a terrible mess of things and—"

"Maggie, if you're going to say let's let bygones be bygones and be friends, save your breath, because I don't want to hear it. It was nice of you to give me the dog, but—"

"So you're going to keep him?"

"Yes, but please don't insult me by saying let's be friends."

"That's why you think I'm here?" Her smile widened.

It was a smile he knew and loved, but he was leaving it up to her to make the first move. "Isn't it?"

"Not even close," she said and shook her head. "I don't just want to be your friend, I want to be your best friend, your lover, your sweetheart, your wife. Not five years from now but right now. I love you with all my heart."

He moved closer. Close enough to see the sparkle in her eyes. "I thought you had to wait because of Albert. What changed?"

"Me. I realized how very much in love with you I am. I was a fool to think there's a timetable for when you're supposed to love again. It happens when it happens. The only real way to judge whether or not the time is right is to listen to your heart."

He lowered his face to hers. For a fleeting moment he thought of asking if she was absolutely certain, but instead he brought his lips to hers and kissed her in a way he'd only dreamt of before. When the kiss ended, he knew he didn't have to ask. He had his answer.

"I love you, Maggie. I've loved you for a long time and—"

A loud crash sounded from the back of the house.

"Oh no."

He headed for the kitchen with Margaret right behind. The garbage can was turned over, and Chance was inside of it. The only part of him still visible was the wagging white-tipped tail.

The Start of a New Life

On New Year's Eve, they went to a tiny French restaurant for dinner, drank champagne, then returned home to ring in the new year with Guy Lombardo. At the stroke of midnight, he pressed his lips to hers and kissed her with a passion that carried them from one year into the next. When the kiss ended, he pulled a ring from his pocket and asked her to marry him. As Margaret answered yes, she knew he could feel the thundering of her heart.

Tom said he'd like the wedding to be as soon as possible and she agreed, but once they began to discuss the logistics of invitations and planning it became a bit more complicated.

"We could get married at City Hall with Josie as witness," he suggested.

"Not in a church?"

"A church would be nice, but then we'll need to allow time for—"

"What about if we have the minister perform the service in the small chapel and just have a tiny wedding?"

"What about your family?" Tom said. "After all the trouble we went through to find them, I thought you'd want them to celebrate with us."

"I do," Margaret said wistfully. "But if it means waiting…"

They sat in silence for a few moments. Tom turned to her with a wide grin. "Rather than wait, let's get married now and celebrate later."

"Celebrate later?"

"Yes. Instead of a formal wedding, we'll have a family reunion and invite everyone to come and celebrate with us."

"I love it," Margaret said. "We can get married in the chapel, and when the weather's warmer we can have an outdoor party in the back yard."

That night they stayed up and talked until dawn. They spoke of the future and the past, of how they'd enjoyed traveling together and would one day drive across the country to visit places like Las Vegas, San Francisco, and Seattle. They thought about planning the first trip in the summer, after the reunion party. After Tom had sold his house and moved in with Margaret. After she'd settled the issues she'd left simmering on the back burner for so long—issues like Jeffrey Schoenfeld, who was now calling almost every day.

⁂

On January 2nd, Tom arrived at the house before eight. They had breakfast together and headed down to City Hall where they applied for a marriage license. Their next stop was the small Wyoming Presbyterian Church Margaret had attended for years. They gathered in Reverend Johnson's office and talked for an hour.

When he asked what their future plans were, Tom answered, "We plan to love each other for as long as we live, never go to bed angry, and always give more than we get." As soon as he'd finished, Margaret nodded her agreement.

The reverend smiled. "Marriage is a sacred vow, and I hate to see it broken. That's why I ask that question. I try to make certain a couple is not entering into marriage with unrealistic expectations."

"And did we pass?" Tom asked.

"With flying colors."

They were married three days later in the back of the small chapel. Margaret wore a pale blue dress she'd worn a number of times before and carried a nosegay of white roses. Josie was the only one in attendance. The wedding was a simple exchange of vows with no pomp and circumstance, yet Reverend Johnson said he'd never seen a happier or more radiant bride.

They invited Josie to join them for dinner, but she refused saying this was one celebration the two of them should enjoy alone.

The evening was a repeat of what they'd done New Year's Eve. They dined at the same restaurant, drank champagne, and returned to the house. Then they climbed into bed together. Unlike that night they'd been stranded 30 miles from nowhere, Tom did not stick to his side of the mattress.

In the weeks that followed, Margaret met with Jeffrey Schoenfeld and agreed to sell him the controlling shares of McCutcheon and Schoenfeld. She'd decided the law firm belonged in the past with Albert, and she no longer had room for it in her life. Because he'd waited so long for her answer, Jeffrey had become worried she might sell to someone else and raised his offering price three times.

Once the details for the sale of the firm were finalized, Margaret began talking about her will and handed him a list of her beneficiaries. There were 47 in all.

Jeffrey's mouth dropped open when he saw the list. "Who are all these people?"

"Mostly family," she answered. "Tom Bateman is my new husband, Josie and her children are friends, and the rest are relatives."

"I thought you said you had no family."

"Turns out I was wrong," Margaret said and smiled.

They went through the specified endowments item by item. The grandchildren in the family all received a fully funded college tuition as did Josie's three. The remainder of the estate was to be divided according to the list she'd drawn up. Margaret half-expected Jeffrey to scowl or make a snide comment about her marrying Tom so soon, but he didn't even mention it. Apparently, he was satisfied with gaining control of the law firm, and what she did was of no consequence. The only thing he said was that he needed 30 days to prepare the paperwork and get back to her.

In early February Margaret's relatives all received an invitation to a family reunion. The invitation said guests would stay at the Heatherwood Court Hotel with all travel and accommodations to be covered by their hosts, Margaret and Tom Bateman. Enclosed was an R.S.V.P. card and return envelope. Before the week was out, they'd received every card back and all of them a yes. In the neat printed hand she'd learned to recognize as Virgil's was written, "Not surprised. We figured you two would be married before long."

They'd decided on the hotel because as large as Margaret's house was with two bedrooms downstairs and five upstairs, it was too small for the number of guests attending.

Jeffrey Schoenfeld returned a few weeks later with a fat folder of papers to be signed and a sizable check. Once the documents were notarized and filed, Margaret invited Josie over. The three of them were seated at the kitchen table, Tom to her side and Josie opposite. Knowing what was to come, it was all she and Tom could do to keep the smiles from their faces.

"Now that Tom and I are married," she said, "a few things around here need to change."

Josie nodded. "I been figuring that. The truth is I ain't pulling my weight 'cause there's not a whole lot that needs doing."

"Oh, but you're wrong," Tom said. "There's something more we're going to need your help with."

Josie wrinkled her nose and looked across the table. "Excuse me? I ain't quite understanding."

"It's Chance. We're going to need someone to take care of him while we're traveling."

"Well, that's no problem. One little bitty dog like him is easy to see to. I can come in the morning, feed him, and—"

"That's a lot of running back and forth," Tom cut in. "We were thinking maybe it'd be easier if you lived here."

Josie's eyes got big and round. "You know I think the world of you and Miss Margaret both, but I got three kids and my Edwin to take care of. I couldn't leave them to—"

"We weren't expecting you to," Margaret said. "We want you to bring your family with you. Your oldest boy graduates high school this year, and he'll be heading off to college."

"Maybe heading off to college. We ain't heard yet whether he's getting that scholarship or not, and if he don't—"

"He's definitely going. As a matter of fact, all three kids are going. Him next year, the girls the year after." Margaret pushed a manila folder across the table. "A tuition fund has been set up for each of them. There's money enough for them to go to any college they want, and as long as they keep up their studies the tuition, room, and board will be paid for."

Josie sat there looking like she'd been shocked out of her skin. "I'm still not understanding. Is this some kind of loan or—"

"It's a gift. A gift to say thank you for all the times you've stood beside me, helped me find my way, listened to my sorrows, and been the best friend I could ever wish for."

"Shoot, I didn't do nothing you wouldn't have done for me."

"Exactly. You might not realize it, Josie, but you were a sister to me when I didn't have one to turn to."

"I appreciate you feeling that way, but this is a powerful lot of money and—"

Margaret laughed. "All that time being bothered by Jeffrey had to come to some good, didn't it? Selling Albert's shares of the practice allowed me to come into a lot of money, and I can't think of a better way to use it than to help someone I love."

Josie looked over to Tom apprehensively. "Seeing as how you're Miss Margaret's husband, you ought to have a say in this and I'm sure—"

Tom shook his head. "Sorry, Josie. I agree with what Maggie's doing."

That look of apprehension was still stuck to Josie's face. "You agree with her spending all this money and saying Edwin and the kids can come live here?"

Again, Tom nodded. "Absolutely."

"Did she tell you Edwin's only got one leg and he ain't much good for working?"

"She did."

"And you still want us to come live here?"

"We do. You see, Josie, if it weren't for you, we probably wouldn't be married."

"I don't get what I've got to do with—"

"The first time I was here Maggie would have let me leave, but you were the one who came running out, asking me to come back in. I was hoping she'd ask me to work on the case, but I don't think she would have done it were it not for you."

Margaret smiled and gave a nod. "That's true, Josie; you know it is."

Josie's grin stretched the full width of her face as she sat there shaking her head. "I hope you folks know what you're in for. Them girls is picky eaters and always on the telephone, and Edwin, he ain't no bargain. My boy, George, he'll do a bit of yard work, but once he goes off to college…"

⁂

It took almost two months for Josie to pack up the apartment and get everybody ready for the move, but they finally arrived lock, stock, and barrel 10 days before the reunion. Most of their furniture went into storage, but Edwin insisted on bringing his La-Z-Boy recliner. As the movers carried the chair in, Josie stood with her hands on her hips.

"Set it in the back bedroom," she said. "Miss Margaret don't want you messing up her family room with that thing."

Margaret laughed. "Nonsense. This is your home now, and Edwin can put his chair wherever he wants. It's high time this house was really lived in."

Josie and Edwin took one of the downstairs bedrooms, George took the upstairs room at the far end of the hall, and the girls moved into the one beside it. Hearing the house filled with laughter and lively conversations was music to Margaret's ears. It was a sound she'd missed for far too long; the sound of family. Two days later, she realized the sadness that had once permeated the house was gone.

⁂

On the weekend of the reunion, the weather was everything they'd hoped for: the sun brilliant, the sky a clear blue, and the magnolia trees gloriously decked out in pink and white blossoms. Margaret threw open the bedroom window and breathed in the scent of fresh-cut grass and hyacinths. The sound of voices came from downstairs and warmed her heart.

Most of the guests were staying at the Heatherwood Courtyard, but

Dewey and Ellen were at the house in the room next to her and Tom. Virgil and Jeanie were next to the twins, and Caldonia was downstairs in the room next to Josie. Every bedroom was full, and the house was more alive than Margaret could ever remember.

By the time they sat down to breakfast, the caterers had arrived and were setting up tents in the back yard. After the tents came tables and folding chairs, then racks of dishes and silverware. Wicker chairs with plump cushions were placed beneath the shade of the oak, and in time the tables were spread with trays of food and buckets of ice alongside pitchers of sweet tea, lemonade, and wine. Lights were strung across the yard, and Chinese lanterns swayed in the soft breezes.

The guests began arriving a few minutes before noon. They came in shorts and colorful shirts, sundresses and sandals, everyone casual, everyone dressed for a good time. Cousins who had never met sat together and discovered an invisible thread that tied them one to another. Brothers and sisters embraced and reminded each other of things once forgotten. Some memories brought laughter, others caused a tear to fall, but happiness and the bond of family was everywhere.

When Virgil told of leaving Coal Creek, Margaret said, "That wasn't what Mama wanted. She did what she had to do, but what she really wanted was to have her family with her." She gave a wistful sigh. "Seeing us gathered together like this would have made Mama so happy. I only wish she could have been here with us."

Everyone sat quietly for a few seconds.

"She is here," Dewey said. "She knows."

Dewey had grown forgetful and sometimes mixed up times and places, but this was no mix-up. Margaret could feel the truth of what he meant. Eliza was there. She was in the eyes of brothers who sat side by side, the laughter of grandchildren she'd never seen, and the hearts she'd touched in her too short and too heavily burdened life. She was here now, and she'd be with them for as long as they held her memory in their hearts.

As the afternoon wore on caterers replenished the food trays, and when the sky grew dusky the lights were lit. Dirty dishes disappeared, and new ones replaced them. Although they'd told Josie she was there as a guest and had only to enjoy herself, she circled through the crowd asking if this one or that one would like a fresh drink or a cozy chair.

The moon was high in the sky when the guests finally began to leave. One by one they hugged Margaret, whispered how she and Tom were so obviously meant for one another, and said they needed to have gatherings such as this more often. Oliver and Claudia suggested they do it next year at their place.

"Our house is nowhere as big as this," she said, "but we can make room."

Later that night, after everyone had retired and the house grown silent, the sights and sounds of the day lingered in Margaret's head. She and Tom climbed into bed, tired but happy. They talked for a while, then kissed goodnight and snapped off the light.

As she snuggled close with her head on Tom's shoulder, she closed her eyes and saw both the past and the future. A year ago, Margaret thought her life was all but over, that she'd never love again, never see her family, never again know happiness. She was so wrong. The sorrow of the past was something she'd forever carry, but the future was more beautiful than anything she could have possibly imagined.

Her life was far from over; in fact, the best years were just beginning.

Acknowledgments

When a reader holds a finished book in hand, they see only the face of the author, but in truth, many people contribute to the successful making of a novel. Even the most skilled storyteller is only as good as the people who support her. I am fortunate to have an advisory team that willingly reads through every draft, unflinchingly tells me where I have gone wrong, and then shows up with wine and a homemade cake to help me find my way to a new and more beautiful storyline. No words could ever express how grateful I am for my Port St. Lucie Posse, Joanne Bliven, Kathy Foslien, Lynn Ontiveros, and Trudy Southe. Such amazing friends are a blessing beyond belief.

I am equally blessed in knowing Ekta Garg, a superb editor, and extremely talented author, who somehow manages to catch my mistakes without ever losing sight of my voice. Ekta's attention to detail constantly pushes me to go deeper into the story and I believe I am better because of this challenge.

Thank you also to Amy Atwell and the team at Author E.M.S. They are like the proverbial Fire Department, always there to help put out the fires. Thank you, Amy, for turning my manuscripts into beautifully formatted pages and for being so wonderfully organized and dependable.

I also owe a huge debt of gratitude to the women of the BFF Clubhouse (Bette's Friends & Fans), they are the loyalist of followers, buy my books, share them with friends and take time to write reviews. Without such fans my stories might grow dusty on the shelf.

Lastly, I am thankful beyond words for my husband Dick, who puts up with my crazy hours, irrational thinking, and late or non-existent dinners. I could not be who I am without him for he is and will always be my sweetheart and greatest blessing.

Award-winning novelist Bette Lee Crosby brings the wit and wisdom of her Southern mama to works of fiction—the result is a delightful blend of humor, mystery and romance. "Storytelling is in my blood", Crosby laughingly admits, "My mom was not a writer, but she was a captivating storyteller, so I find myself using bits and pieces of her voice in almost everything I write."

A *USA Today* bestselling author, Crosby has twenty-two published novels, including *Spare Change* and the Wyattsville series. She has been the recipient of the Reader's Favorite Gold Medal, Reviewer's Choice Award, FPA President's Book Award and International Book Award, among many others. Her 2016 novel, *Baby Girl*, was named Best Chick Lit of the Year by *Huffington Post*. Her 2018 novel *The Summer of New Beginnings*, published by Lake Union, took First Place in the Royal Palm Literary Award for Women's Fiction and was a runner-up for book of the year. Her 2019 release, *Emily, Gone* was a winner of the Benjamin Franklin Literary Award.

Crosby currently lives on the East Coast of Florida with her husband and a feisty Bichon Frise who is supposedly her muse.

To learn more about Bette Lee, visit her website at:
https://betteleecrosby.com

CPSIA information can be obtained
at www.ICGtesting.com
Printed in the USA
LVHW111445140521
687356LV00016B/652